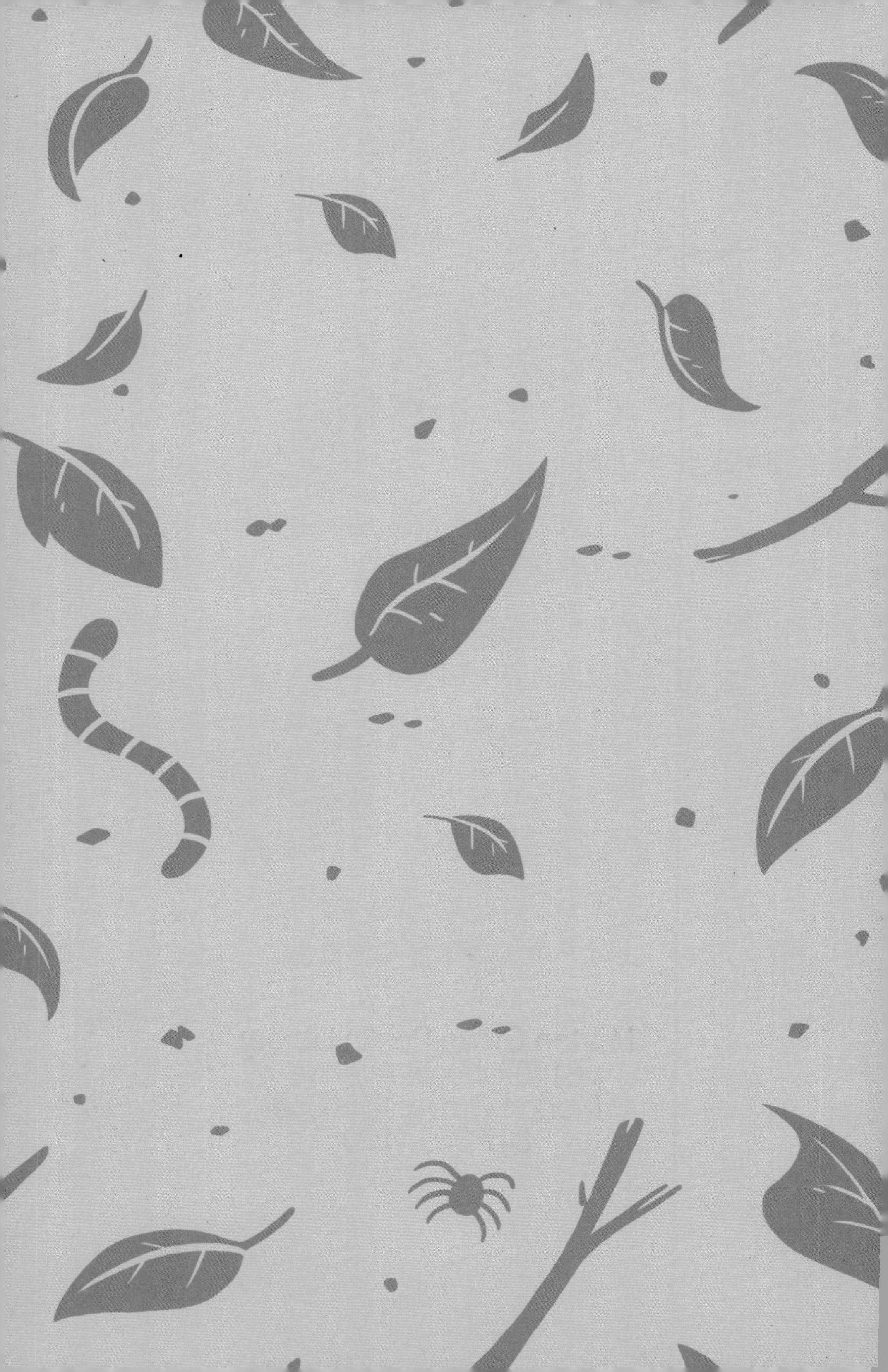

"A simply wonderful tale of friendship and whimsy,
masterfully constructed with depth and moxie."
—*Kirkus Reviews*

"Sophisticated and thoughtful,
this comic also has plenty of child appeal."
—*School Library Journal*

"I'm addicted to Jellaby! Kean Soo's
storytelling is irresistable."
—Scott McCloud, author of *Understanding Comics*

"Jellaby will win your heart."
—Jeff Smith, creator of *Bone*

Eisner Award nominee
for Best Digital Comic

Joe Shuster Award winner
for Best Comic for Kids

Monster in the City

Kean Soo

Stone Arch Books
a capstone imprint

Acknowledgements:
Special thanks to Calista Brill, Roberta Pressel,
Judy Hansen, Hope Larson, David & Nicolas Seigneret, Ben
Hu, Jason Turner, Clio Chiang, Kazu Kibuishi, and of course,
all my friends and family for their love and support
over the years. A very special thank-you to the Canada
Council for the Arts for their support of this work.

Jellaby is published by Stone Arch Books
a capstone imprint
1710 Roe Crest Drive
North Mankato, Minnesota 56003
www.capstonepub.com

Cataloging-in-Publication Data is available on the Library of Congress website.
ISBN: 978-1-4342-9196-7 (library binding)

Summary:
Ten-year-old Portia Bennett and her friend Jason continue their journey
through the city of Toronto. They're one step closer to finding the home
of their lost friend, a sweet, silent creature named Jellaby. Unfortunately,
dangers await, including a tentacled beast with a taste for children. To succeed
in her quest -- and save her friends -- Portia must step up and
kick some monster butt.

Cover Design: Kean Soo & Kazu Kibuishi

Printed in China.
032014   008080RRDF14

Foreword

As a kid, I didn't spend much time in "the city." My family lived in an apartment complex just barely within San Francisco city limits, and my parents preferred suburban conveniences like ample parking and large supermarkets. City visits were reserved for special occasions like my grandparents visiting from Hawaii, or going to see the lights at Christmastime.

One year, during a field trip to see a play downtown, my classmates decided it would be funny to ditch me. They took off down the street, leaving me in a crowd of tourists, cable car noise, homeless people, and utter confusion. I still remember how terrifying it felt to be alone in the center of the city. A friend would've come in handy right about then.

Thankfully, the people I surround myself with now are a little kinder. I've known Kean since 2004, by way of comic conventions, Livejournal posts, and message boards. We forged a bond over our love of comics, as well as our shared interest in food. Some of my fondest memories involve riding around Toronto in the backseat of Kean's tiny Volkswagen, listening to indie rock and looking for the best ice cream, sushi, or Hungarian meat stacks. Conversation usually steers back to our work, and we've spent many hours discussing braces, monsters, and middle school.

My readers constantly look to me for graphic novel recommendations, and despite the kids' graphic novel boom of the last decade or so, I'm often hard-pressed to come up with age-appropriate titles that have that perfect combination of great art, solid cartooning, and wonderful storytelling. Jellaby is the complete package, and I'm unabashedly pleased to recommend the book you hold in your hands.

Get ready to soar over the city, explore its dark underground tunnels, and find yourself among friends.

~ Raina Telgemeier,
creator of Smile and Drama

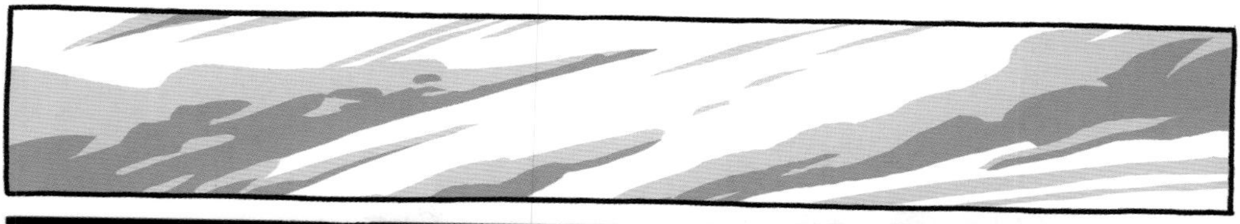

CHAPTER ONE

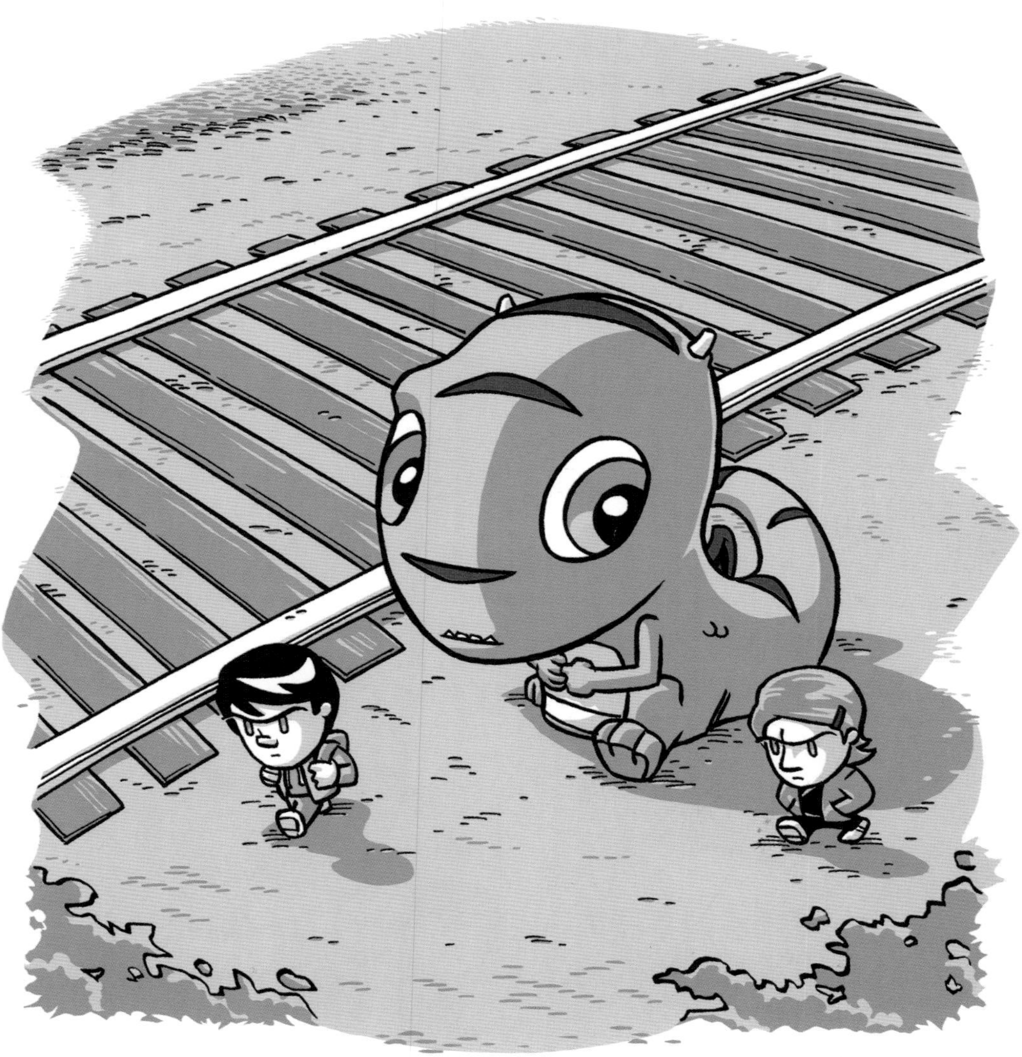

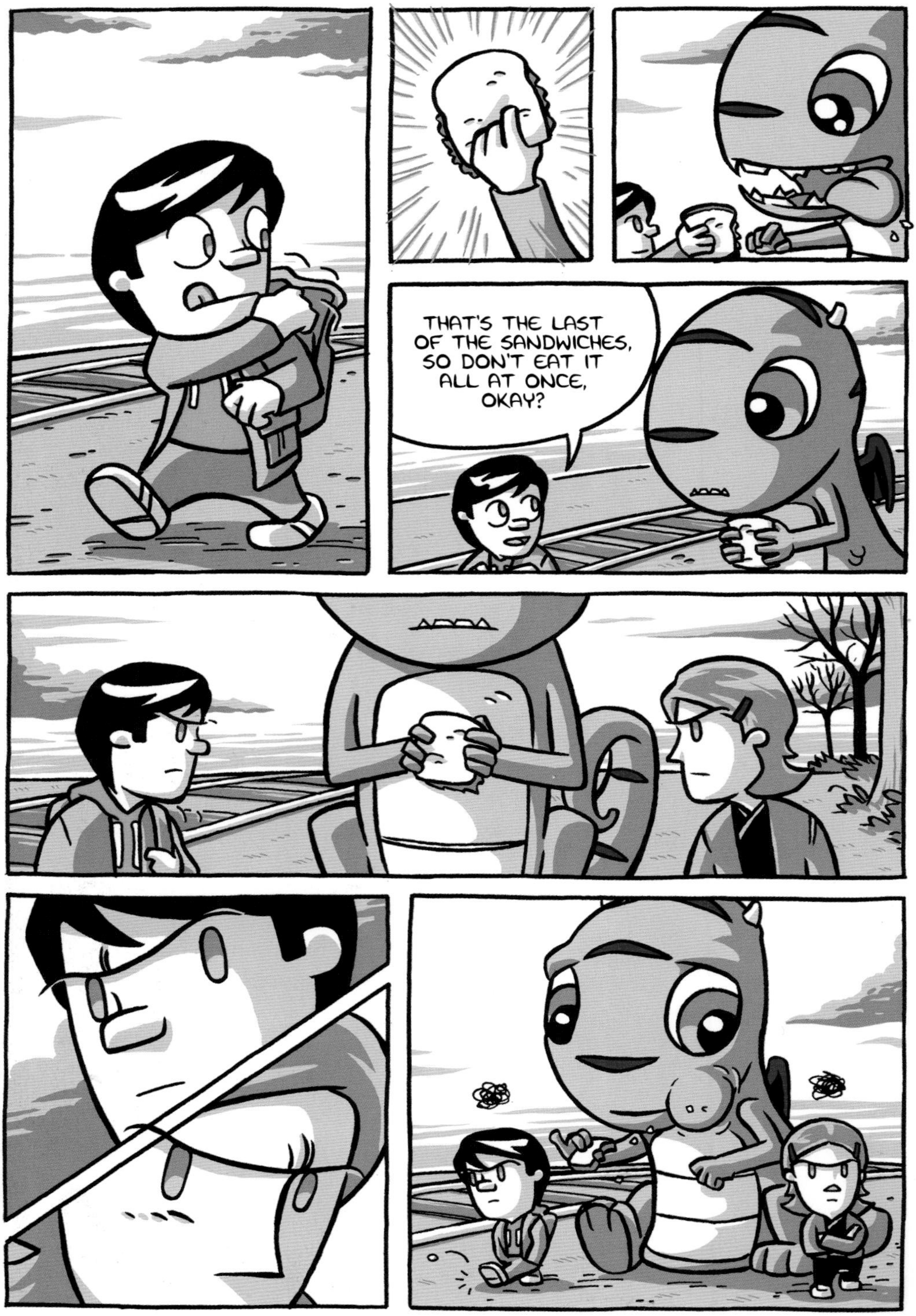
THAT'S THE LAST OF THE SANDWICHES, SO DON'T EAT IT ALL AT ONCE, OKAY?

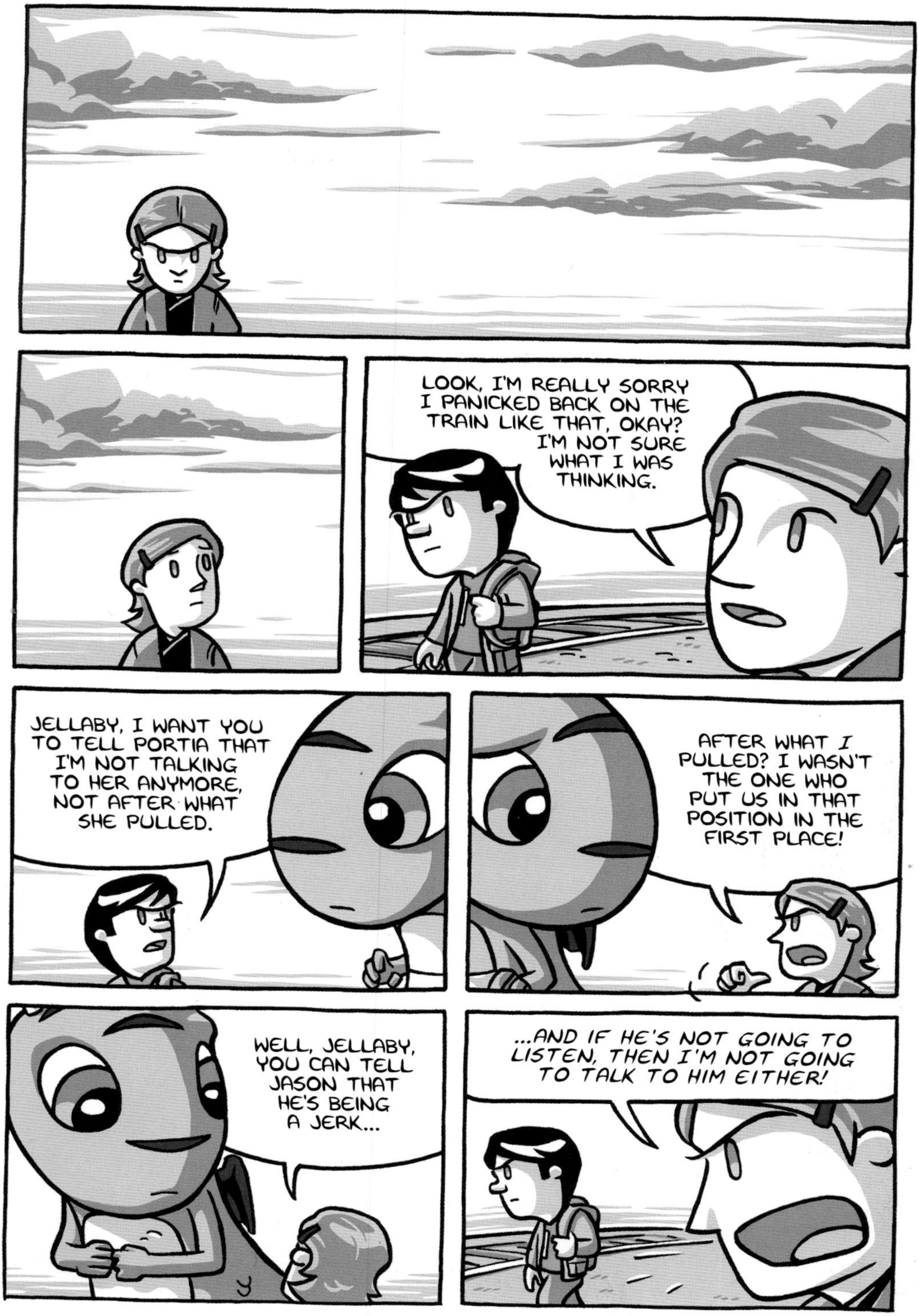
LOOK, I'M REALLY SORRY I PANICKED BACK ON THE TRAIN LIKE THAT, OKAY? I'M NOT SURE WHAT I WAS THINKING.
JELLABY, I WANT YOU TO TELL PORTIA THAT I'M NOT TALKING TO HER ANYMORE, NOT AFTER WHAT SHE PULLED.
AFTER WHAT *I* PULLED? I WASN'T THE ONE WHO PUT US IN THAT POSITION IN THE FIRST PLACE!
WELL, JELLABY, YOU CAN TELL JASON THAT HE'S BEING A JERK...
...AND IF HE'S NOT GOING TO LISTEN, THEN I'M NOT GOING TO TALK TO HIM EITHER!

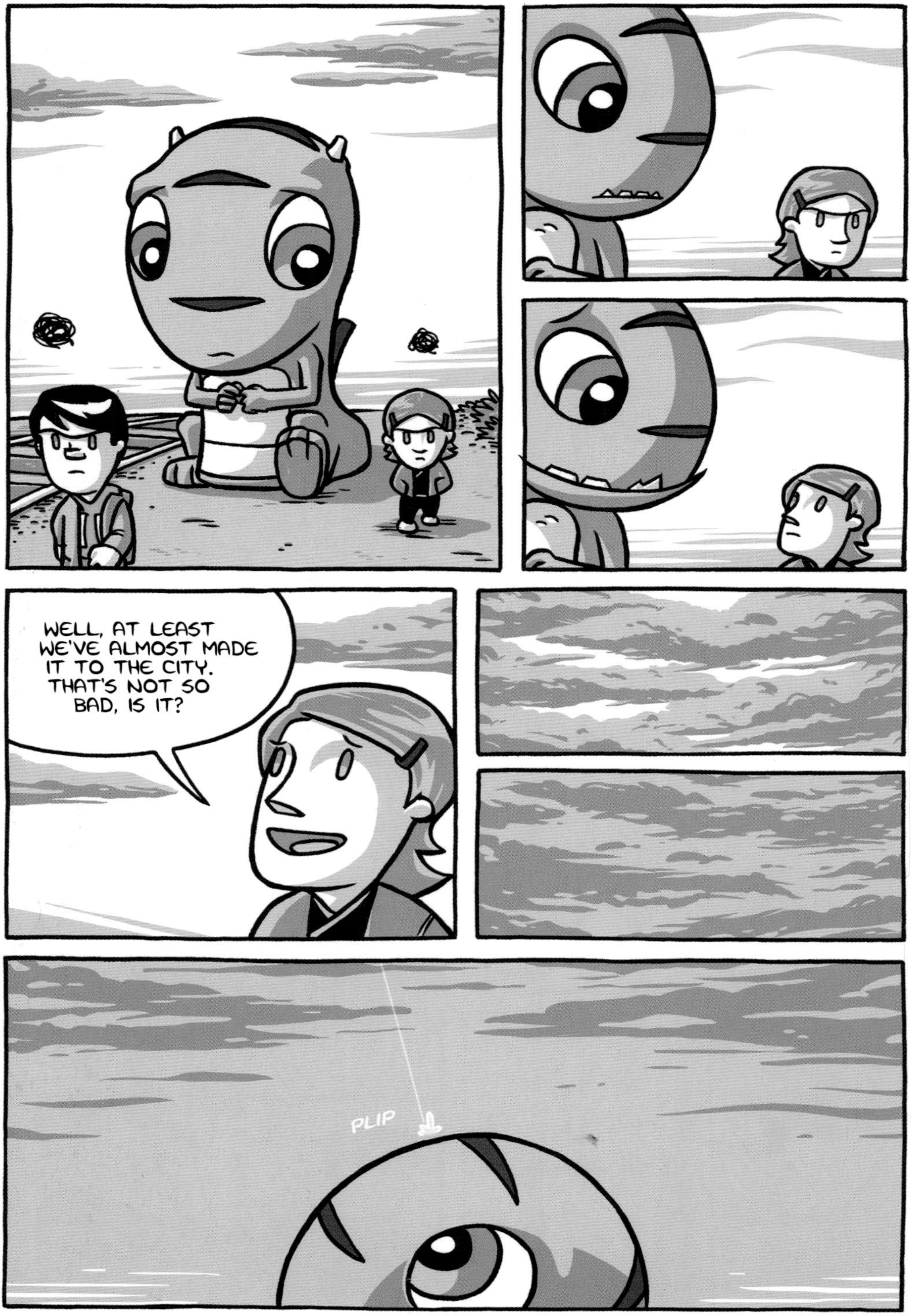
WELL, AT LEAST WE'VE ALMOST MADE IT TO THE CITY. THAT'S NOT SO BAD, IS IT?
PLIP

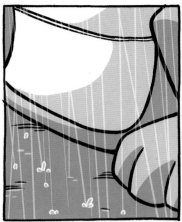

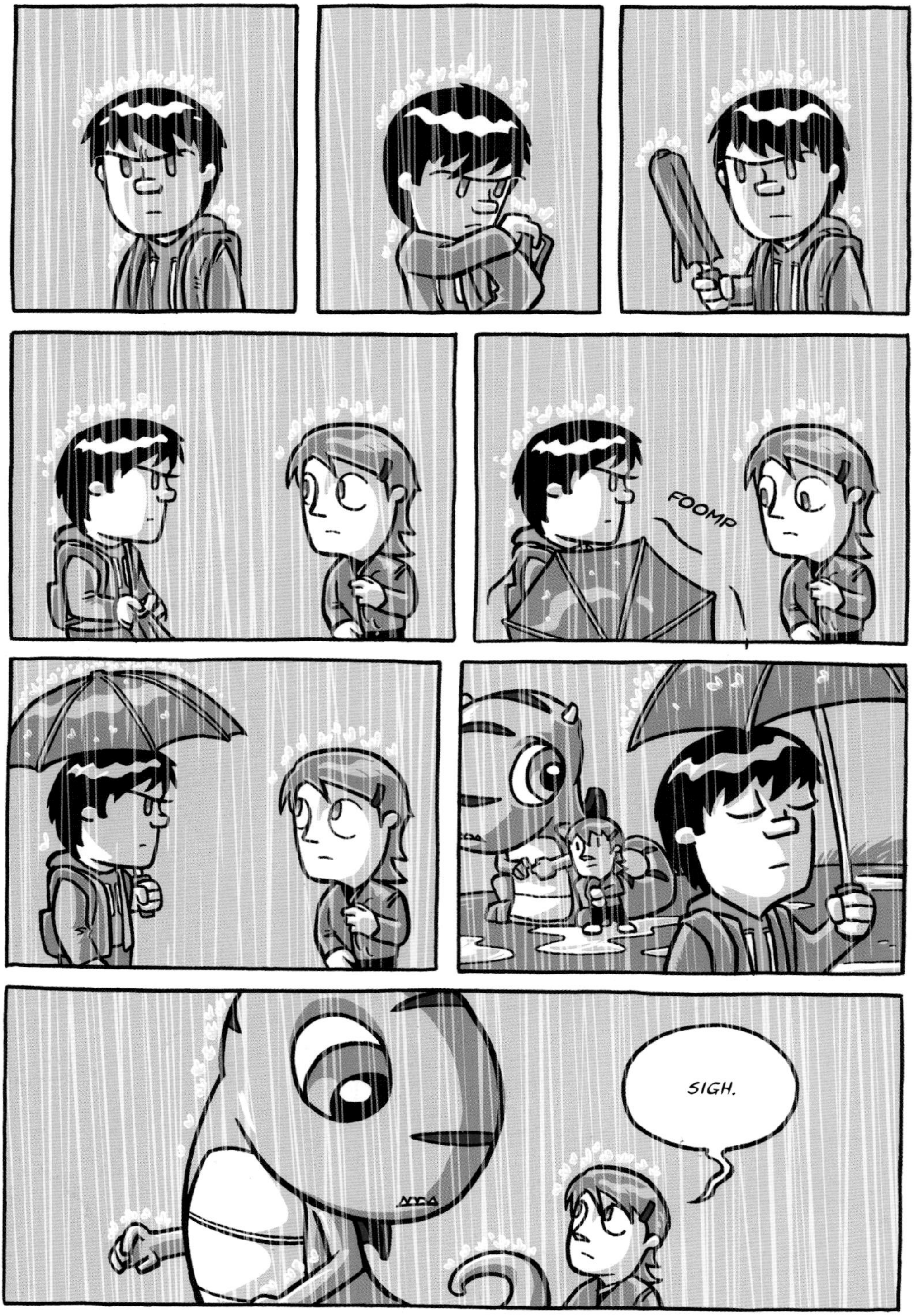
FOOMP
SIGH.

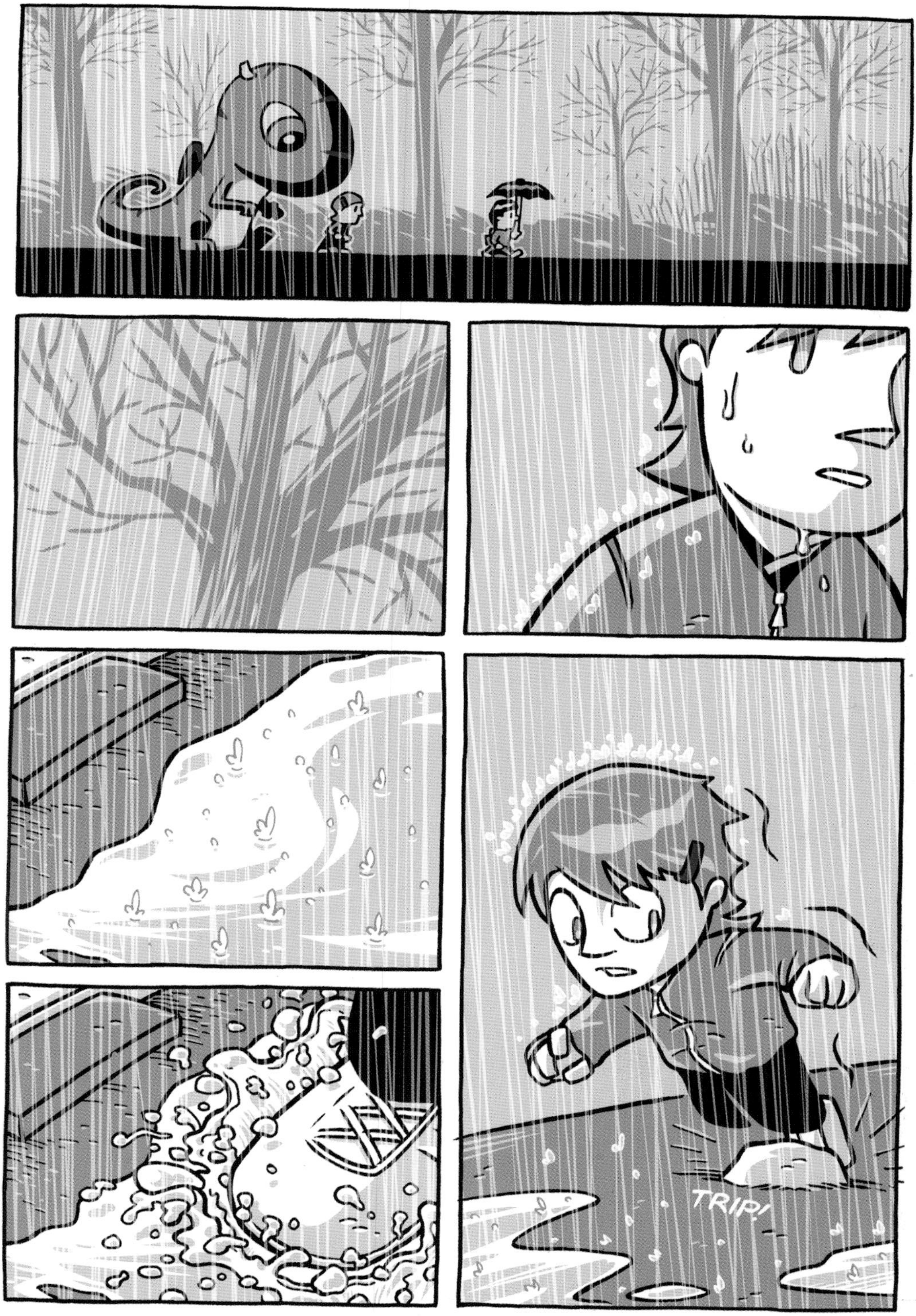
TRIP!

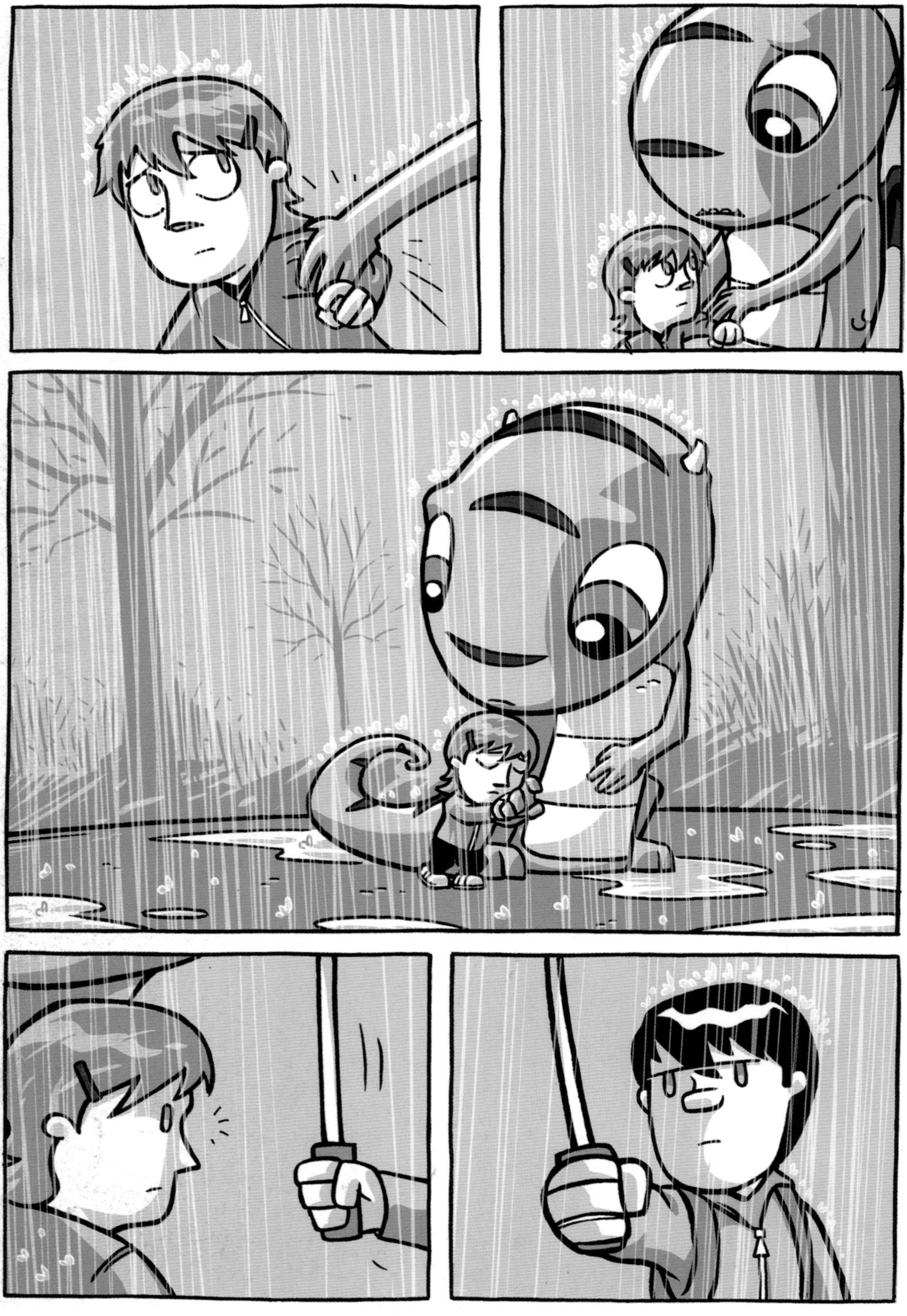

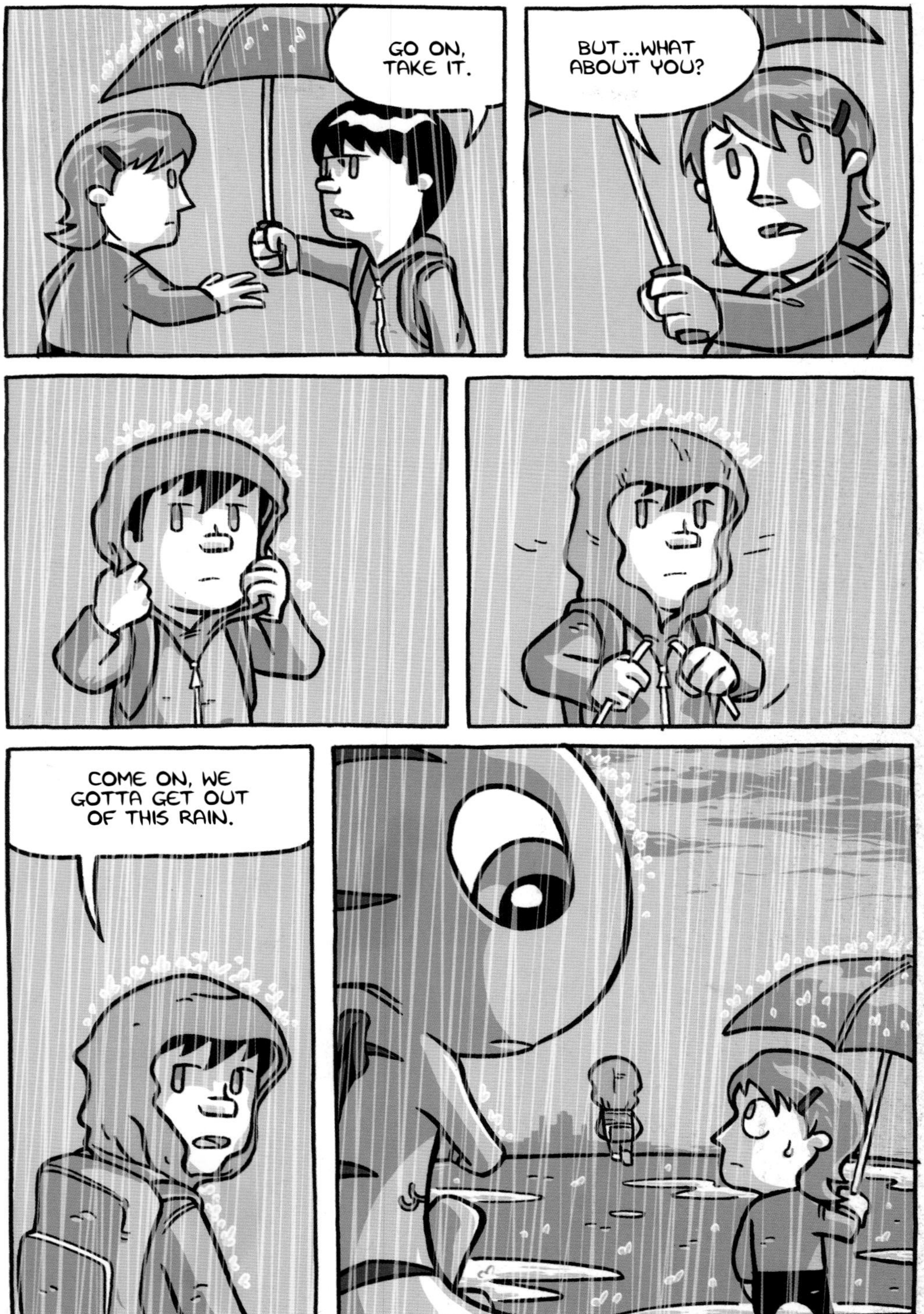
GO ON, TAKE IT.
BUT...WHAT ABOUT YOU?
COME ON, WE GOTTA GET OUT OF THIS RAIN.

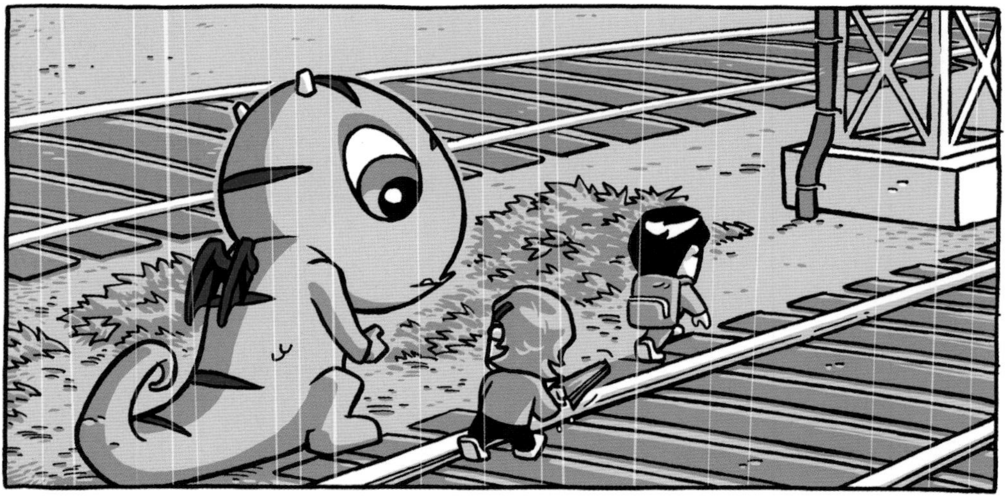

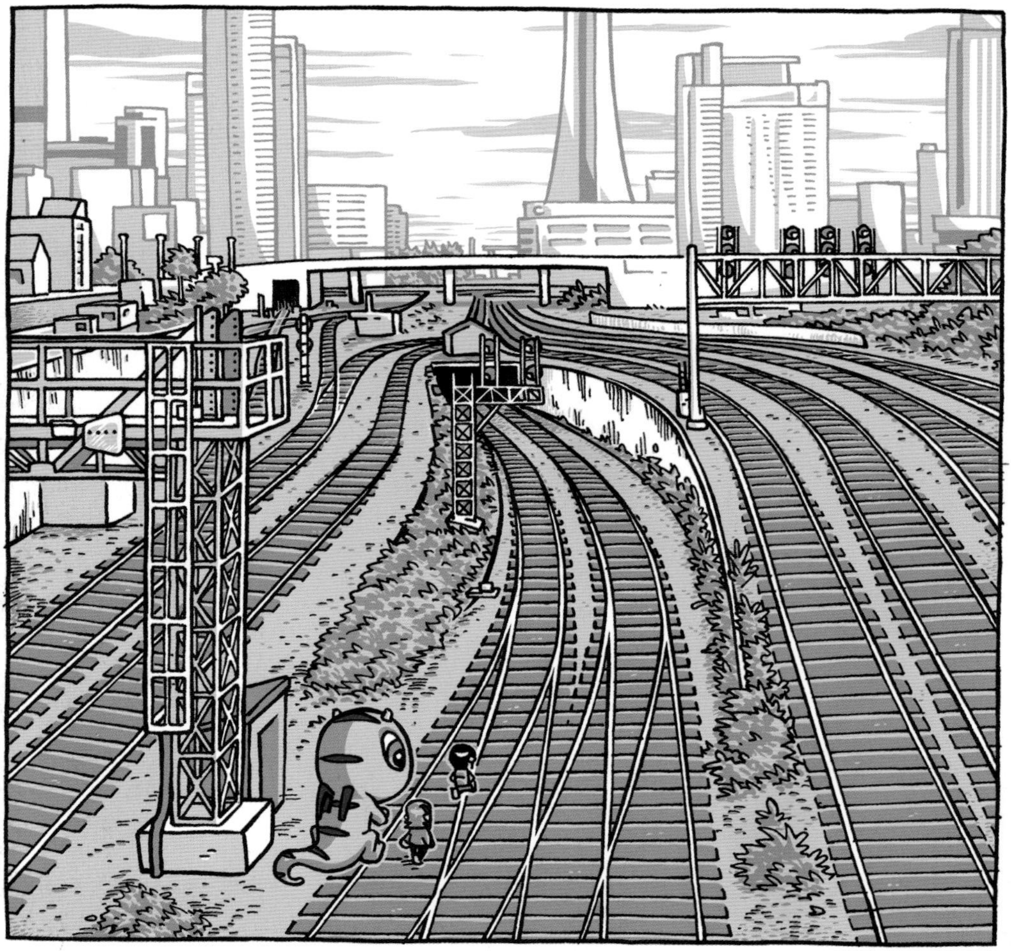

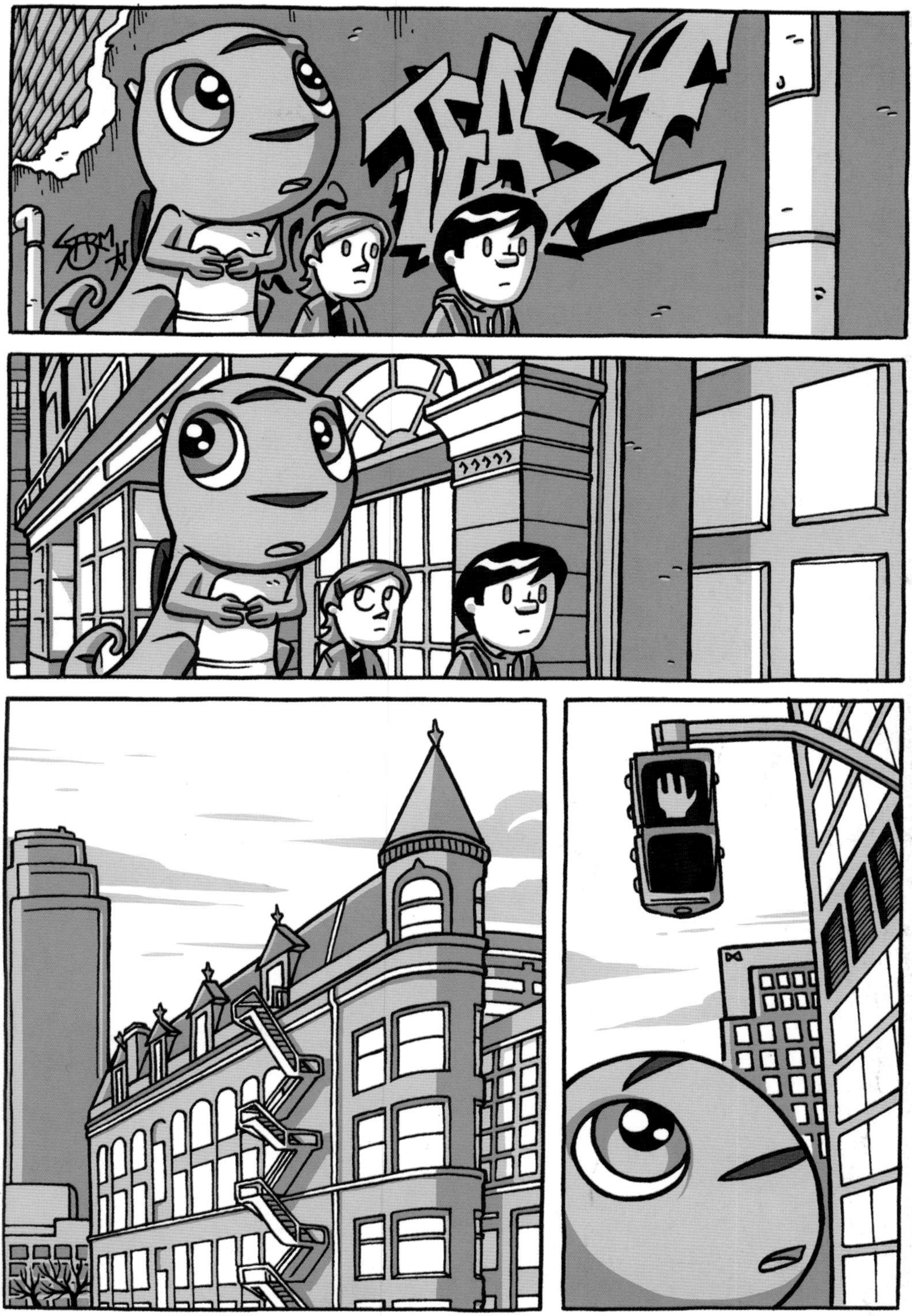

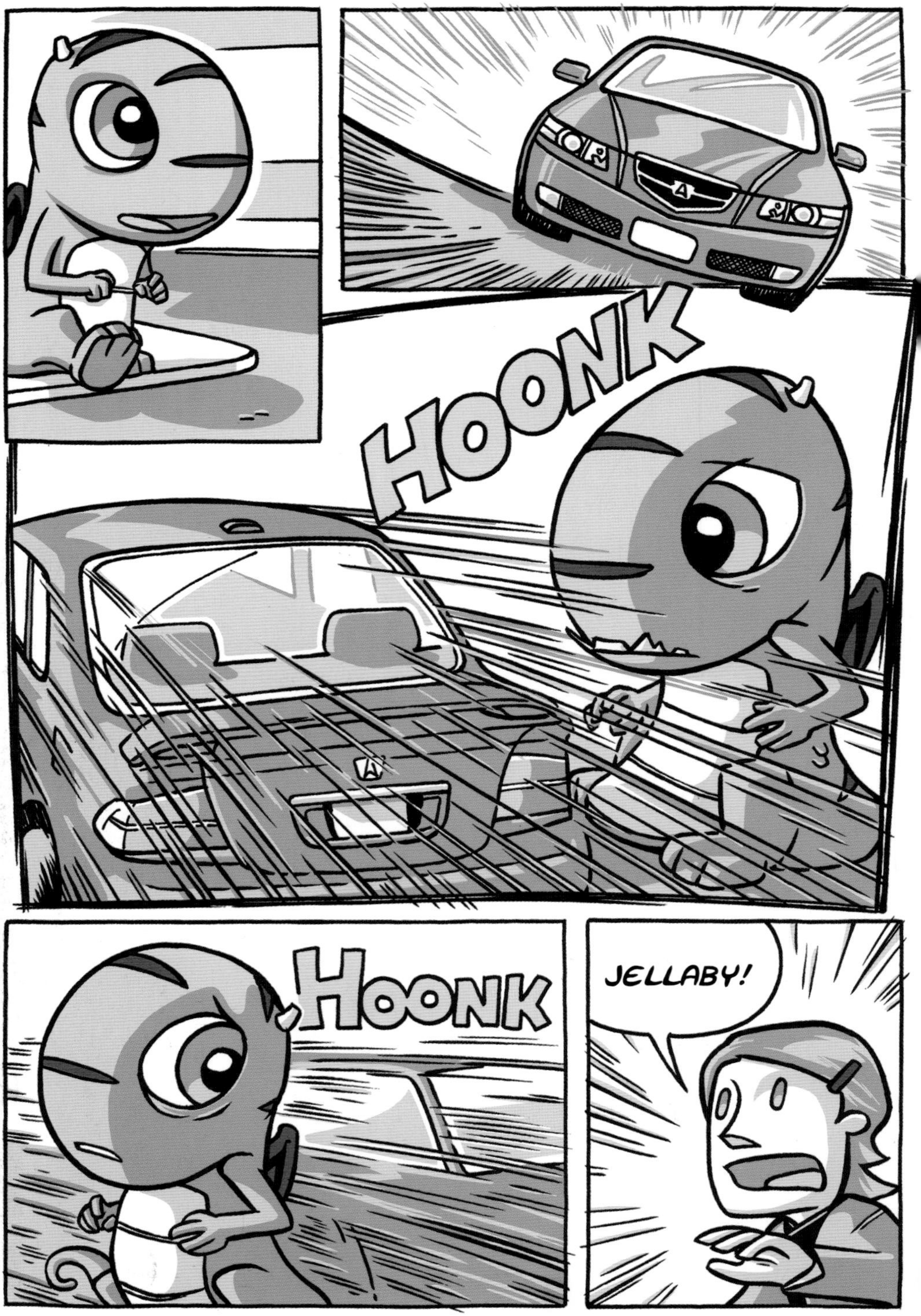
HOONK
HOONK
JELLABY!

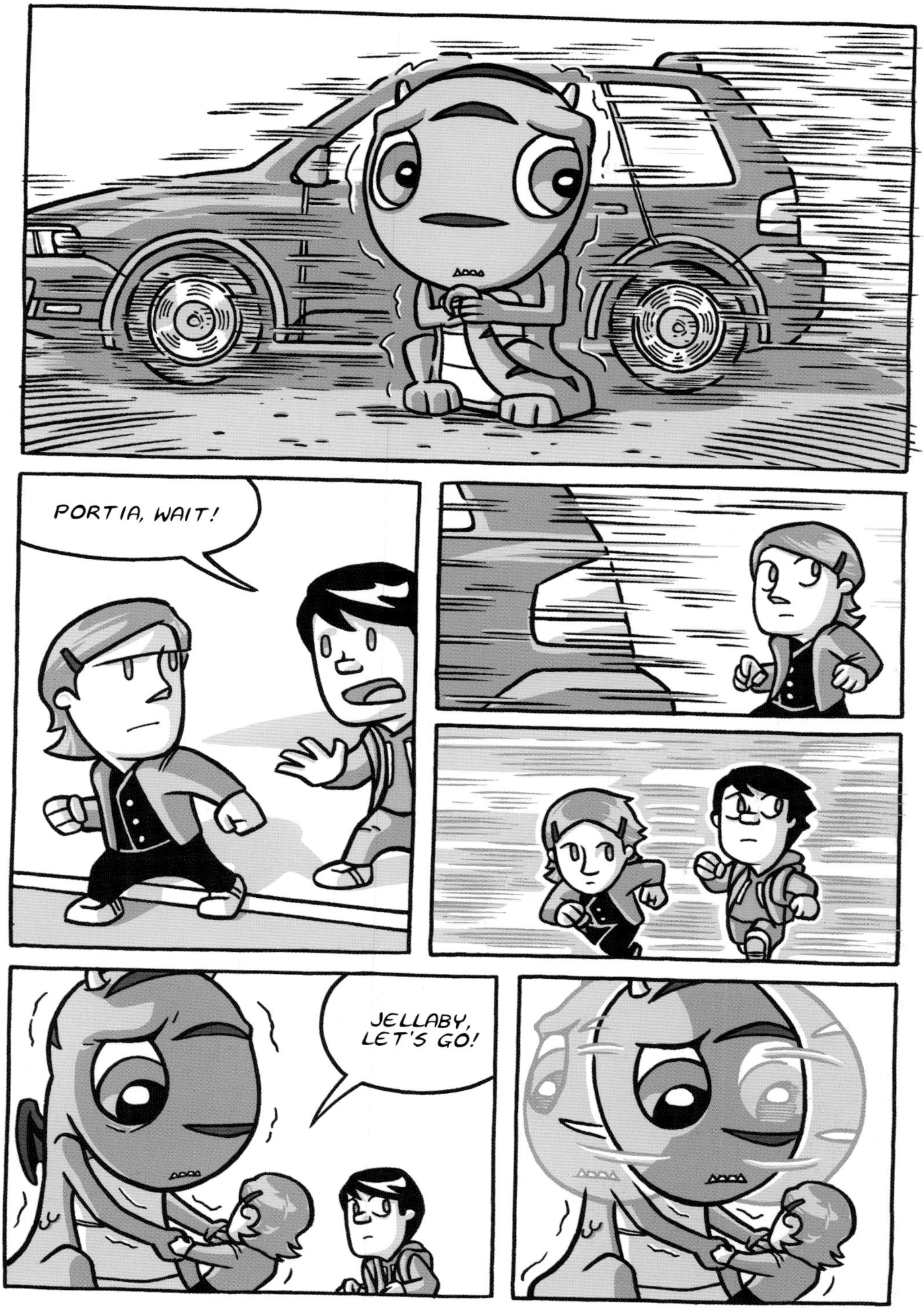
PORTIA, WAIT!
JELLABY, LET'S GO!

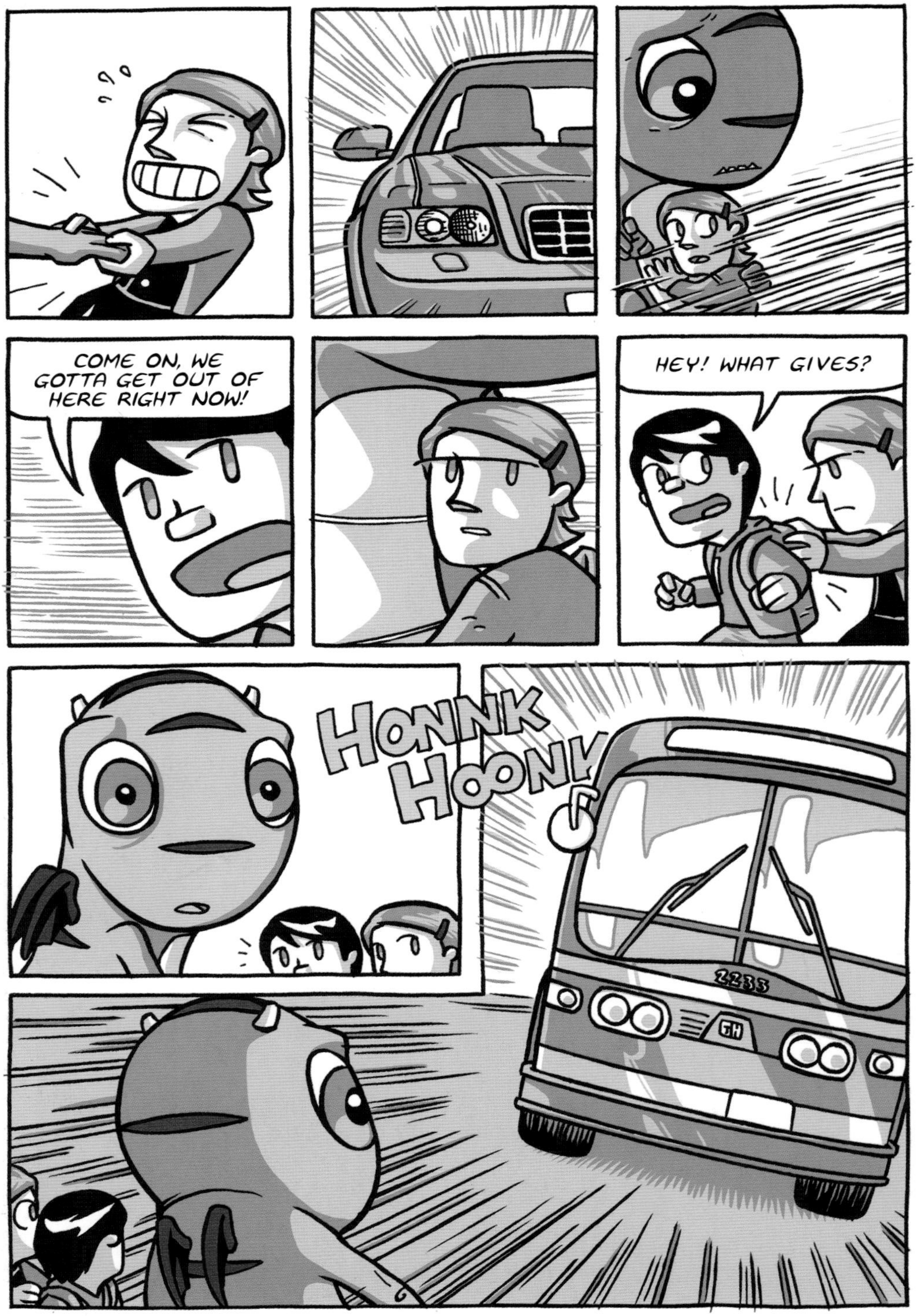
COME ON, WE GOTTA GET OUT OF HERE RIGHT NOW!
HEY! WHAT GIVES?
HONNK
HOONK
2233

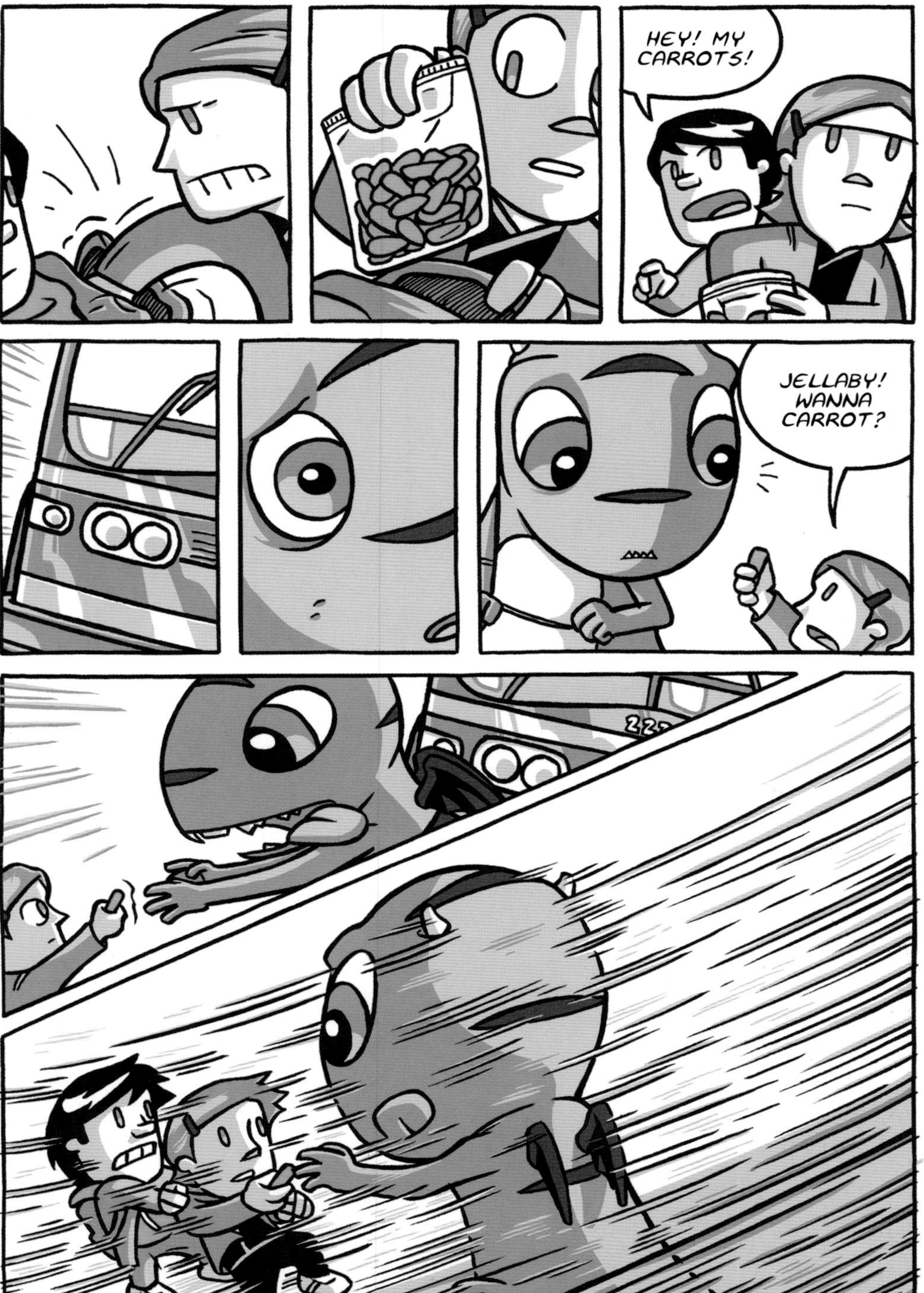
HEY! MY CARROTS!
JELLABY! WANNA CARROT?

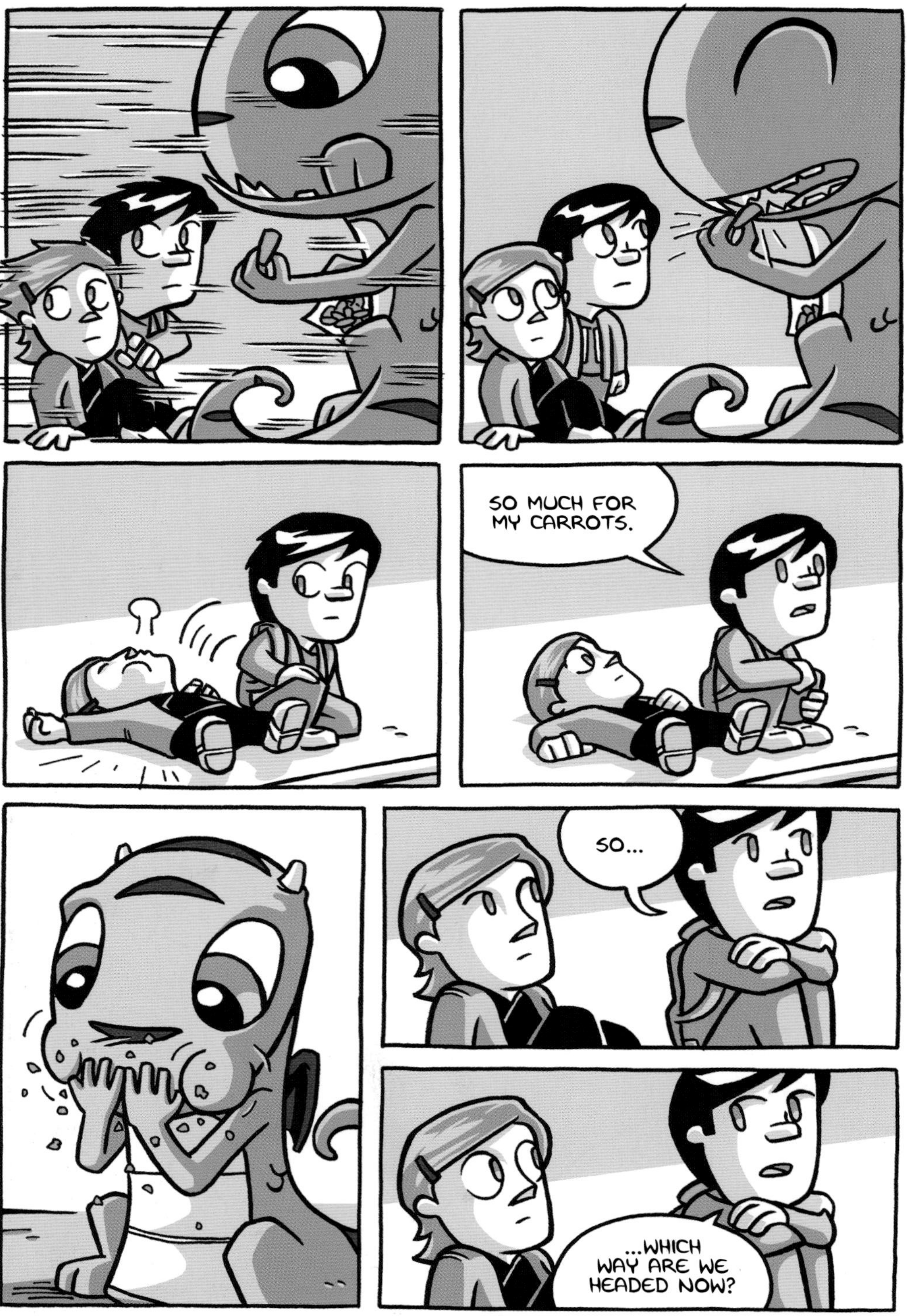

SO MUCH FOR MY CARROTS.
SO...
...WHICH WAY ARE WE HEADED NOW?

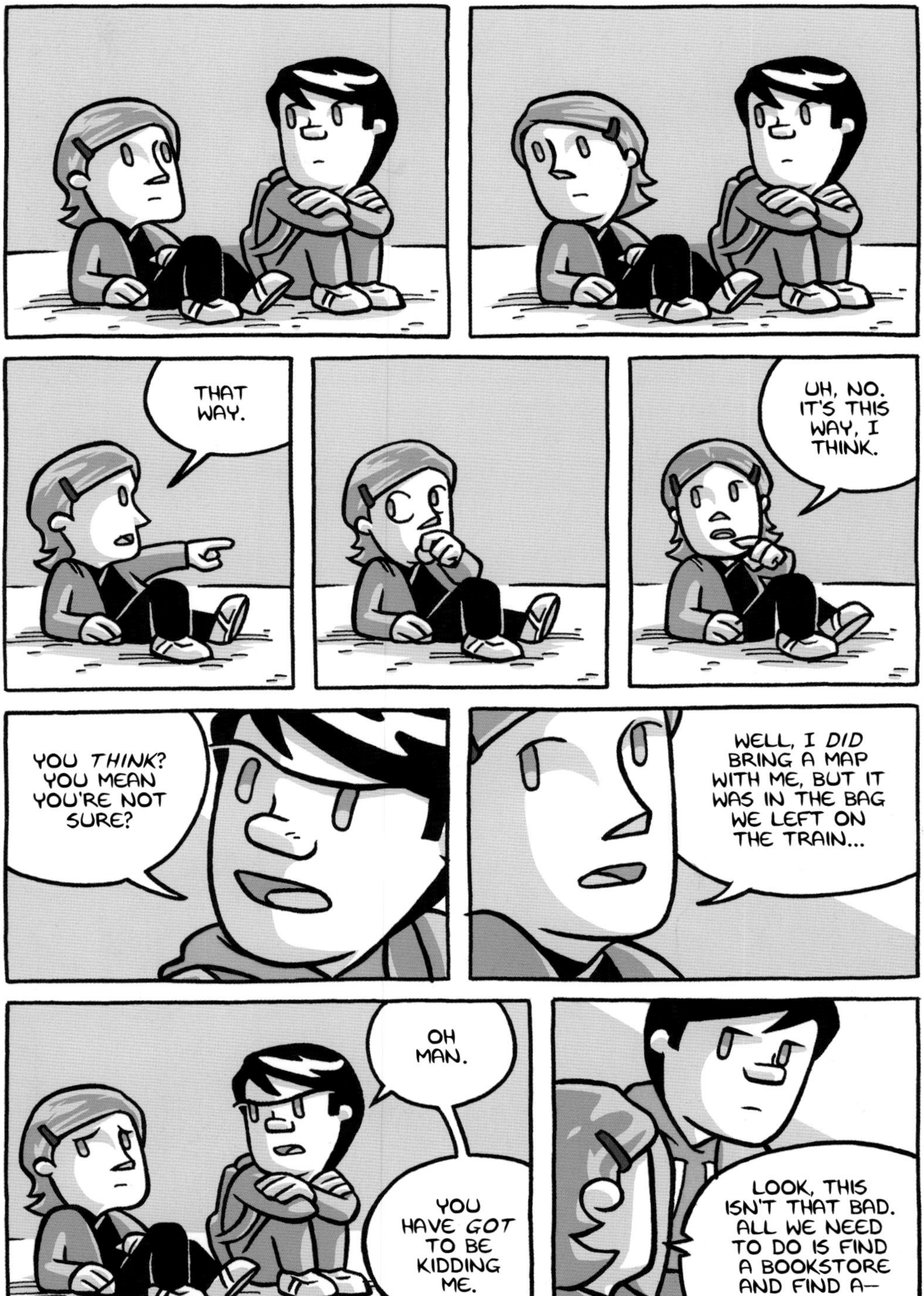
THAT WAY.
UH, NO. IT'S THIS WAY, I THINK.
YOU *THINK*? YOU MEAN YOU'RE NOT SURE?
WELL, I *DID* BRING A MAP WITH ME, BUT IT WAS IN THE BAG WE LEFT ON THE TRAIN...
OH MAN.
YOU HAVE *GOT* TO BE KIDDING ME.
LOOK, THIS ISN'T THAT BAD. ALL WE NEED TO DO IS FIND A BOOKSTORE AND FIND A—

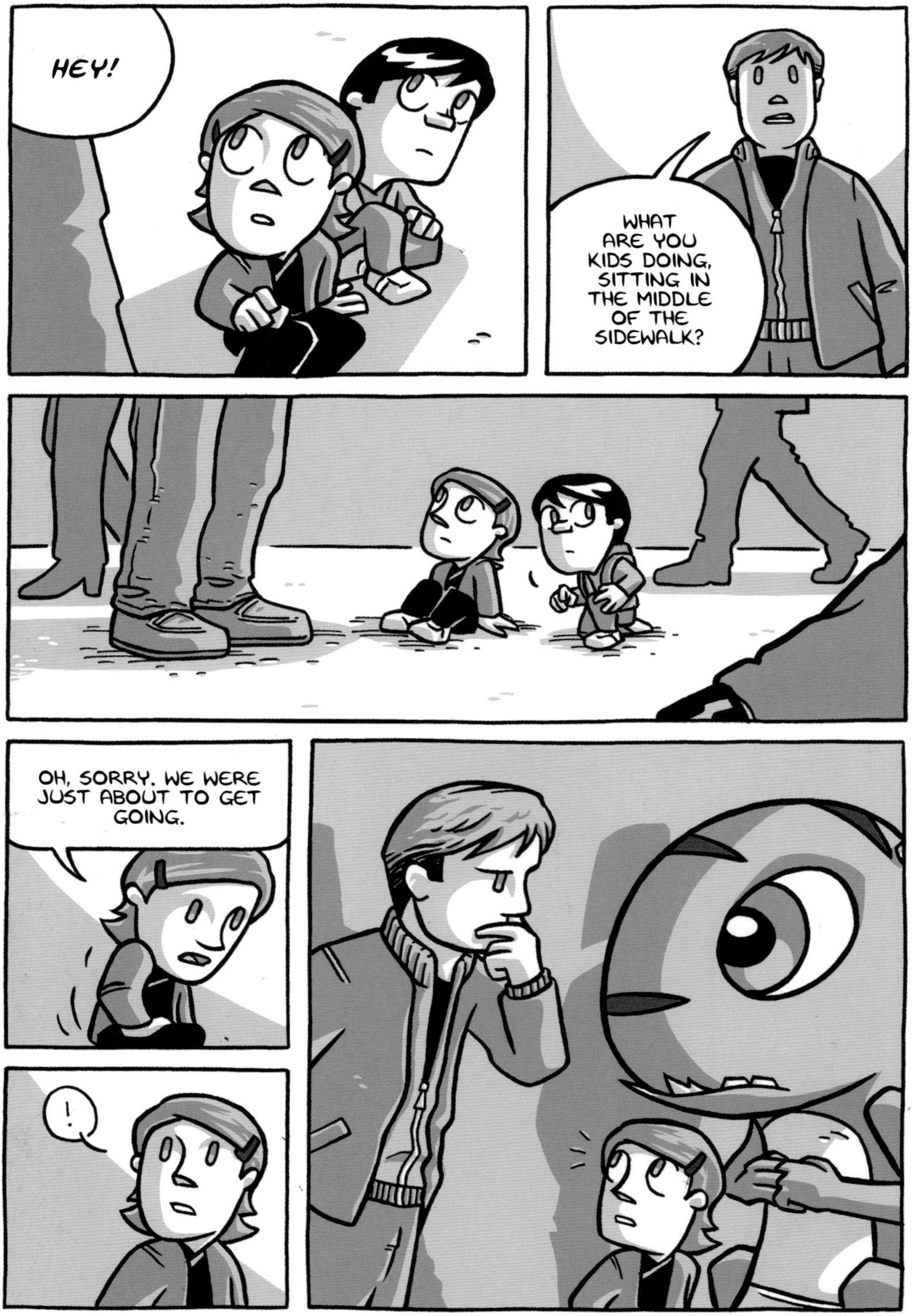
HEY!
WHAT ARE YOU KIDS DOING, SITTING IN THE MIDDLE OF THE SIDEWALK?
OH, SORRY. WE WERE JUST ABOUT TO GET GOING.
!

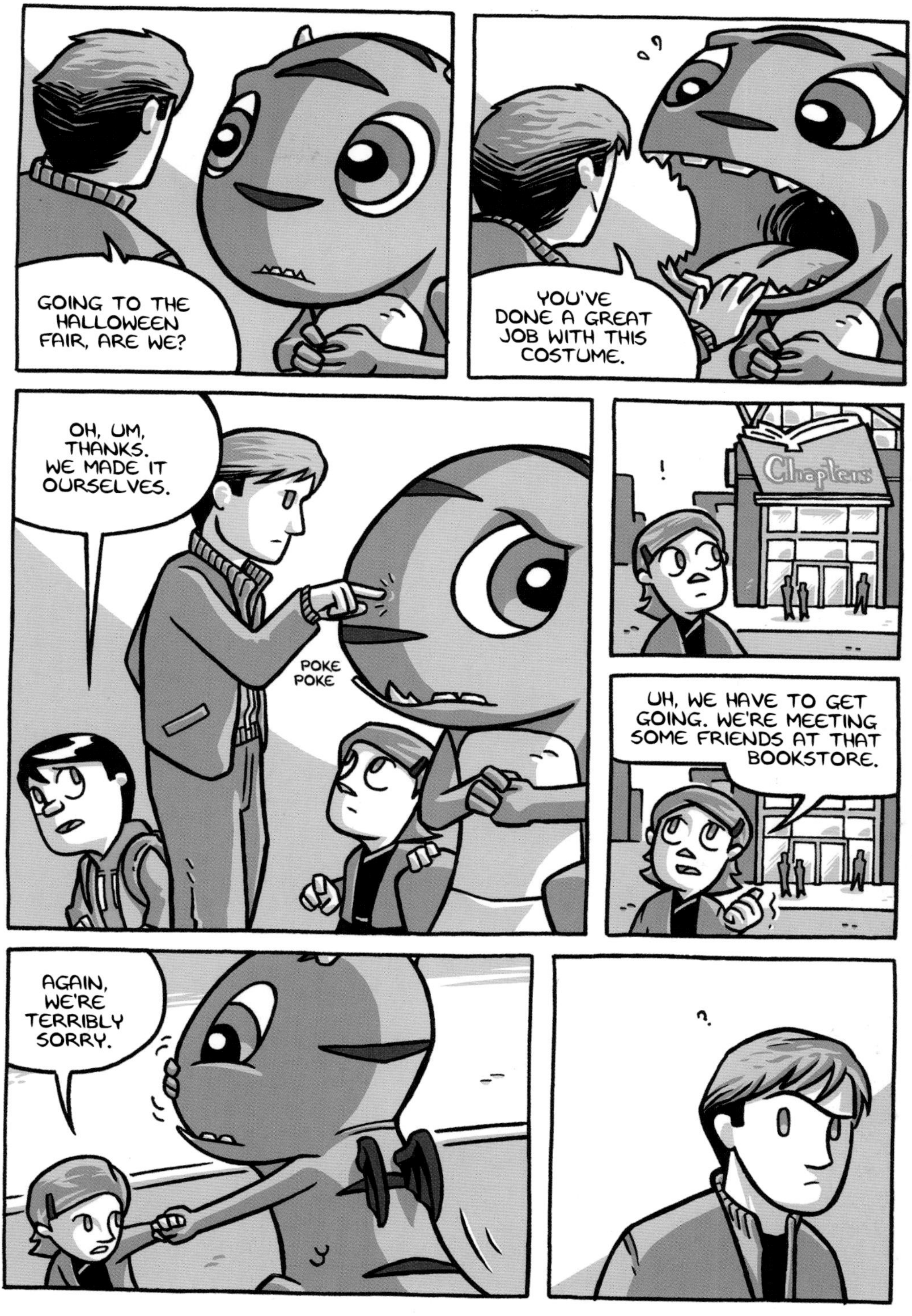
GOING TO THE HALLOWEEN FAIR, ARE WE?
YOU'VE DONE A GREAT JOB WITH THIS COSTUME.
OH, UM, THANKS. WE MADE IT OURSELVES.
POKE POKE
Chapters
!
UH, WE HAVE TO GET GOING. WE'RE MEETING SOME FRIENDS AT THAT BOOKSTORE.
AGAIN, WE'RE TERRIBLY SORRY.

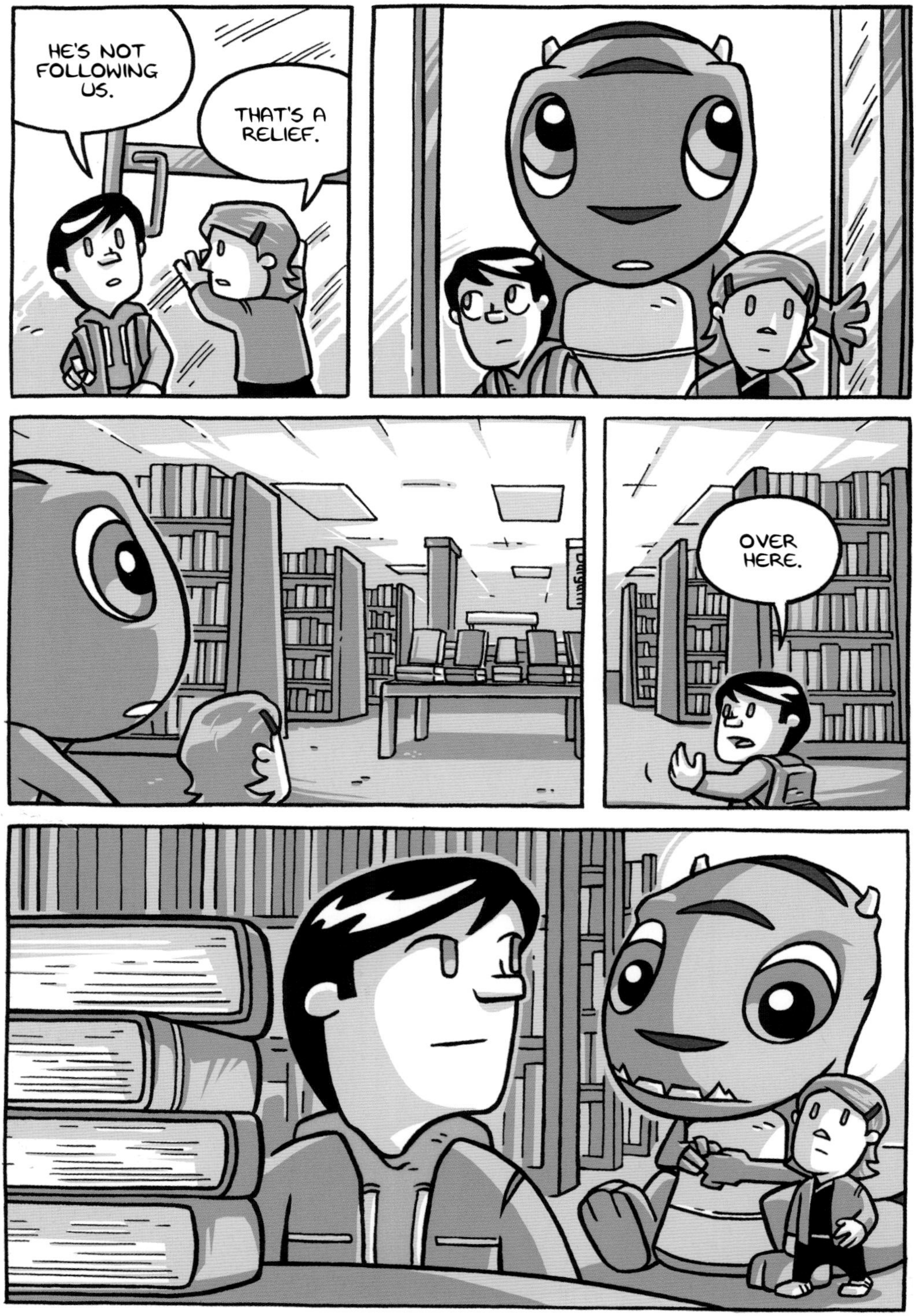
HE'S NOT FOLLOWING US.
THAT'S A RELIEF.
OVER HERE.

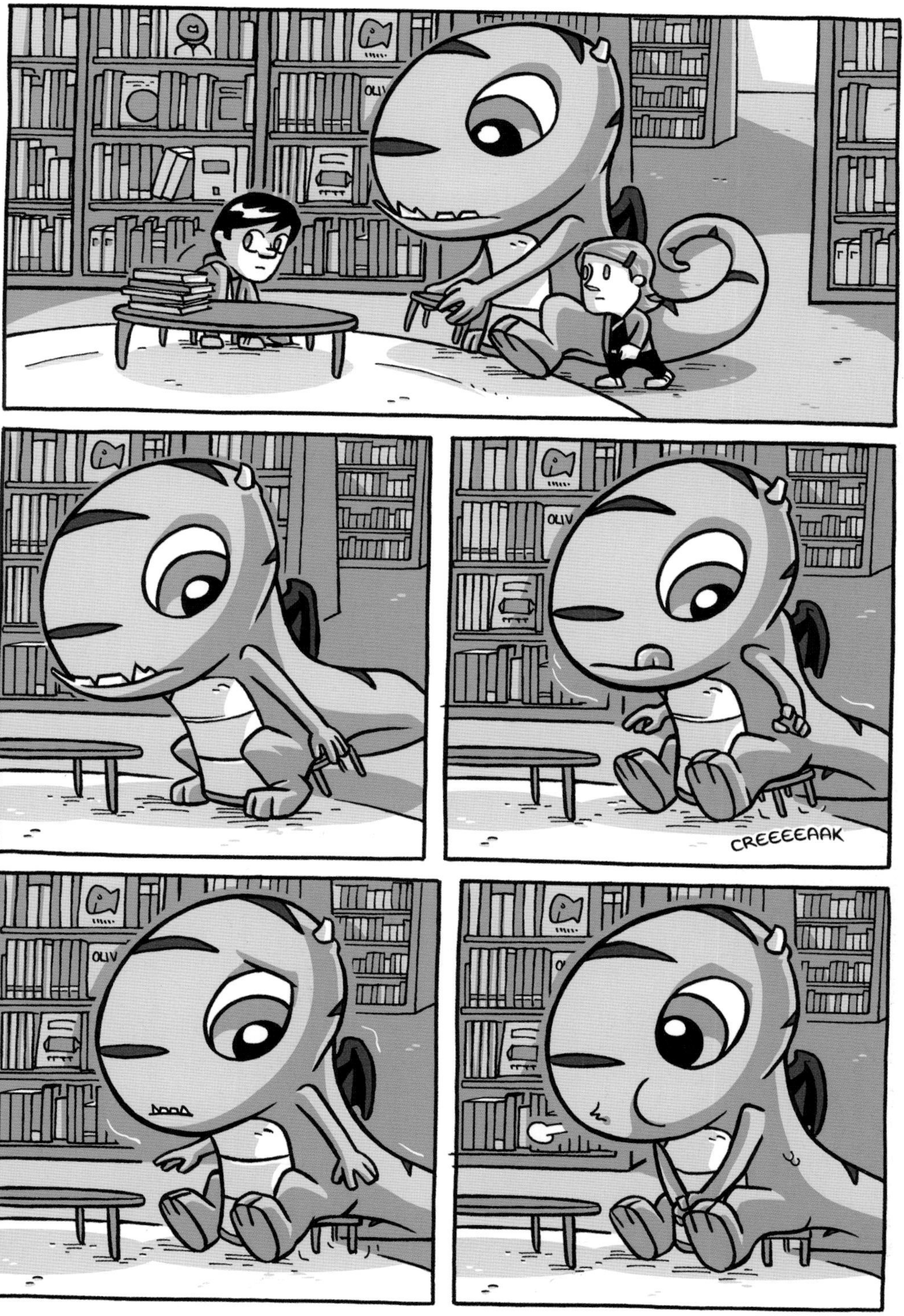
OLIV
OLIV
CREEEEAAK
OLIV

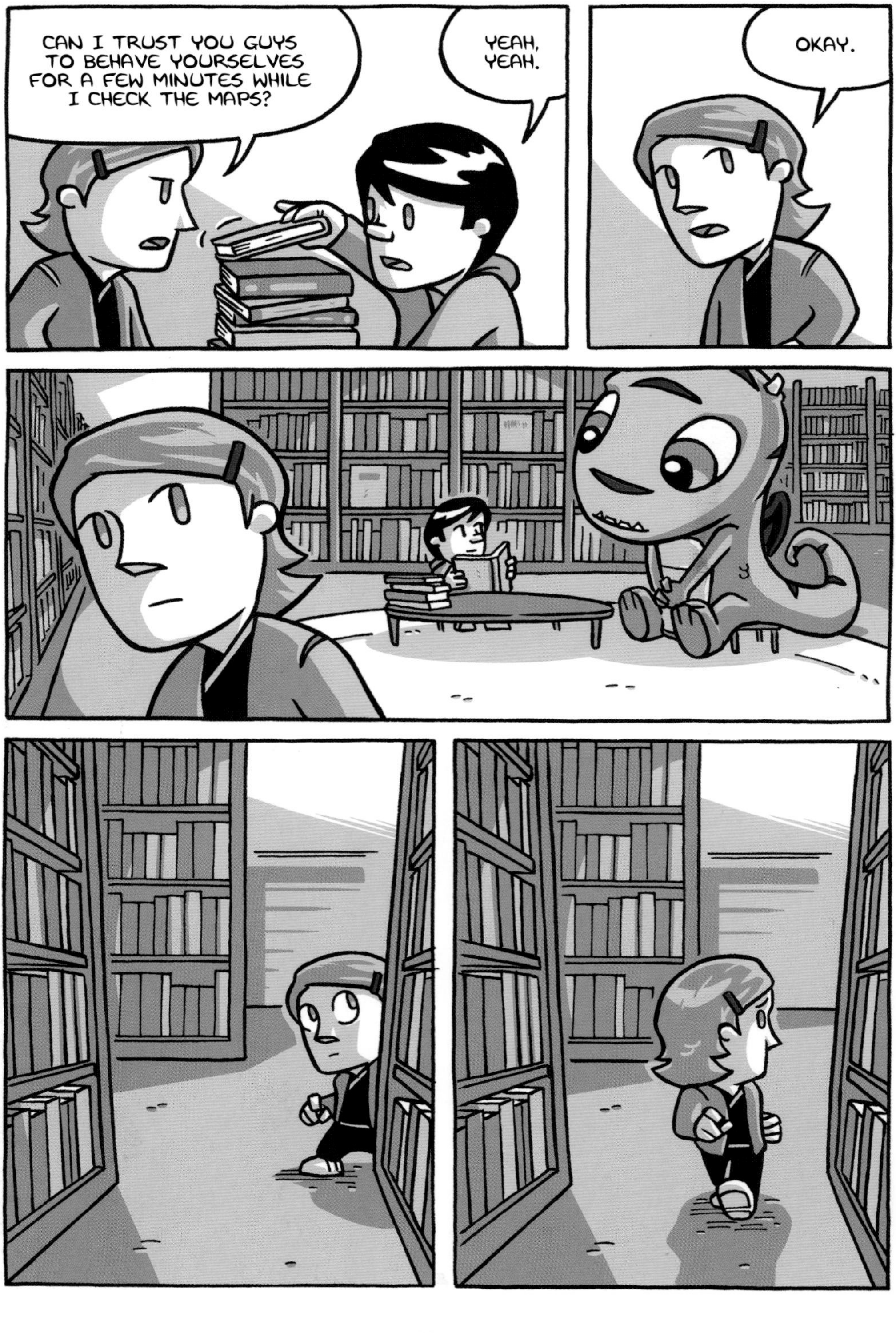
CAN I TRUST YOU GUYS TO BEHAVE YOURSELVES FOR A FEW MINUTES WHILE I CHECK THE MAPS?
YEAH, YEAH.
OKAY.

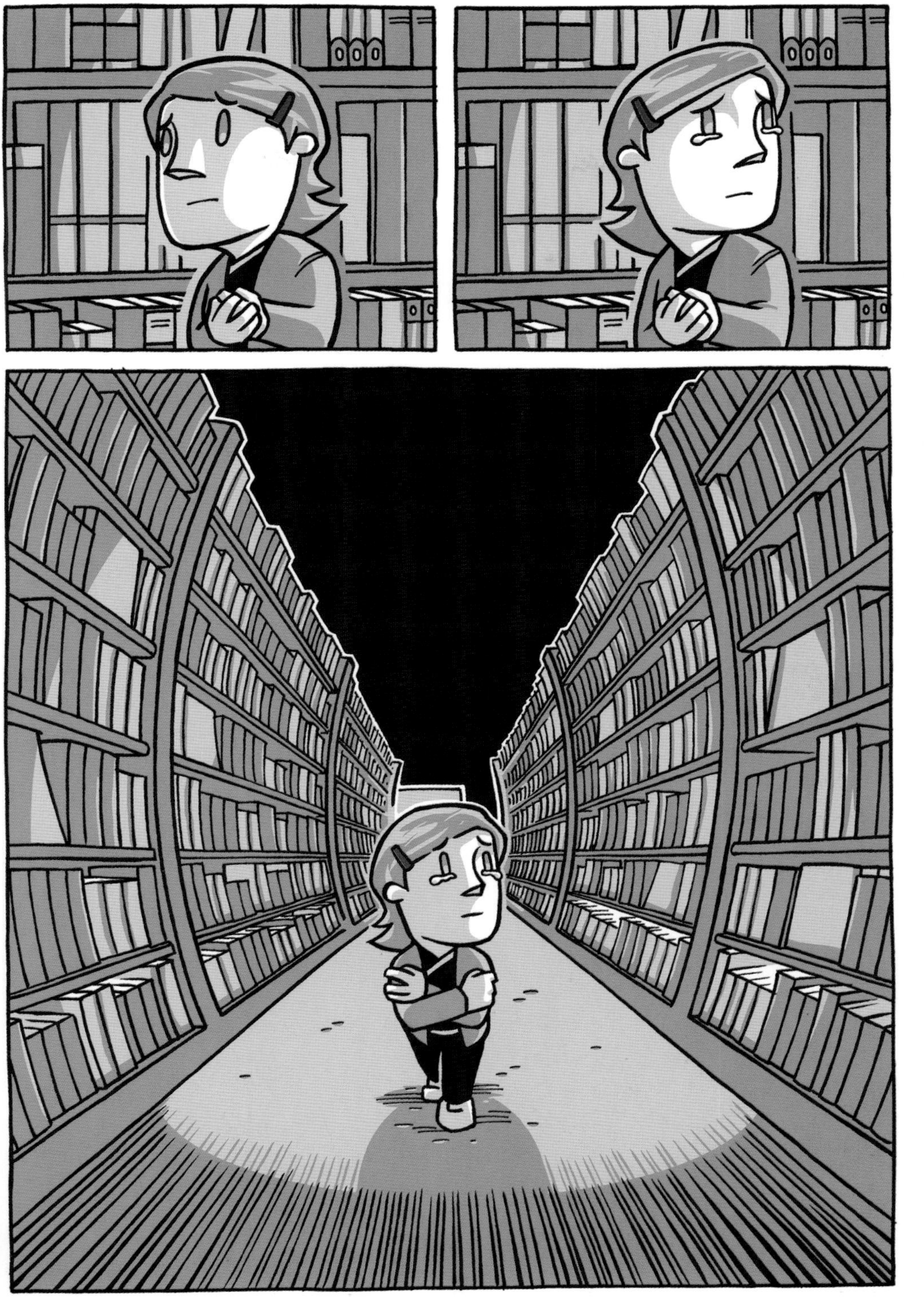

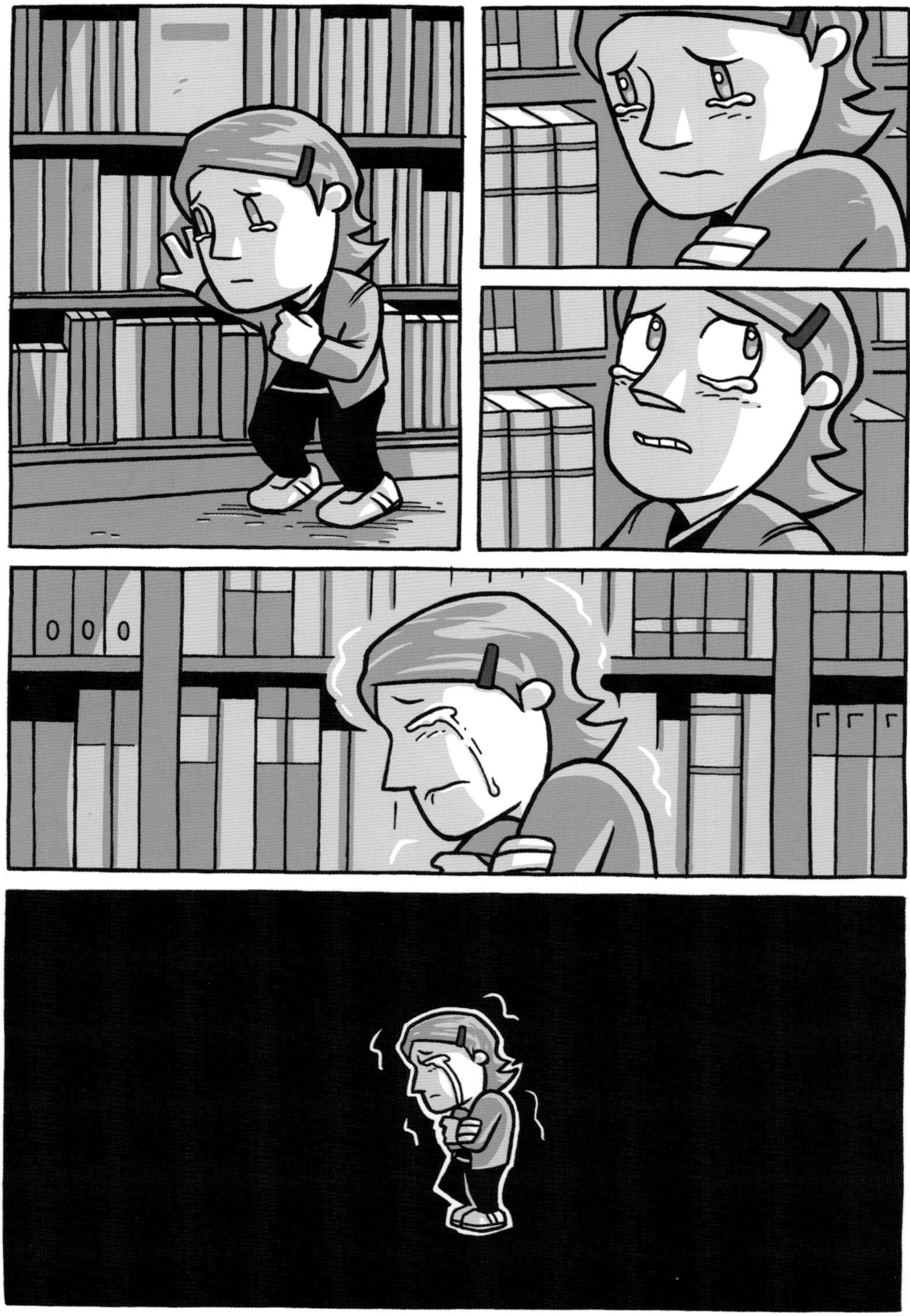

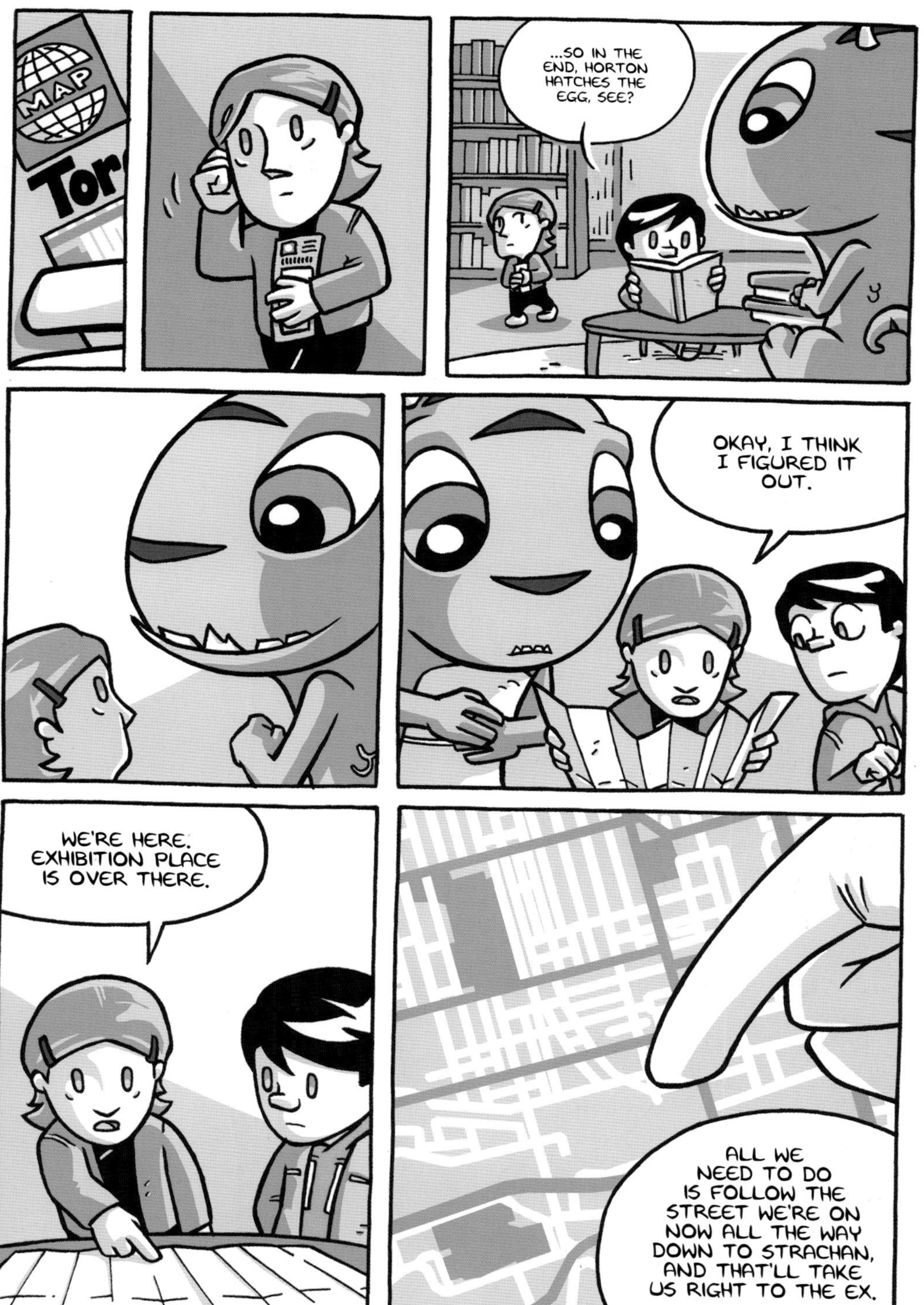
MAP
Tor
...SO IN THE END, HORTON HATCHES THE EGG, SEE?
OKAY, I THINK I FIGURED IT OUT.
WE'RE HERE. EXHIBITION PLACE IS OVER THERE.
ALL WE NEED TO DO IS FOLLOW THE STREET WE'RE ON NOW ALL THE WAY DOWN TO STRACHAN, AND THAT'LL TAKE US RIGHT TO THE EX.

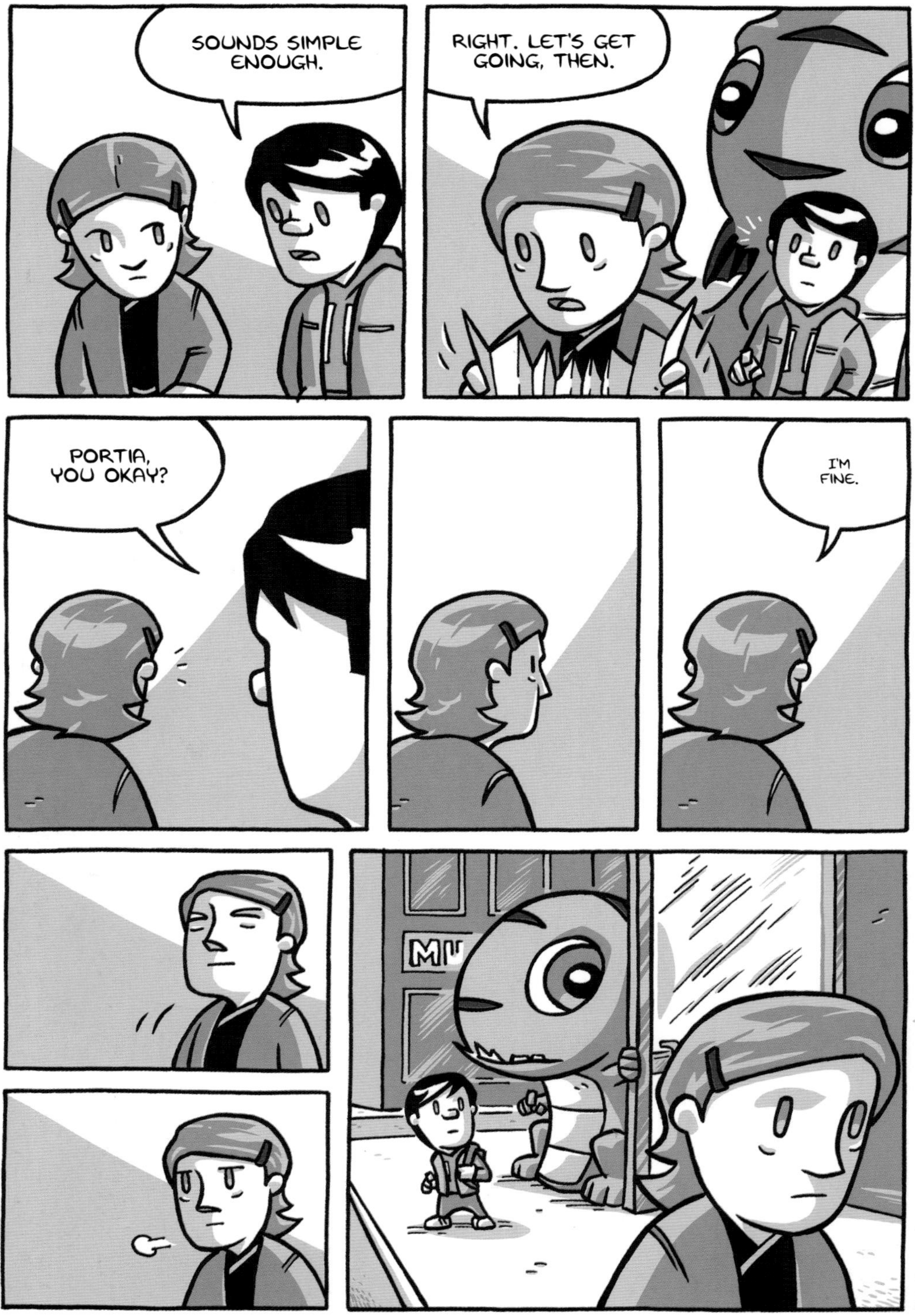
SOUNDS SIMPLE ENOUGH.
RIGHT. LET'S GET GOING, THEN.
PORTIA, YOU OKAY?
I'M FINE.
MU

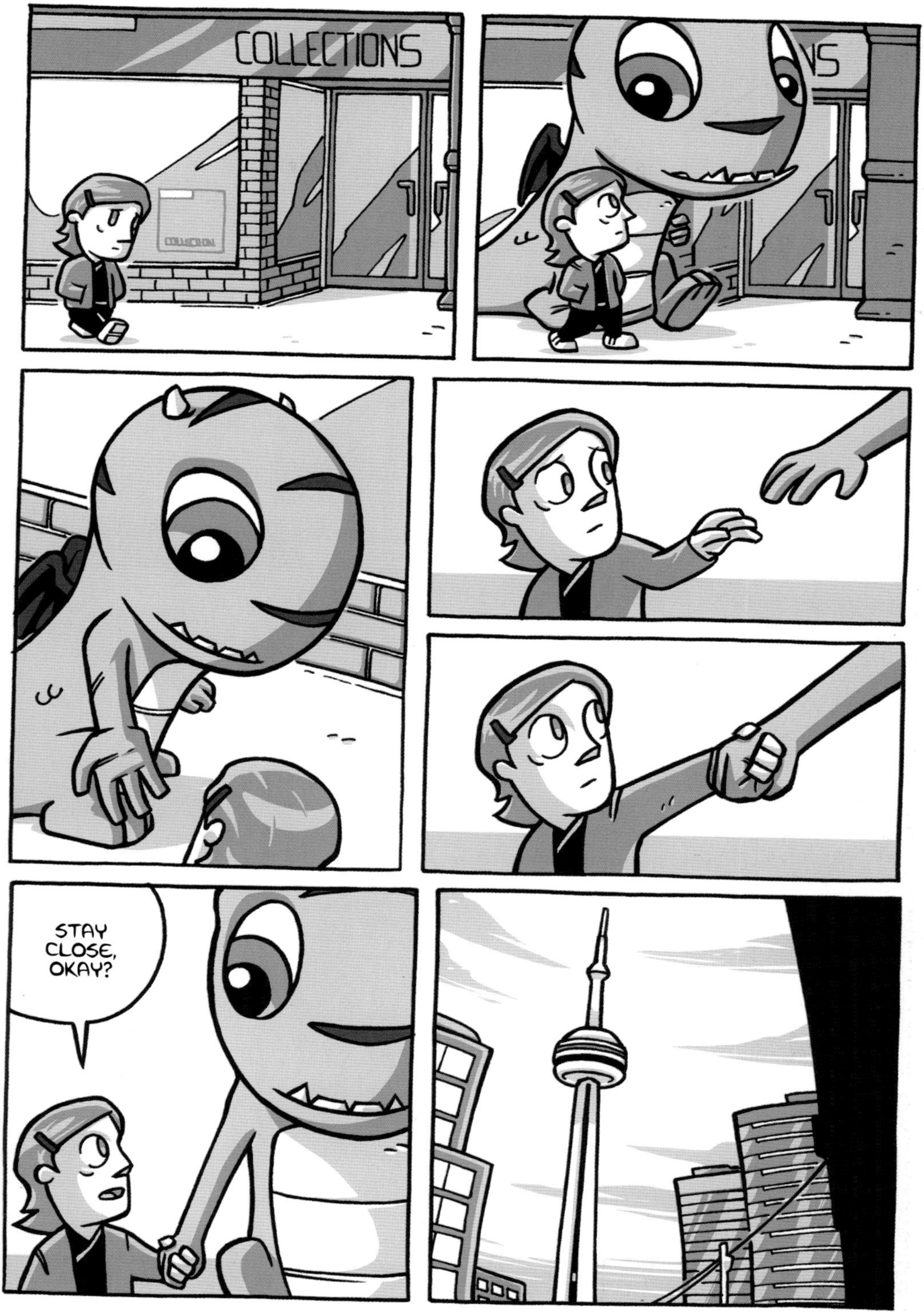
COLLECTIONS
STAY CLOSE, OKAY?

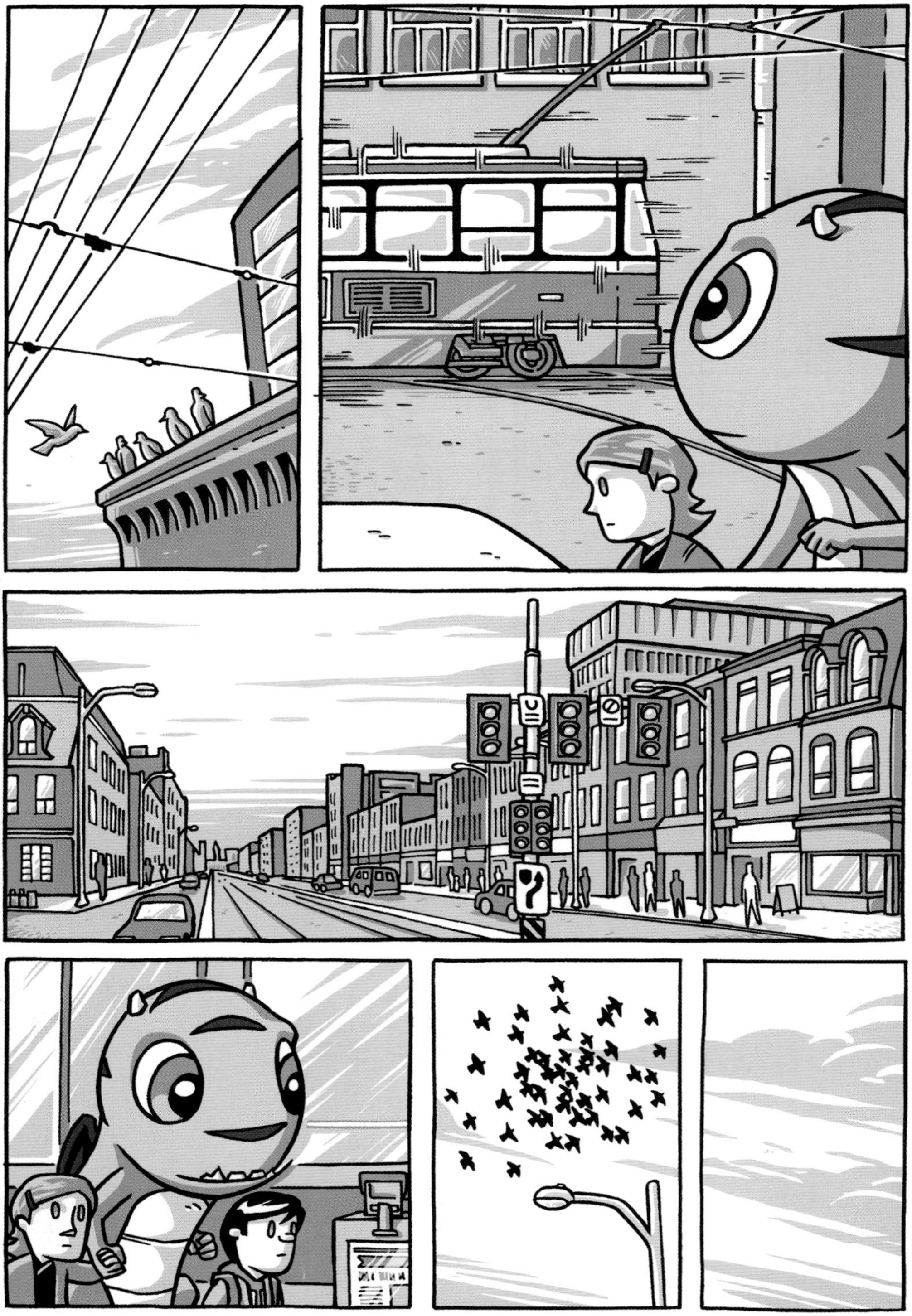

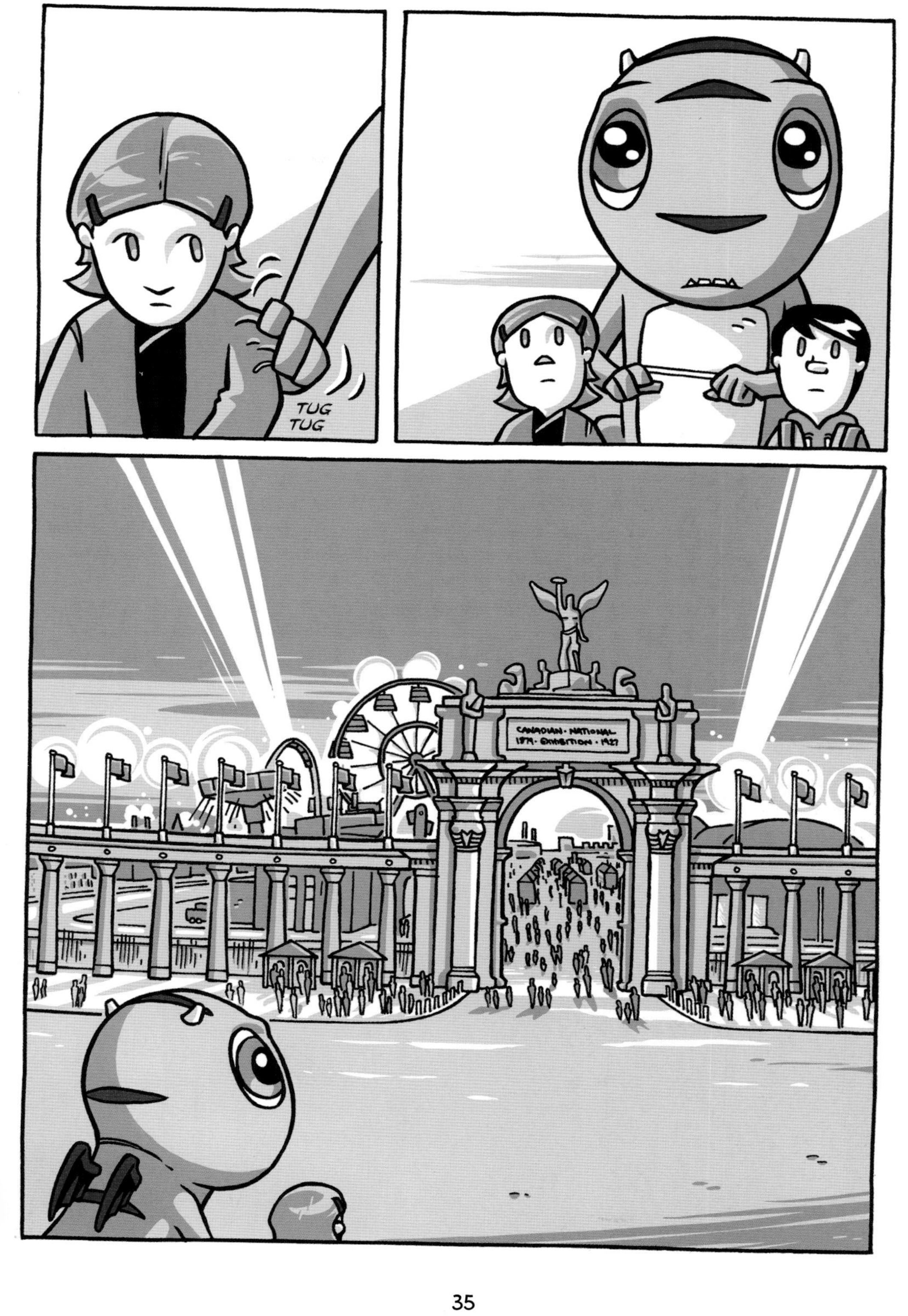
TUG TUG
CANADIAN · NATIONAL
1879 · EXHIBITION · 1927

CHAPTER TWO

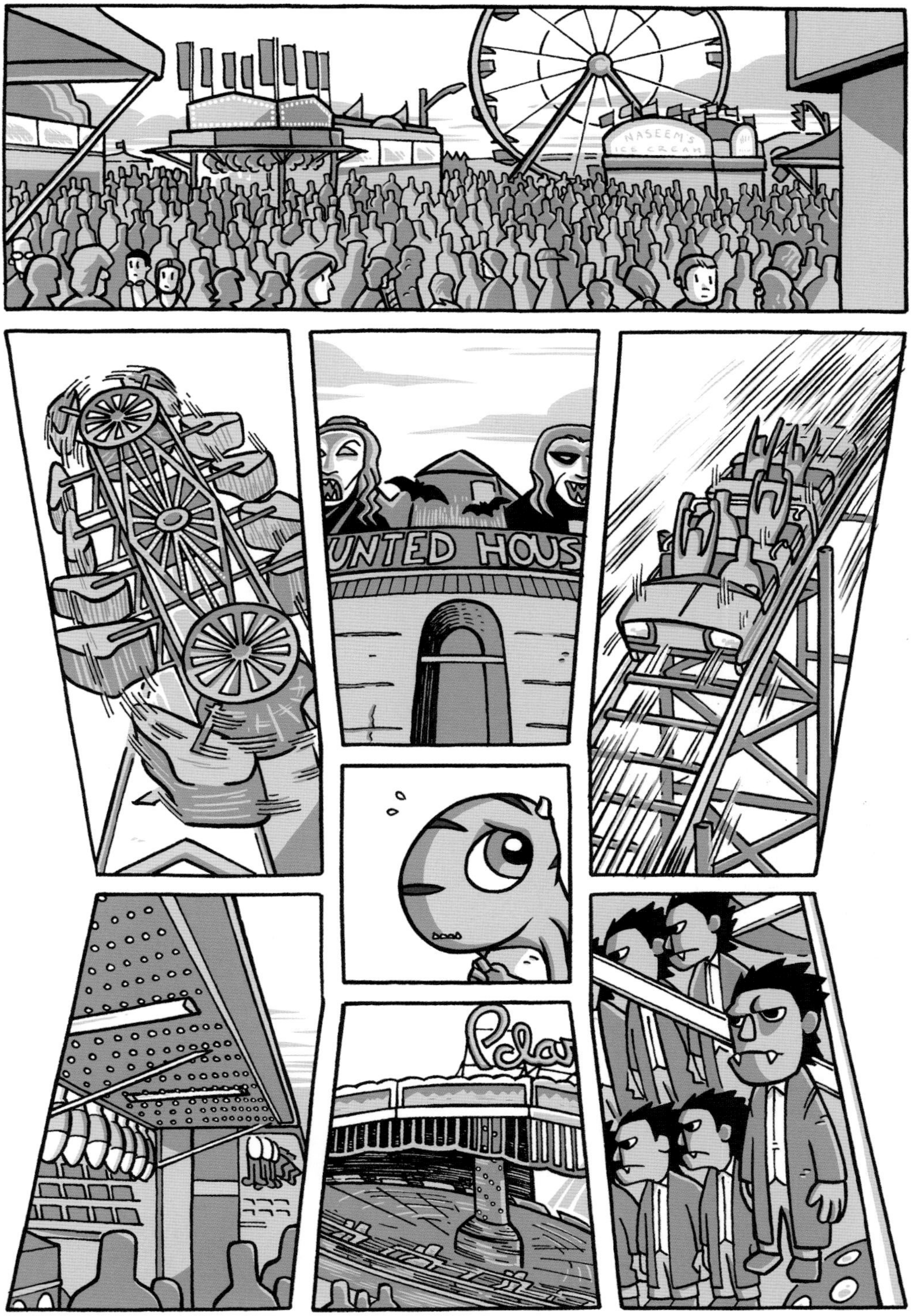
NASEEM'S
ICE CREAM
UNTED HOUS

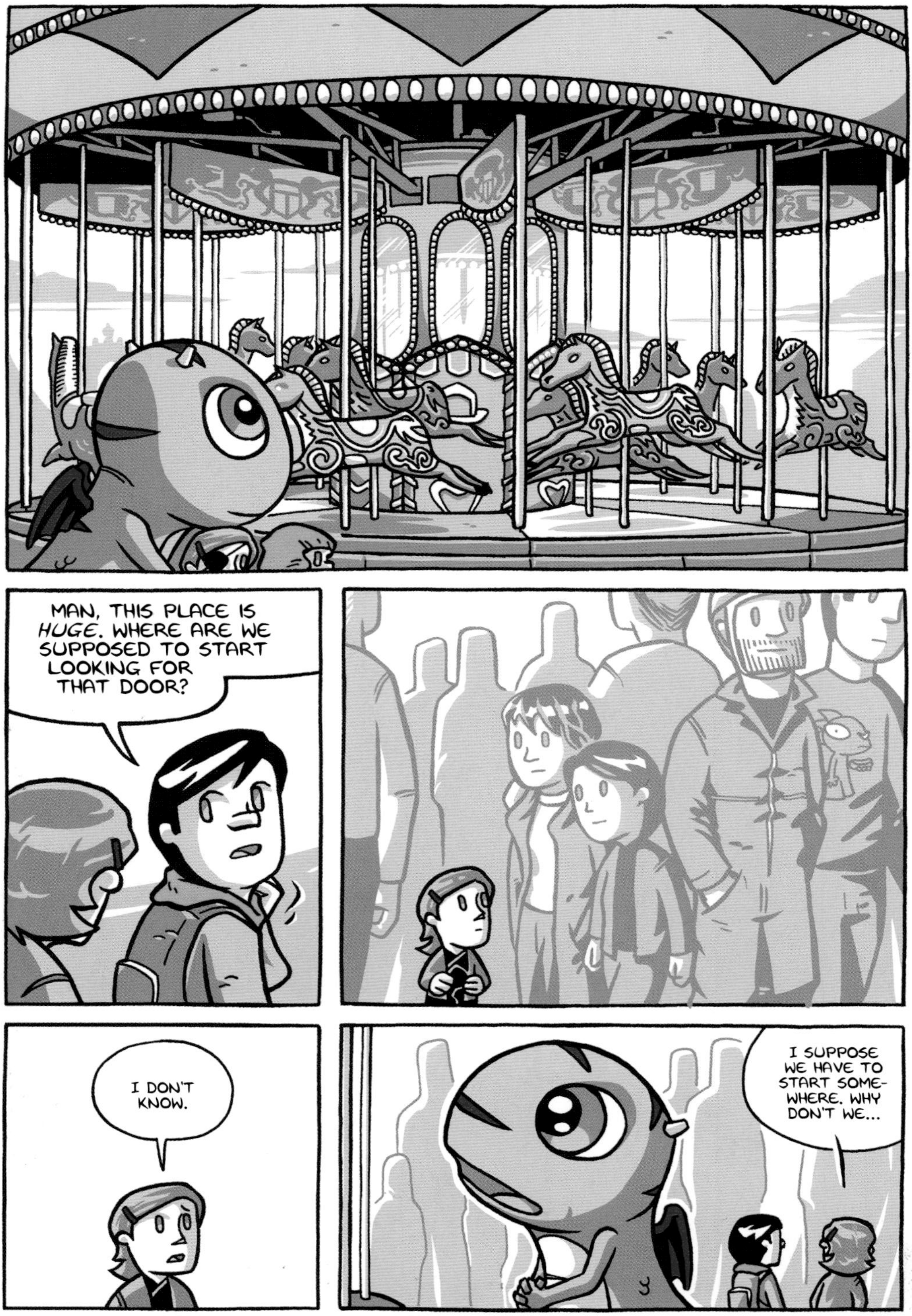
MAN, THIS PLACE IS *HUGE*. WHERE ARE WE SUPPOSED TO START LOOKING FOR THAT DOOR?
I DON'T KNOW.
I SUPPOSE WE HAVE TO START SOME-WHERE. WHY DON'T WE...

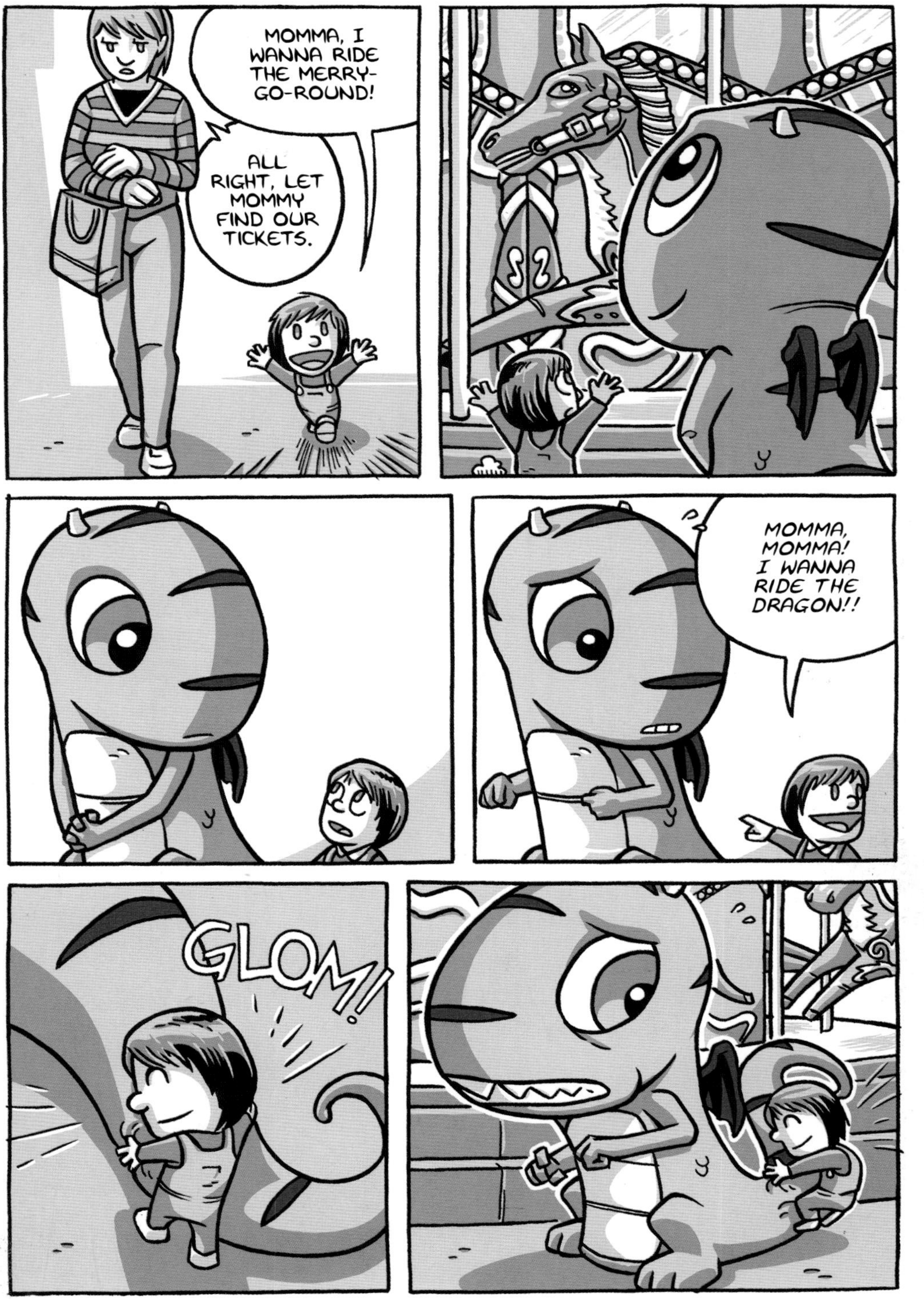

MOMMA, I WANNA RIDE THE MERRY-GO-ROUND!
ALL RIGHT, LET MOMMY FIND OUR TICKETS.
MOMMA, MOMMA! I WANNA RIDE THE DRAGON!!
GLOM!

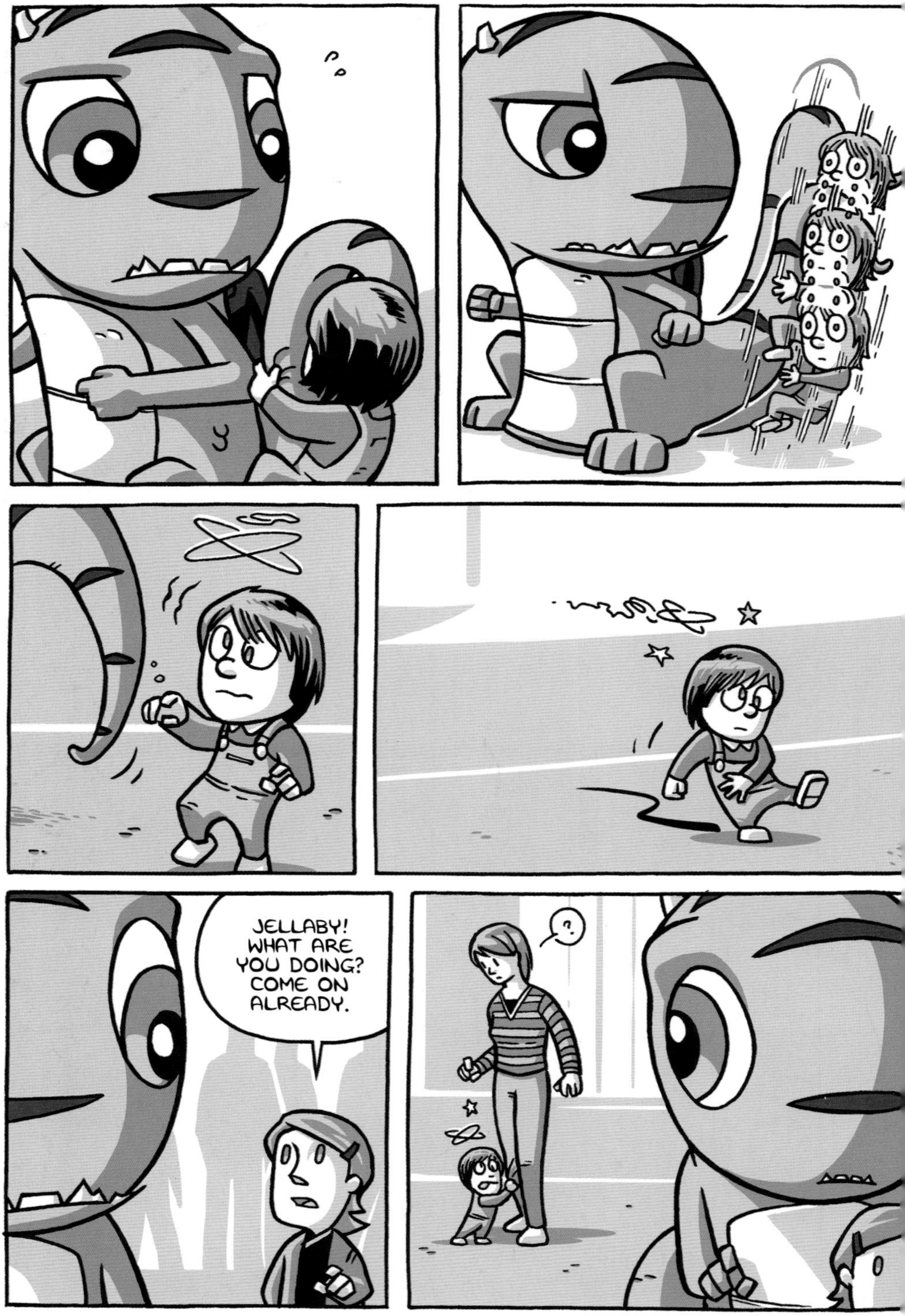
JELLABY! WHAT ARE YOU DOING? COME ON ALREADY.
?

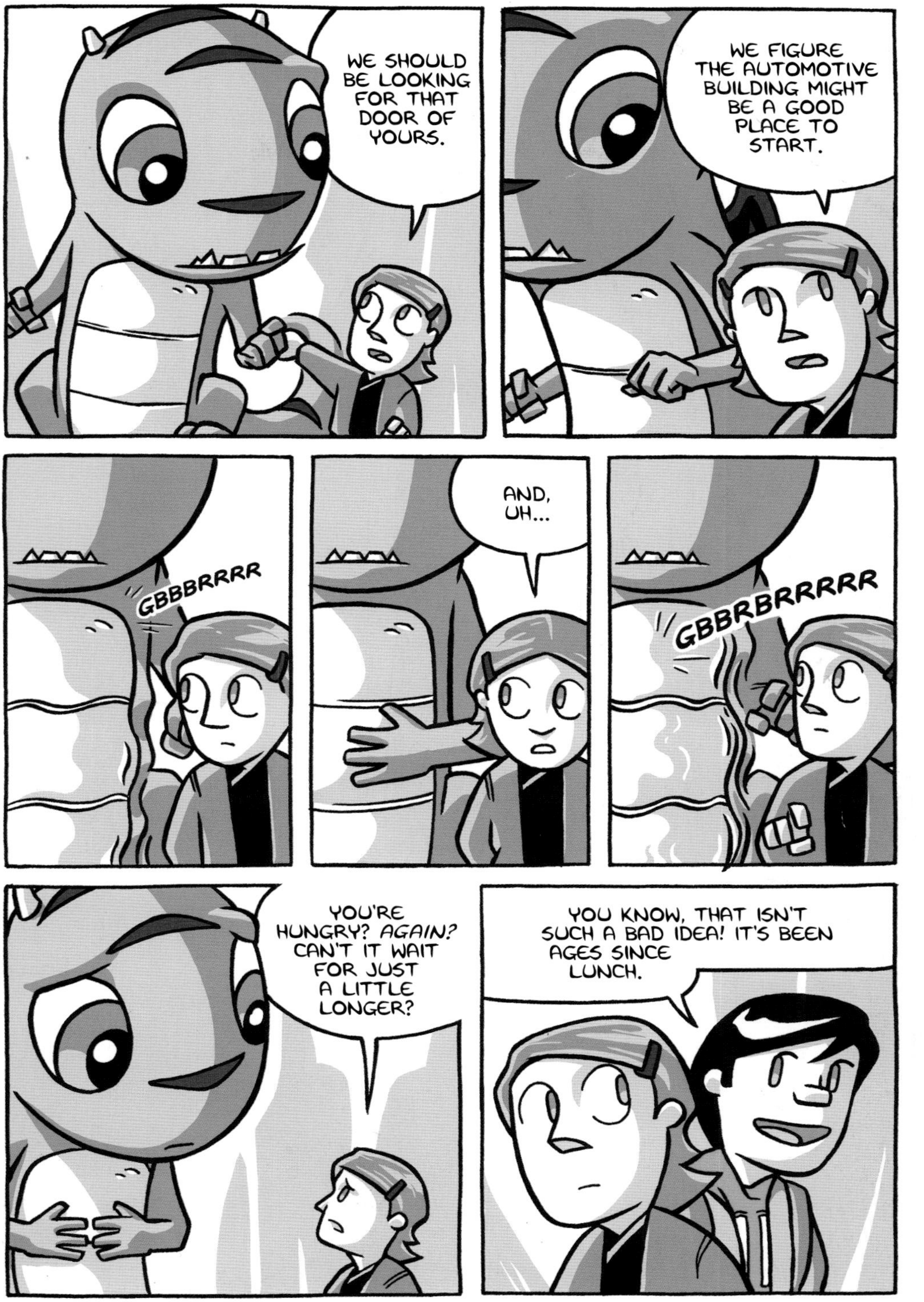
WE SHOULD BE LOOKING FOR THAT DOOR OF YOURS.
WE FIGURE THE AUTOMOTIVE BUILDING MIGHT BE A GOOD PLACE TO START.
GBBBRRRR
AND, UH...
GBBRBRRRRR
YOU'RE HUNGRY? *AGAIN?* CAN'T IT WAIT FOR JUST A LITTLE LONGER?
YOU KNOW, THAT ISN'T SUCH A BAD IDEA! IT'S BEEN AGES SINCE LUNCH.

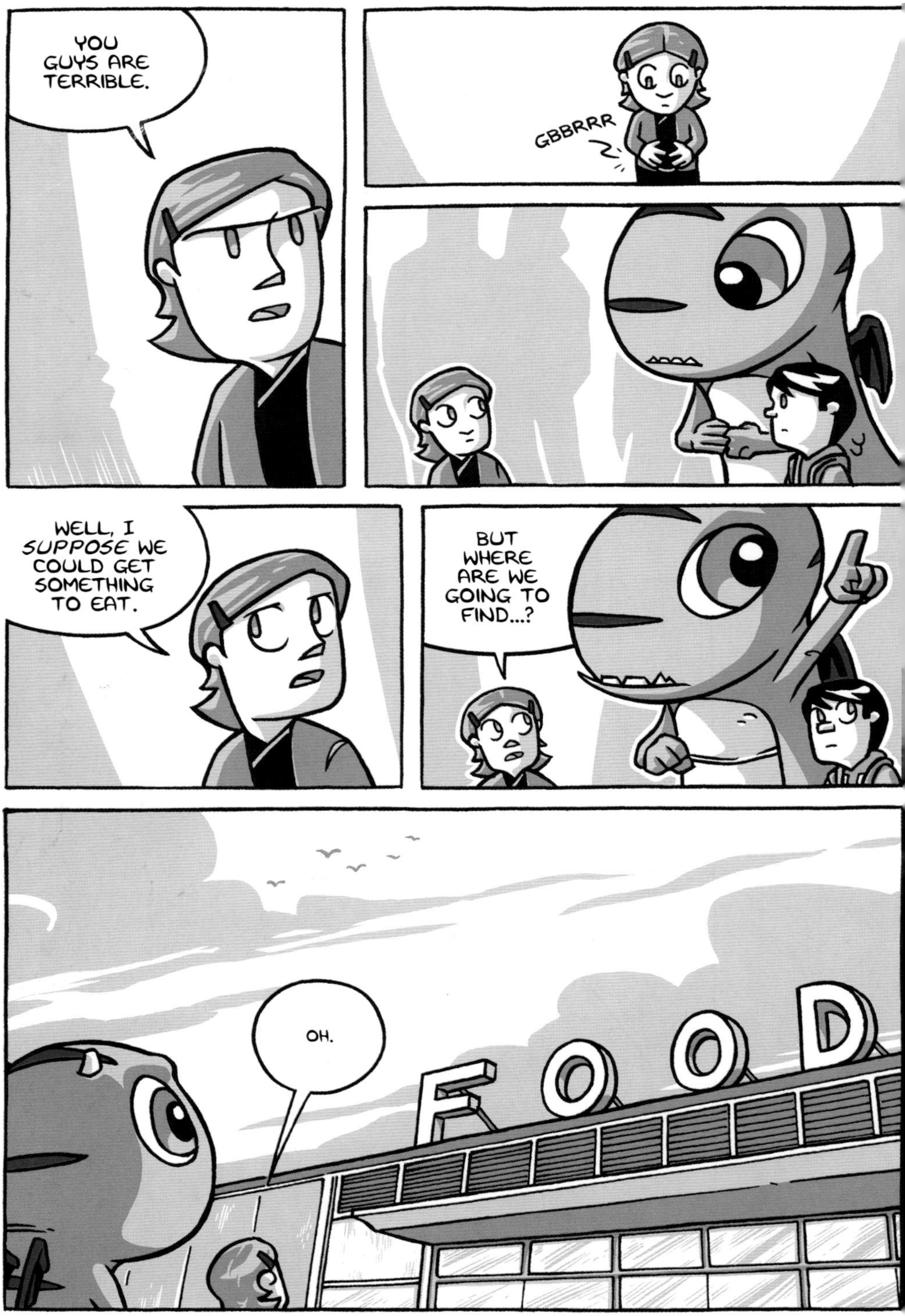
YOU GUYS ARE TERRIBLE.
GBBRRR
WELL, I *SUPPOSE* WE COULD GET SOMETHING TO EAT.
BUT WHERE ARE WE GOING TO FIND...?
OH.
FOOD

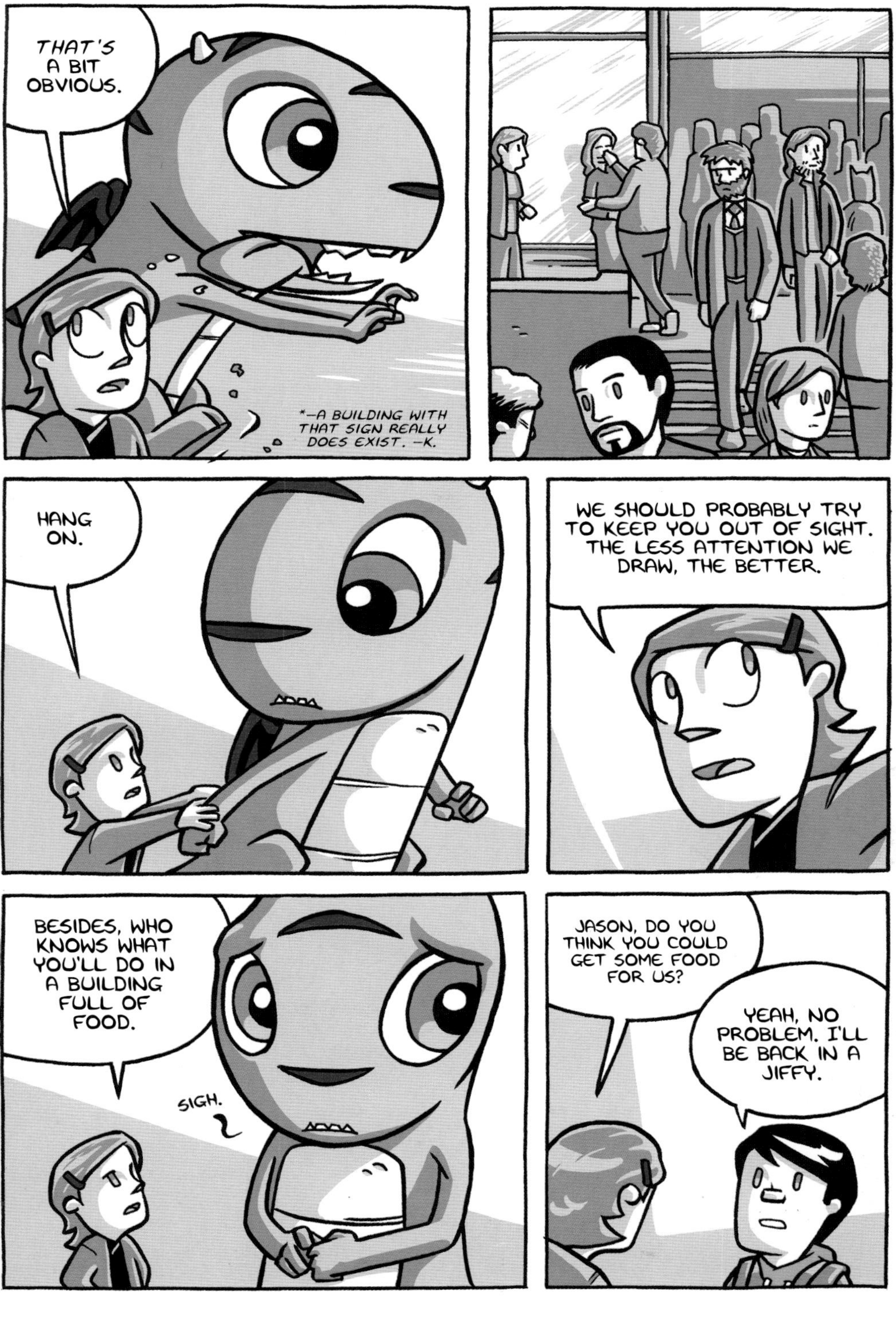
THAT'S A BIT OBVIOUS.
*—A BUILDING WITH THAT SIGN REALLY DOES EXIST. —K.
HANG ON.
WE SHOULD PROBABLY TRY TO KEEP YOU OUT OF SIGHT. THE LESS ATTENTION WE DRAW, THE BETTER.
BESIDES, WHO KNOWS WHAT YOU'LL DO IN A BUILDING FULL OF FOOD.
SIGH.
JASON, DO YOU THINK YOU COULD GET SOME FOOD FOR US?
YEAH, NO PROBLEM. I'LL BE BACK IN A JIFFY.

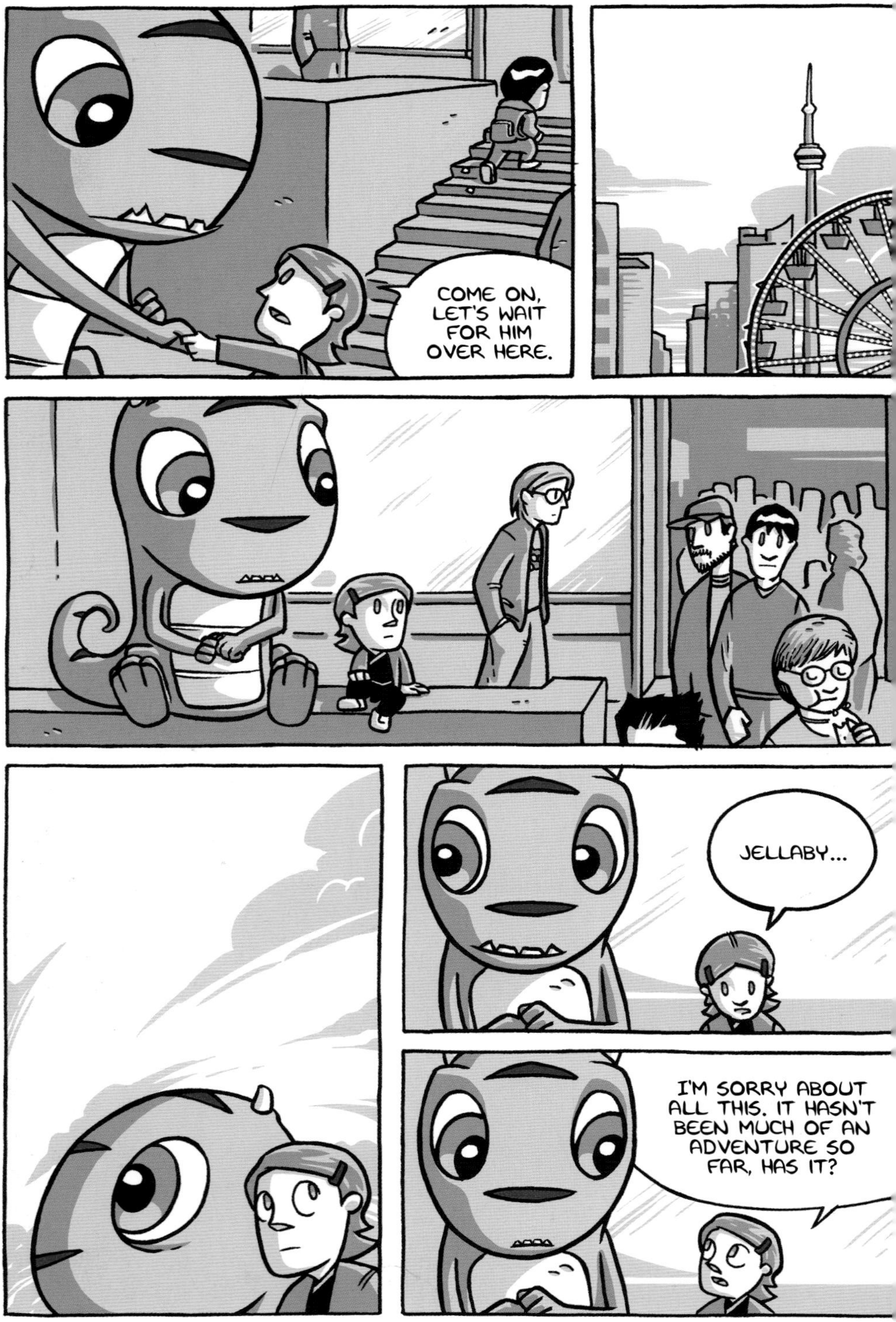
COME ON, LET'S WAIT FOR HIM OVER HERE.
JELLABY...
I'M SORRY ABOUT ALL THIS. IT HASN'T BEEN MUCH OF AN ADVENTURE SO FAR, HAS IT?

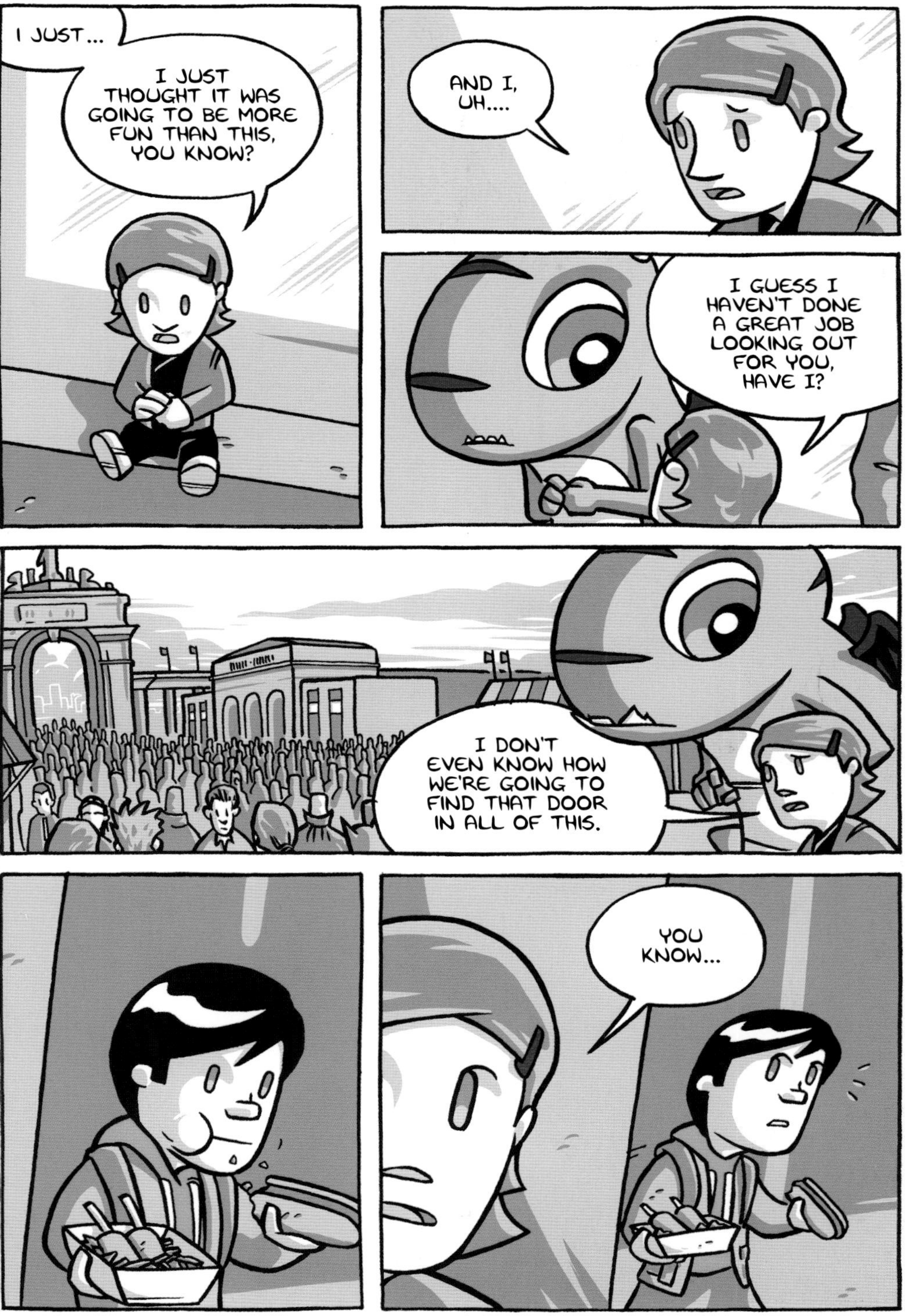
I JUST...
I JUST THOUGHT IT WAS GOING TO BE MORE FUN THAN THIS, YOU KNOW?
AND I, UH....
I GUESS I HAVEN'T DONE A GREAT JOB LOOKING OUT FOR YOU, HAVE I?
I DON'T EVEN KNOW HOW WE'RE GOING TO FIND THAT DOOR IN ALL OF THIS.
YOU KNOW...

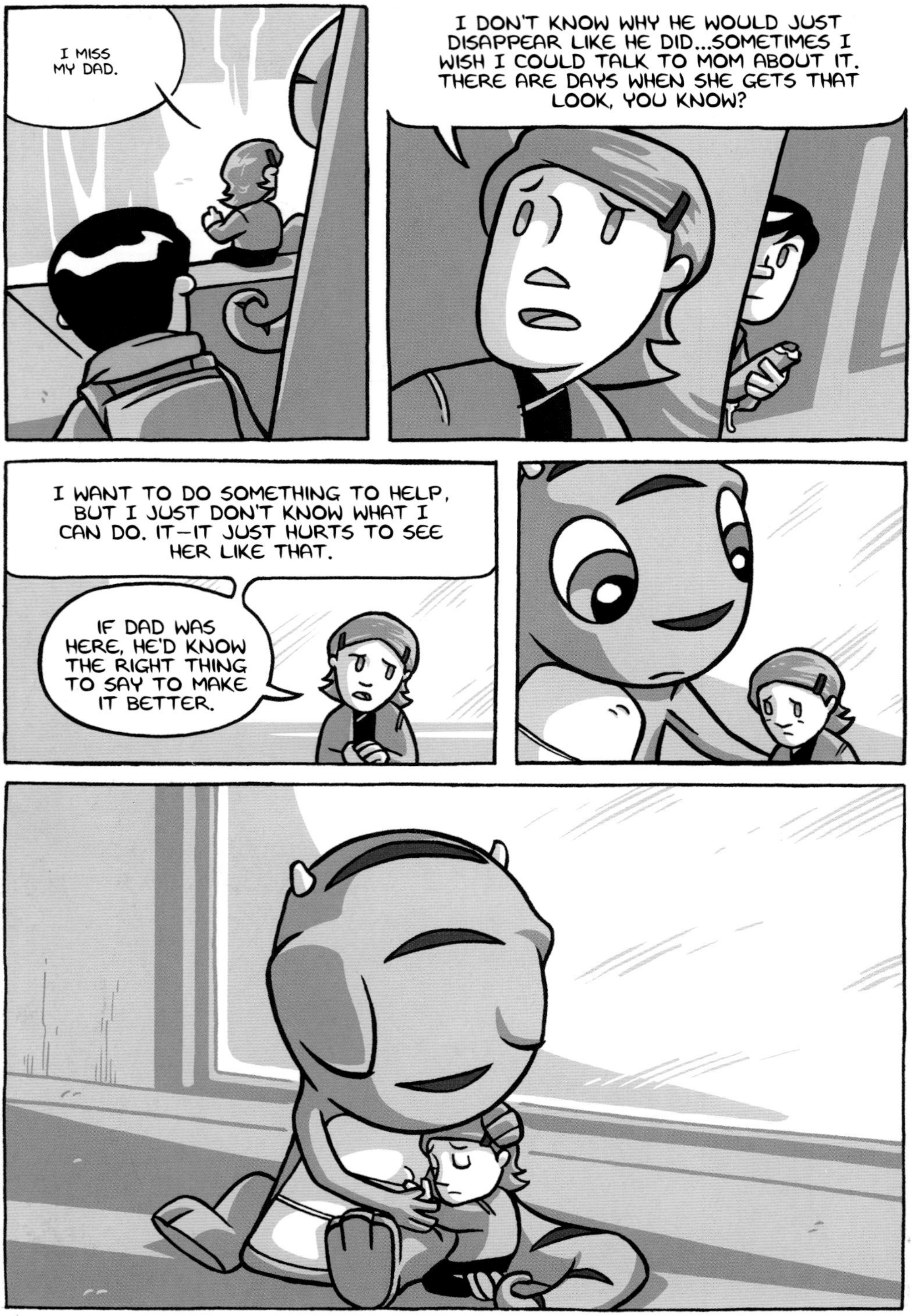
I MISS MY DAD.
I DON'T KNOW WHY HE WOULD JUST DISAPPEAR LIKE HE DID...SOMETIMES I WISH I COULD TALK TO MOM ABOUT IT. THERE ARE DAYS WHEN SHE GETS THAT LOOK, YOU KNOW?
I WANT TO DO SOMETHING TO HELP, BUT I JUST DON'T KNOW WHAT I CAN DO. IT—IT JUST HURTS TO SEE HER LIKE THAT.
IF DAD WAS HERE, HE'D KNOW THE RIGHT THING TO SAY TO MAKE IT BETTER.

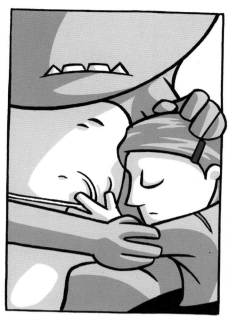

HERE, I
WANT YOU
TO HAVE
THIS.

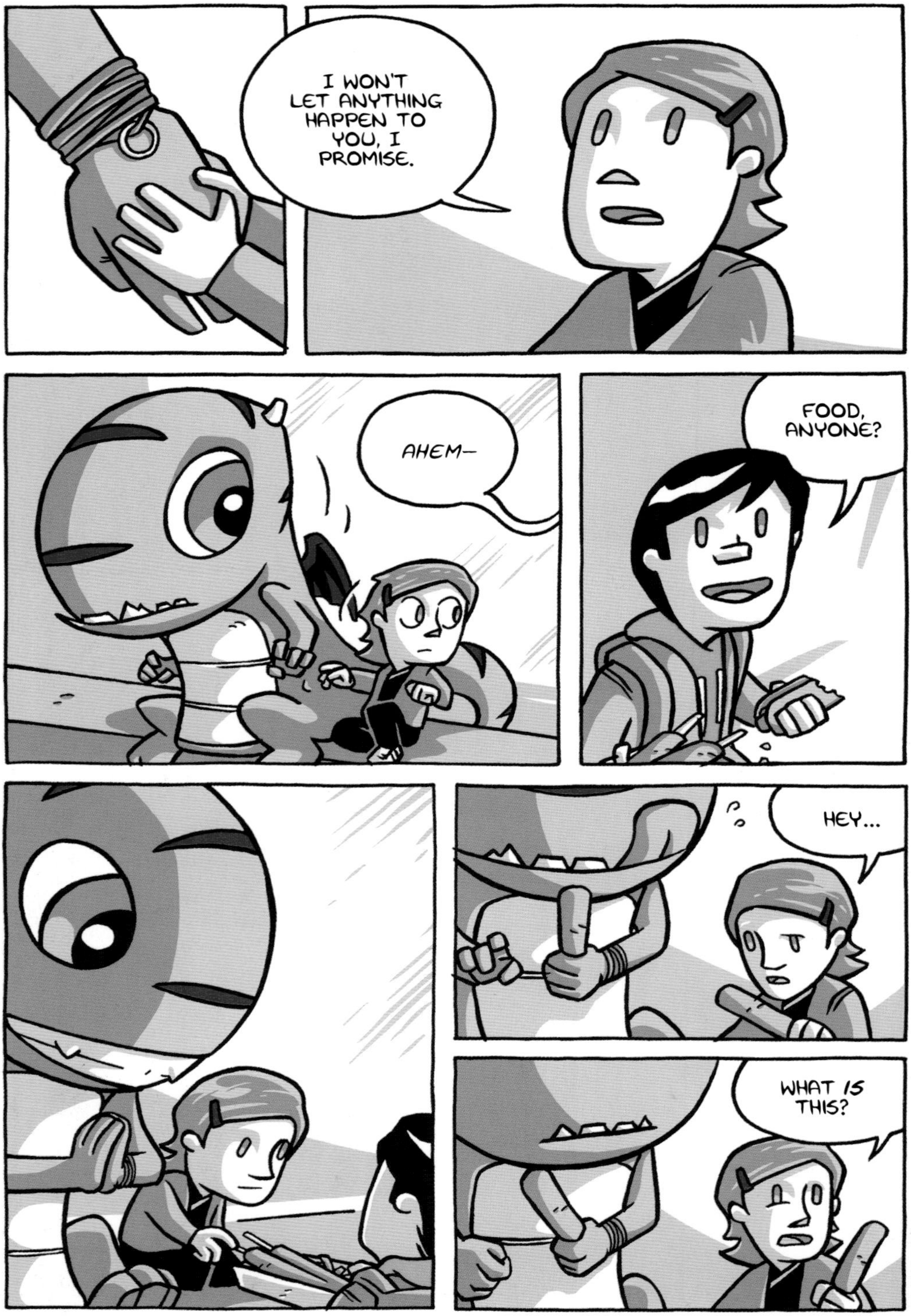
I WON'T LET ANYTHING HAPPEN TO YOU, I PROMISE.
AHEM–
FOOD, ANYONE?
HEY...
WHAT IS THIS?

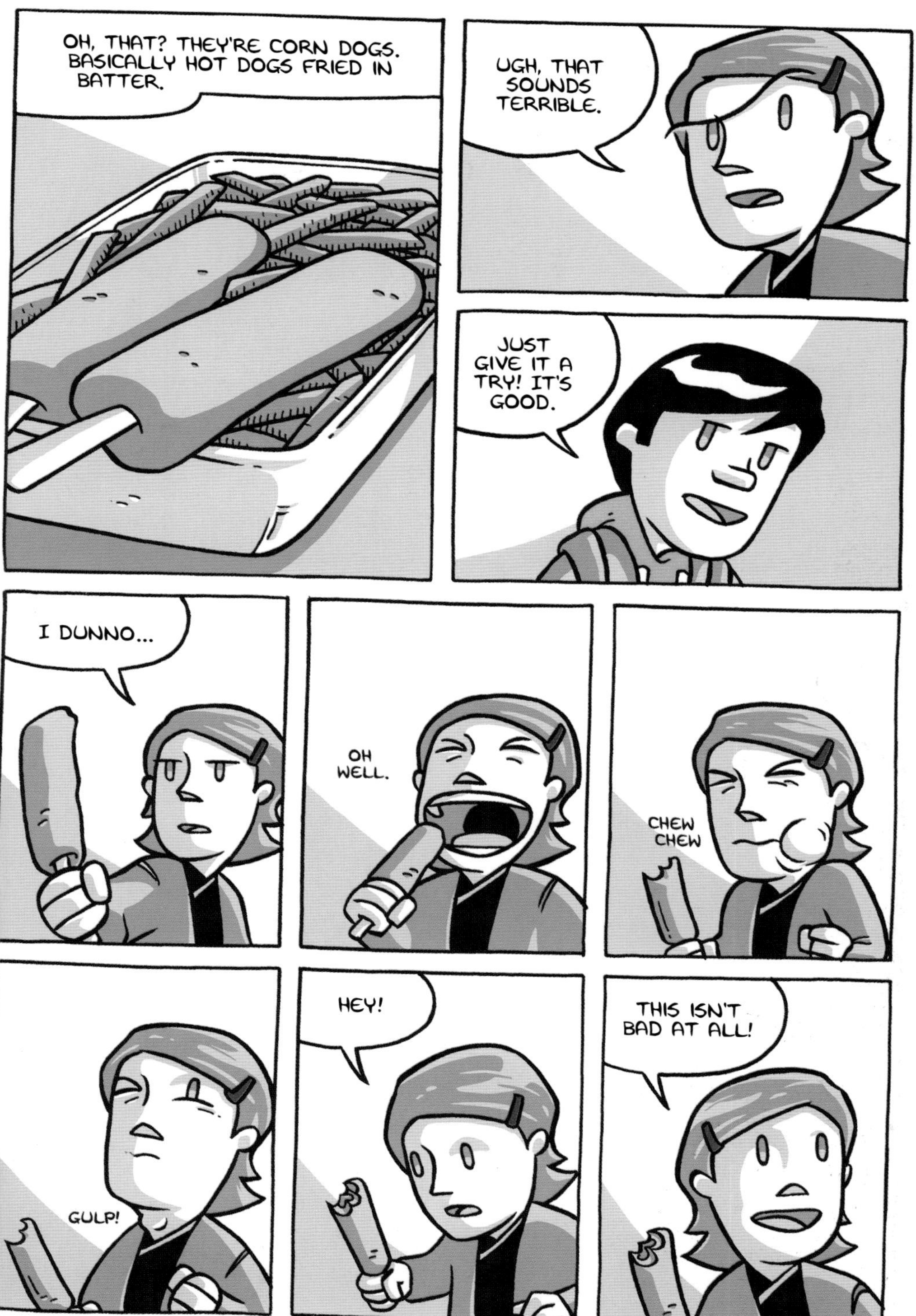
OH, THAT? THEY'RE CORN DOGS. BASICALLY HOT DOGS FRIED IN BATTER.
UGH, THAT SOUNDS TERRIBLE.
JUST GIVE IT A TRY! IT'S GOOD.
I DUNNO...
OH WELL.
CHEW CHEW
GULP!
HEY!
THIS ISN'T BAD AT ALL!

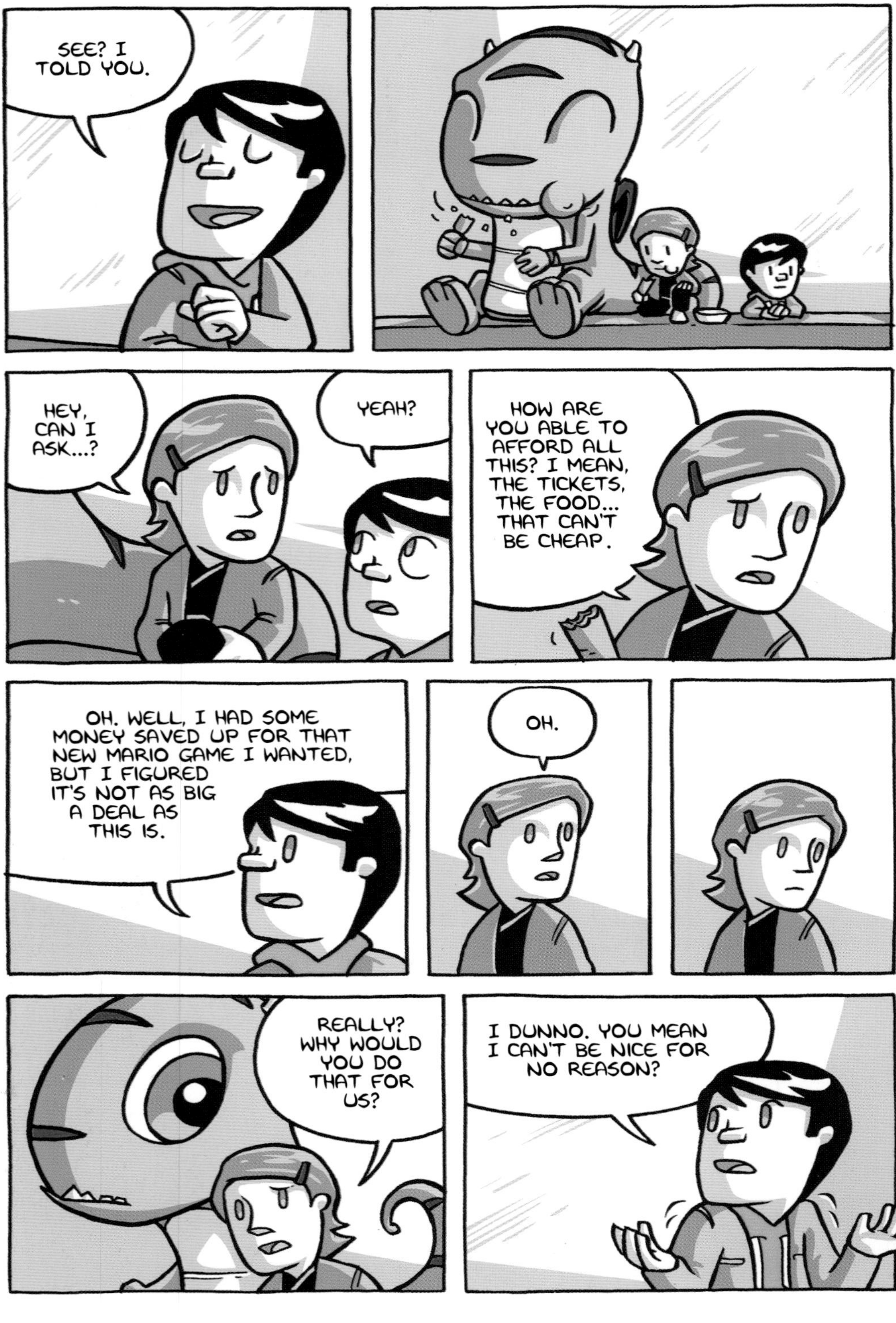
SEE? I TOLD YOU.
HEY, CAN I ASK...?
YEAH?
HOW ARE YOU ABLE TO AFFORD ALL THIS? I MEAN, THE TICKETS, THE FOOD... THAT CAN'T BE CHEAP.
OH. WELL, I HAD SOME MONEY SAVED UP FOR THAT NEW MARIO GAME I WANTED, BUT I FIGURED IT'S NOT AS BIG A DEAL AS THIS IS.
OH.
REALLY? WHY WOULD YOU DO THAT FOR US?
I DUNNO. YOU MEAN I CAN'T BE NICE FOR NO REASON?

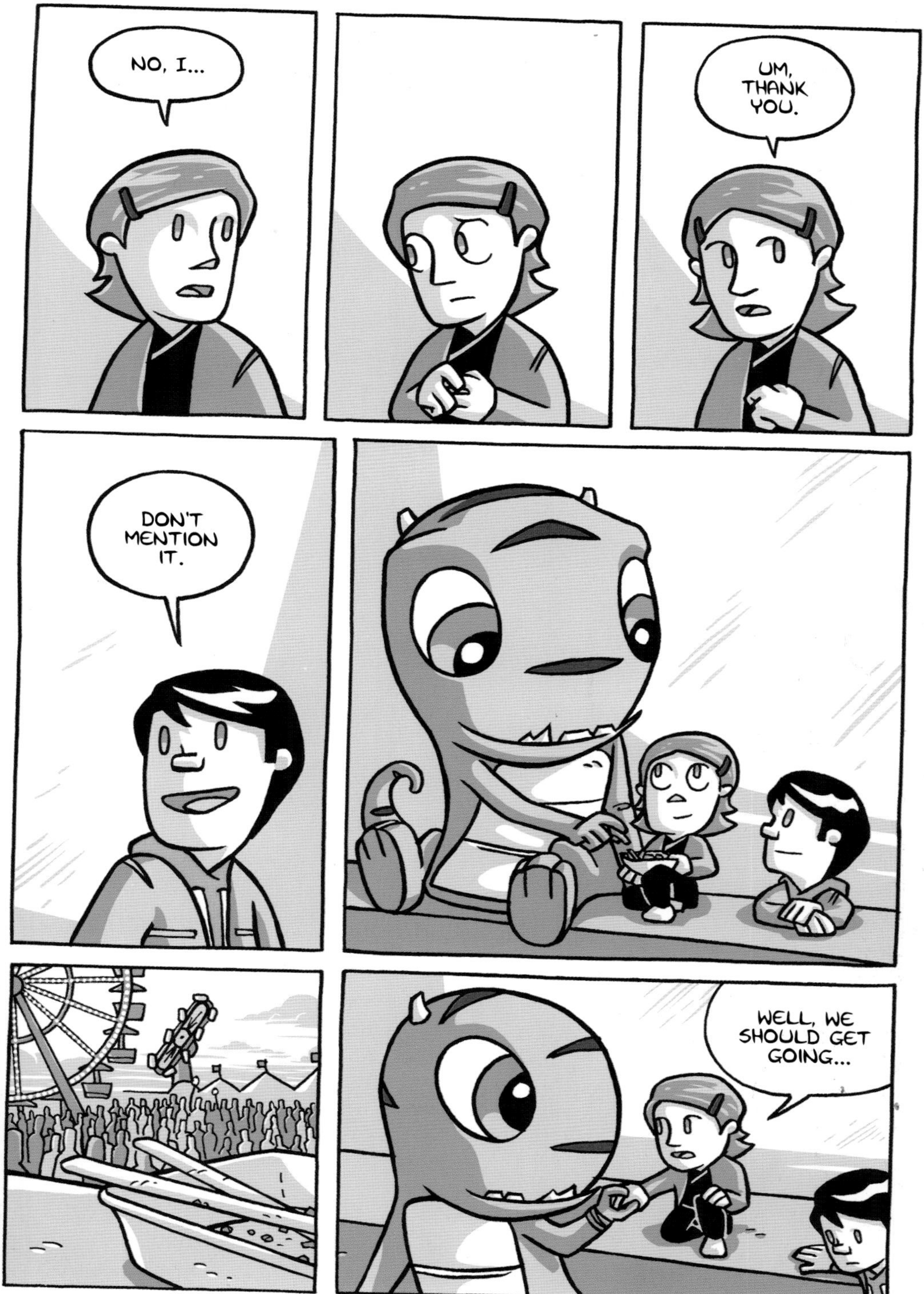
NO, I...
UM, THANK YOU.
DON'T MENTION IT.
WELL, WE SHOULD GET GOING...

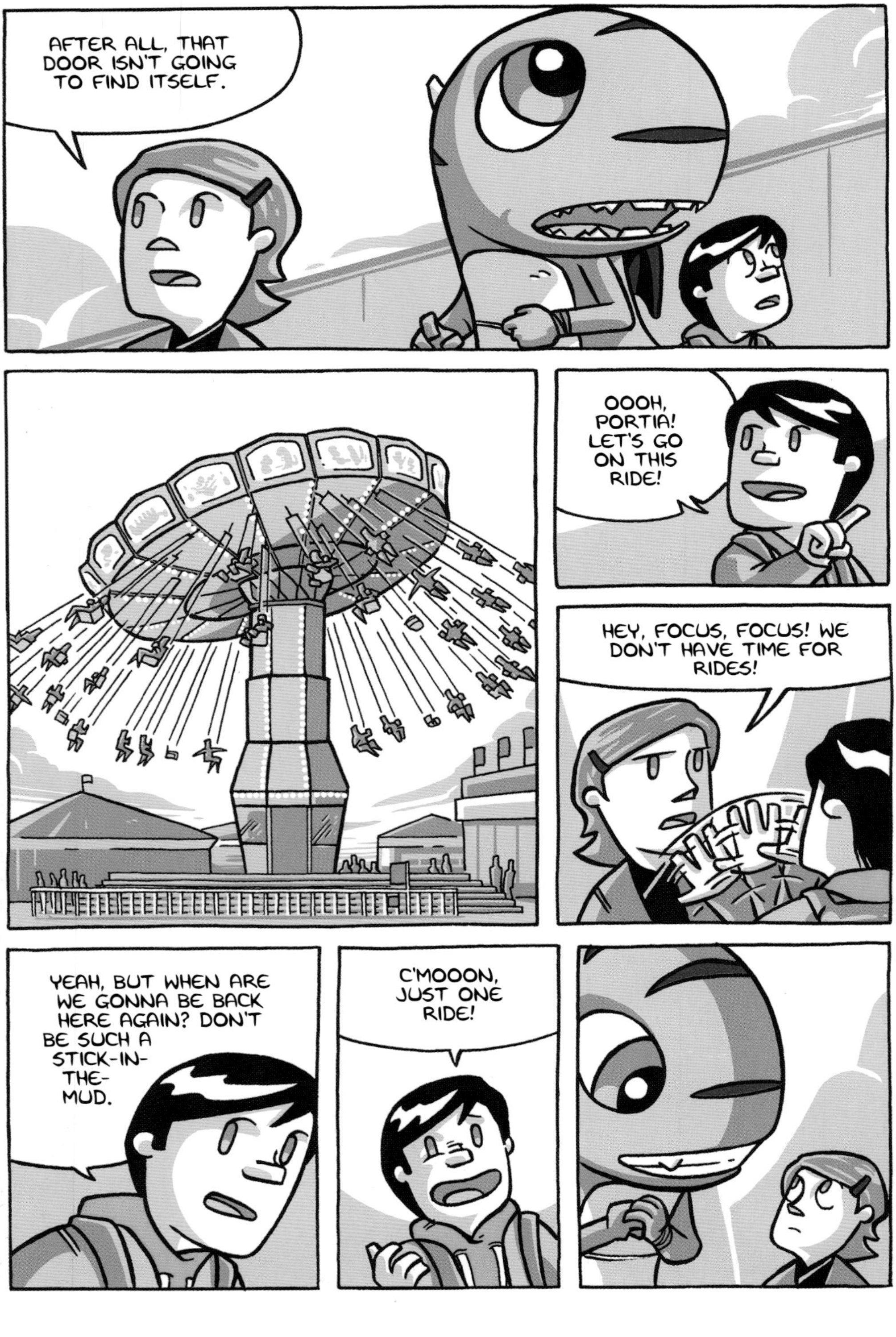
AFTER ALL, THAT DOOR ISN'T GOING TO FIND ITSELF.
OOOH, PORTIA! LET'S GO ON THIS RIDE!
HEY, FOCUS, FOCUS! WE DON'T HAVE TIME FOR RIDES!
YEAH, BUT WHEN ARE WE GONNA BE BACK HERE AGAIN? DON'T BE SUCH A STICK-IN-THE-MUD.
C'MOOON, JUST ONE RIDE!

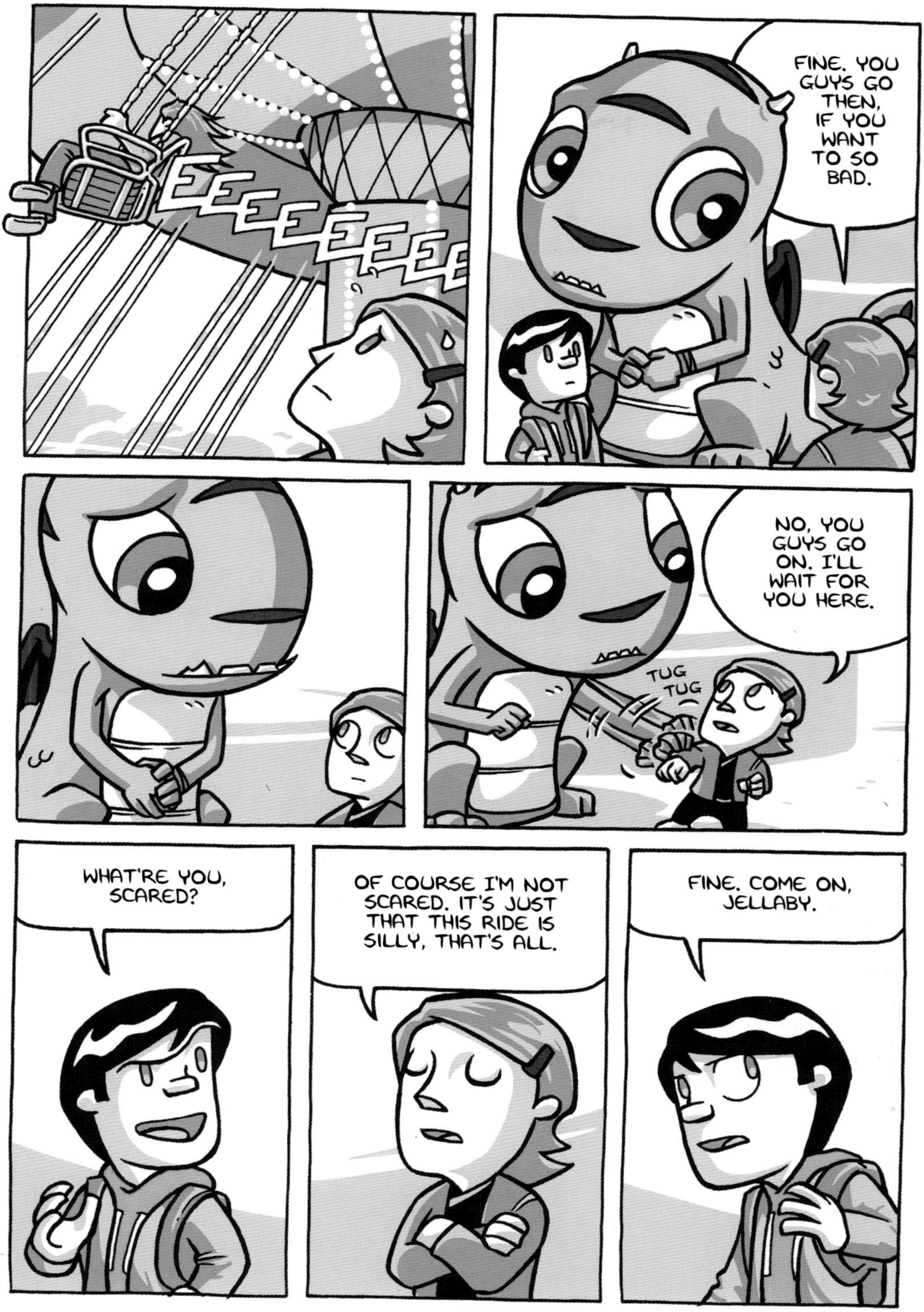
EEEEEEEEE
FINE. YOU GUYS GO THEN, IF YOU WANT TO SO BAD.
NO, YOU GUYS GO ON. I'LL WAIT FOR YOU HERE.
TUG TUG
WHAT'RE YOU, SCARED?
OF COURSE I'M NOT SCARED. IT'S JUST THAT THIS RIDE IS SILLY, THAT'S ALL.
FINE. COME ON, JELLABY.

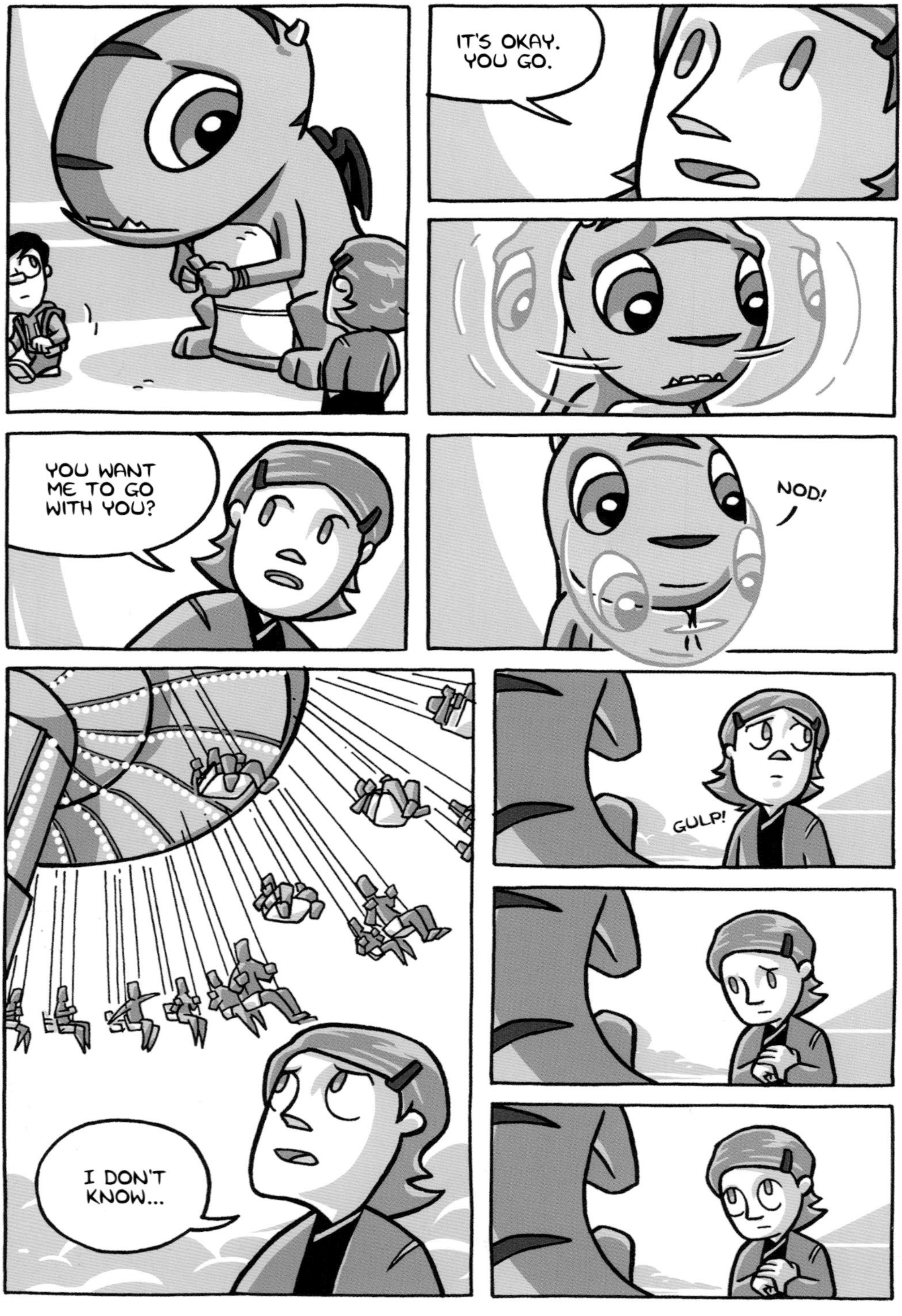
IT'S OKAY. YOU GO.
YOU WANT ME TO GO WITH YOU?
NOD!
GULP!
I DON'T KNOW...

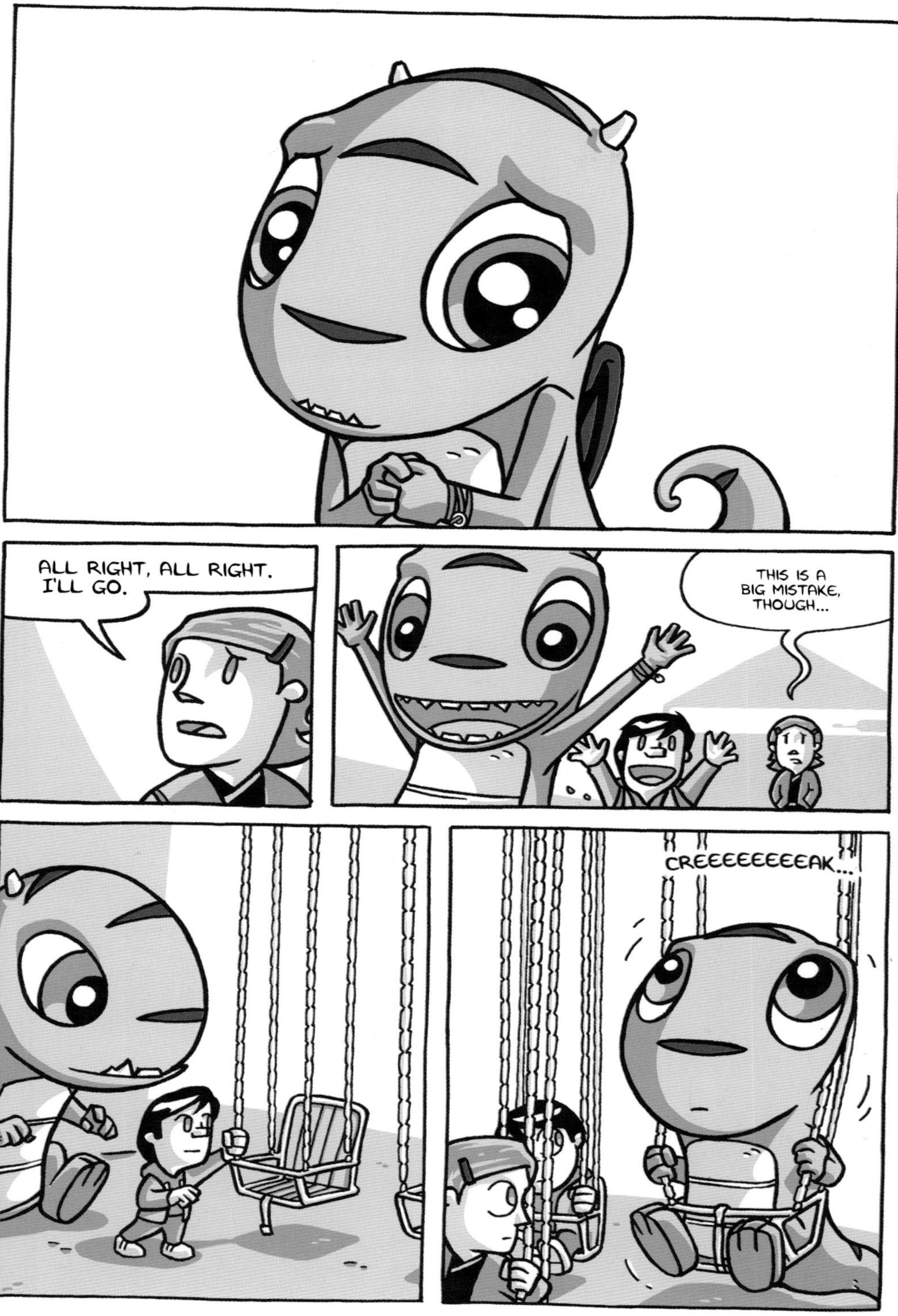
ALL RIGHT, ALL RIGHT. I'LL GO.
THIS IS A BIG MISTAKE, THOUGH...
CREEEEEEEEEAK...

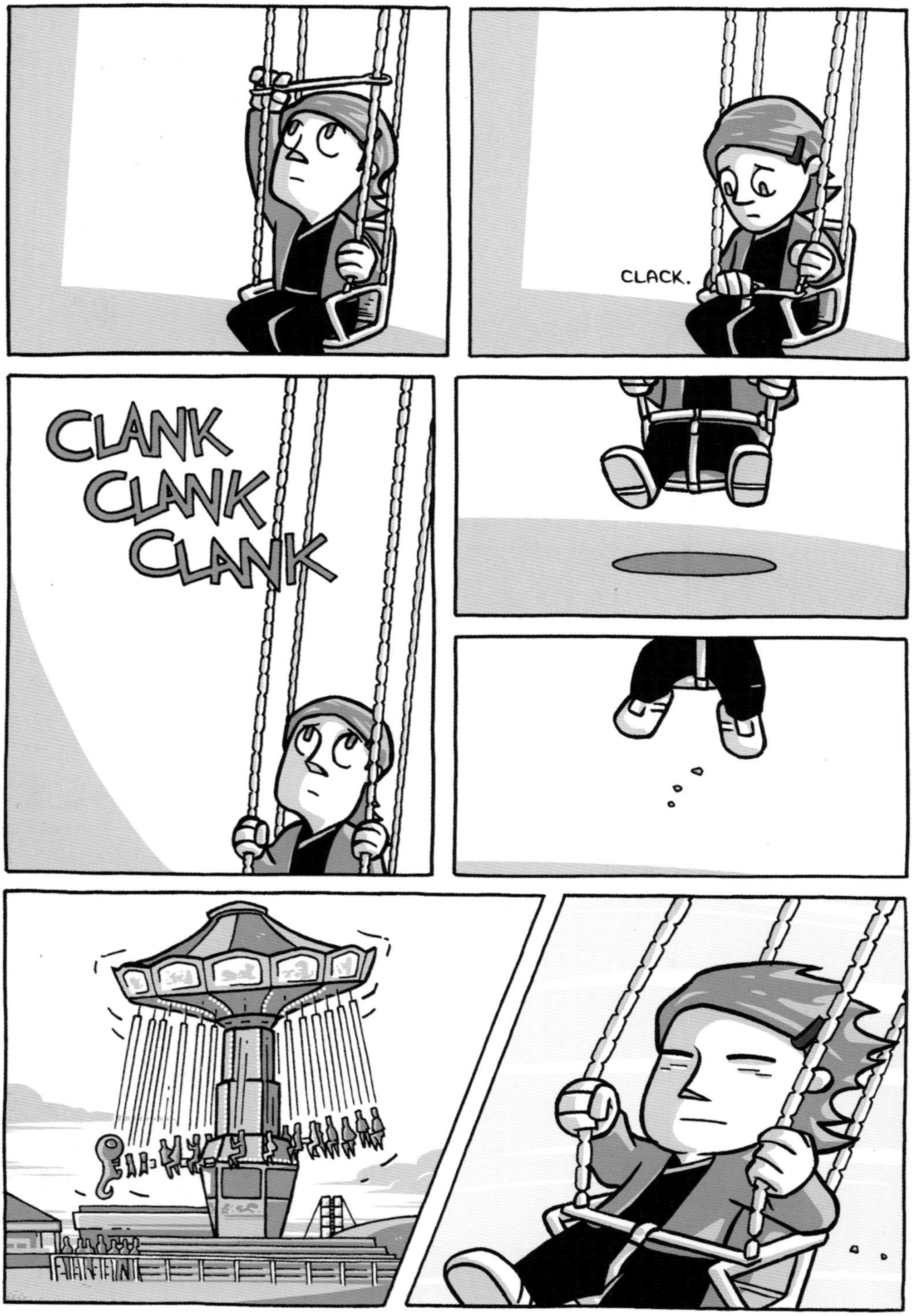
CLACK.
CLANK
CLANK
CLANK

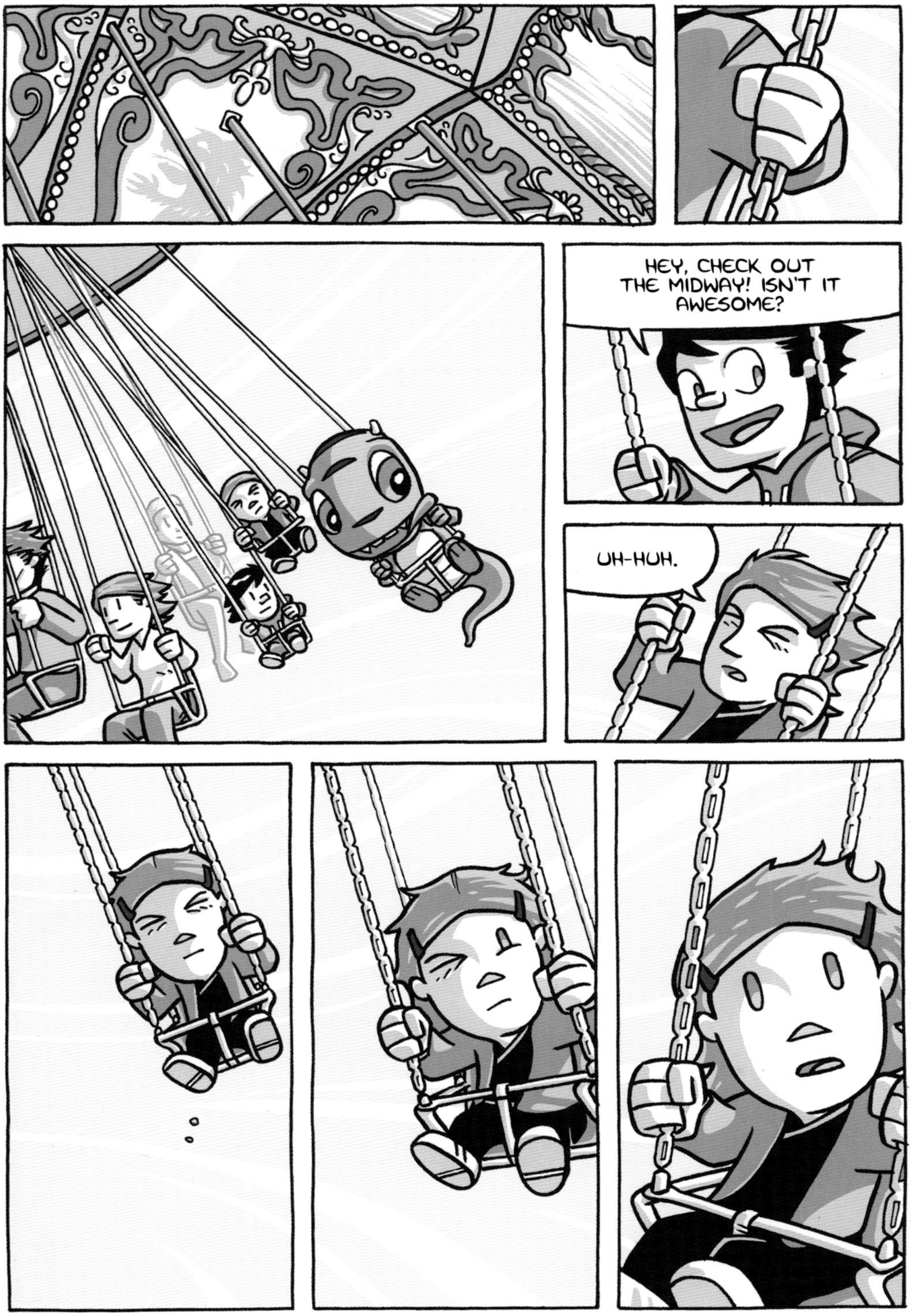
HEY, CHECK OUT THE MIDWAY! ISN'T IT AWESOME?
UH-HUH.

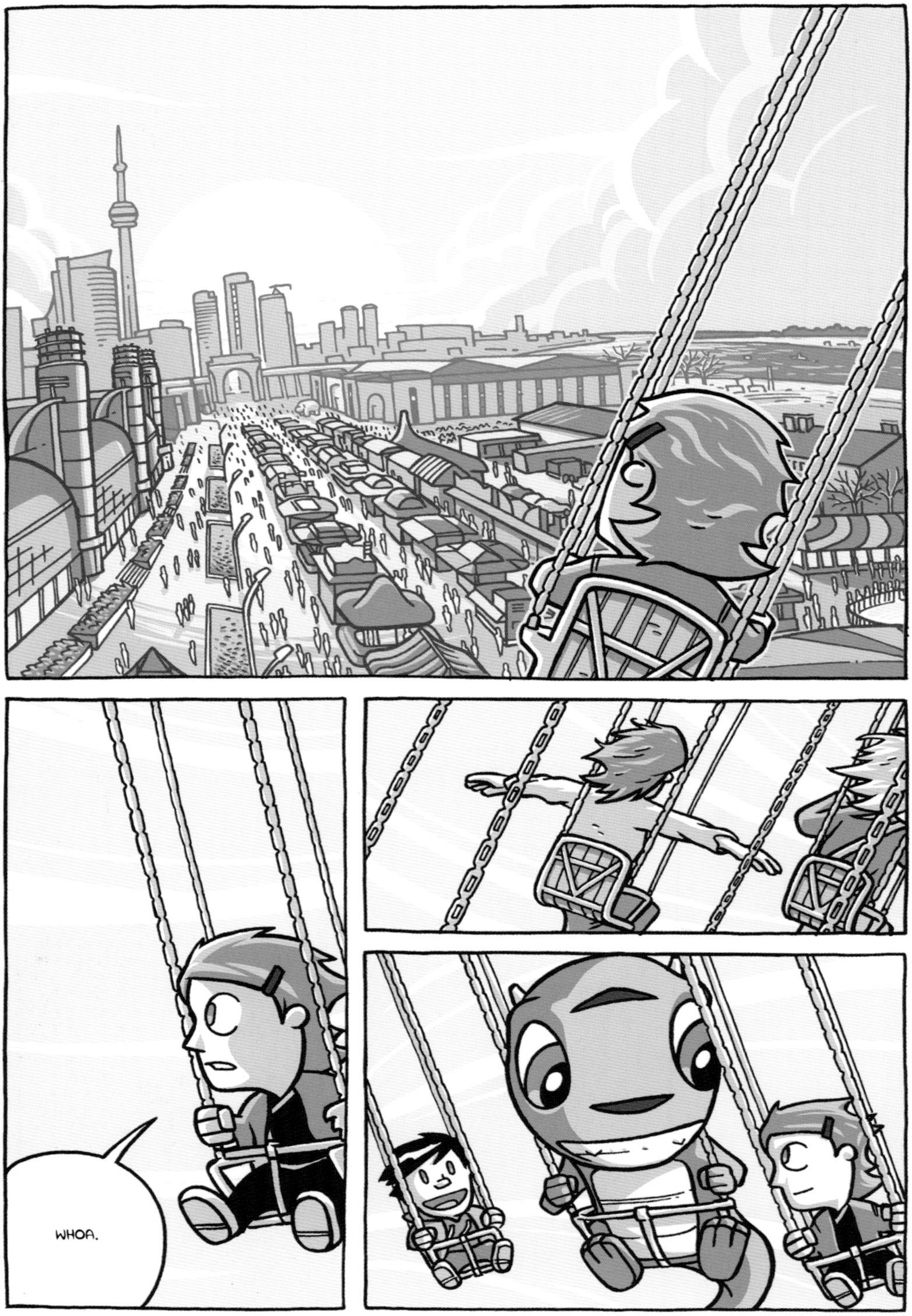
WHOA.

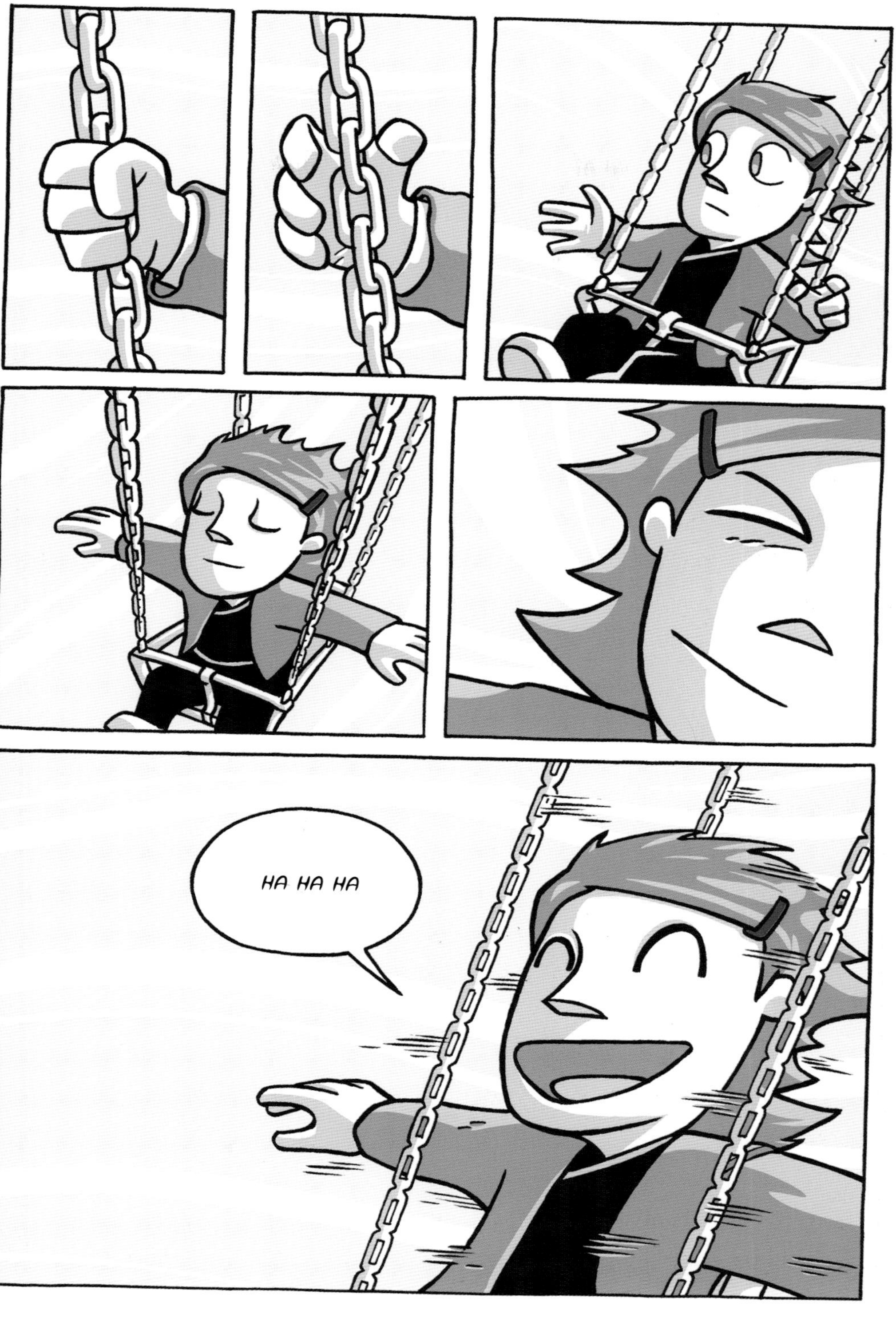
HA HA HA

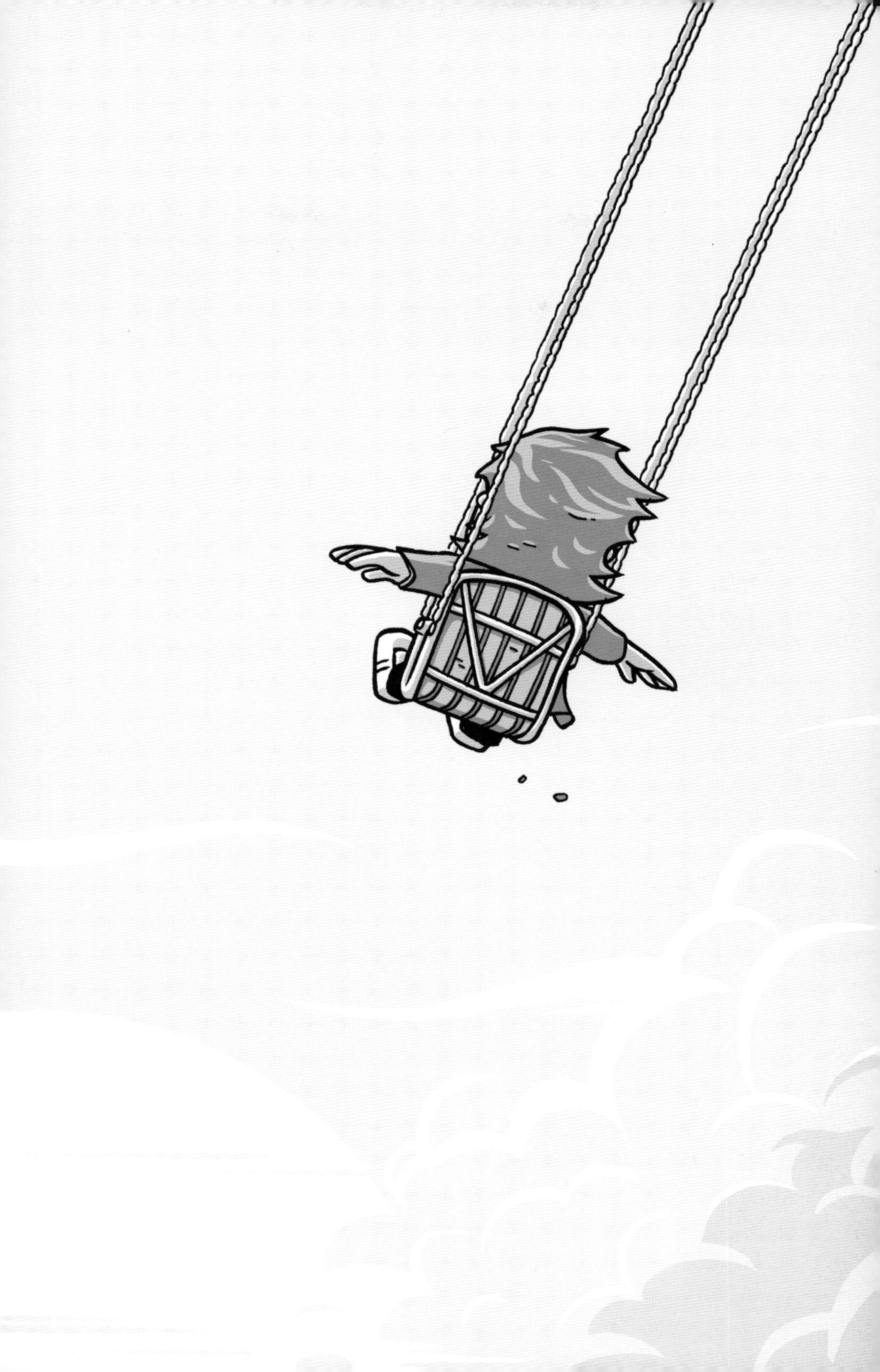

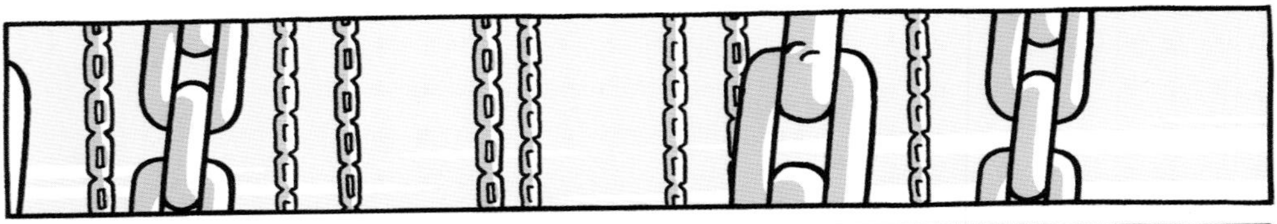

CHAPTER THREE

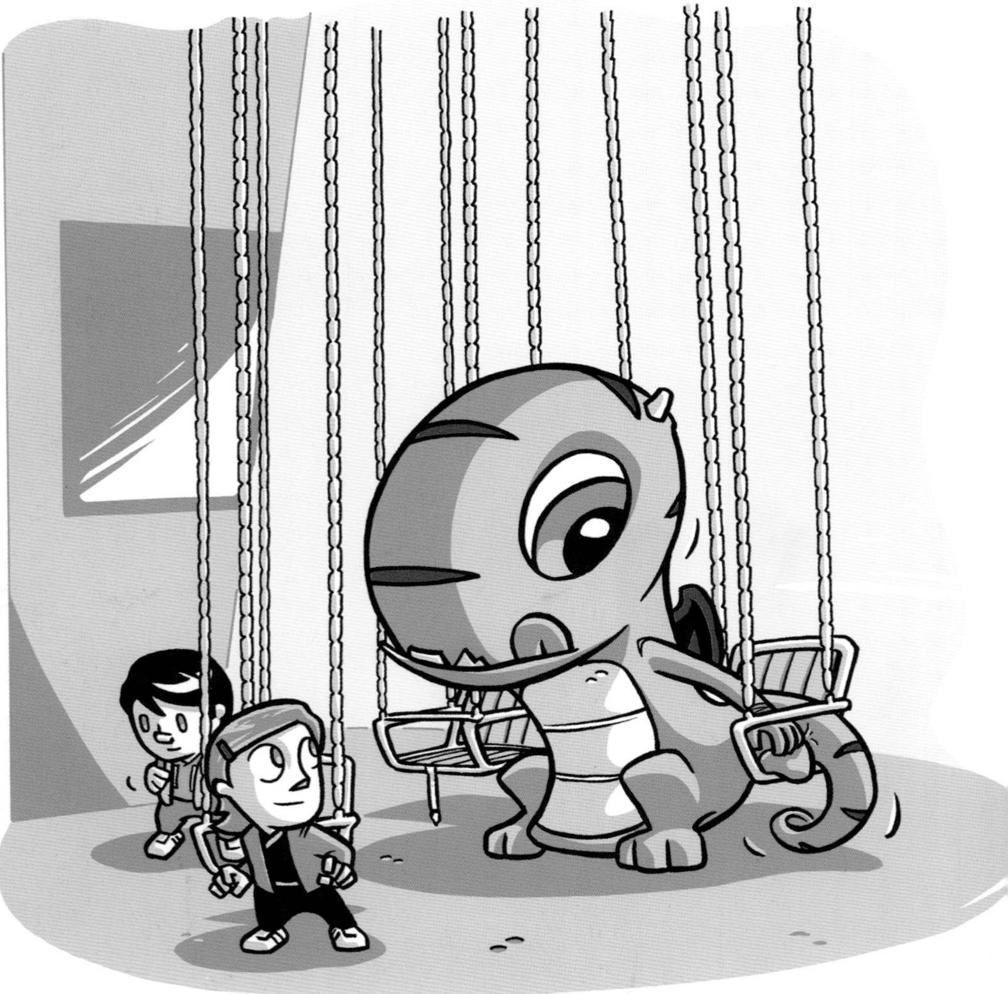

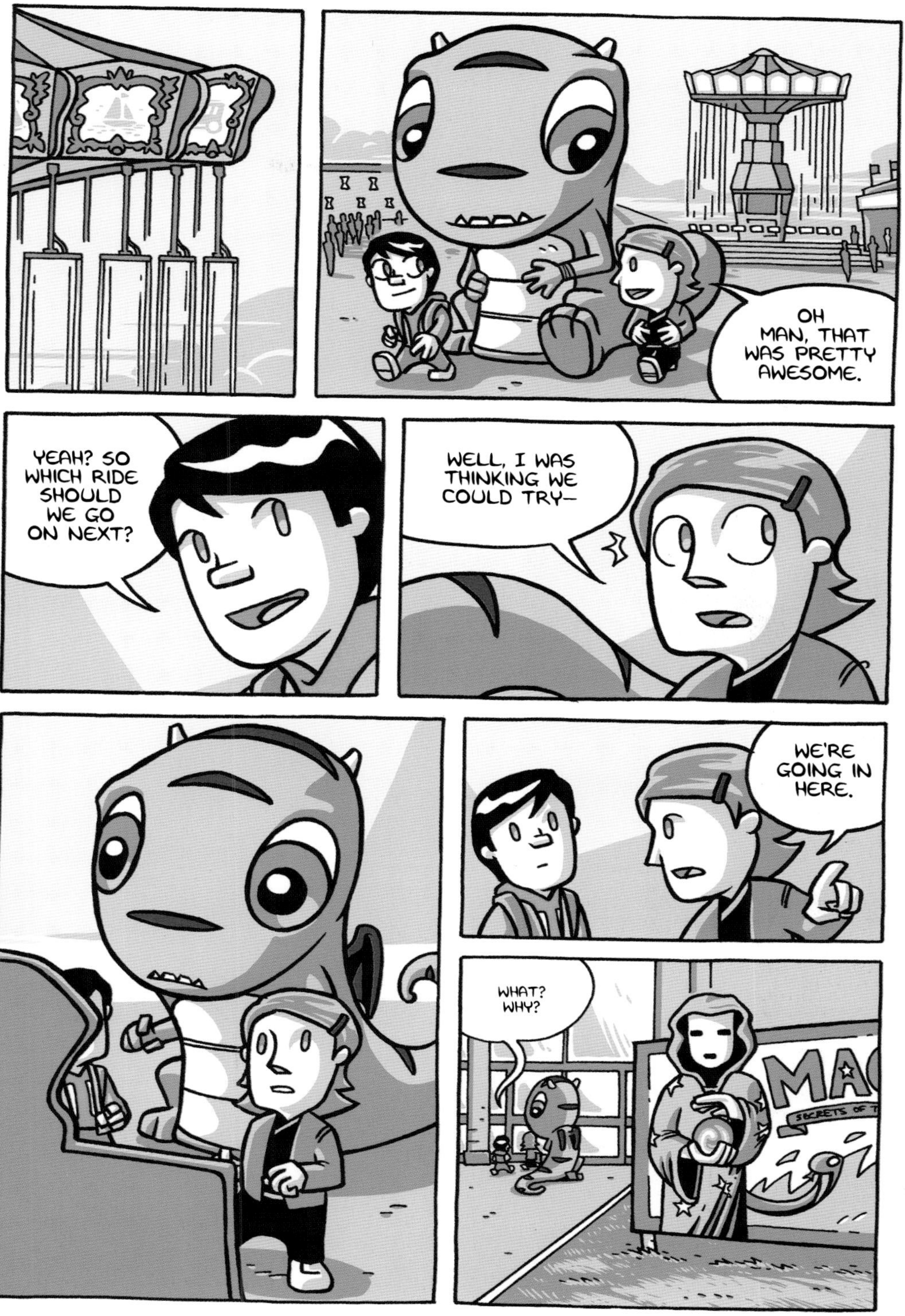
OH MAN, THAT WAS PRETTY AWESOME.
YEAH? SO WHICH RIDE SHOULD WE GO ON NEXT?
WELL, I WAS THINKING WE COULD TRY—
WE'RE GOING IN HERE.
WHAT? WHY?

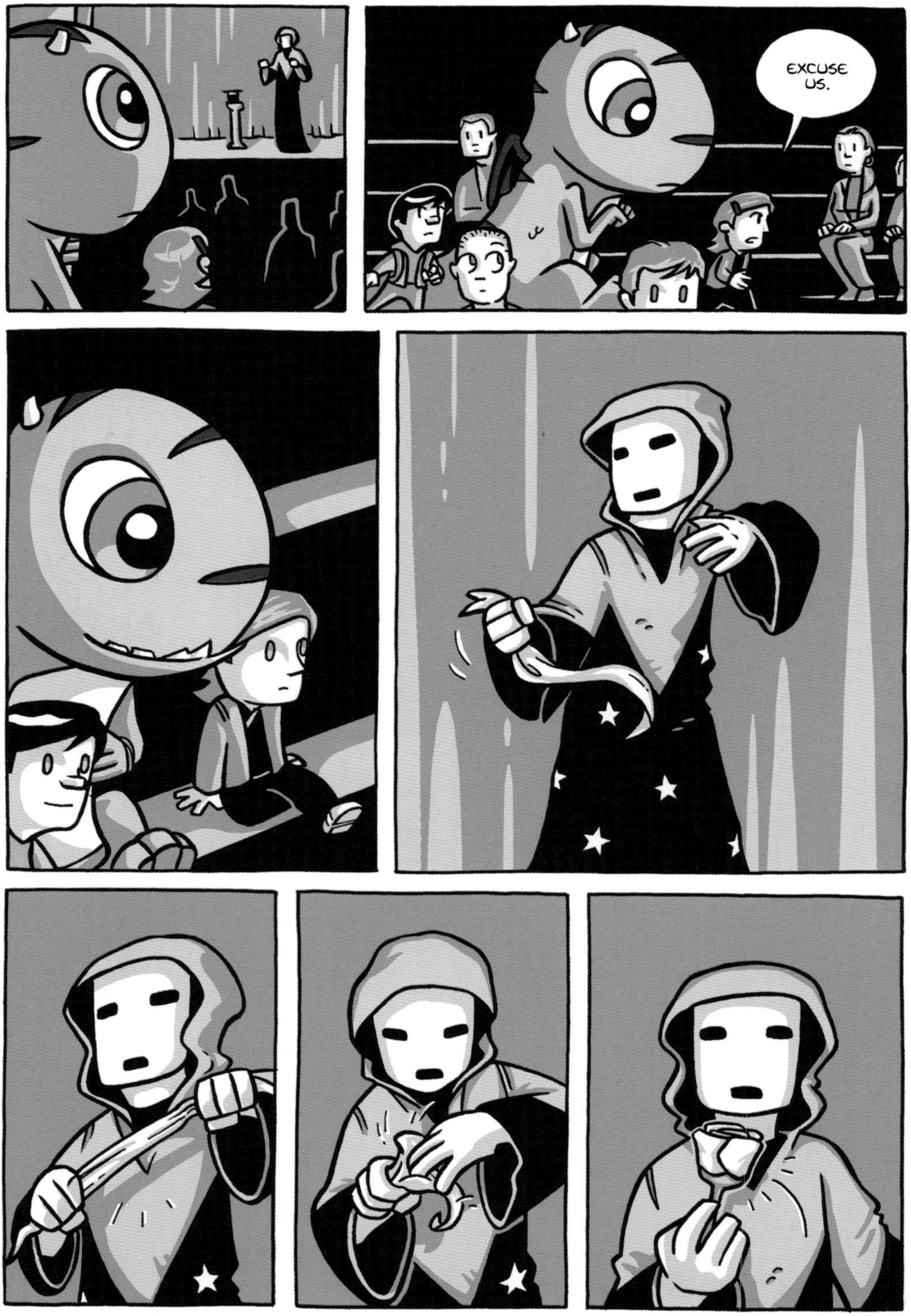
EXCUSE US.

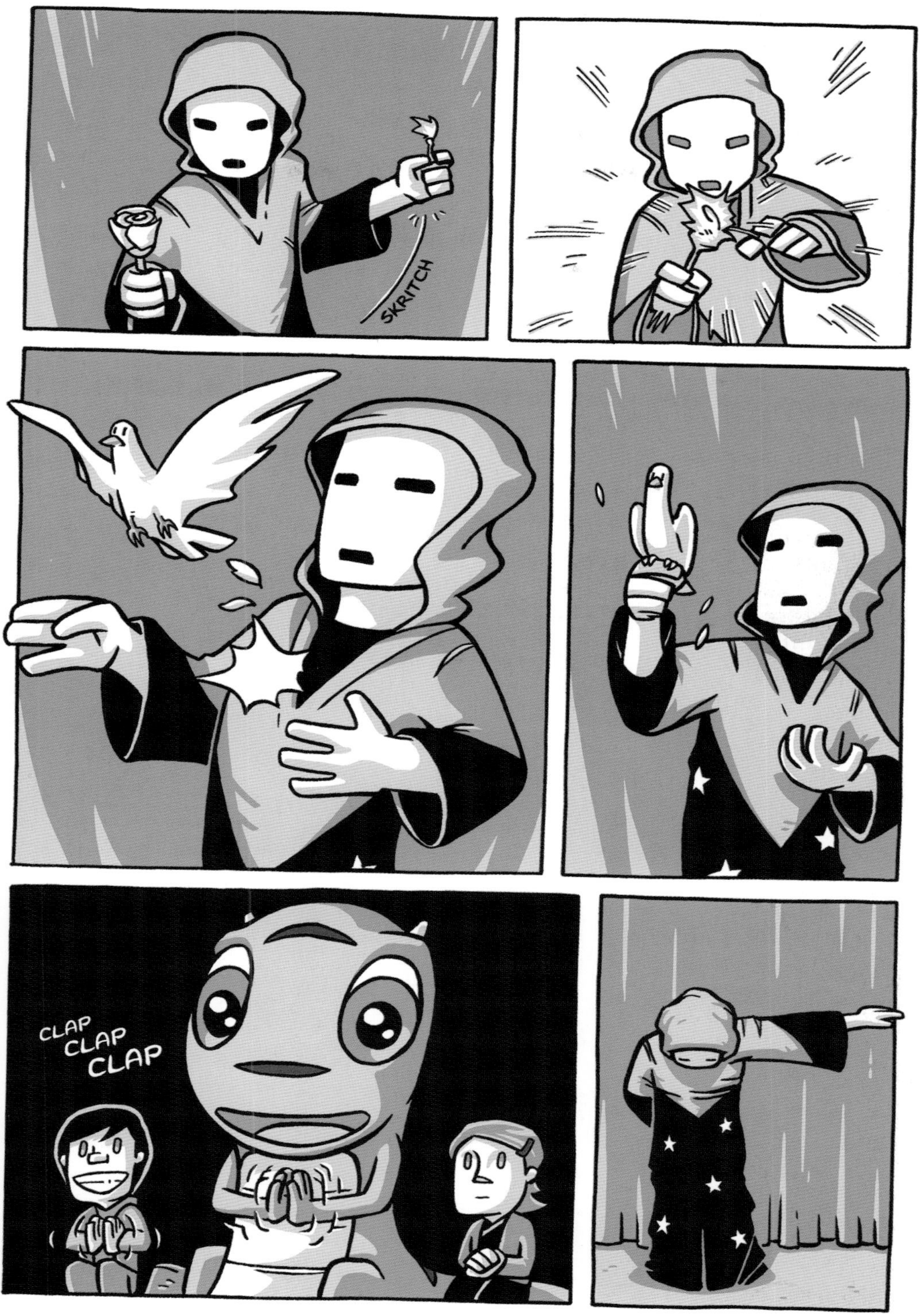
SKRITCH
CLAP
CLAP
CLAP

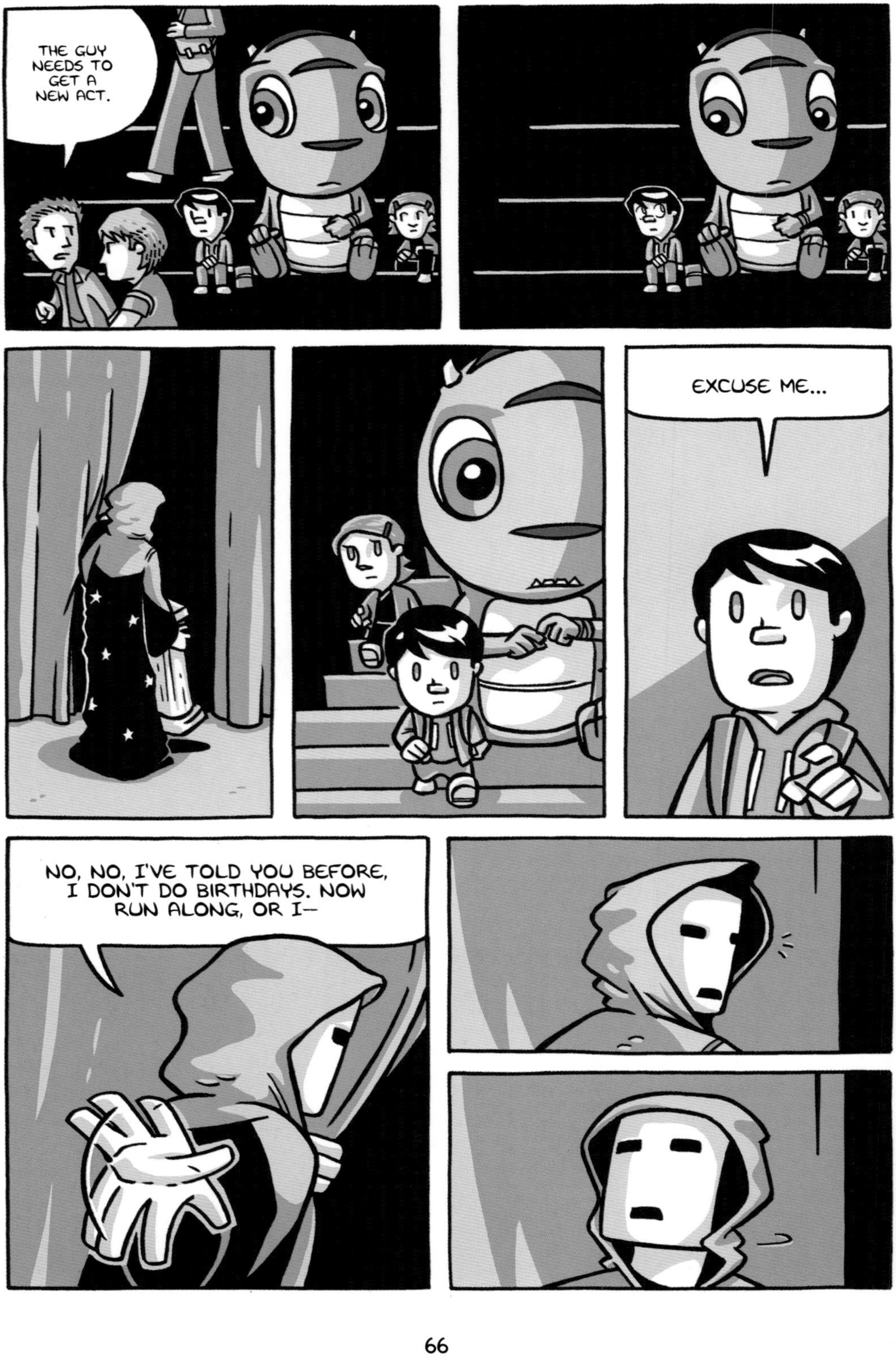
THE GUY NEEDS TO GET A NEW ACT.
EXCUSE ME...
NO, NO, I'VE TOLD YOU BEFORE, I DON'T DO BIRTHDAYS. NOW RUN ALONG, OR I—

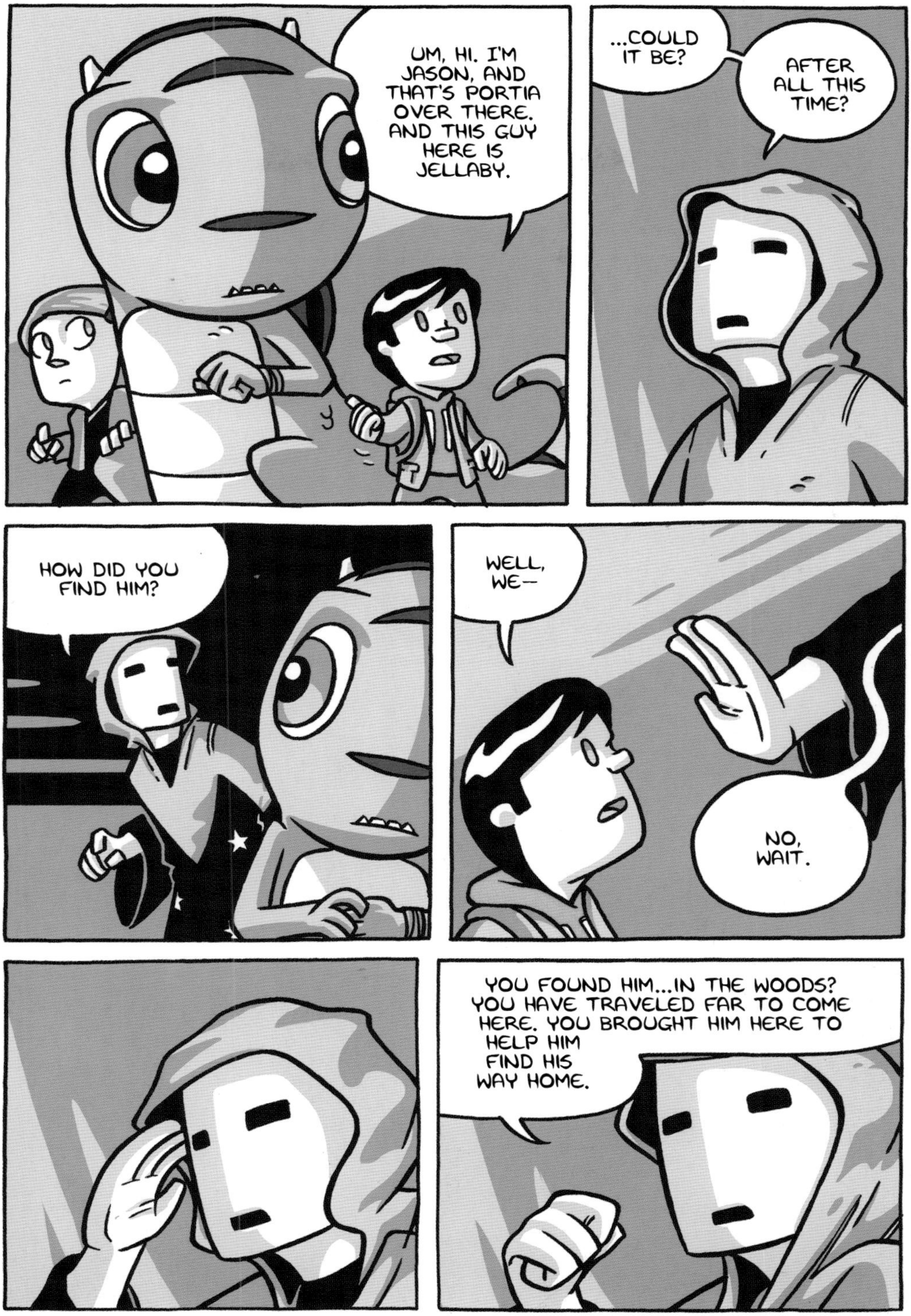

UM, HI. I'M JASON, AND THAT'S PORTIA OVER THERE. AND THIS GUY HERE IS JELLABY.
...COULD IT BE?
AFTER ALL THIS TIME?
HOW DID YOU FIND HIM?
WELL, WE—
NO, WAIT.
YOU FOUND HIM...IN THE WOODS? YOU HAVE TRAVELED FAR TO COME HERE. YOU BROUGHT HIM HERE TO HELP HIM FIND HIS WAY HOME.

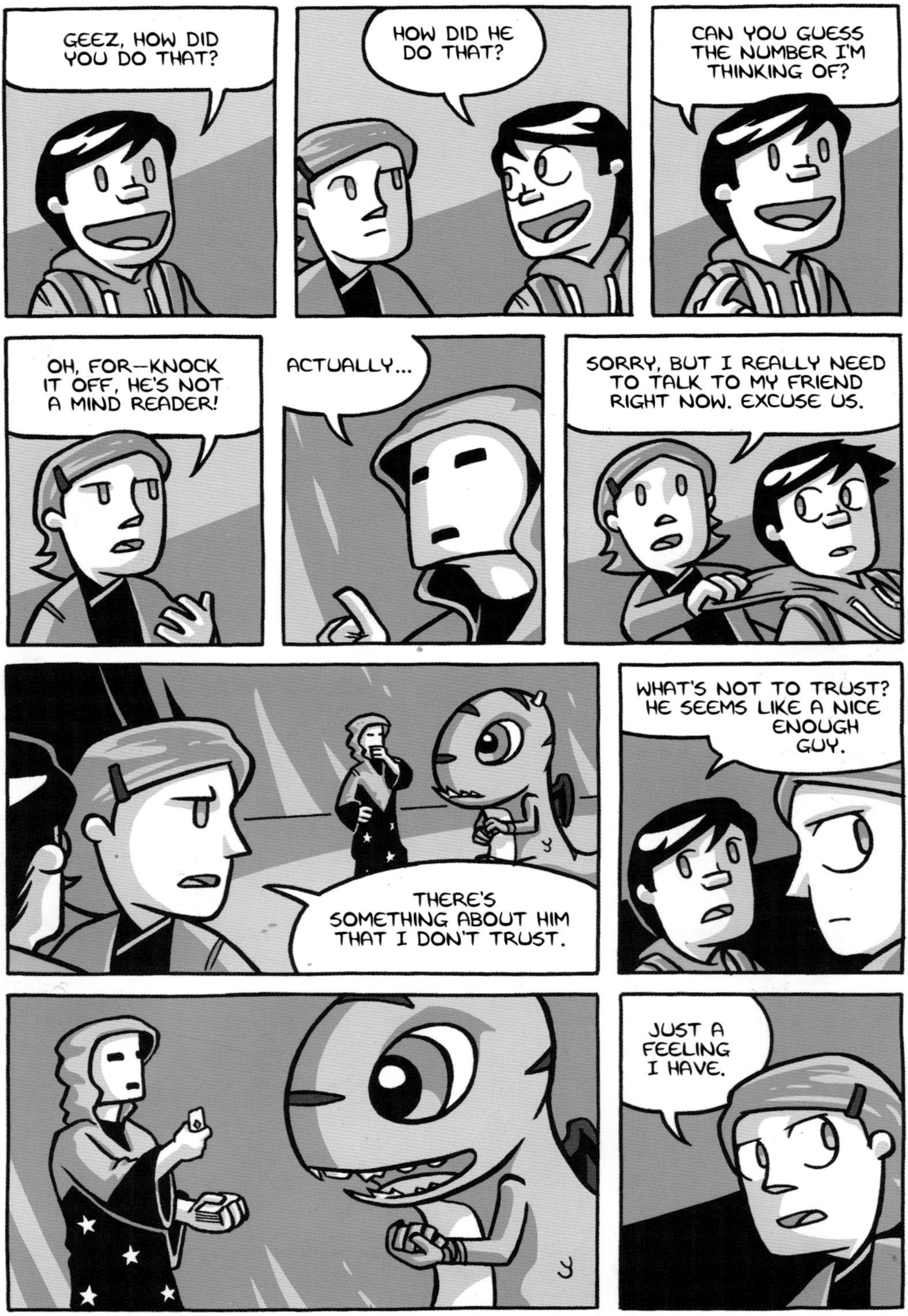
GEEZ, HOW DID YOU DO THAT?
HOW DID HE DO THAT?
CAN YOU GUESS THE NUMBER I'M THINKING OF?
OH, FOR—KNOCK IT OFF, HE'S NOT A MIND READER!
ACTUALLY...
SORRY, BUT I REALLY NEED TO TALK TO MY FRIEND RIGHT NOW. EXCUSE US.
THERE'S SOMETHING ABOUT HIM THAT I DON'T TRUST.
WHAT'S NOT TO TRUST? HE SEEMS LIKE A NICE ENOUGH GUY.
JUST A FEELING I HAVE.

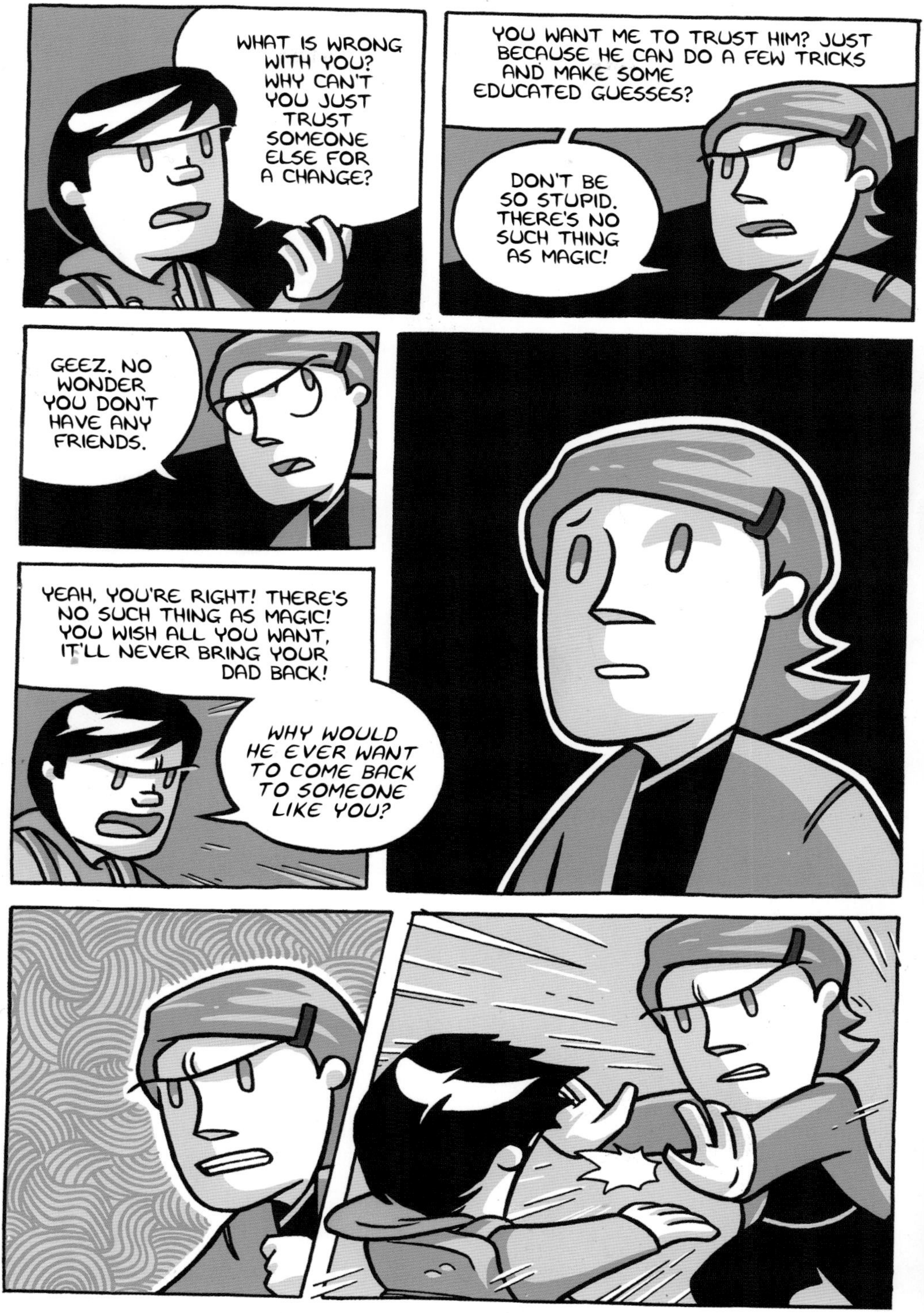
WHAT IS WRONG WITH YOU? WHY CAN'T YOU JUST TRUST SOMEONE ELSE FOR A CHANGE?
YOU WANT ME TO TRUST HIM? JUST BECAUSE HE CAN DO A FEW TRICKS AND MAKE SOME EDUCATED GUESSES?
DON'T BE SO STUPID. THERE'S NO SUCH THING AS MAGIC!
GEEZ. NO WONDER YOU DON'T HAVE ANY FRIENDS.
YEAH, YOU'RE RIGHT! THERE'S NO SUCH THING AS MAGIC! YOU WISH ALL YOU WANT, IT'LL NEVER BRING YOUR DAD BACK!
WHY WOULD HE EVER WANT TO COME BACK TO SOMEONE LIKE YOU?

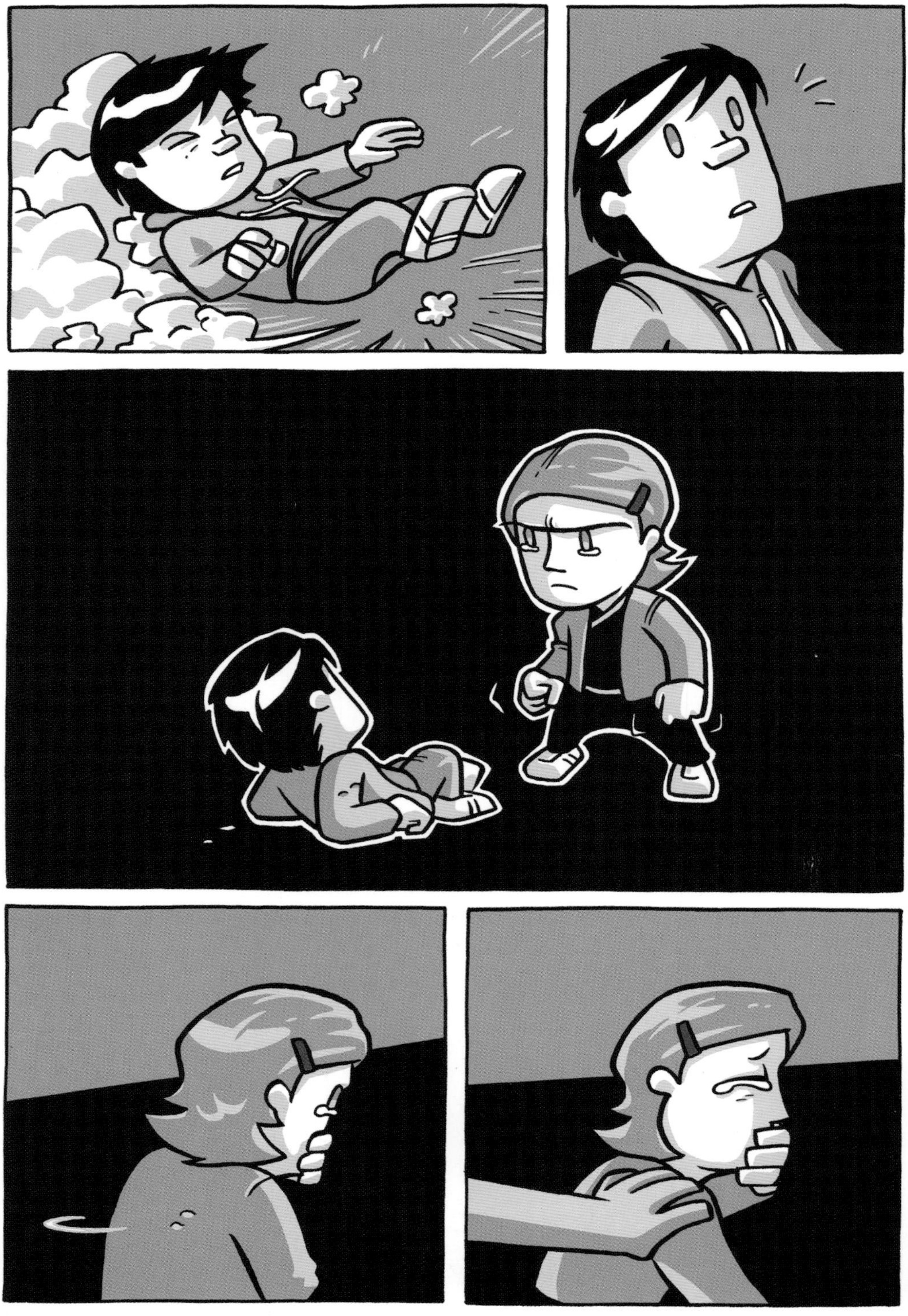

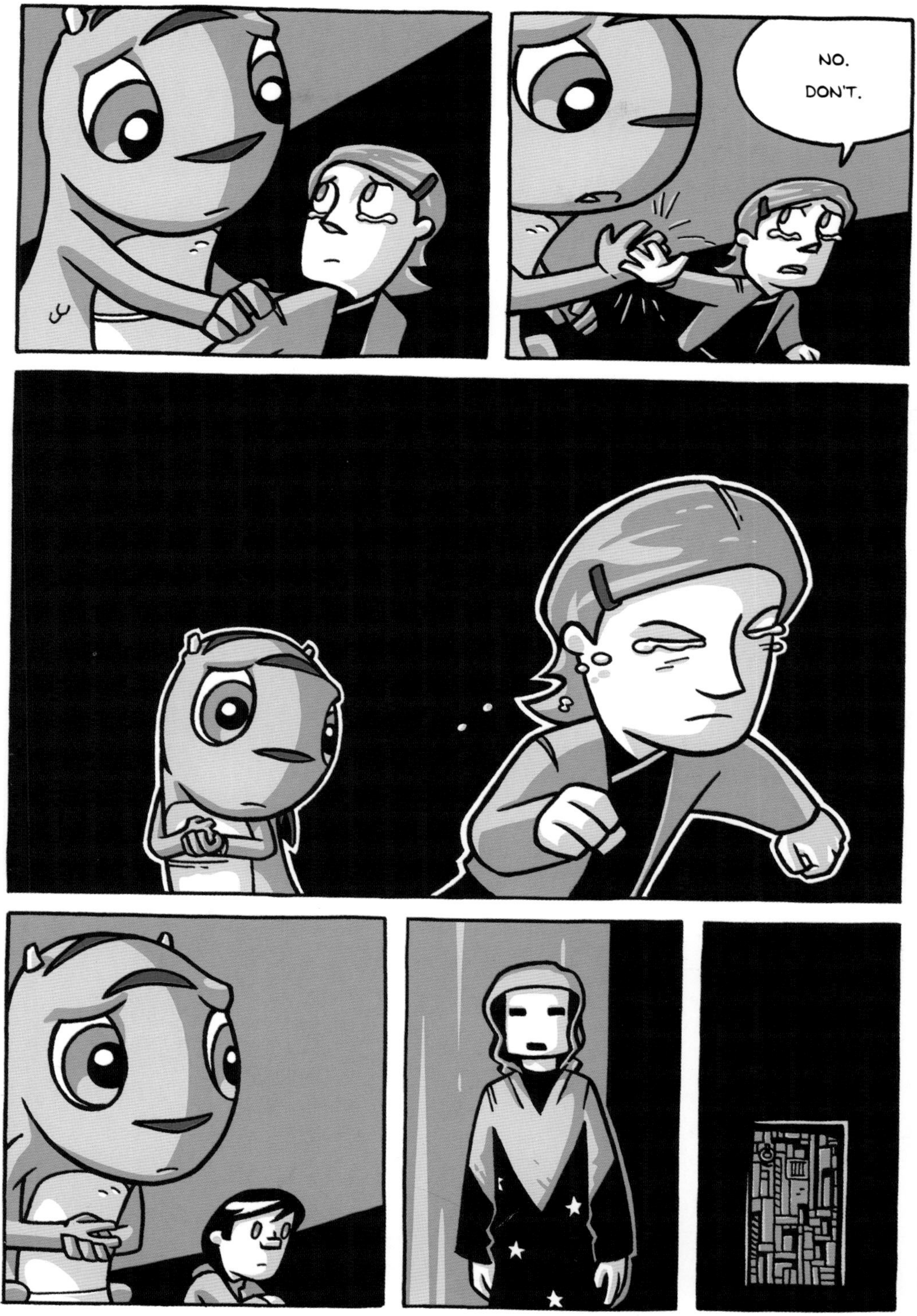
NO.
DON'T.

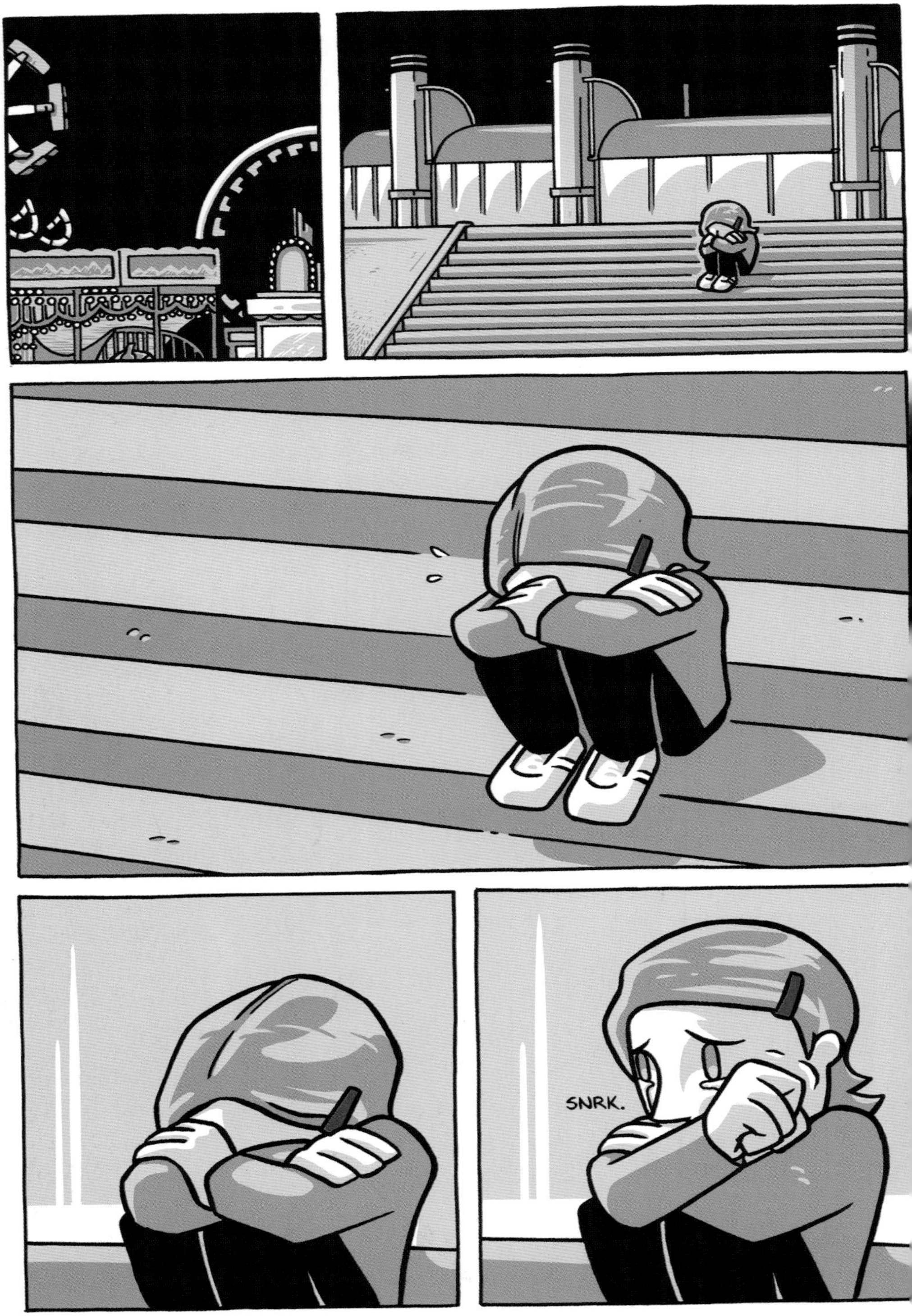
SNRK.

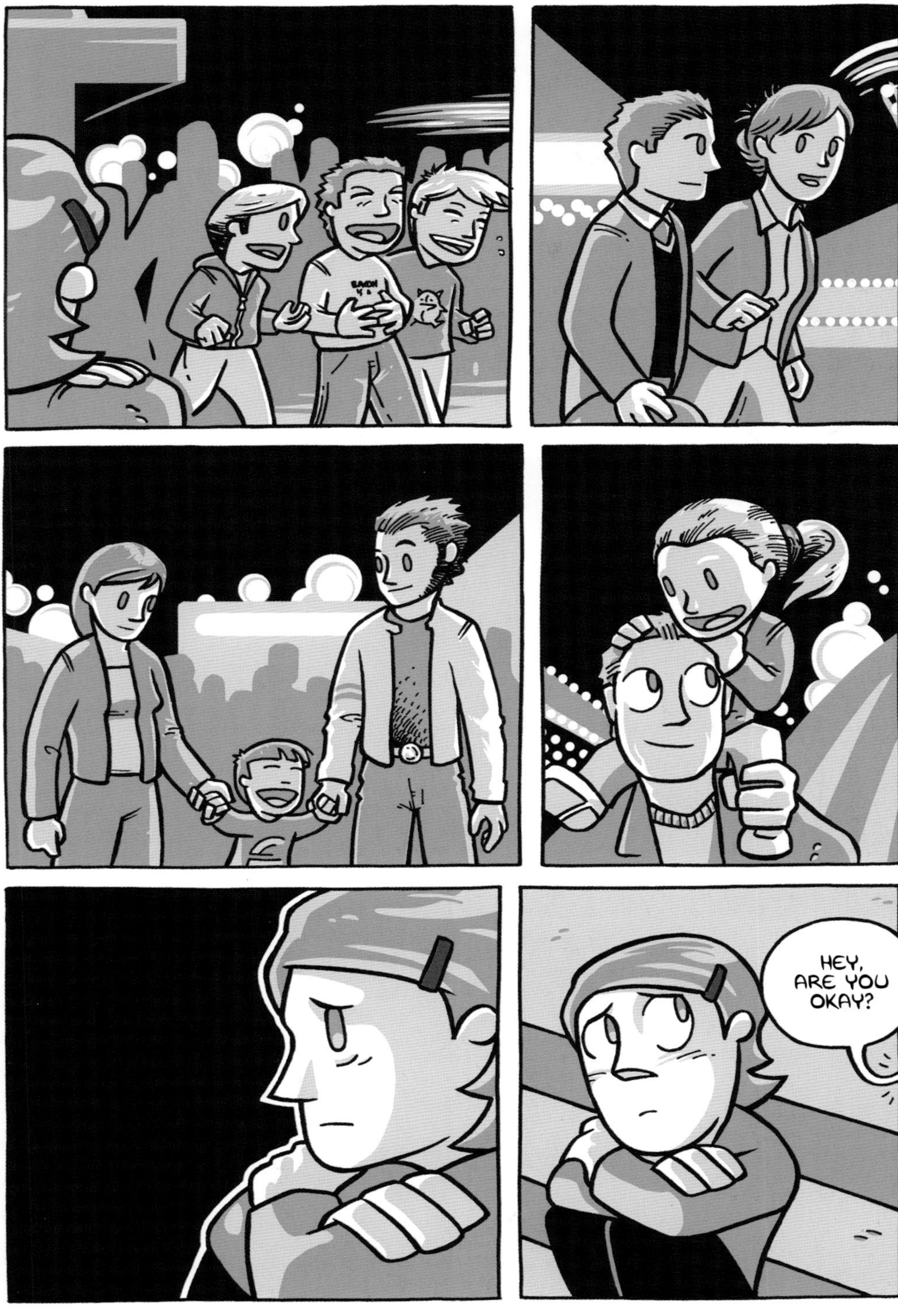
HEY,
ARE YOU
OKAY?

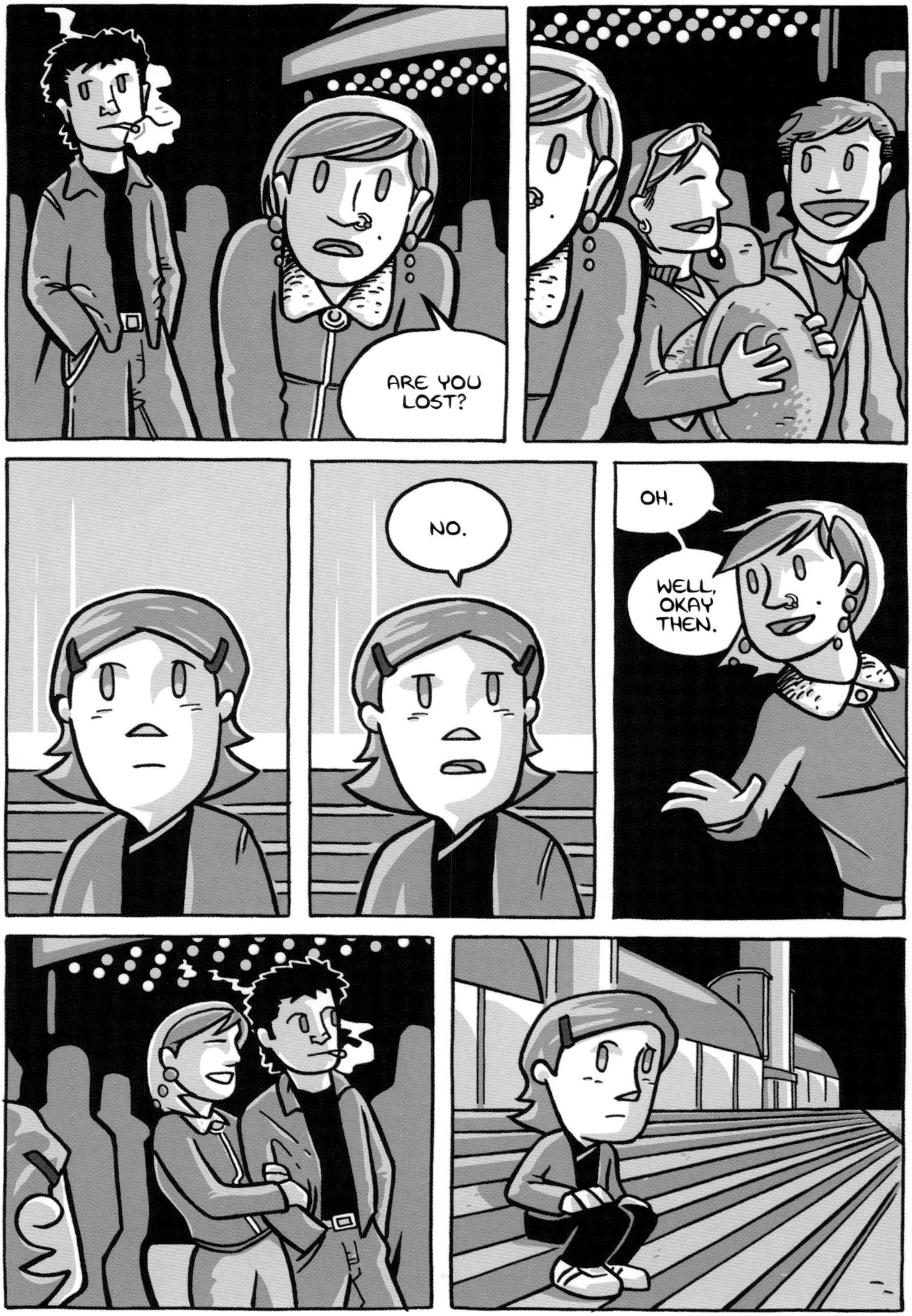
ARE YOU LOST?
NO.
OH.
WELL, OKAY THEN.

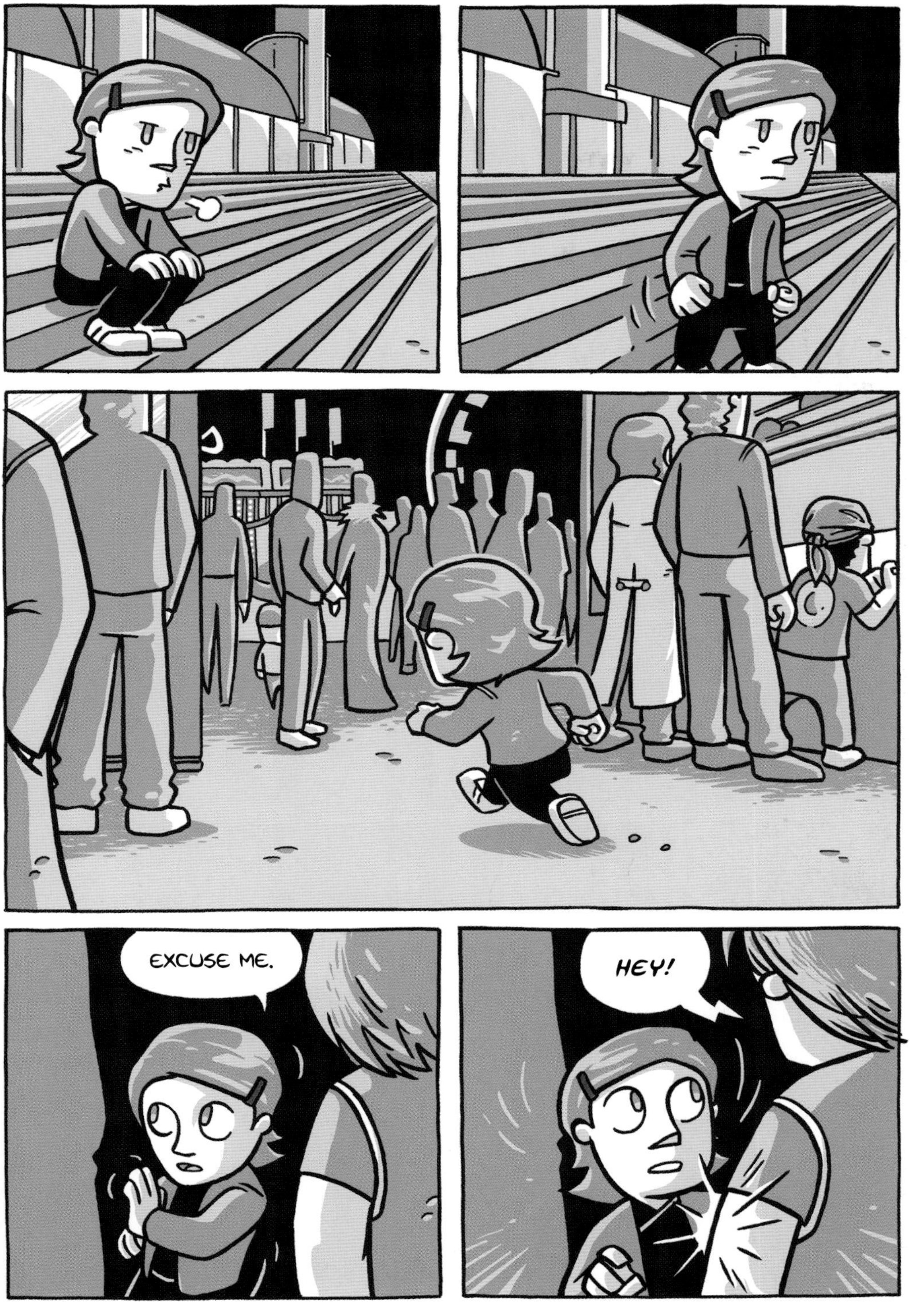
EXCUSE ME.
HEY!

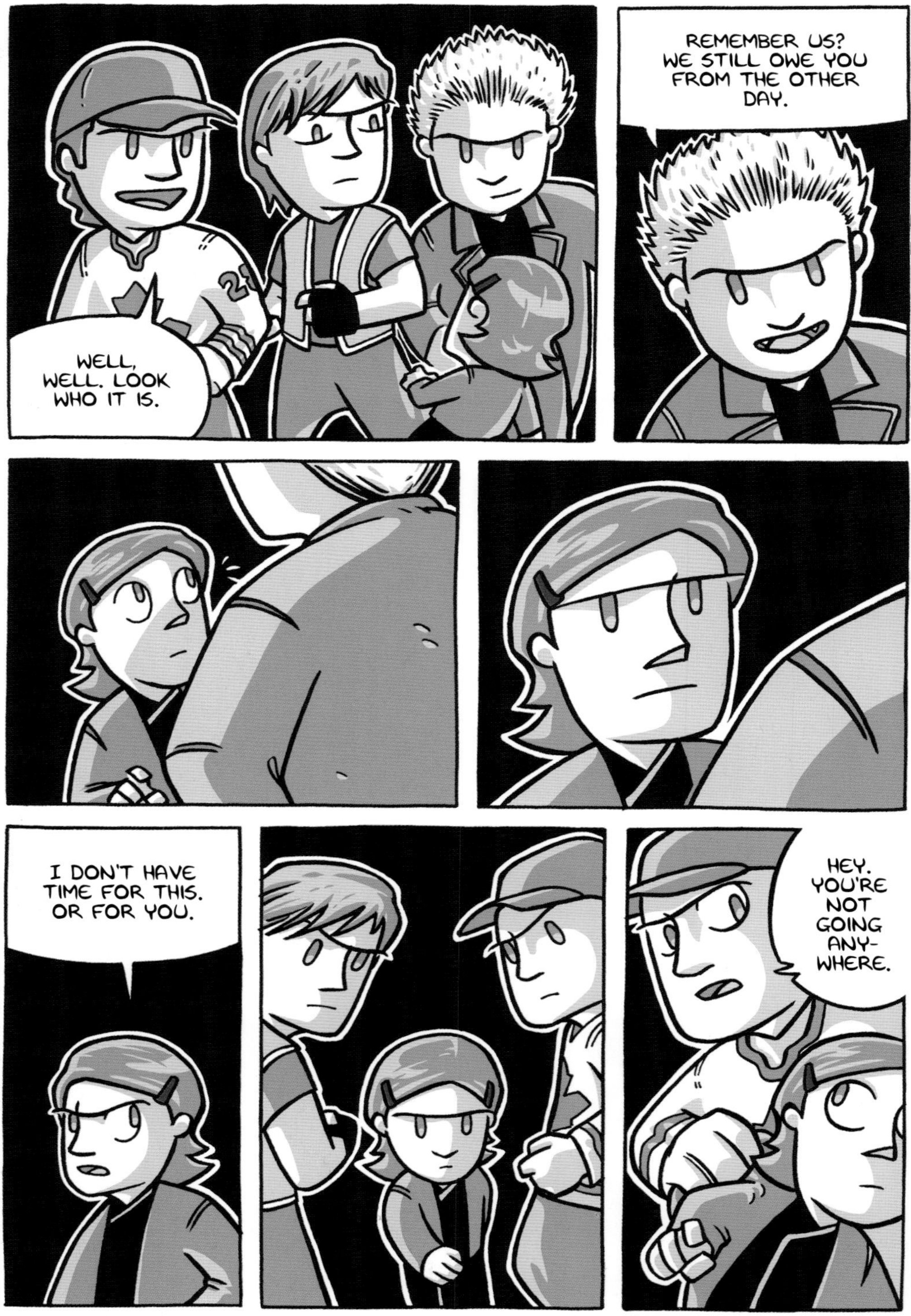
WELL, WELL. LOOK WHO IT IS.
REMEMBER US? WE STILL OWE YOU FROM THE OTHER DAY.
I DON'T HAVE TIME FOR THIS. OR FOR YOU.
HEY. YOU'RE NOT GOING ANY-WHERE.

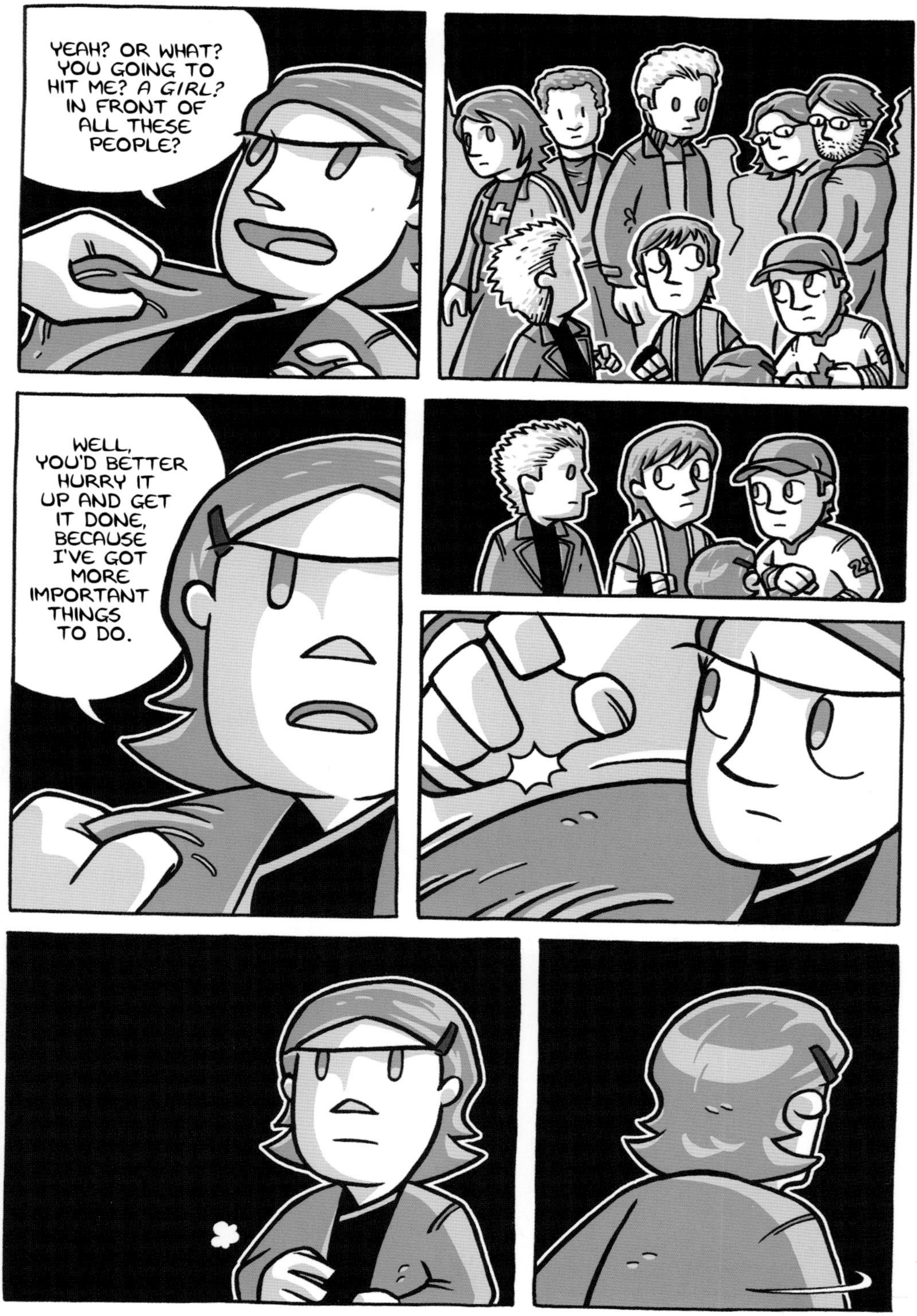
YEAH? OR WHAT? YOU GOING TO HIT ME? A *GIRL?* IN FRONT OF ALL THESE PEOPLE?
WELL, YOU'D BETTER HURRY IT UP AND GET IT DONE, BECAUSE I'VE GOT MORE IMPORTANT THINGS TO DO.

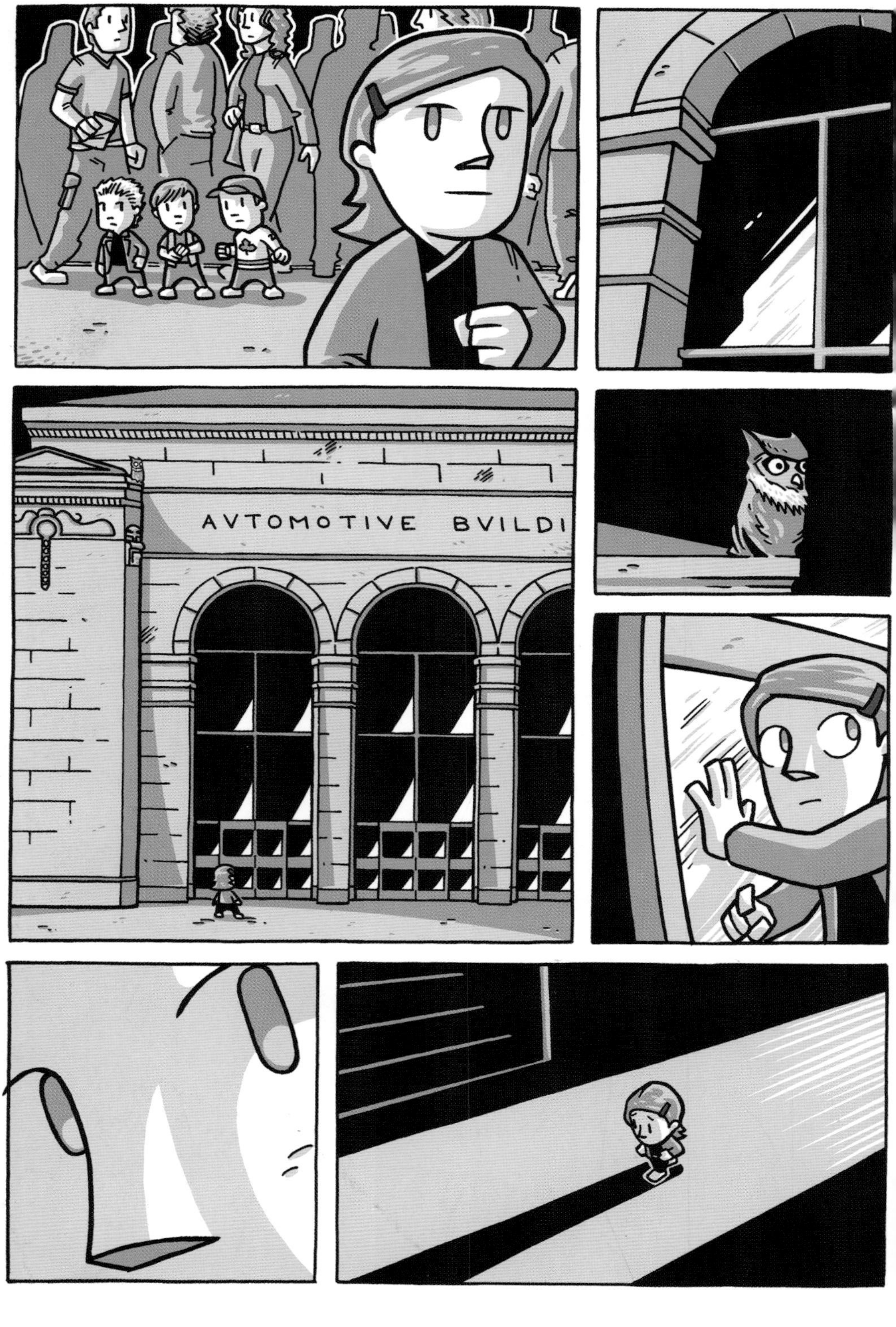
AVTOMOTIVE BVILDI

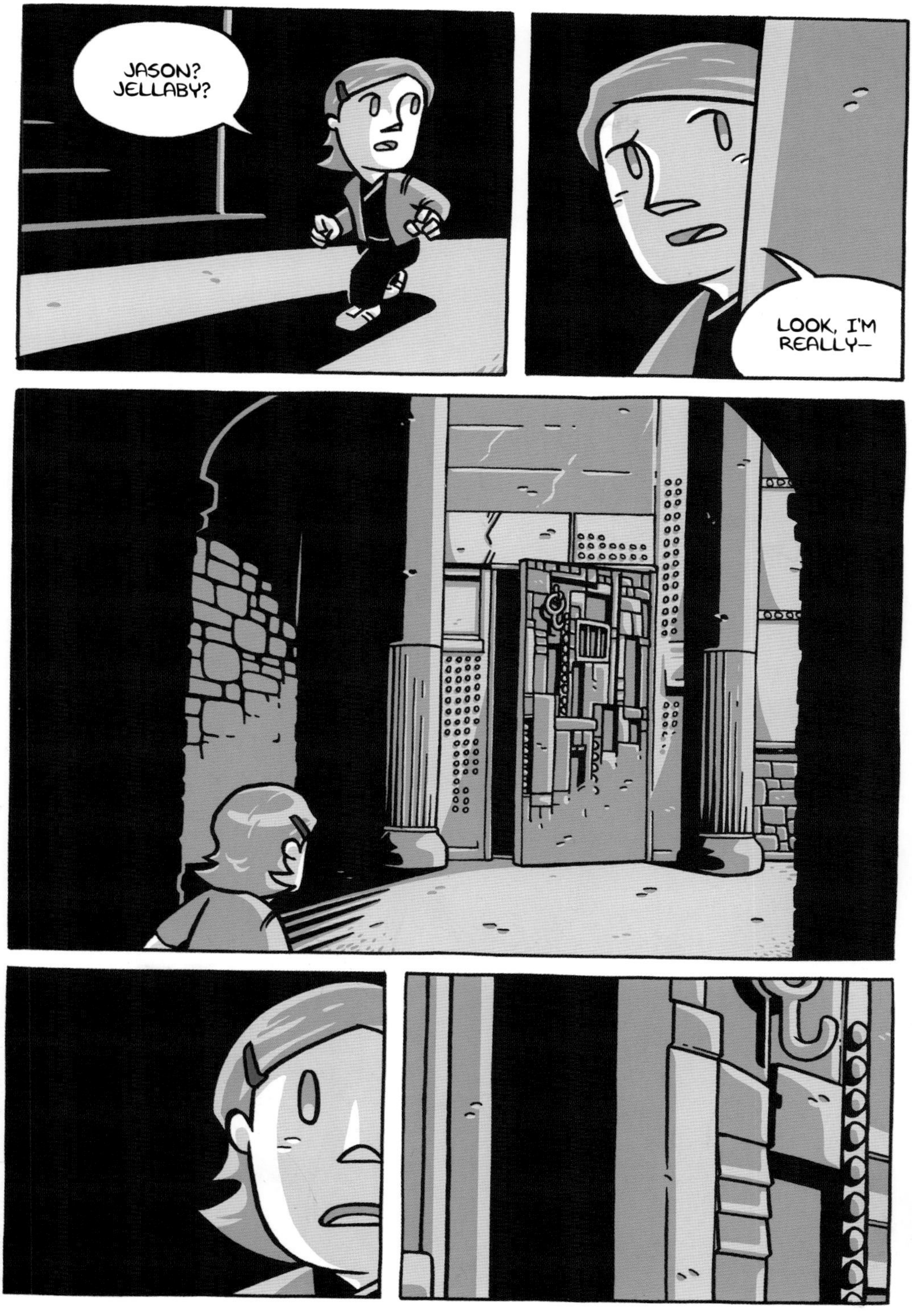
JASON? JELLABY?
LOOK, I'M REALLY–

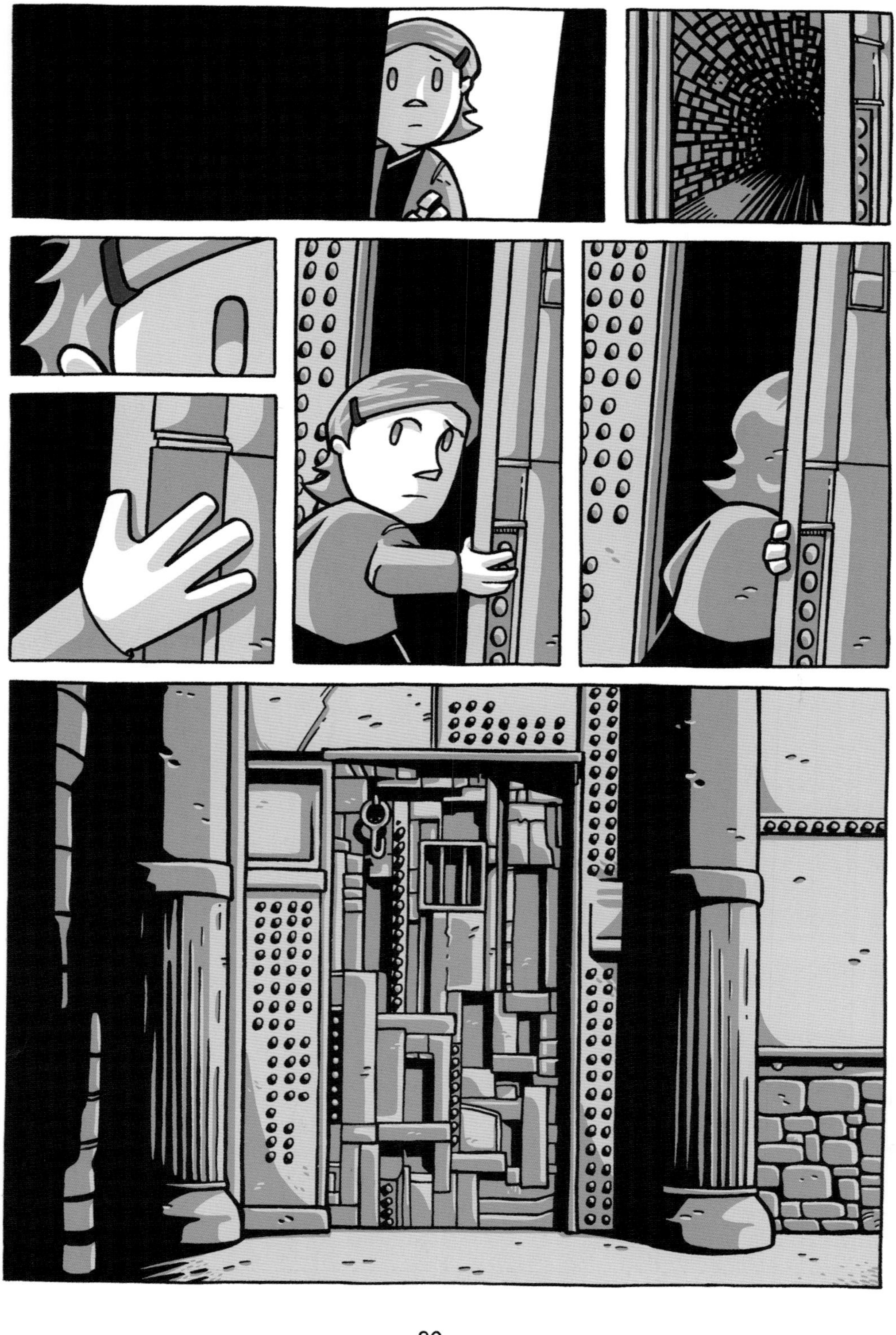

CHAPTER FOUR

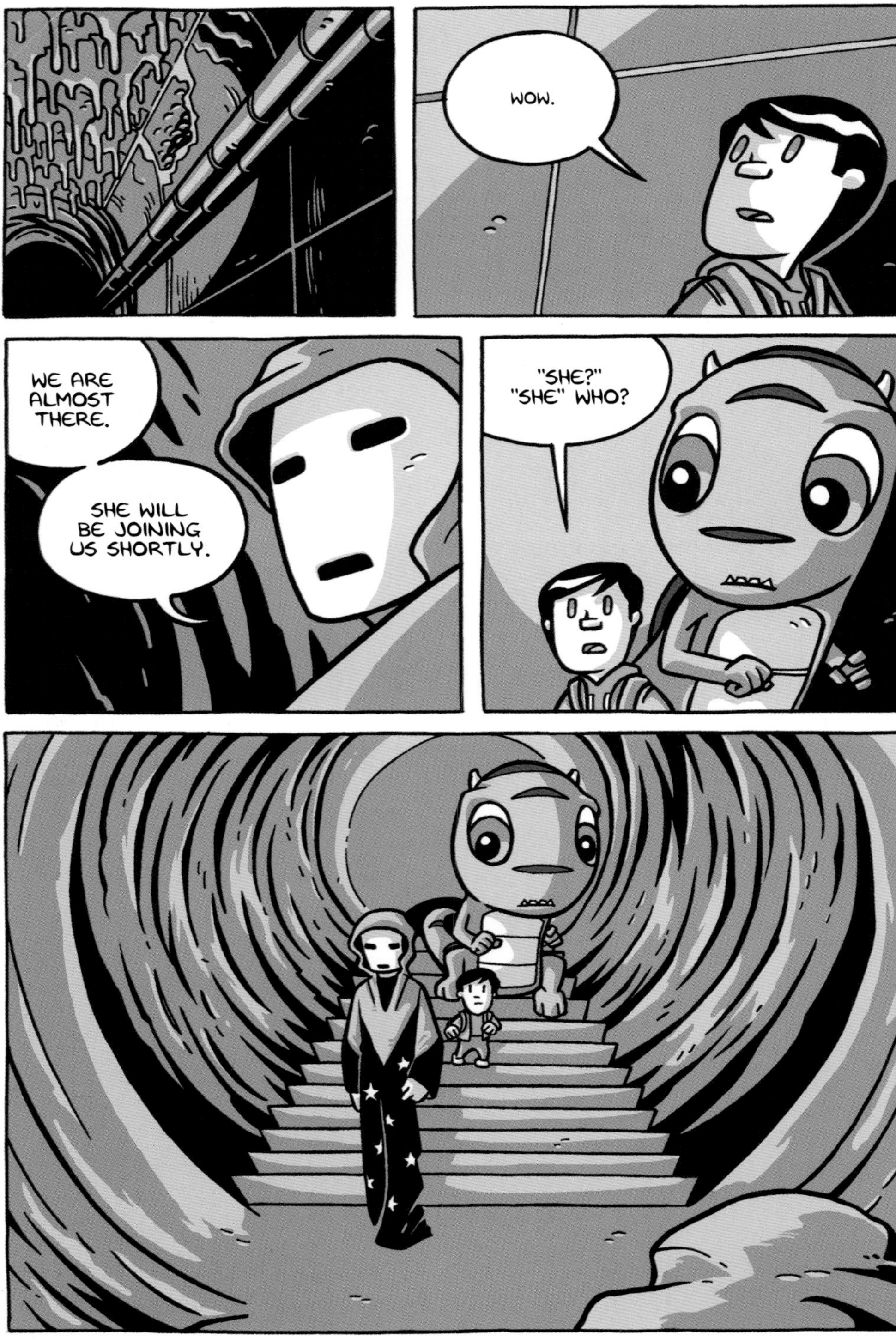
WOW.
WE ARE ALMOST THERE.
SHE WILL BE JOINING US SHORTLY.
"SHE?" "SHE" WHO?

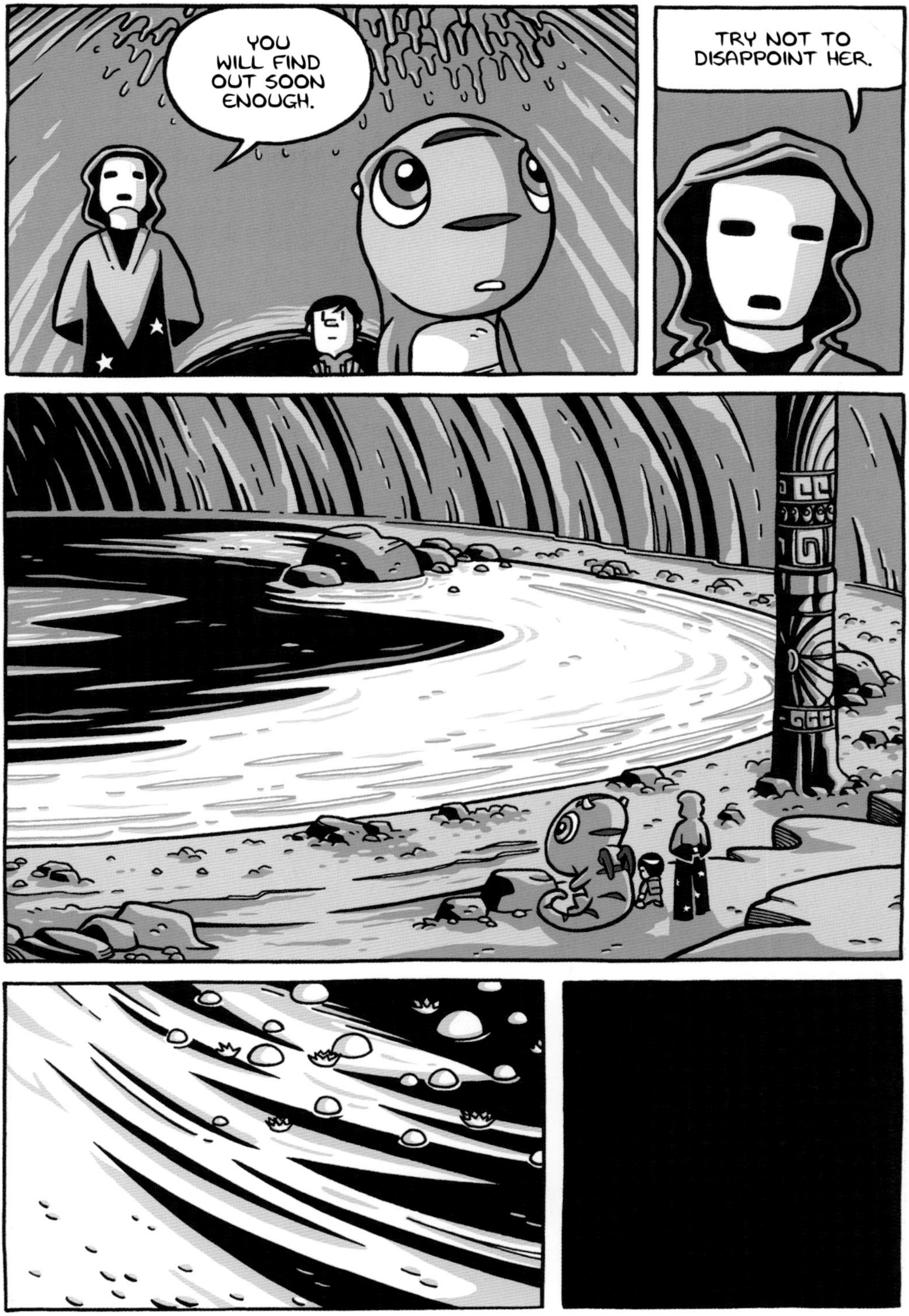
YOU WILL FIND OUT SOON ENOUGH.
TRY NOT TO DISAPPOINT HER.

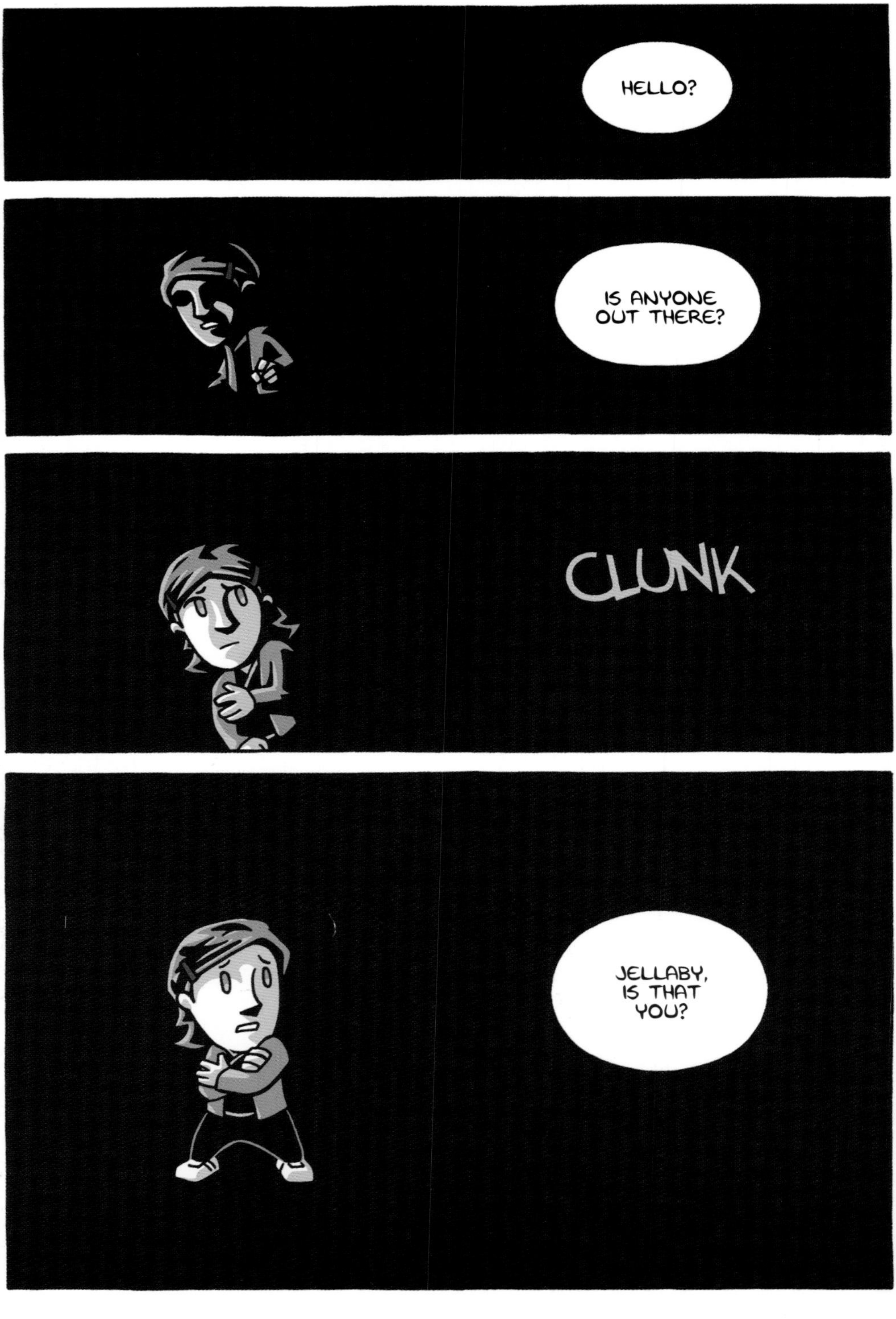
HELLO?
IS ANYONE OUT THERE?
CLUNK
JELLABY, IS THAT YOU?

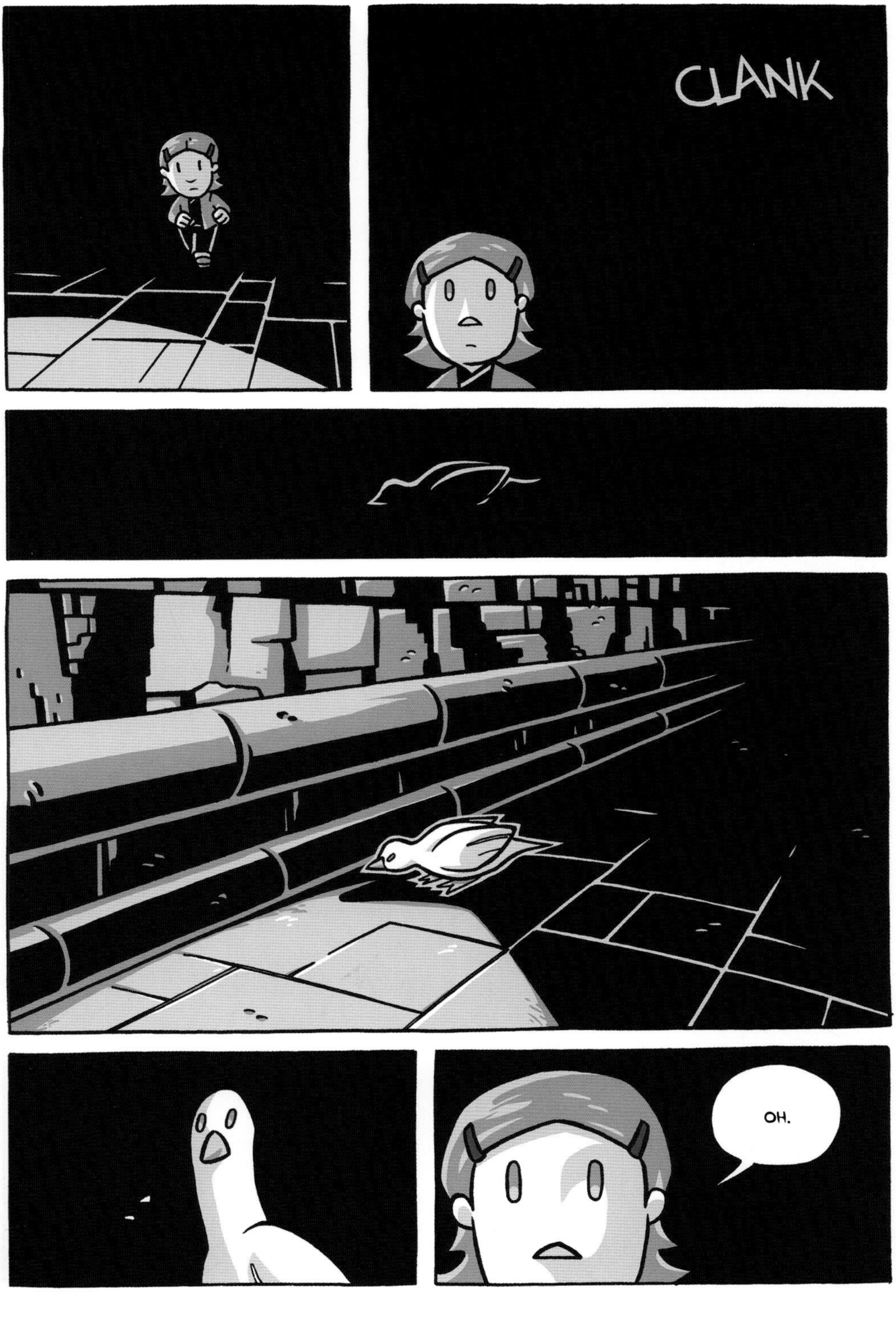
CLANK
OH.

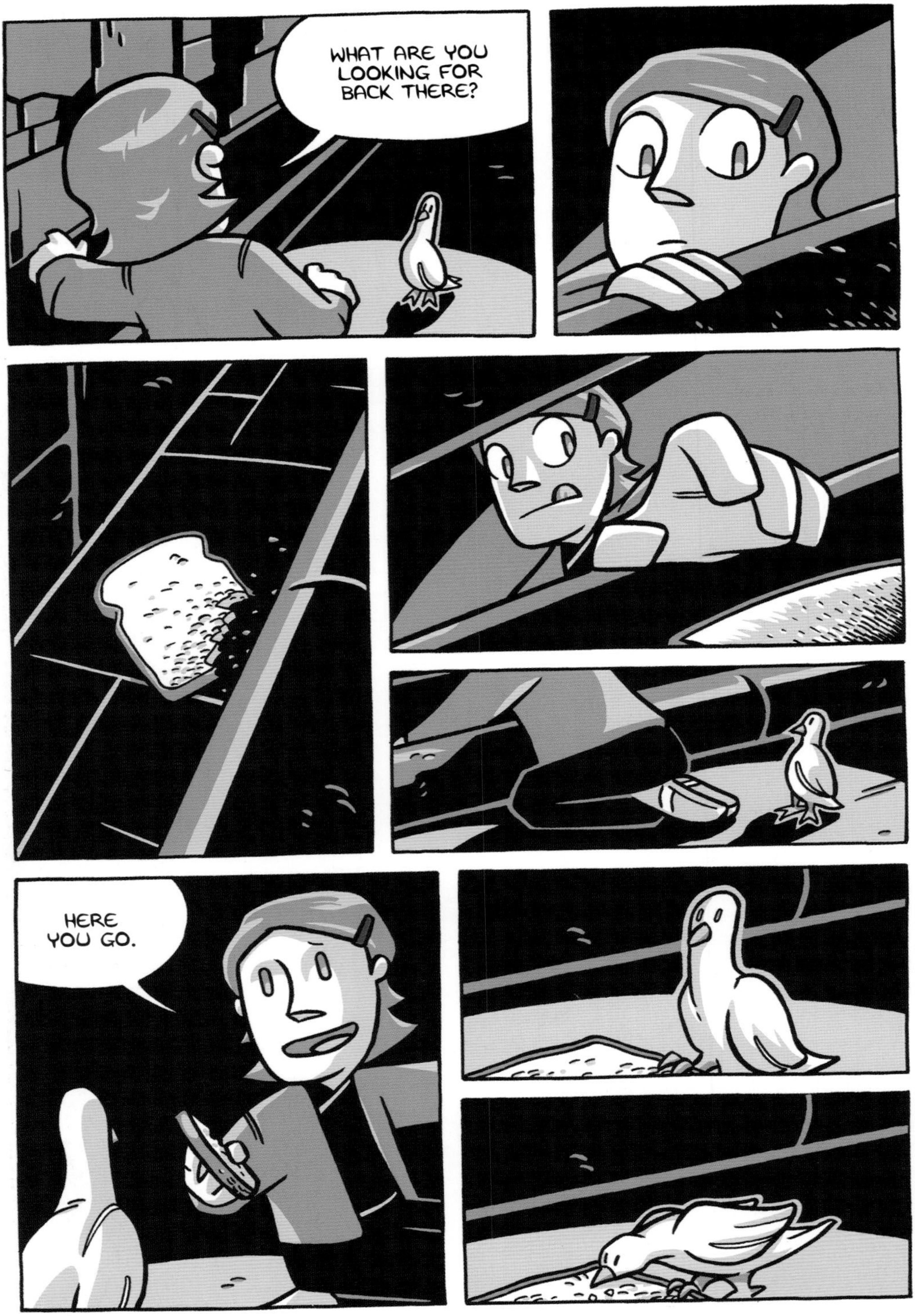
WHAT ARE YOU LOOKING FOR BACK THERE?
HERE YOU GO.

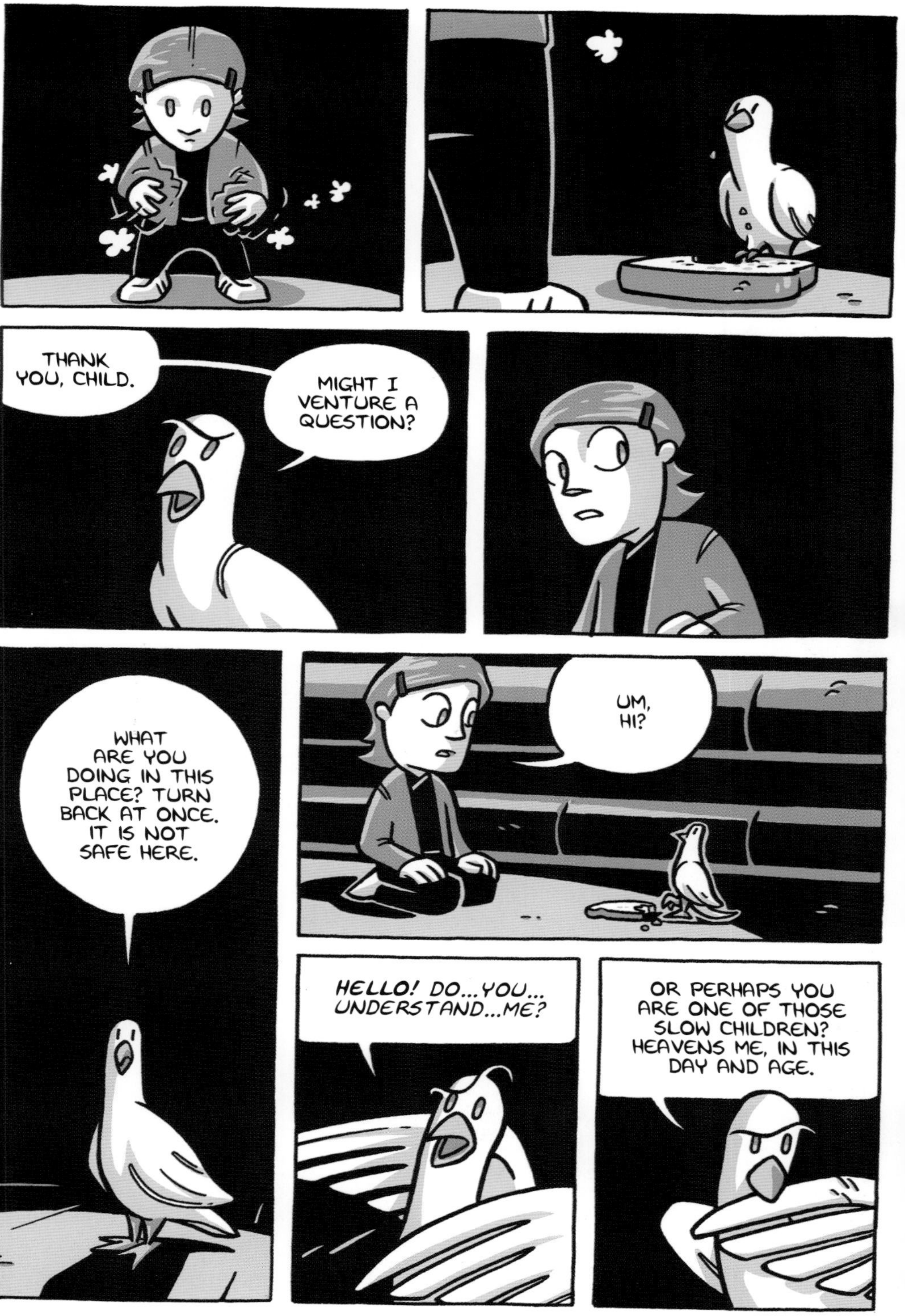
THANK YOU, CHILD.
MIGHT I VENTURE A QUESTION?
WHAT ARE YOU DOING IN THIS PLACE? TURN BACK AT ONCE. IT IS NOT SAFE HERE.
UM, HI?
HELLO! DO...YOU... UNDERSTAND...ME?
OR PERHAPS YOU ARE ONE OF THOSE SLOW CHILDREN? HEAVENS ME, IN THIS DAY AND AGE.

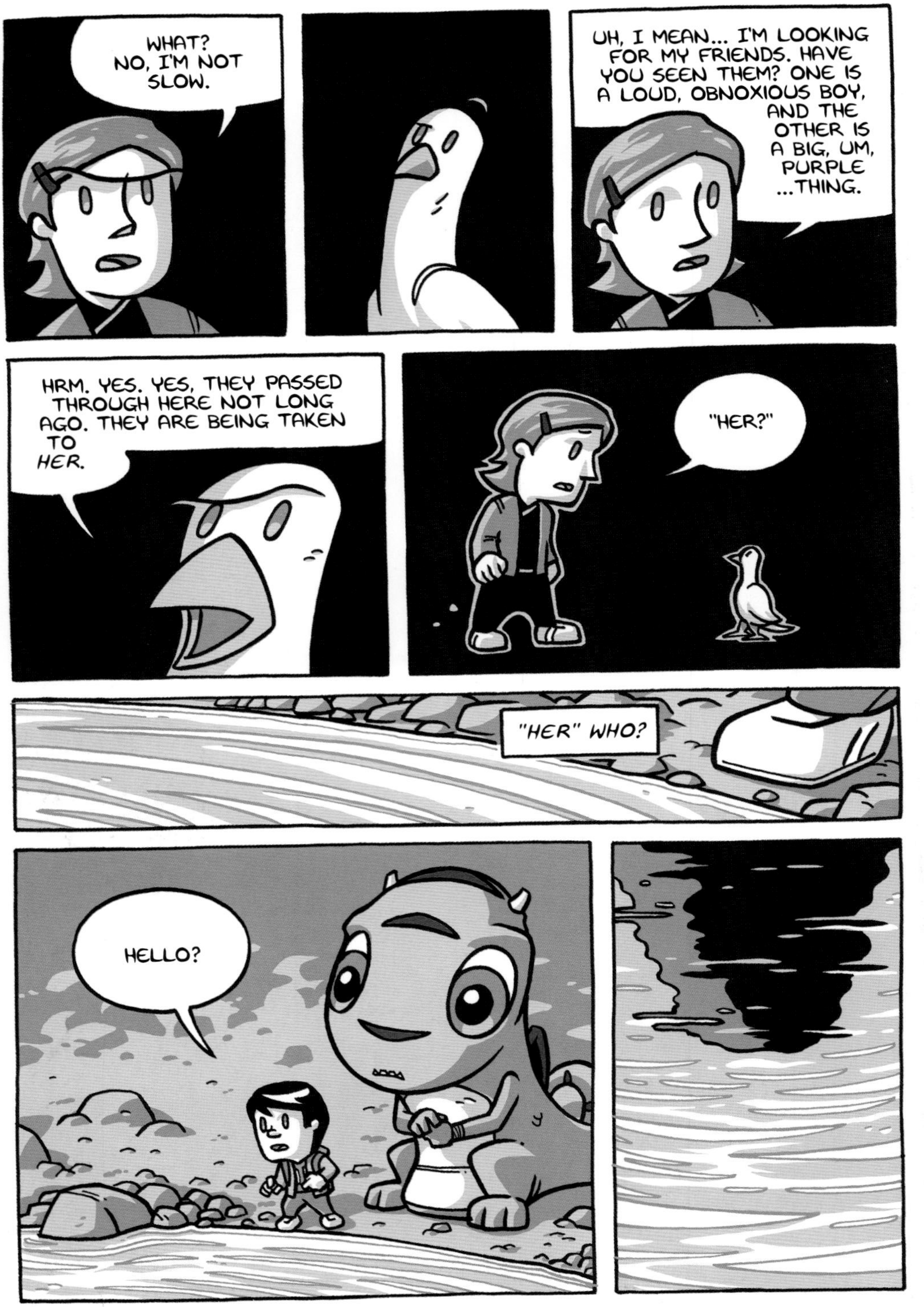
WHAT? NO, I'M NOT SLOW.
UH, I MEAN... I'M LOOKING FOR MY FRIENDS. HAVE YOU SEEN THEM? ONE IS A LOUD, OBNOXIOUS BOY, AND THE OTHER IS A BIG, UM, PURPLE ...THING.
HRM. YES. YES, THEY PASSED THROUGH HERE NOT LONG AGO. THEY ARE BEING TAKEN TO *HER*.
"HER?"
"HER" WHO?
HELLO?

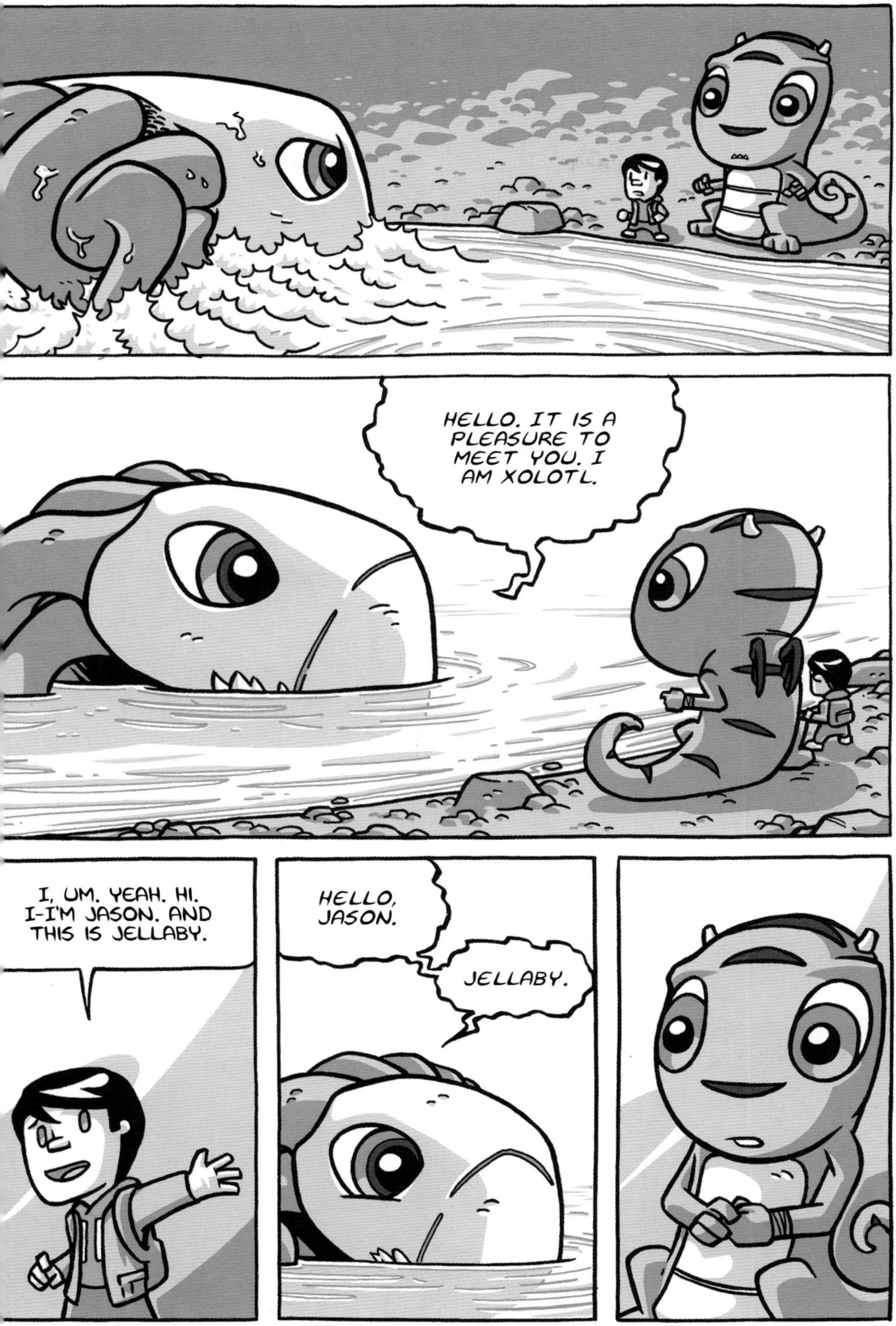
HELLO. IT IS A PLEASURE TO MEET YOU. I AM XOLOTL.
I, UM. YEAH. HI. I-I'M JASON. AND THIS IS JELLABY.
HELLO, JASON.
JELLABY.

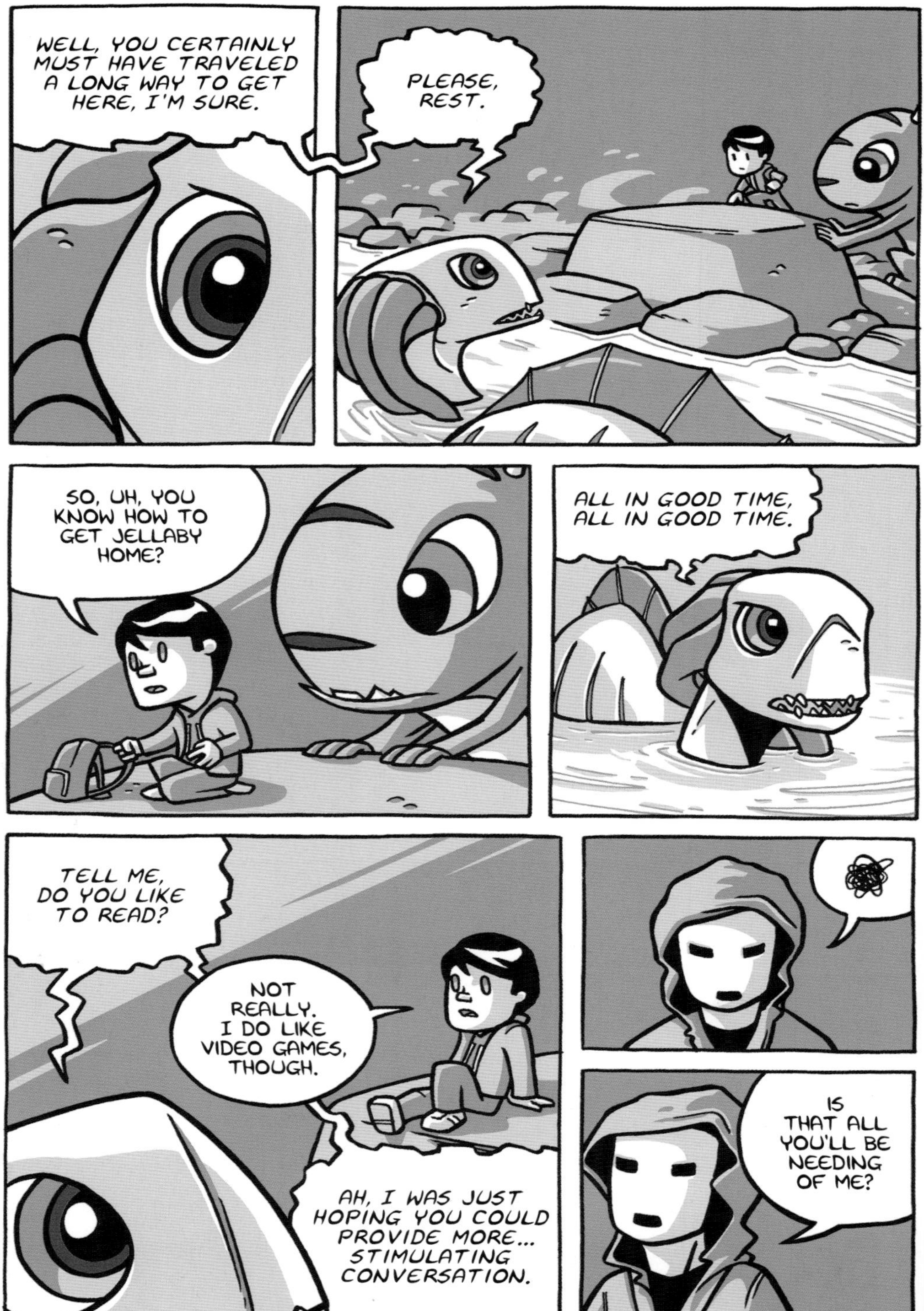
WELL, YOU CERTAINLY MUST HAVE TRAVELED A LONG WAY TO GET HERE, I'M SURE.
PLEASE, REST.
SO, UH, YOU KNOW HOW TO GET JELLABY HOME?
ALL IN GOOD TIME, ALL IN GOOD TIME.
TELL ME, DO YOU LIKE TO READ?
NOT REALLY. I DO LIKE VIDEO GAMES, THOUGH.
AH, I WAS JUST HOPING YOU COULD PROVIDE MORE... STIMULATING CONVERSATION.
IS THAT ALL YOU'LL BE NEEDING OF ME?

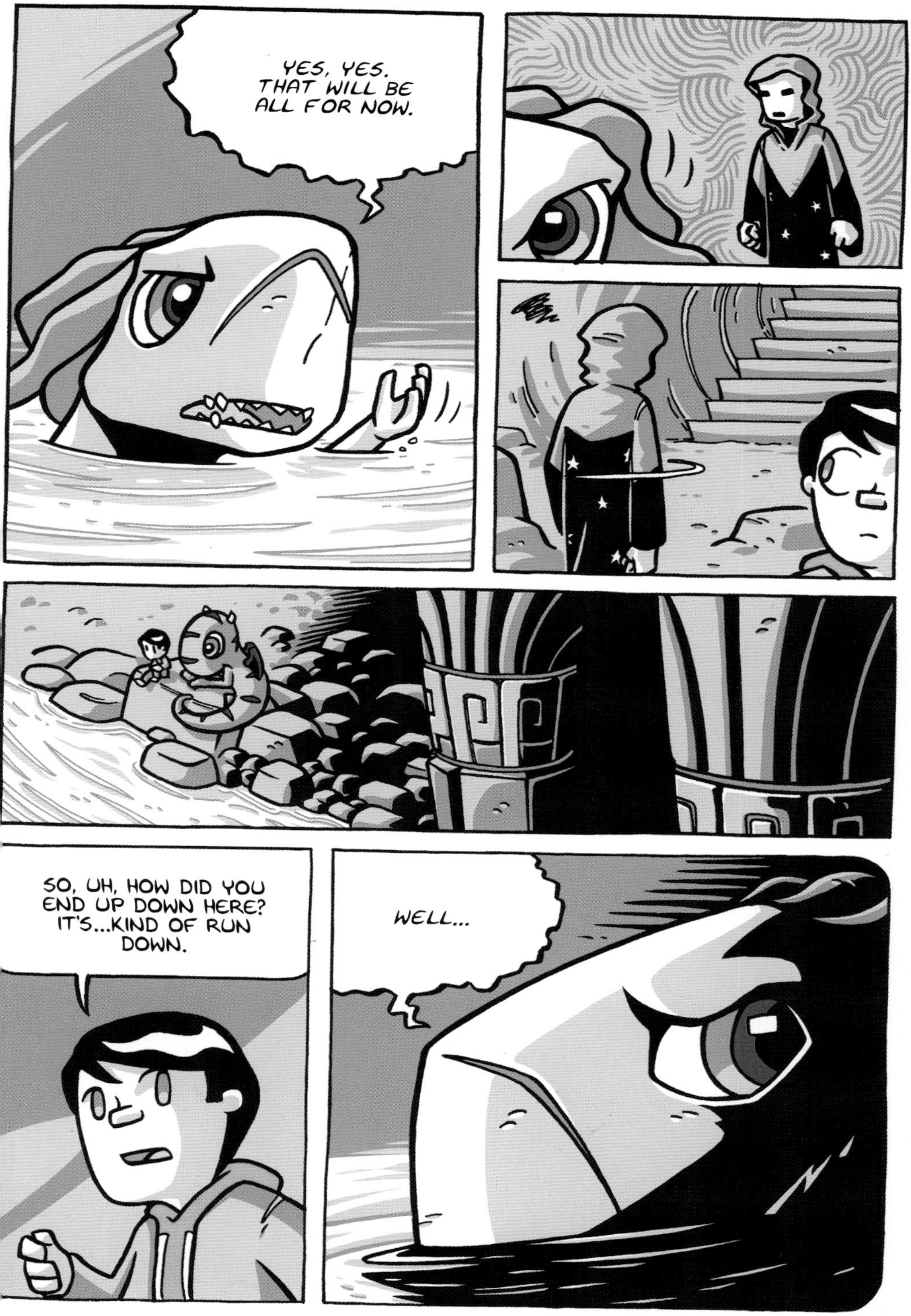
YES, YES. THAT WILL BE ALL FOR NOW.
SO, UH, HOW DID YOU END UP DOWN HERE? IT'S...KIND OF RUN DOWN.
WELL...

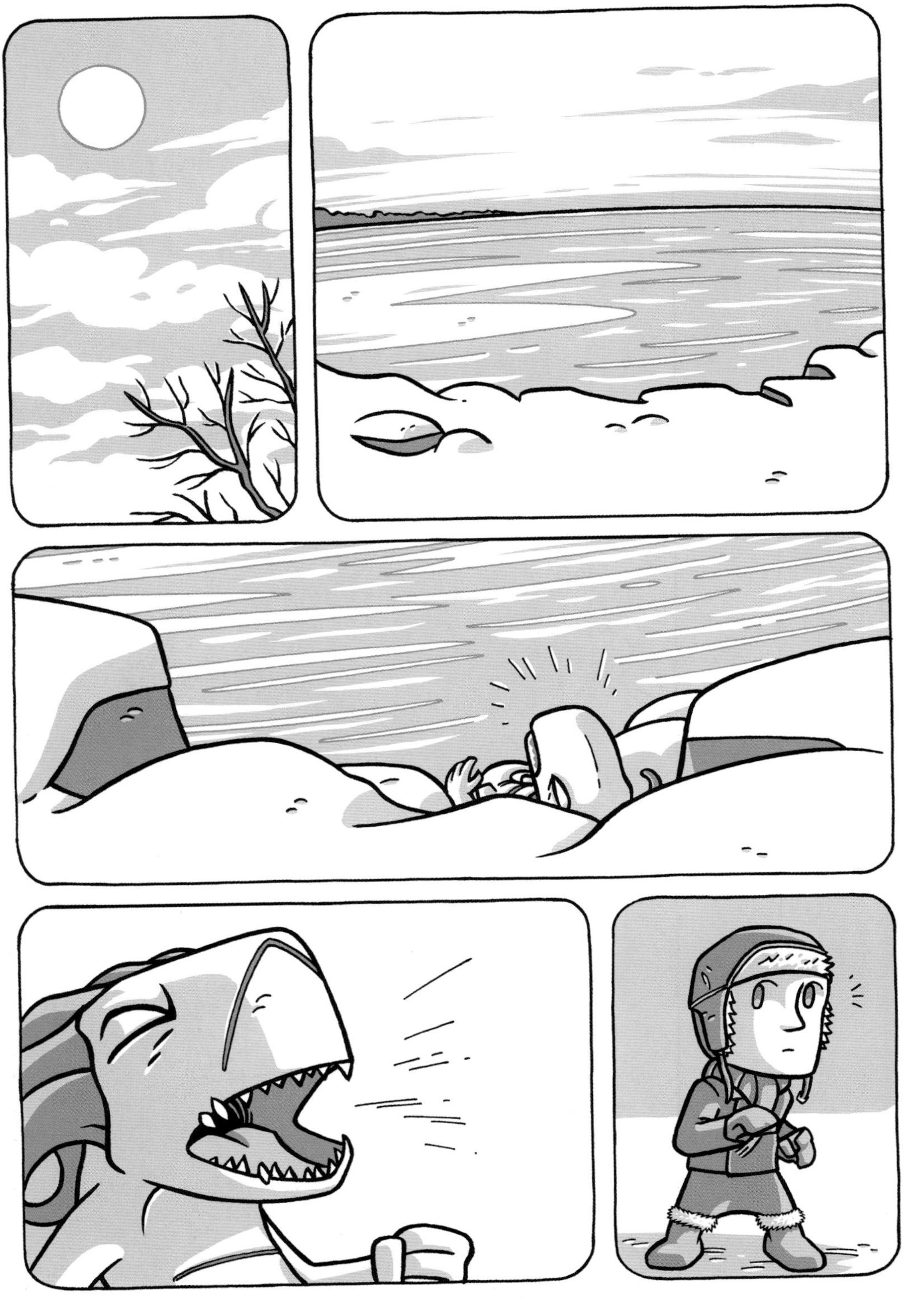

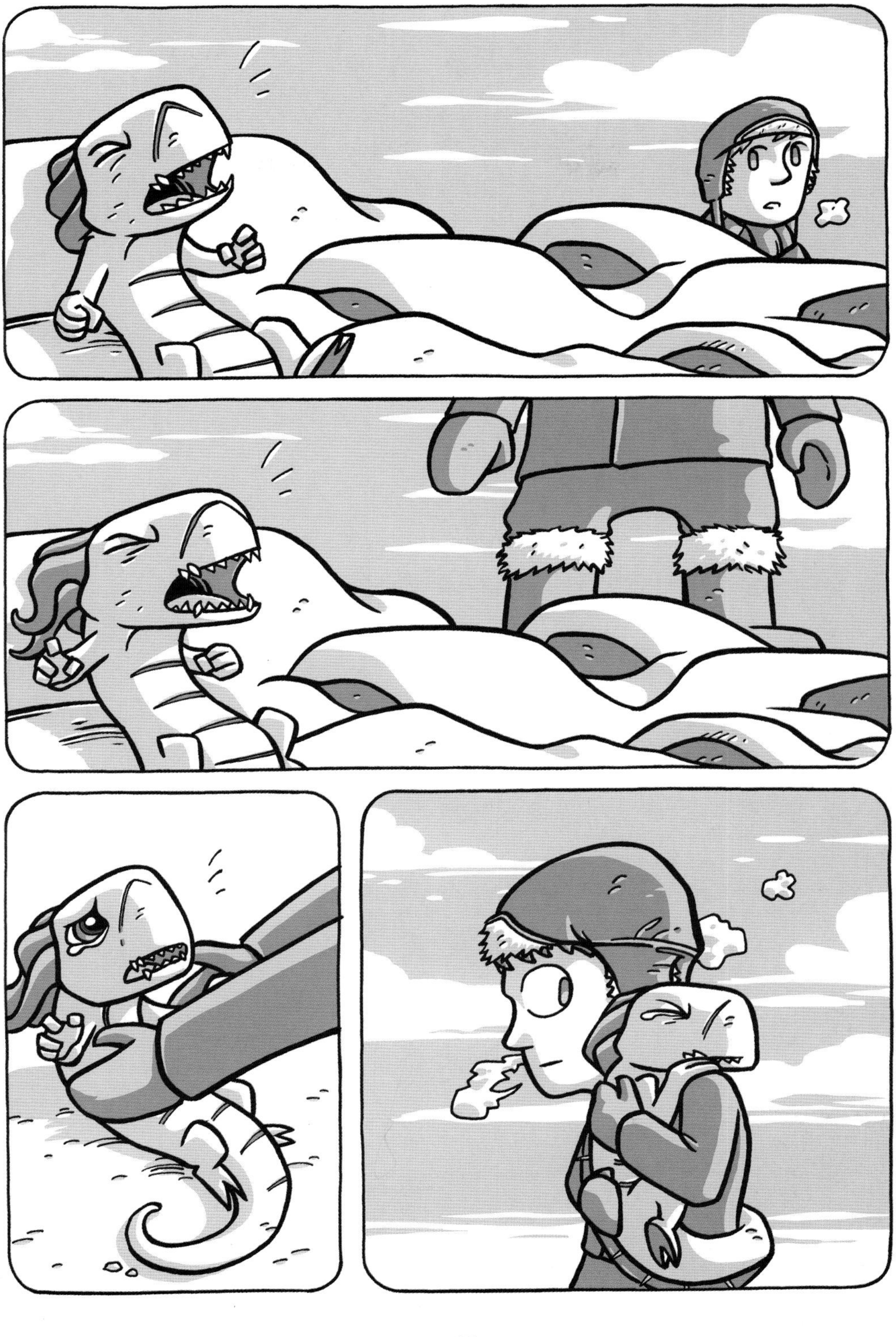

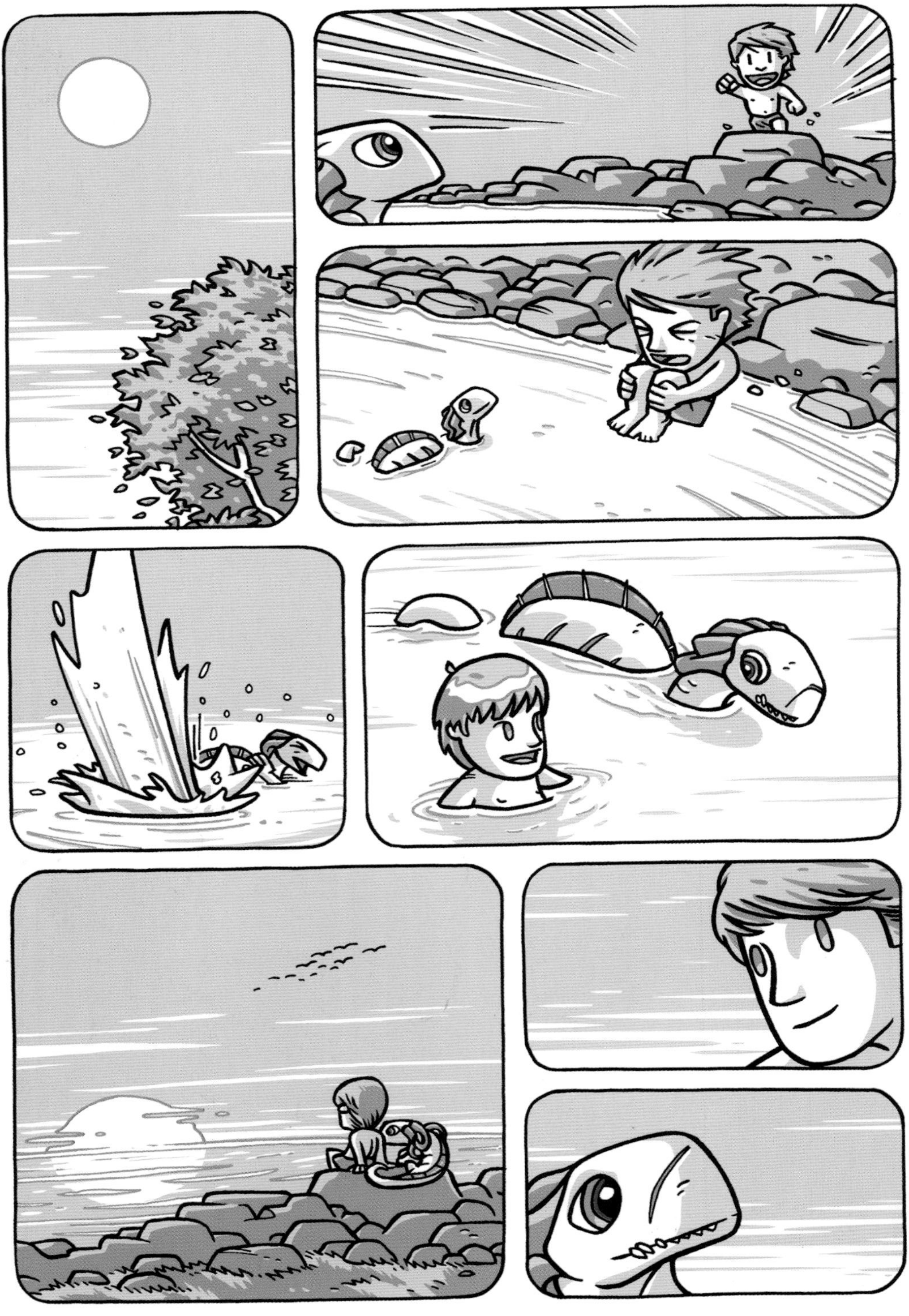

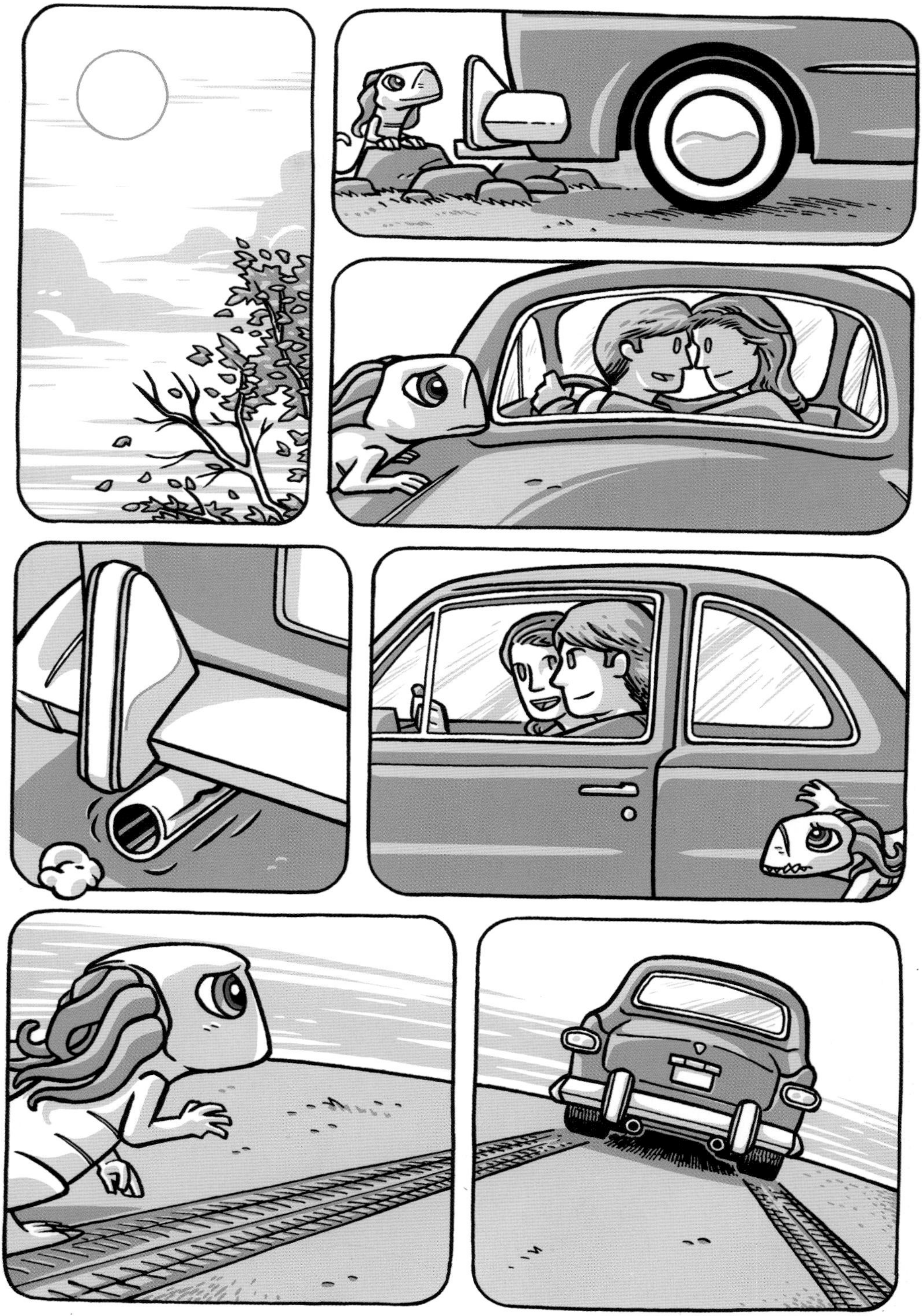

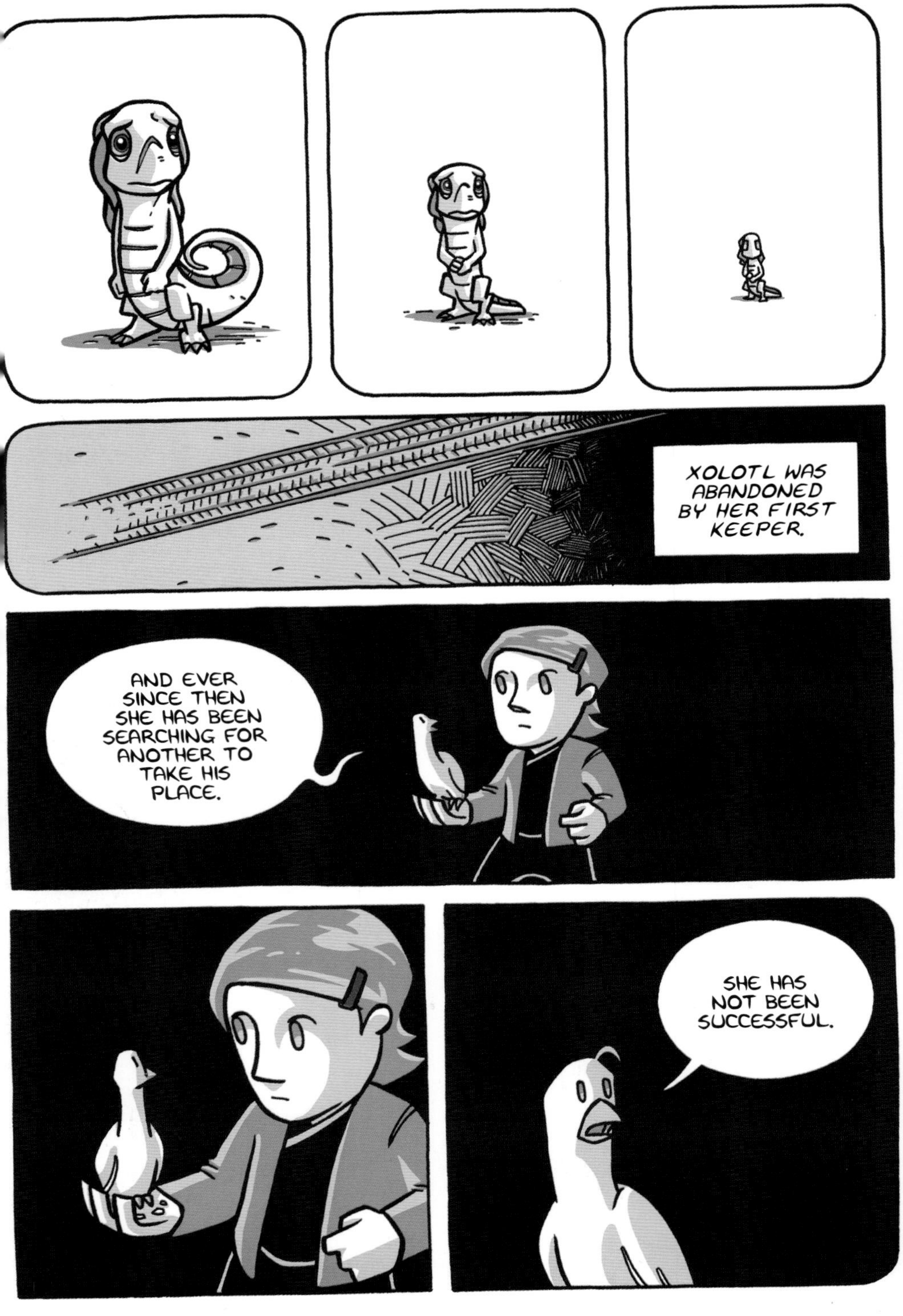
XOLOTL WAS ABANDONED BY HER FIRST KEEPER.
AND EVER SINCE THEN SHE HAS BEEN SEARCHING FOR ANOTHER TO TAKE HIS PLACE.
SHE HAS NOT BEEN SUCCESSFUL.

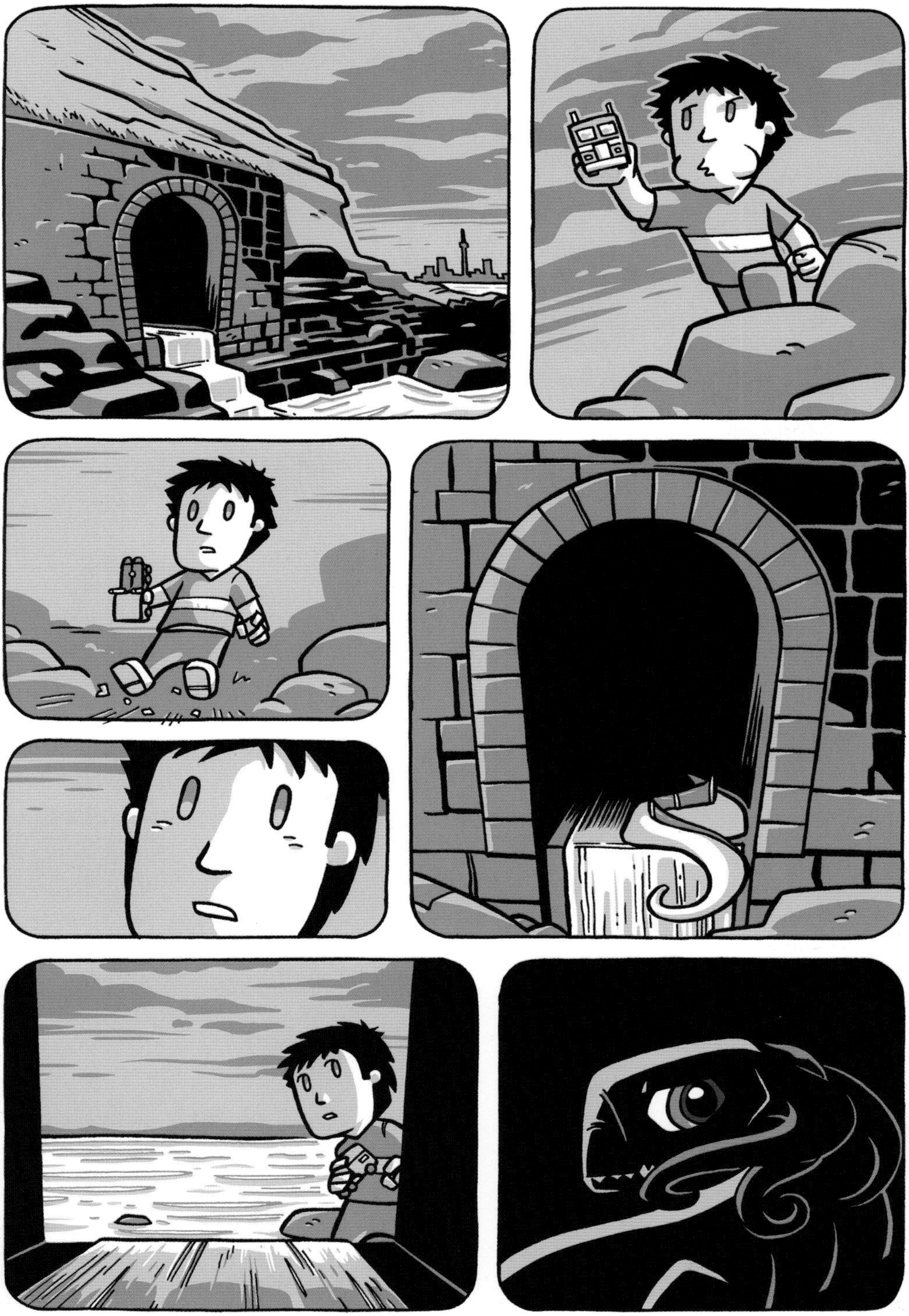

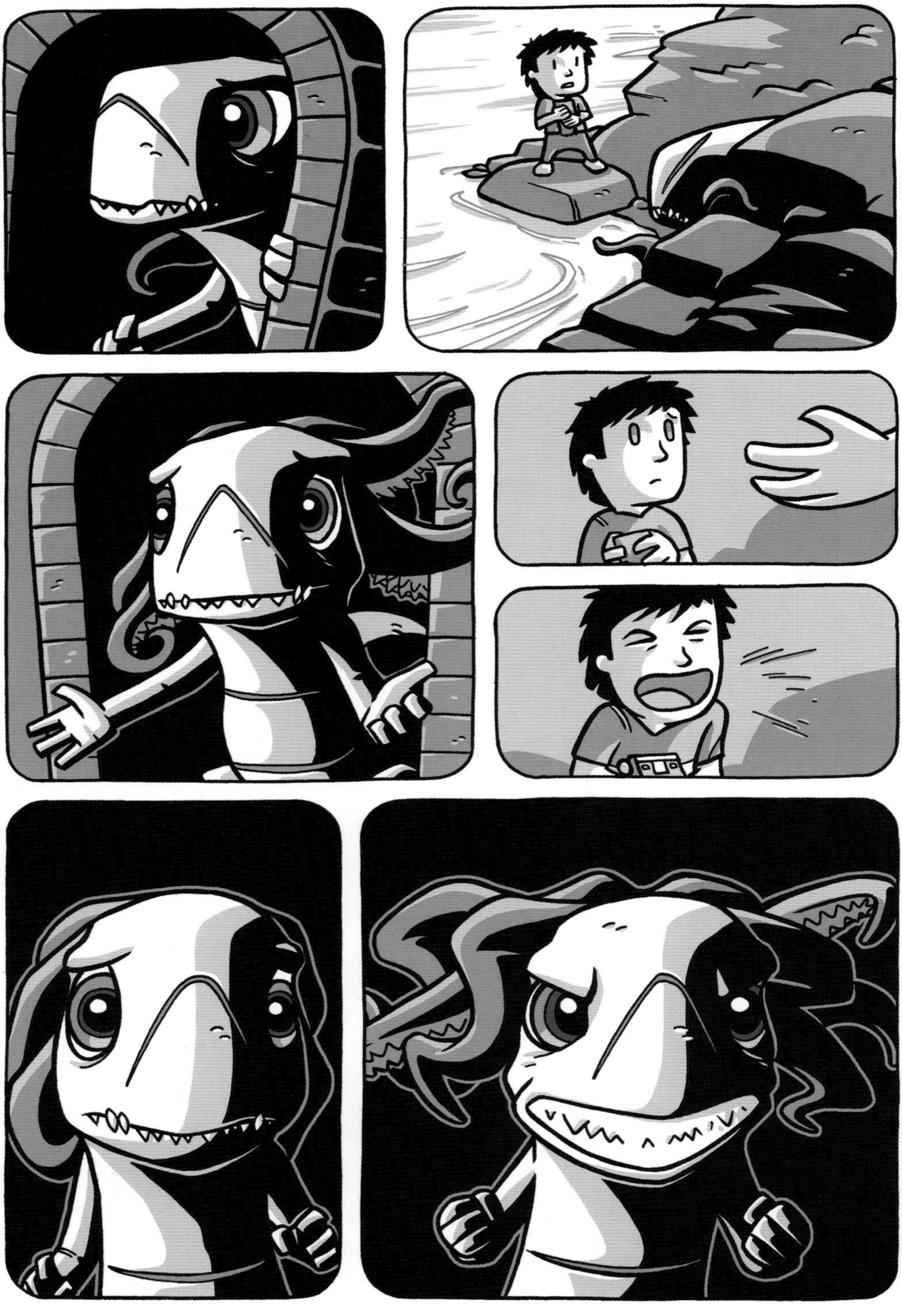

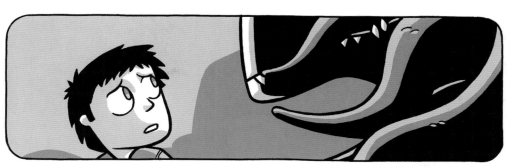

XOLOTL IS MUCH OLDER NOW. DECADES AGO, SHE FOUND THIS PLACE HIDDEN UNDER THE GROUND AND HID HERSELF FROM THE WORLD. BUT HER ANGER STILL REMAINS.

AND IT IS HER TEMPER THAT MAKES HER TRULY DANGEROUS.

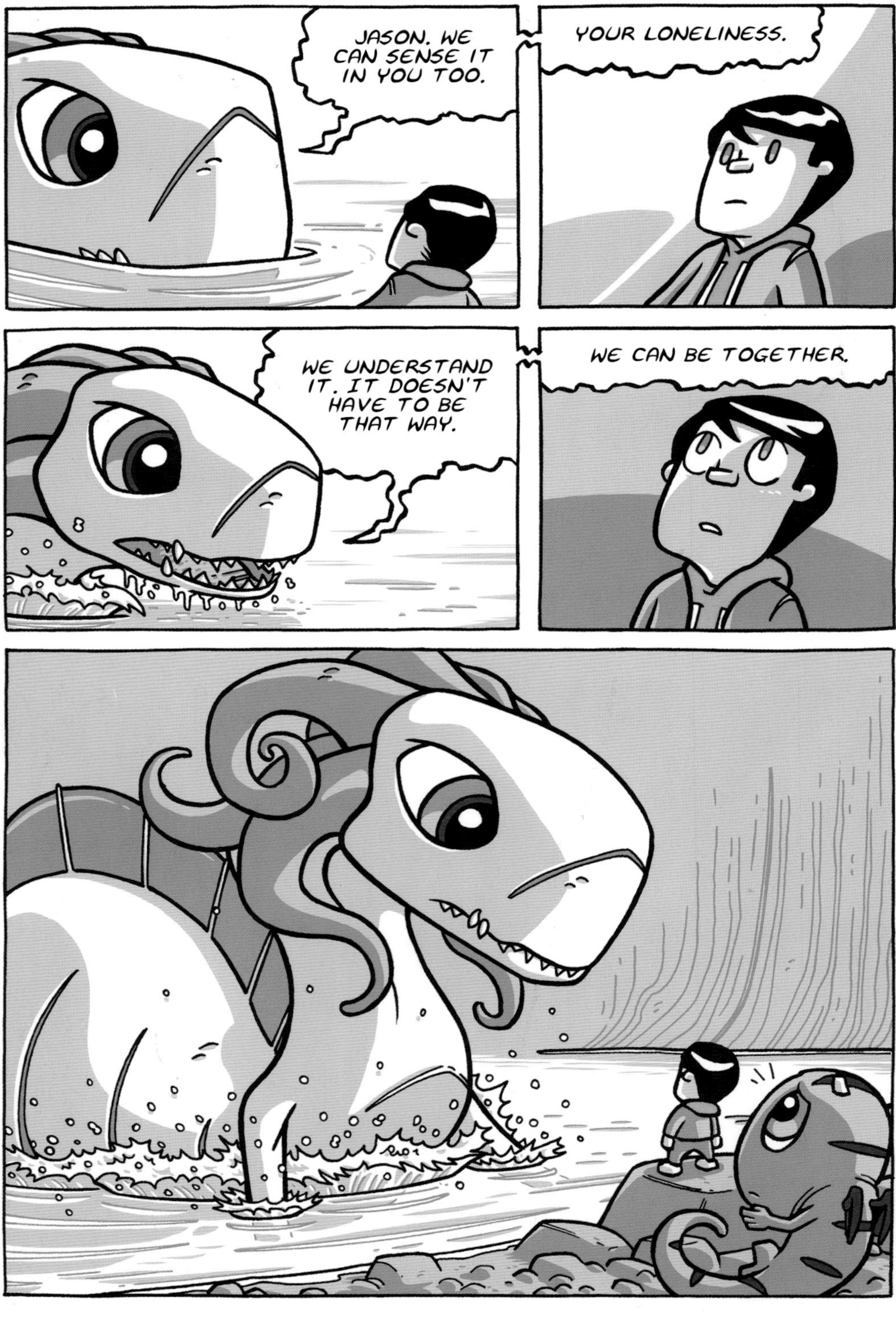
JASON. WE CAN SENSE IT IN YOU TOO.
YOUR LONELINESS.
WE UNDERSTAND IT. IT DOESN'T HAVE TO BE THAT WAY.
WE CAN BE TOGETHER.

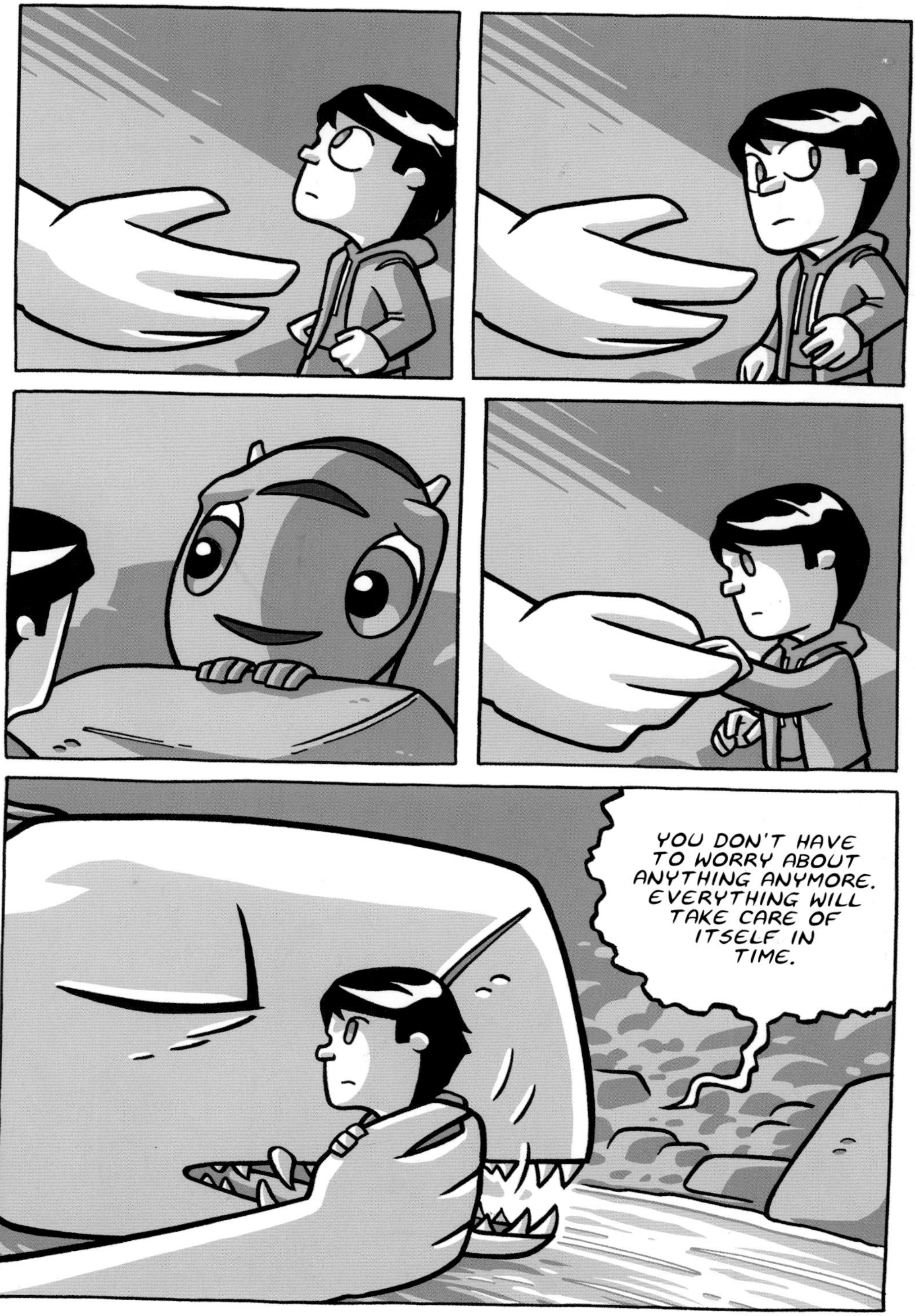
YOU DON'T HAVE TO WORRY ABOUT ANYTHING ANYMORE. EVERYTHING WILL TAKE CARE OF ITSELF IN TIME.

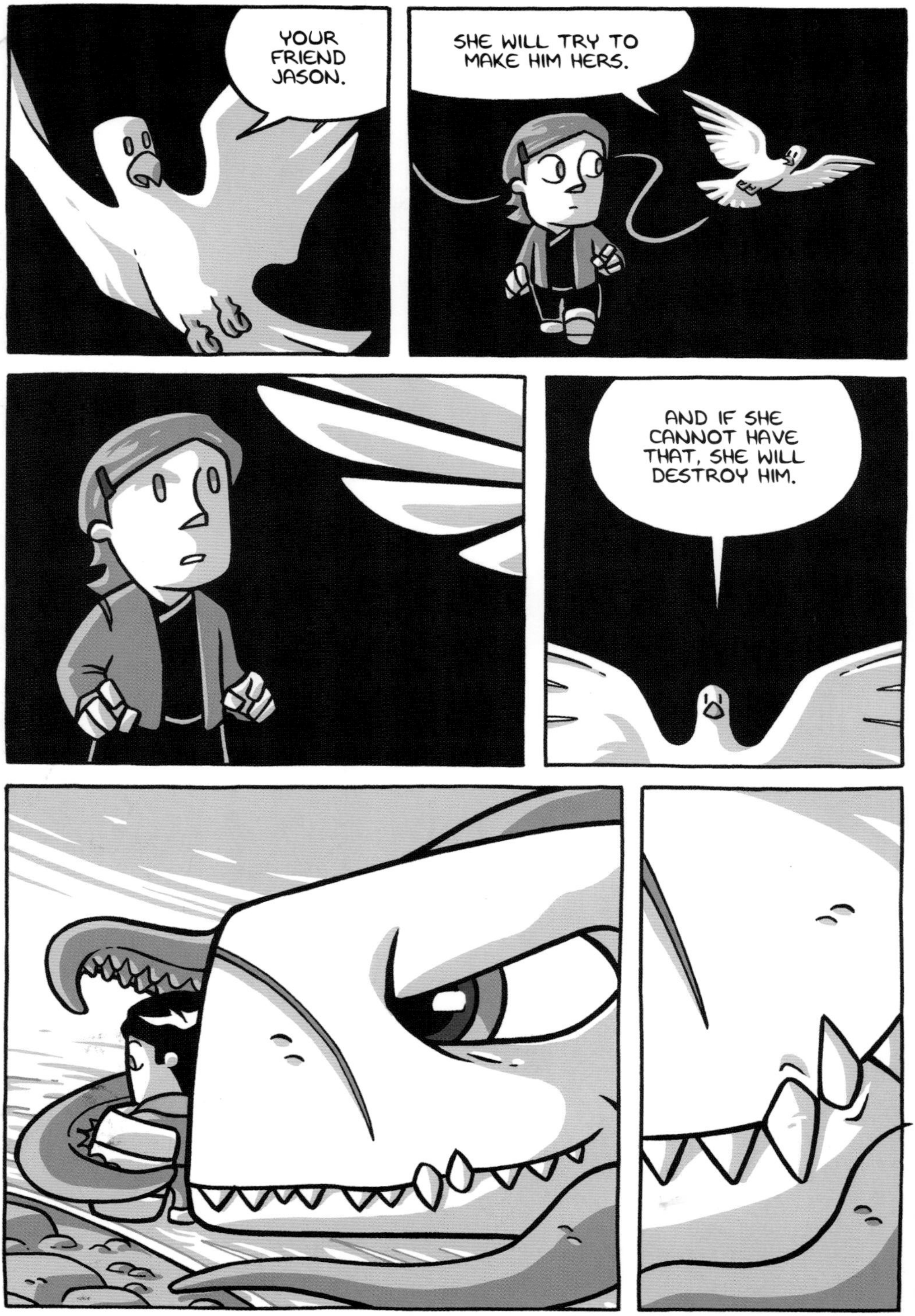
YOUR FRIEND JASON.
SHE WILL TRY TO MAKE HIM HERS.
AND IF SHE CANNOT HAVE THAT, SHE WILL DESTROY HIM.

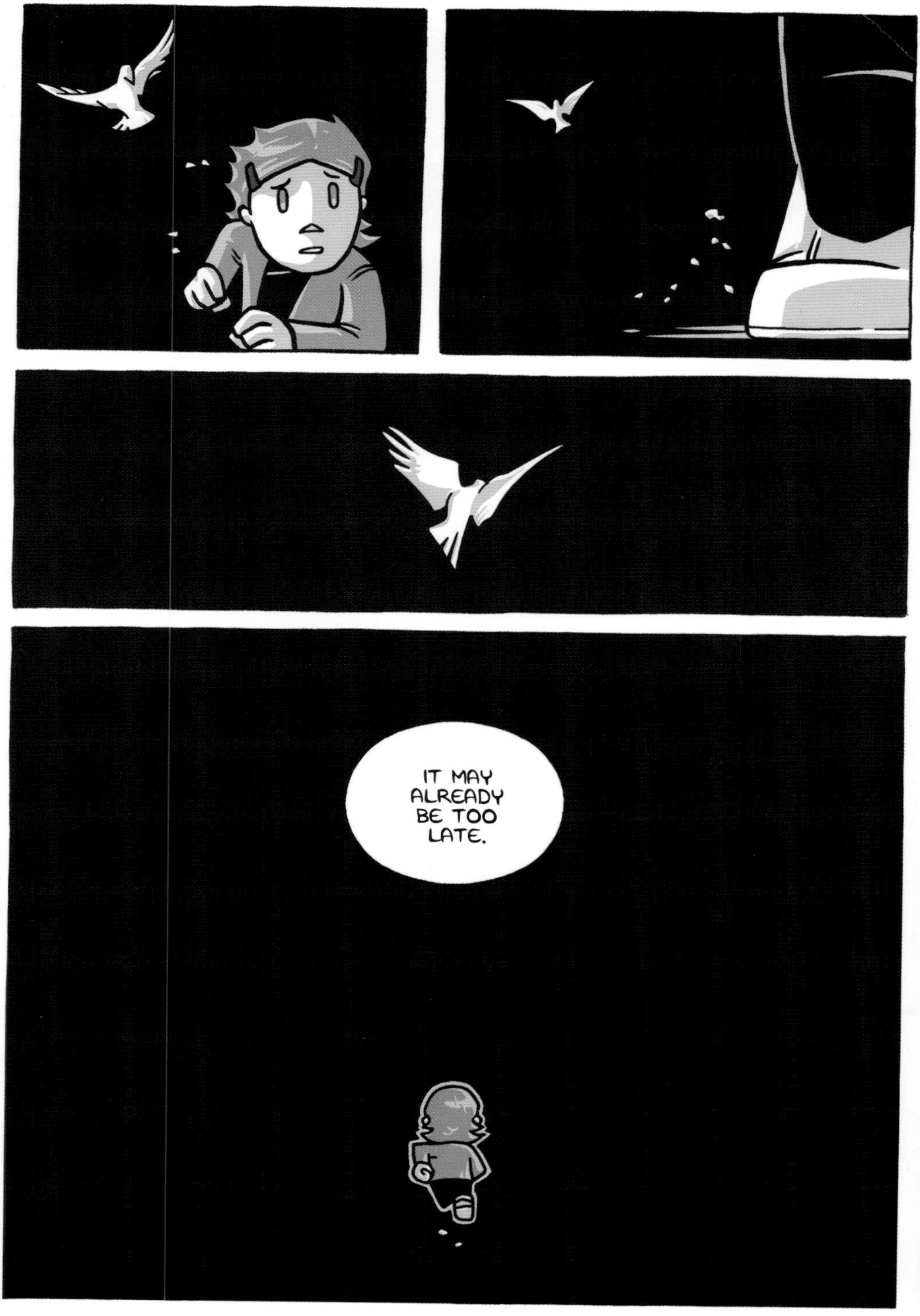
IT MAY ALREADY BE TOO LATE.

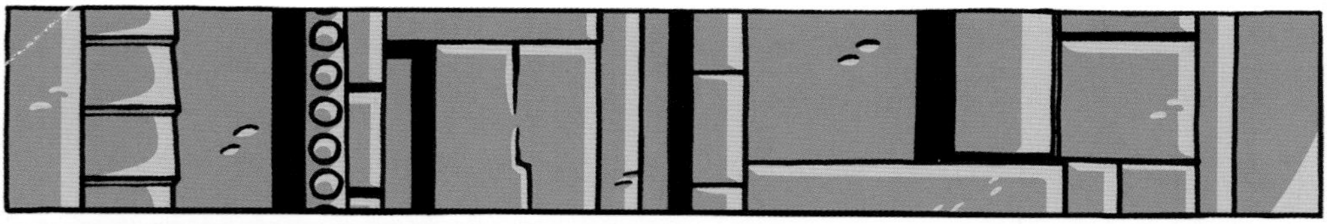

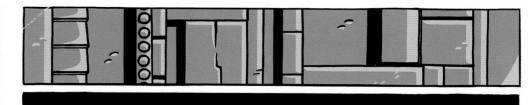

CHAPTER FIVE

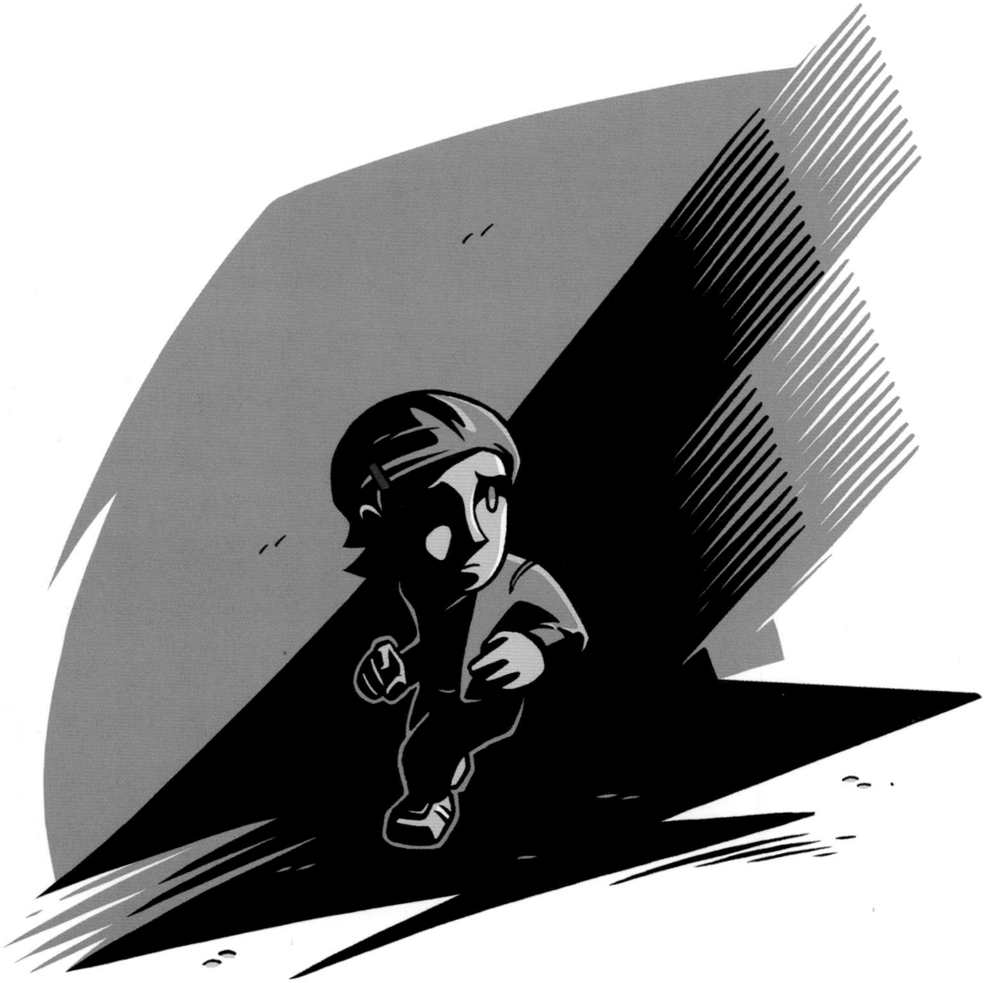

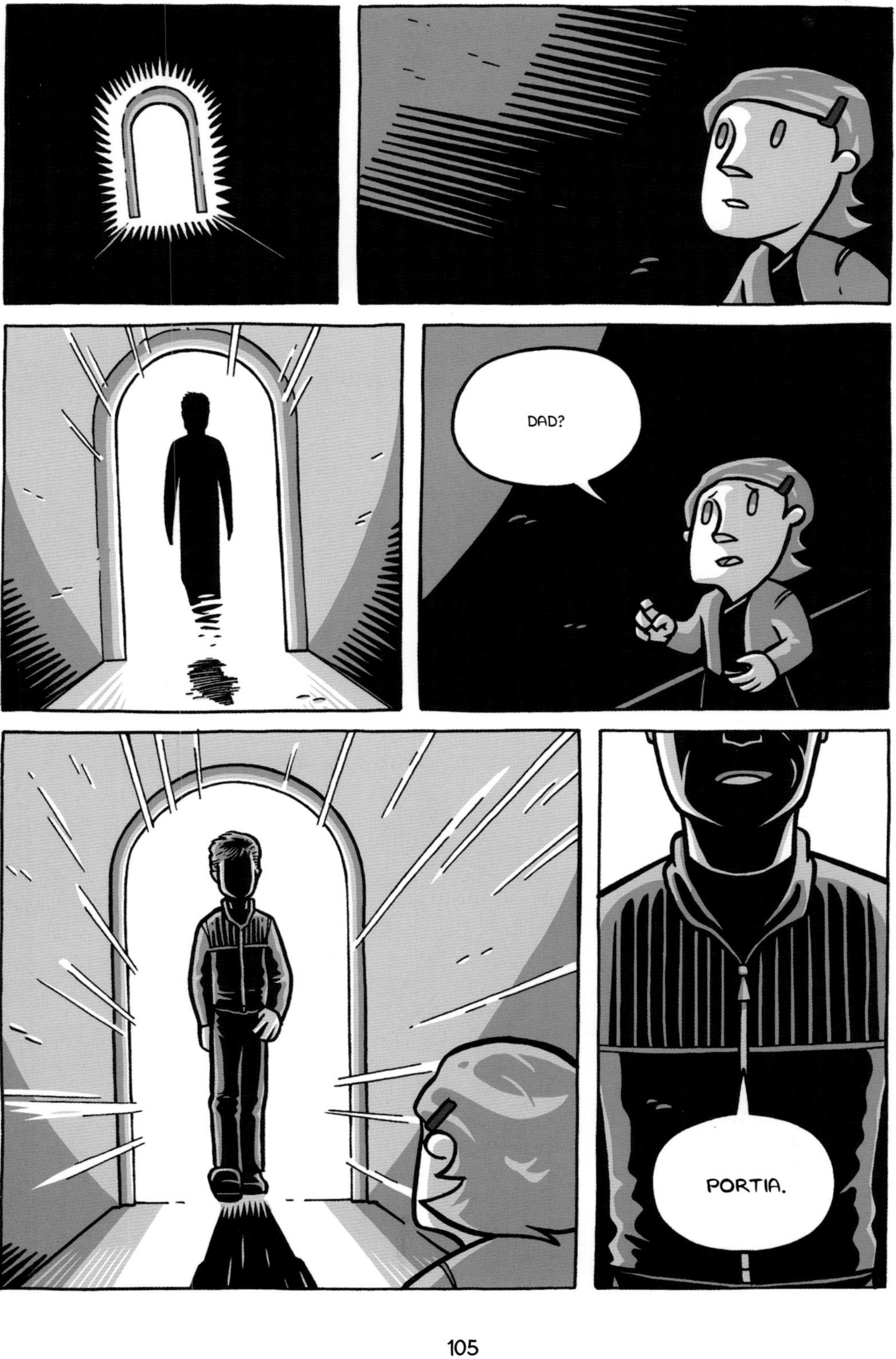
DAD?
PORTIA.

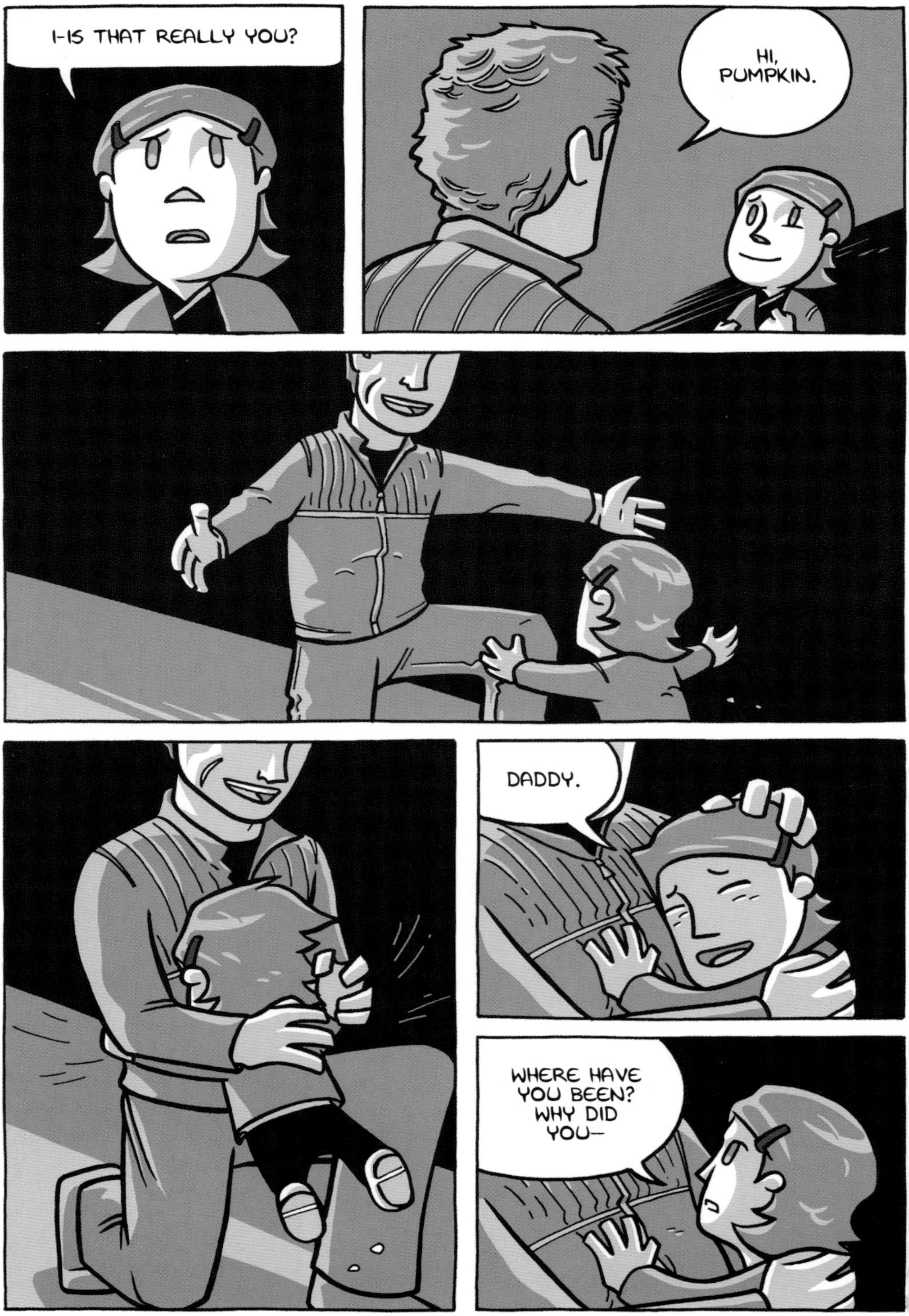
I-IS THAT REALLY YOU?
HI, PUMPKIN.
DADDY.
WHERE HAVE YOU BEEN? WHY DID YOU–

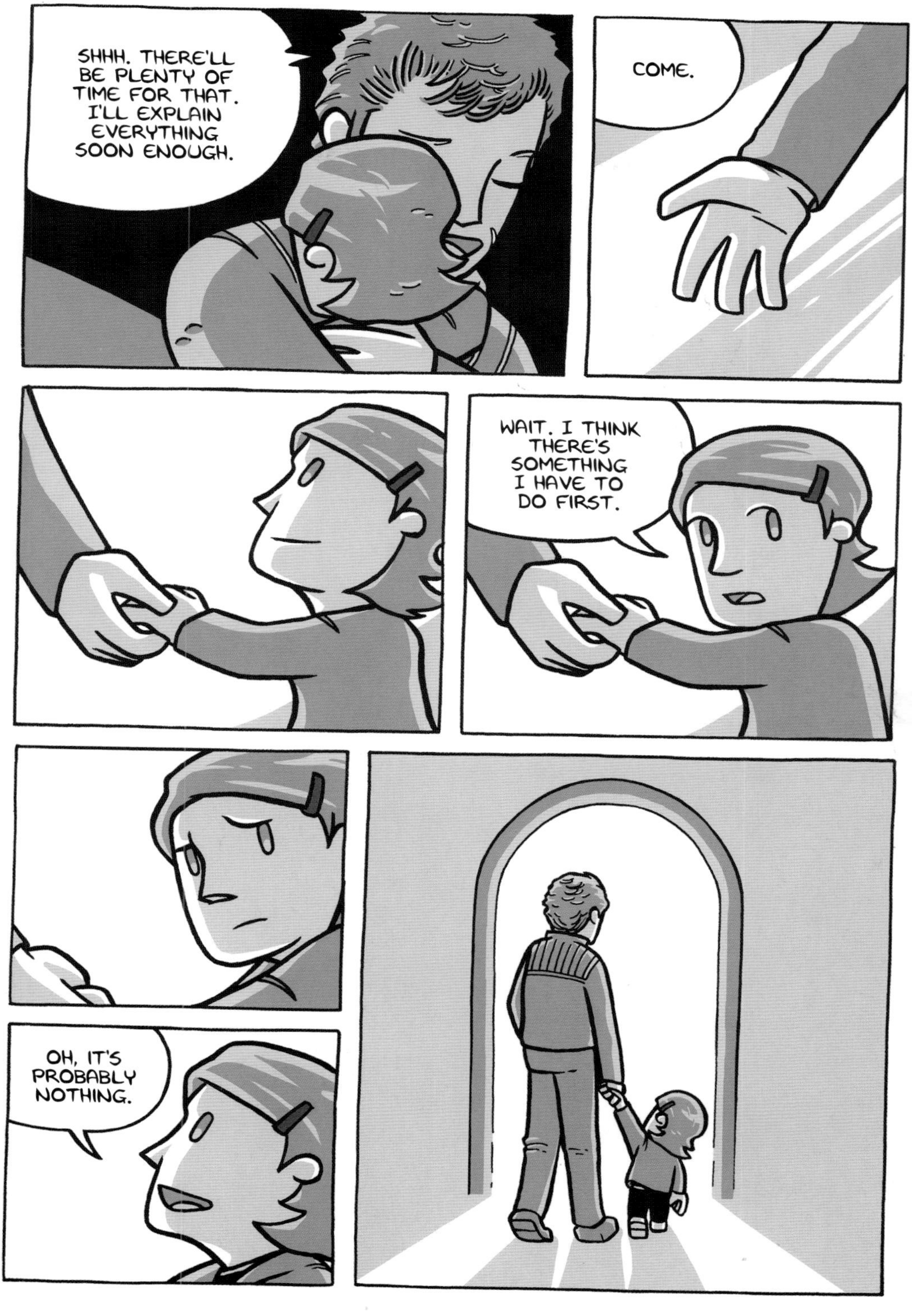
SHHH. THERE'LL BE PLENTY OF TIME FOR THAT. I'LL EXPLAIN EVERYTHING SOON ENOUGH.
COME.
WAIT. I THINK THERE'S SOMETHING I HAVE TO DO FIRST.
OH, IT'S PROBABLY NOTHING.

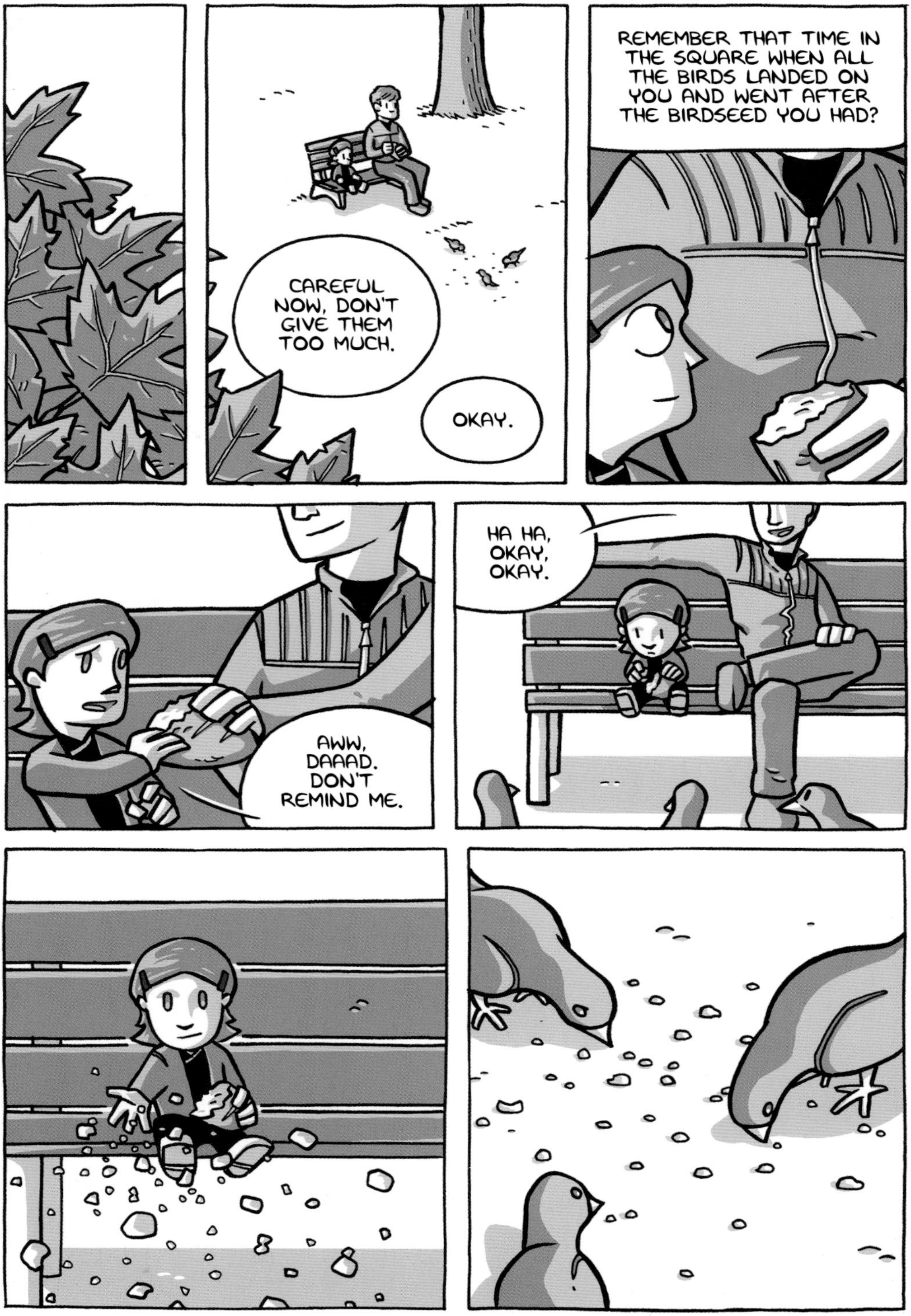
CAREFUL NOW, DON'T GIVE THEM TOO MUCH.
OKAY.
REMEMBER THAT TIME IN THE SQUARE WHEN ALL THE BIRDS LANDED ON YOU AND WENT AFTER THE BIRDSEED YOU HAD?
AWW, DAAAD. DON'T REMIND ME.
HA HA, OKAY, OKAY.

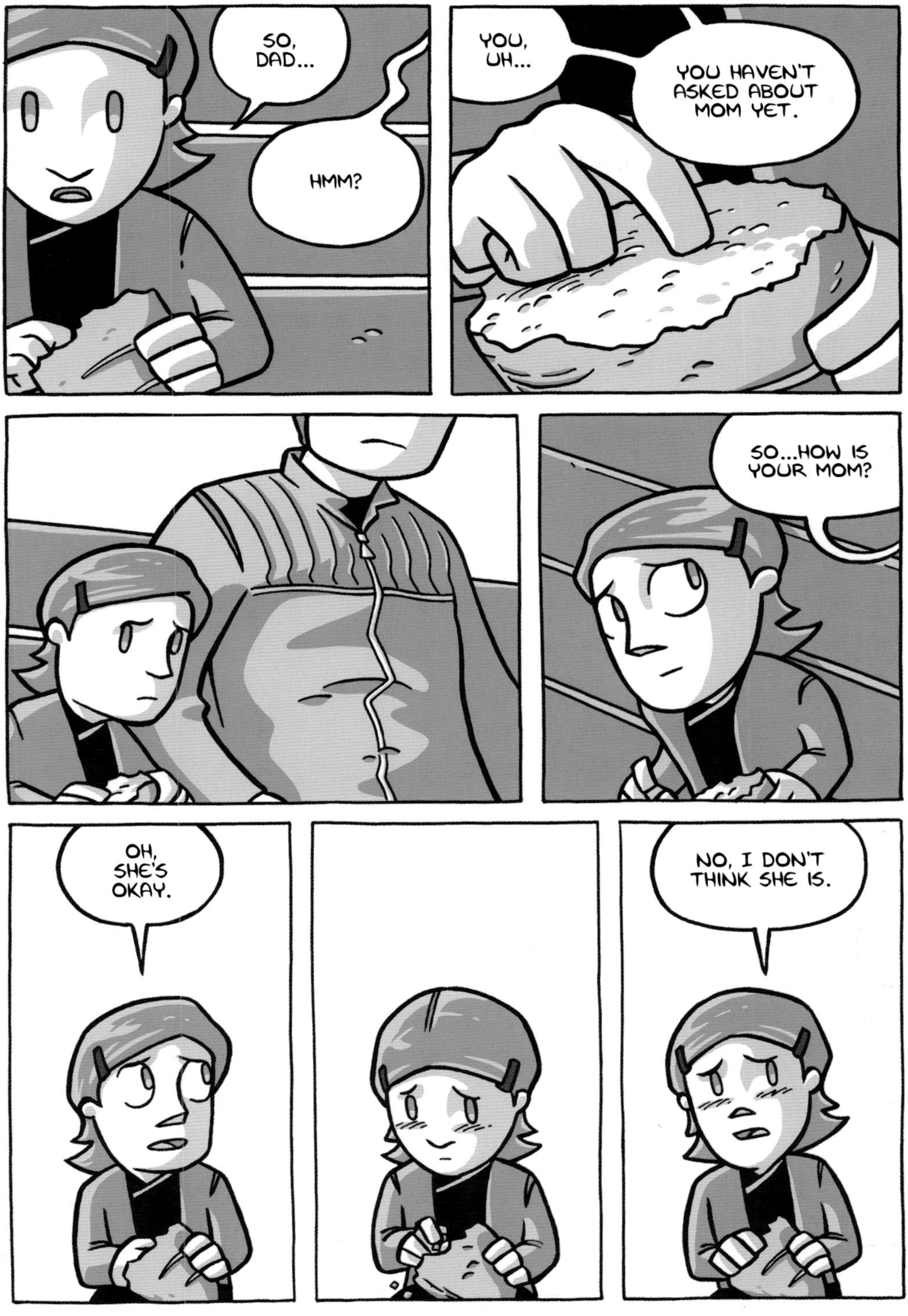
SO, DAD...
HMM?
YOU, UH...
YOU HAVEN'T ASKED ABOUT MOM YET.
SO...HOW IS YOUR MOM?
OH, SHE'S OKAY.
NO, I DON'T THINK SHE IS.

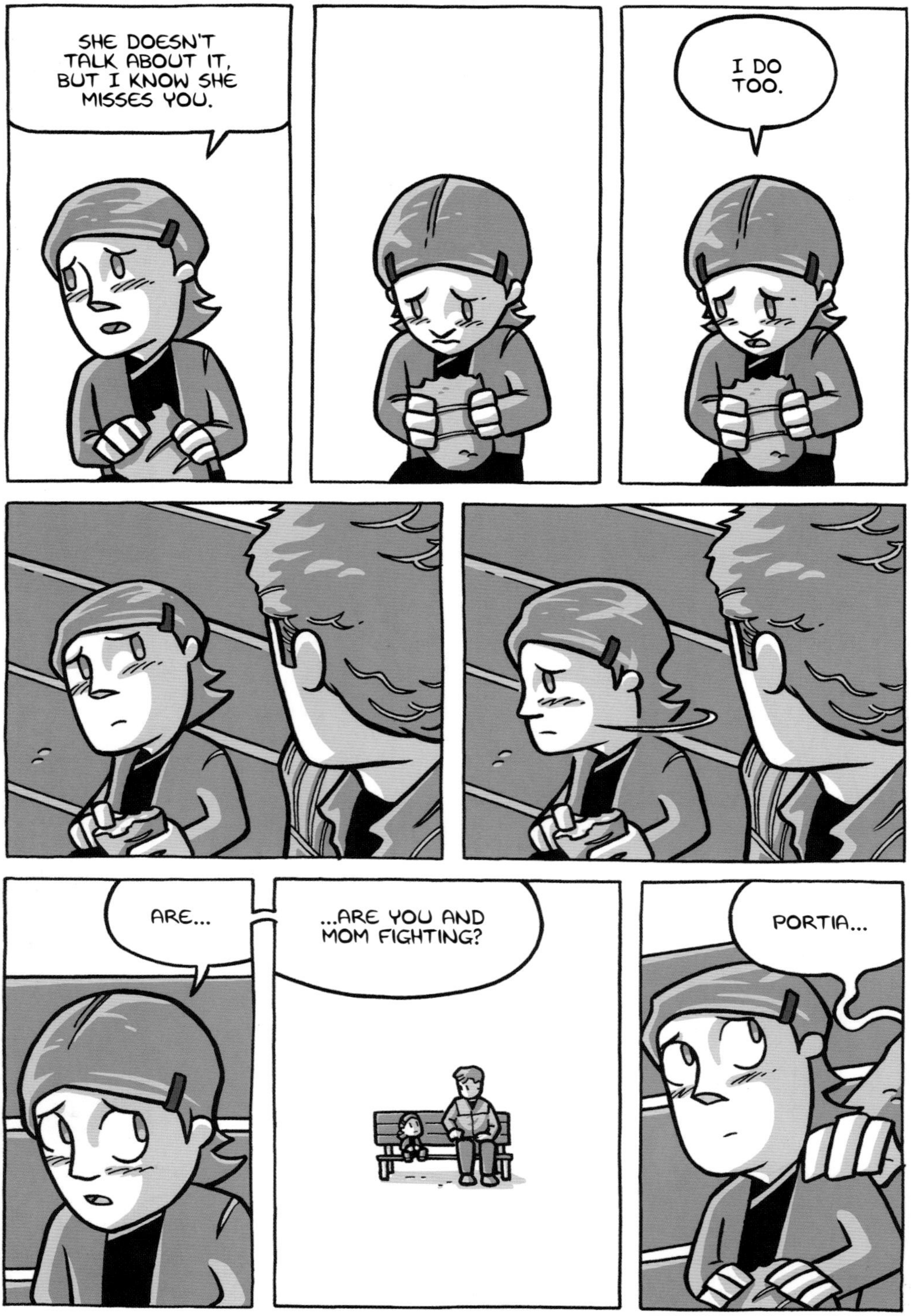
SHE DOESN'T TALK ABOUT IT, BUT I KNOW SHE MISSES YOU.
I DO TOO.
ARE...
...ARE YOU AND MOM FIGHTING?
PORTIA...

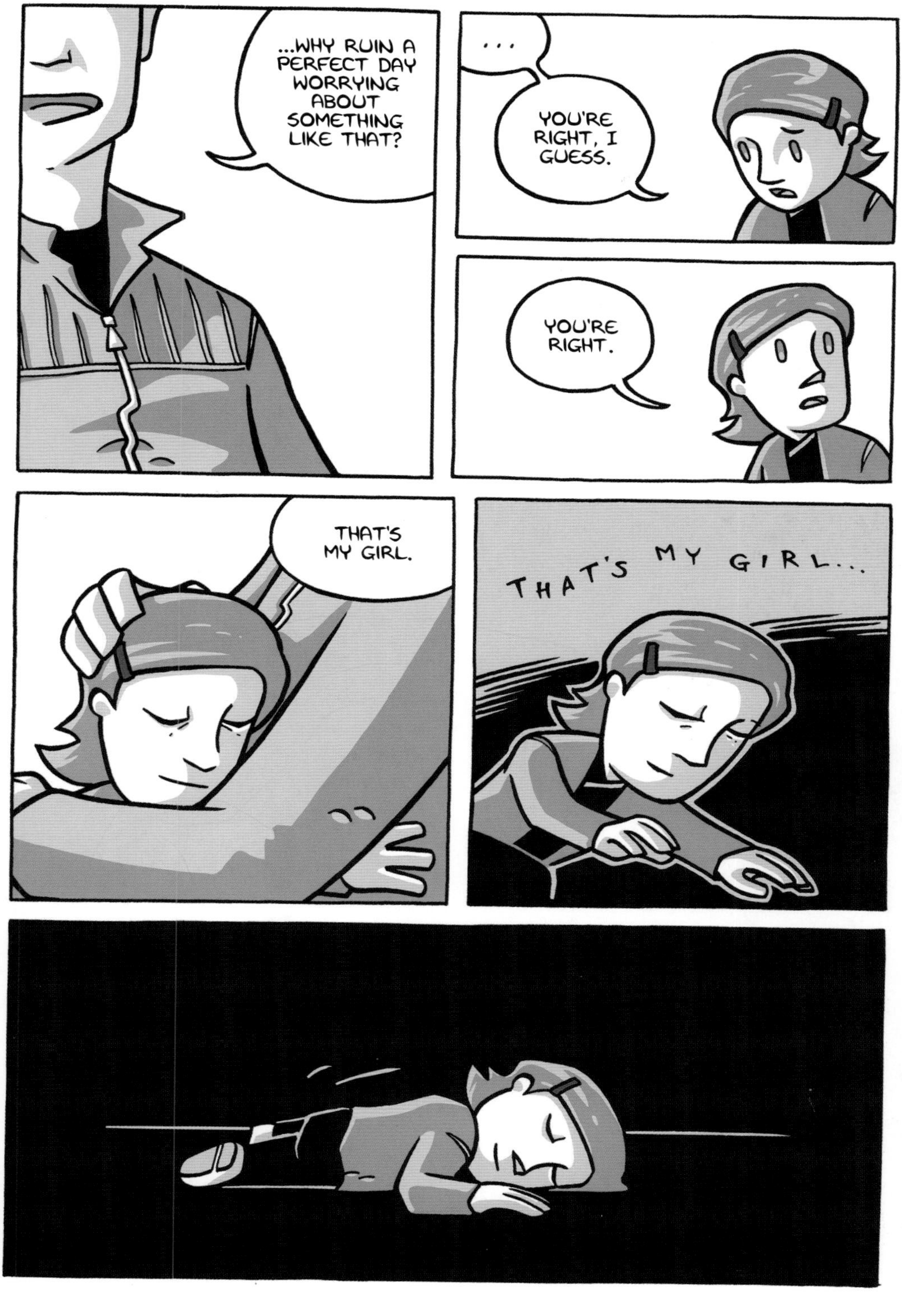
...WHY RUIN A PERFECT DAY WORRYING ABOUT SOMETHING LIKE THAT?
...
YOU'RE RIGHT, I GUESS.
YOU'RE RIGHT.
THAT'S MY GIRL.
THAT'S MY GIRL...

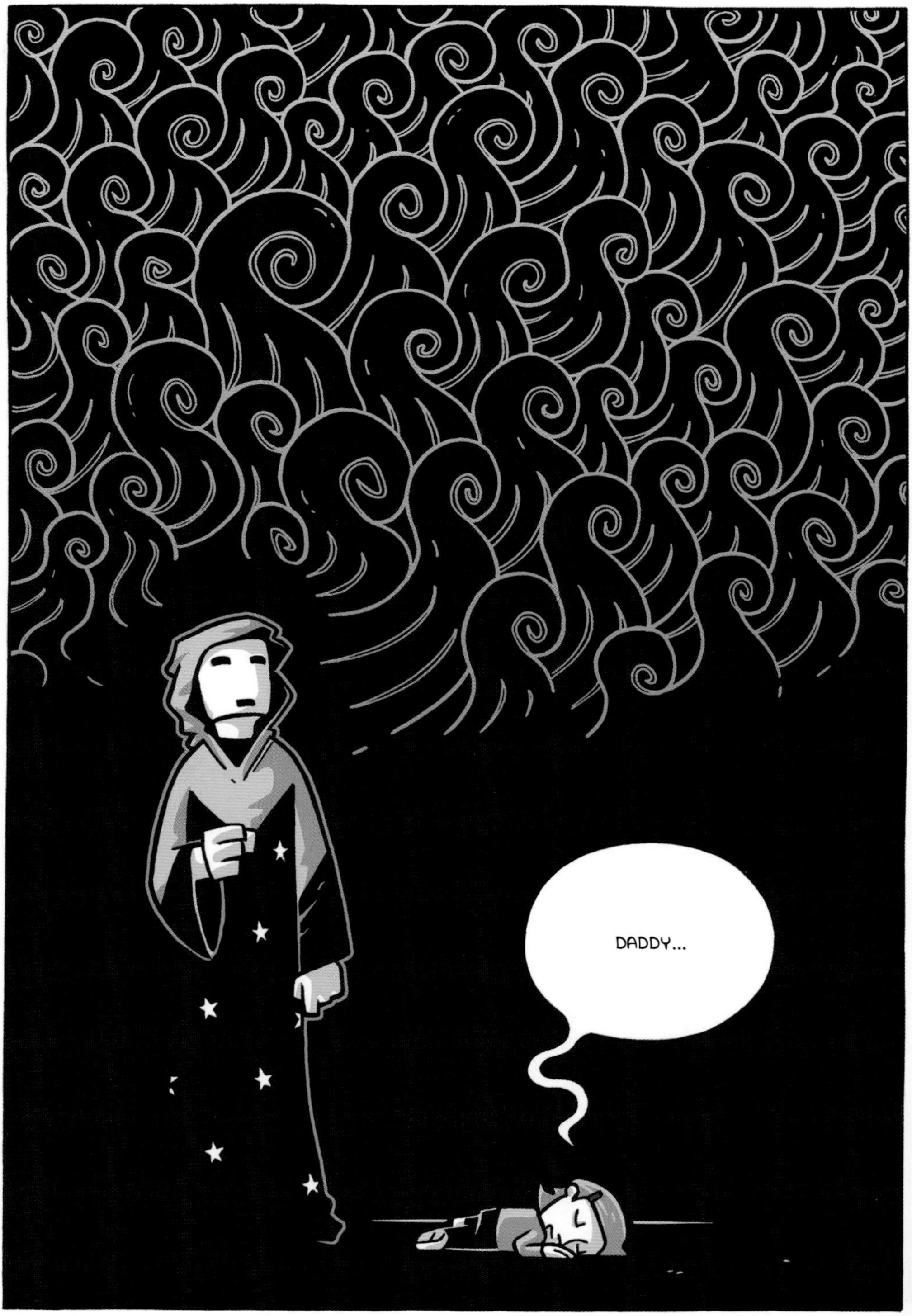
DADDY...

...AND THESE CARVINGS I MADE MYSELF.

HUH. THAT'S... NICE.

AND THERE IS PLENTY TO EXPLORE AROUND HERE.

THE TUNNELS DOWN HERE ARE SO MAZELIKE THAT YOU COULD LOSE YOURSELF IN THEM FOR MONTHS, AND STILL NEVER SEE IT ALL.

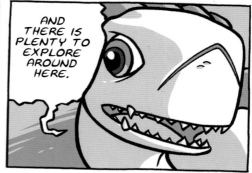

THAT DOES SOUND KIND OF COOL.

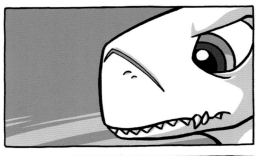

SO, UH... WHEN ARE WE GOING TO BE TAKING JELLABY HOME?

HOME? HA HA HA! OH MY DEAR BOY, THAT IS PRECIOUS.

WAIT, WHAT?

DON'T YOU THINK IF I HAD THE SLIGHTEST IDEA AS TO WHERE "HOME" WAS, THAT I WOULD'VE LEFT THIS PLACE BY NOW?

W-WHAT ARE YOU SAYING?

DO YOU ACTUALLY THINK IT WAS A COINCIDENCE THAT YOU ENDED UP HERE, ONLY TO FIND ME?

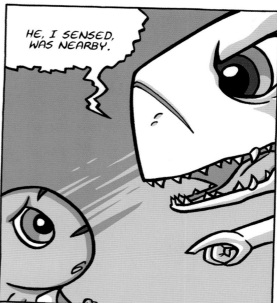

HE, I SENSED, WAS NEARBY.

AND WITH THOSE LIKE HIM, THERE ARE ALWAYS CHILDREN.

YOU...YOU PLANNED THIS?

WHY, OF COURSE. MY DEAR BOY, I HAVE WAYS OF BRINGING YOU HERE.

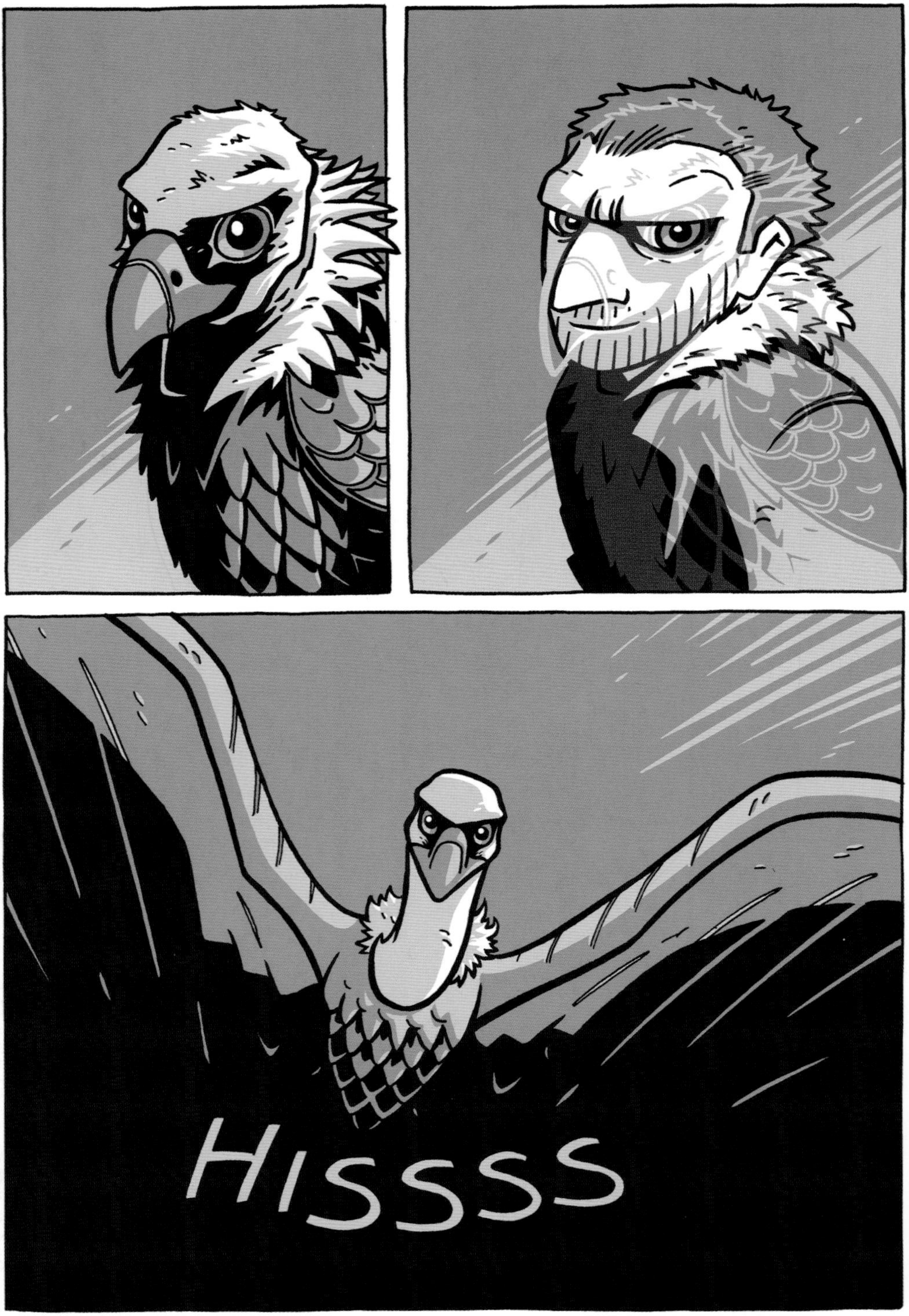
HISSSS

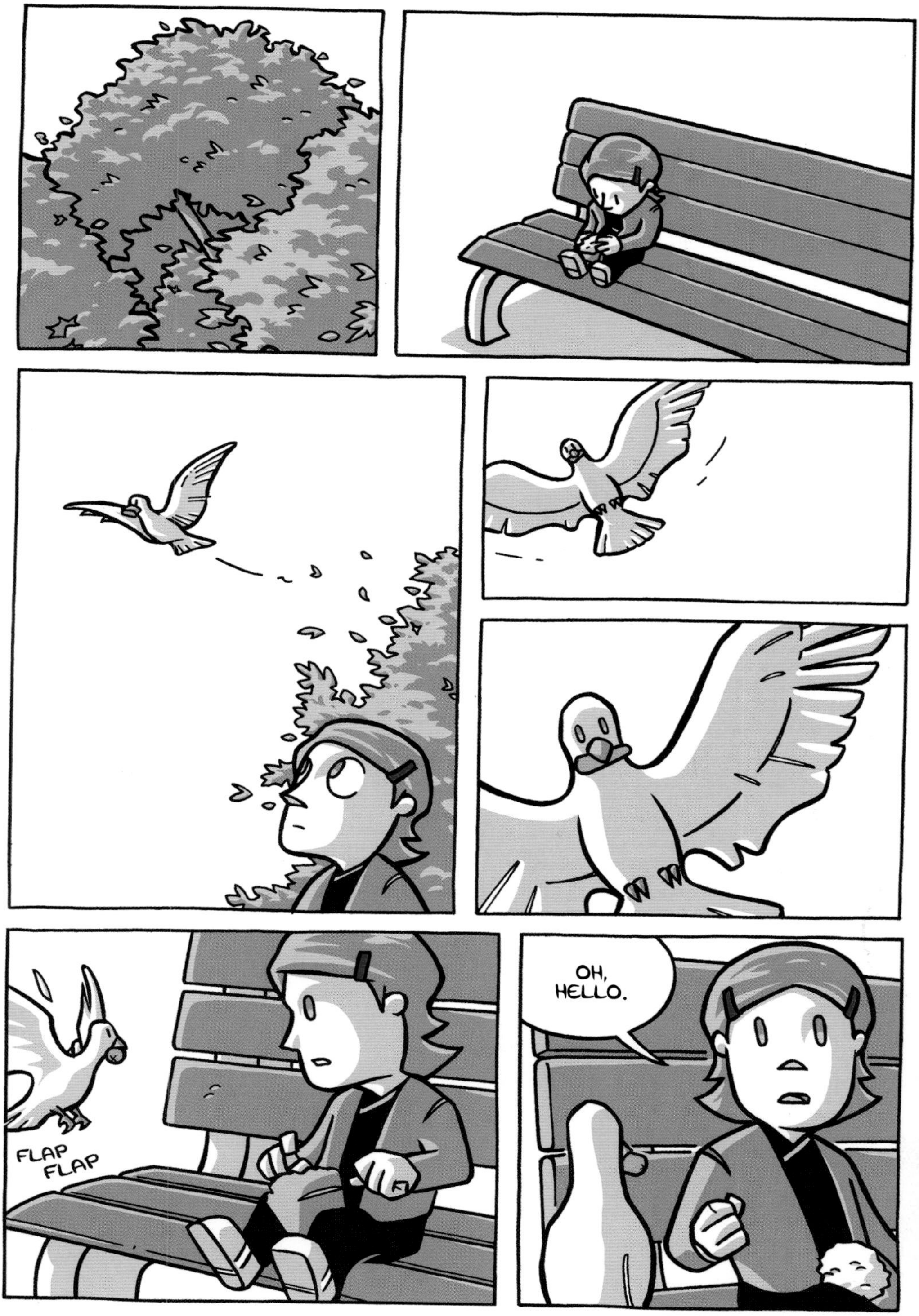
FLAP
FLAP
OH, HELLO.

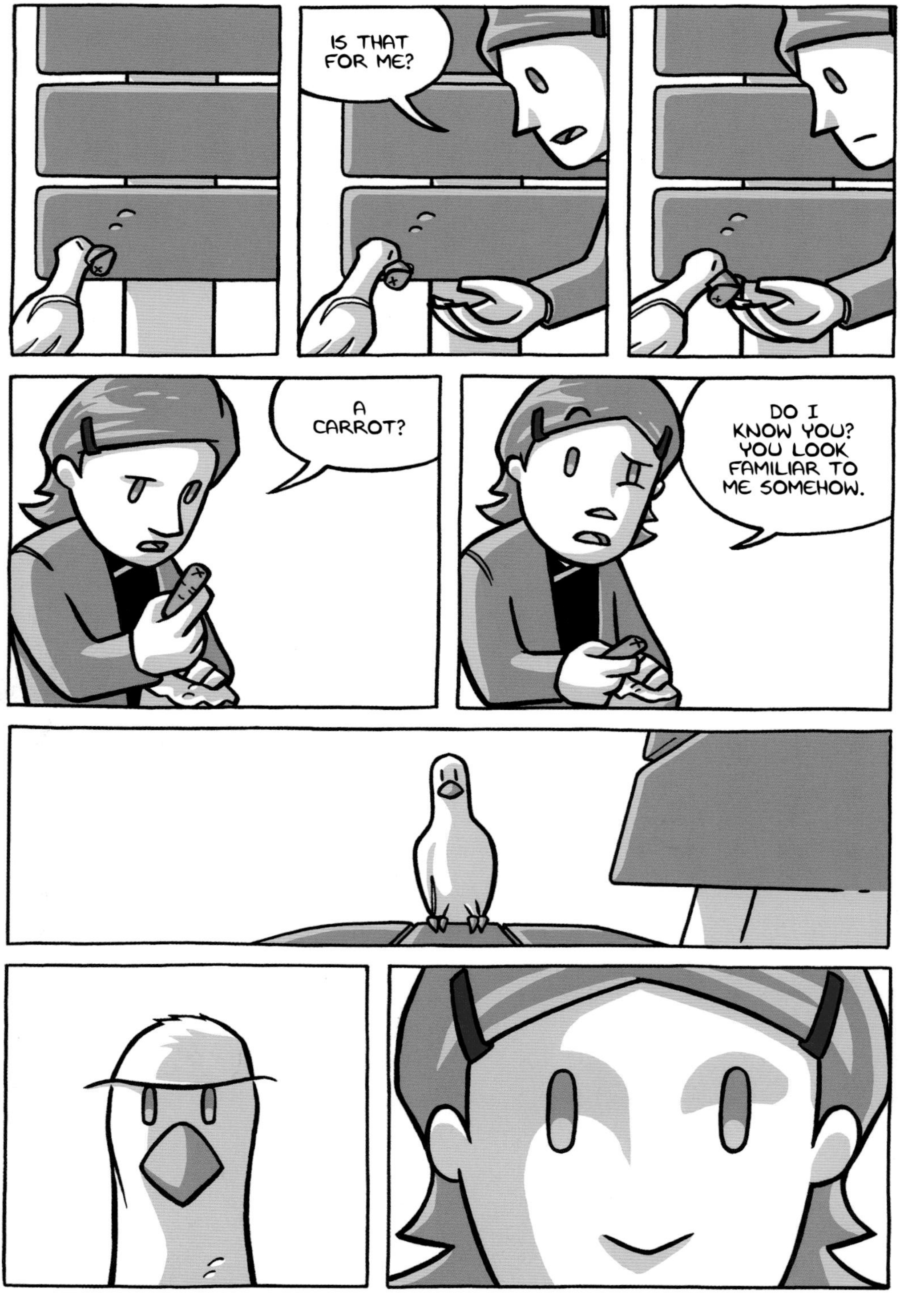
IS THAT FOR ME?
A CARROT?
DO I KNOW YOU? YOU LOOK FAMILIAR TO ME SOMEHOW.

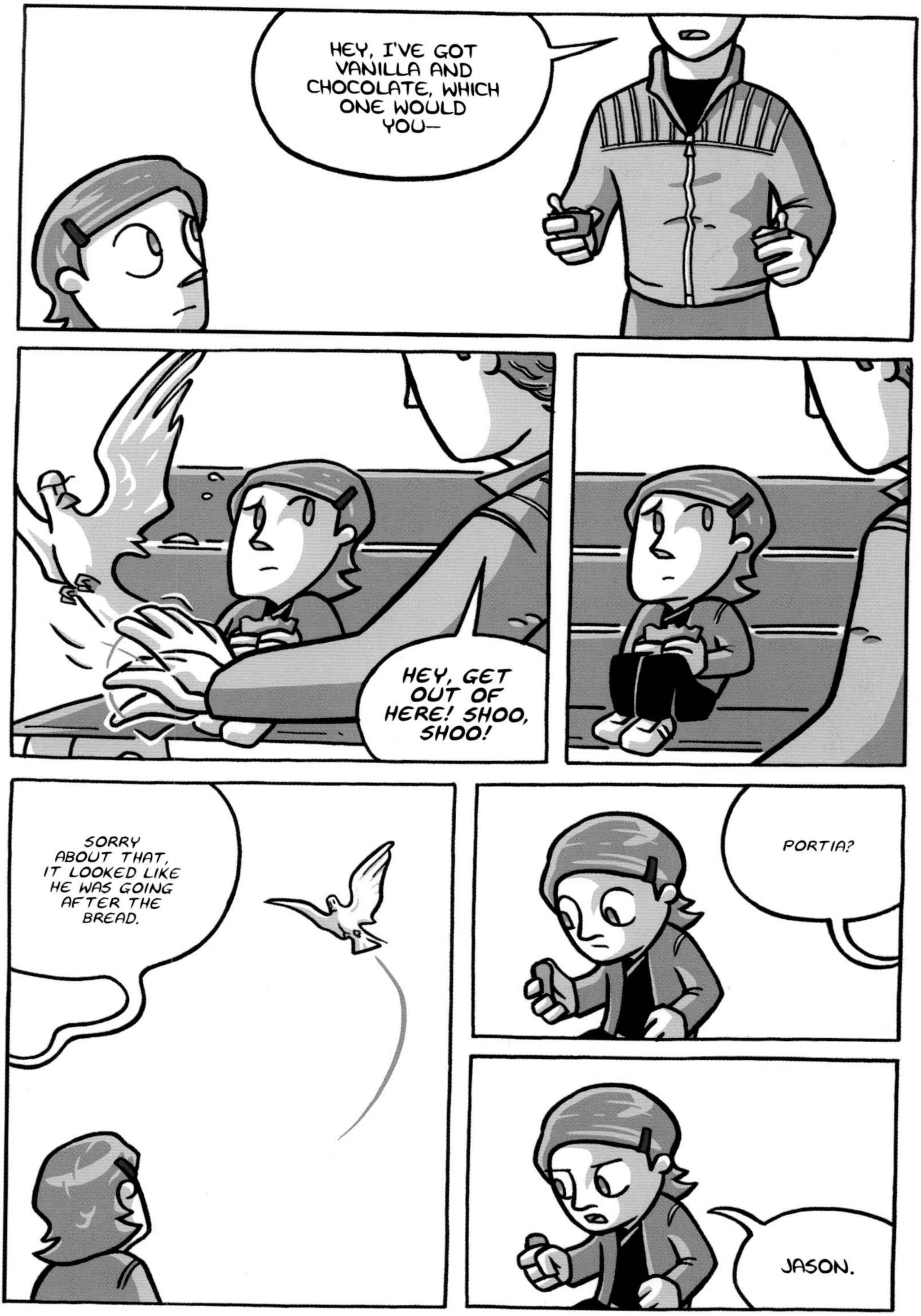
HEY, I'VE GOT VANILLA AND CHOCOLATE, WHICH ONE WOULD YOU—
HEY, GET OUT OF HERE! SHOO, SHOO!
SORRY ABOUT THAT, IT LOOKED LIKE HE WAS GOING AFTER THE BREAD.
PORTIA?
JASON.

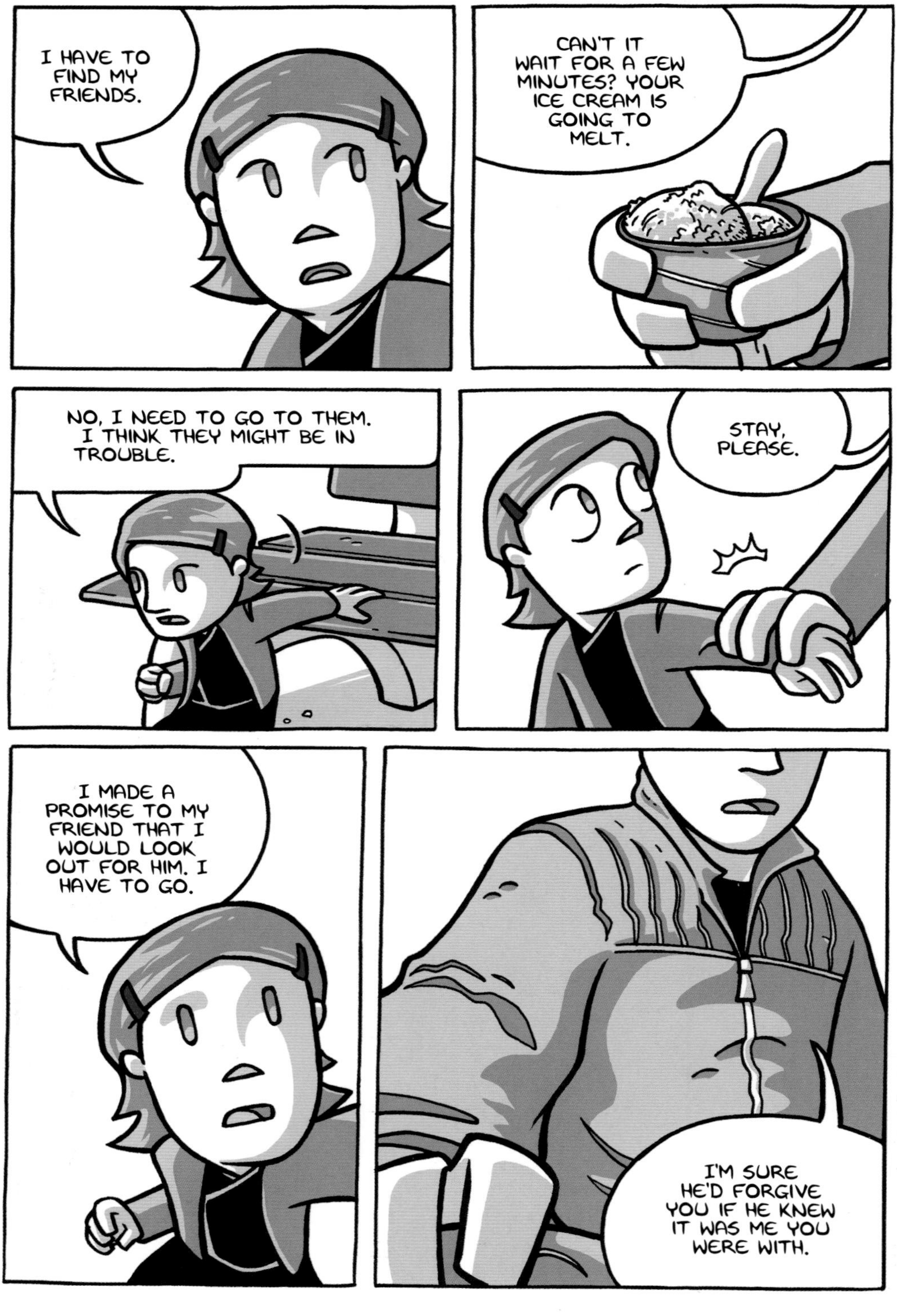
I HAVE TO FIND MY FRIENDS.
CAN'T IT WAIT FOR A FEW MINUTES? YOUR ICE CREAM IS GOING TO MELT.
NO, I NEED TO GO TO THEM. I THINK THEY MIGHT BE IN TROUBLE.
STAY, PLEASE.
I MADE A PROMISE TO MY FRIEND THAT I WOULD LOOK OUT FOR HIM. I HAVE TO GO.
I'M SURE HE'D FORGIVE YOU IF HE KNEW IT WAS ME YOU WERE WITH.

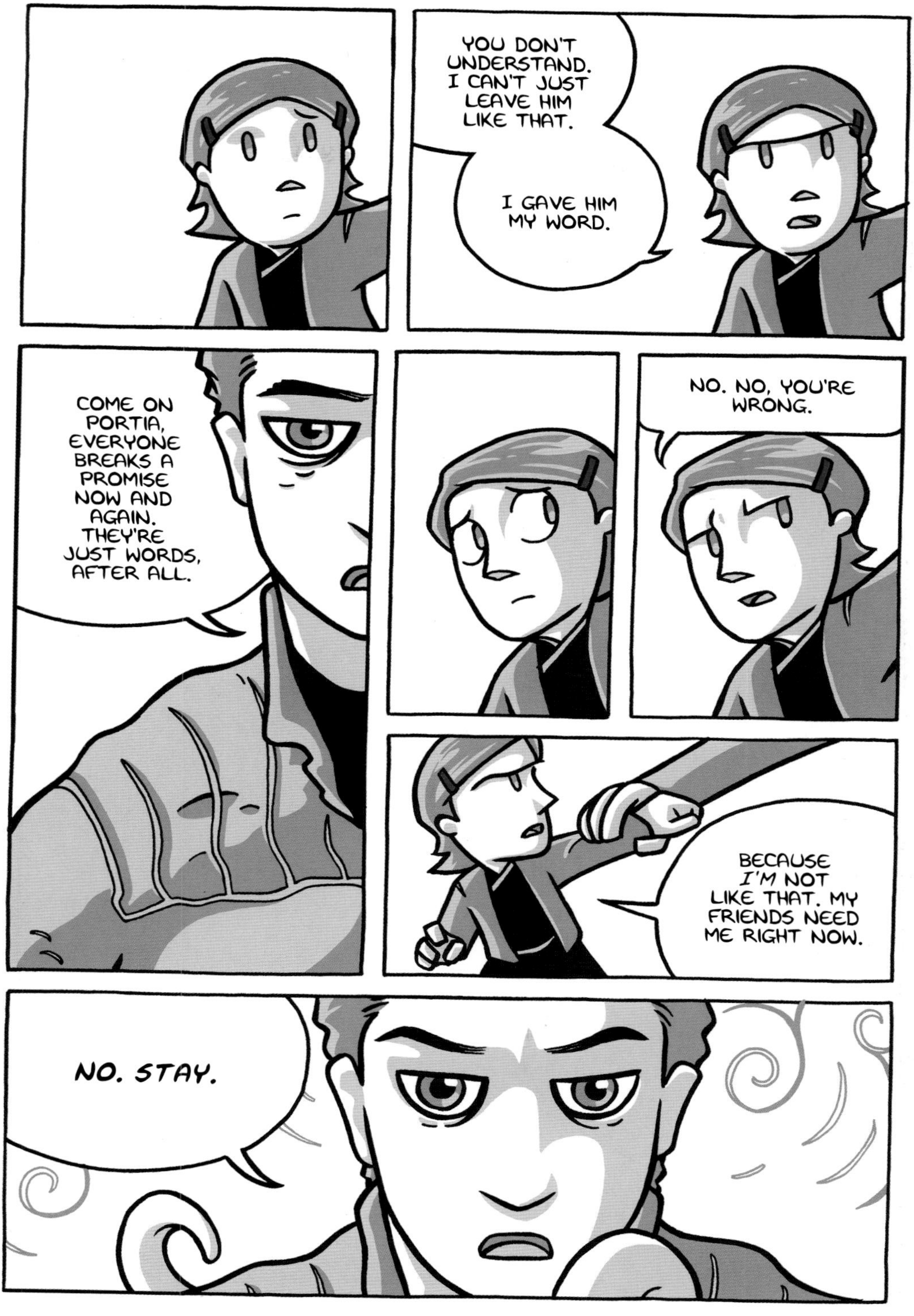
YOU DON'T UNDERSTAND. I CAN'T JUST LEAVE HIM LIKE THAT.
I GAVE HIM MY WORD.
COME ON PORTIA, EVERYONE BREAKS A PROMISE NOW AND AGAIN. THEY'RE JUST WORDS, AFTER ALL.
NO. NO, YOU'RE WRONG.
BECAUSE *I'M* NOT LIKE THAT. MY FRIENDS NEED ME RIGHT NOW.
NO. STAY.

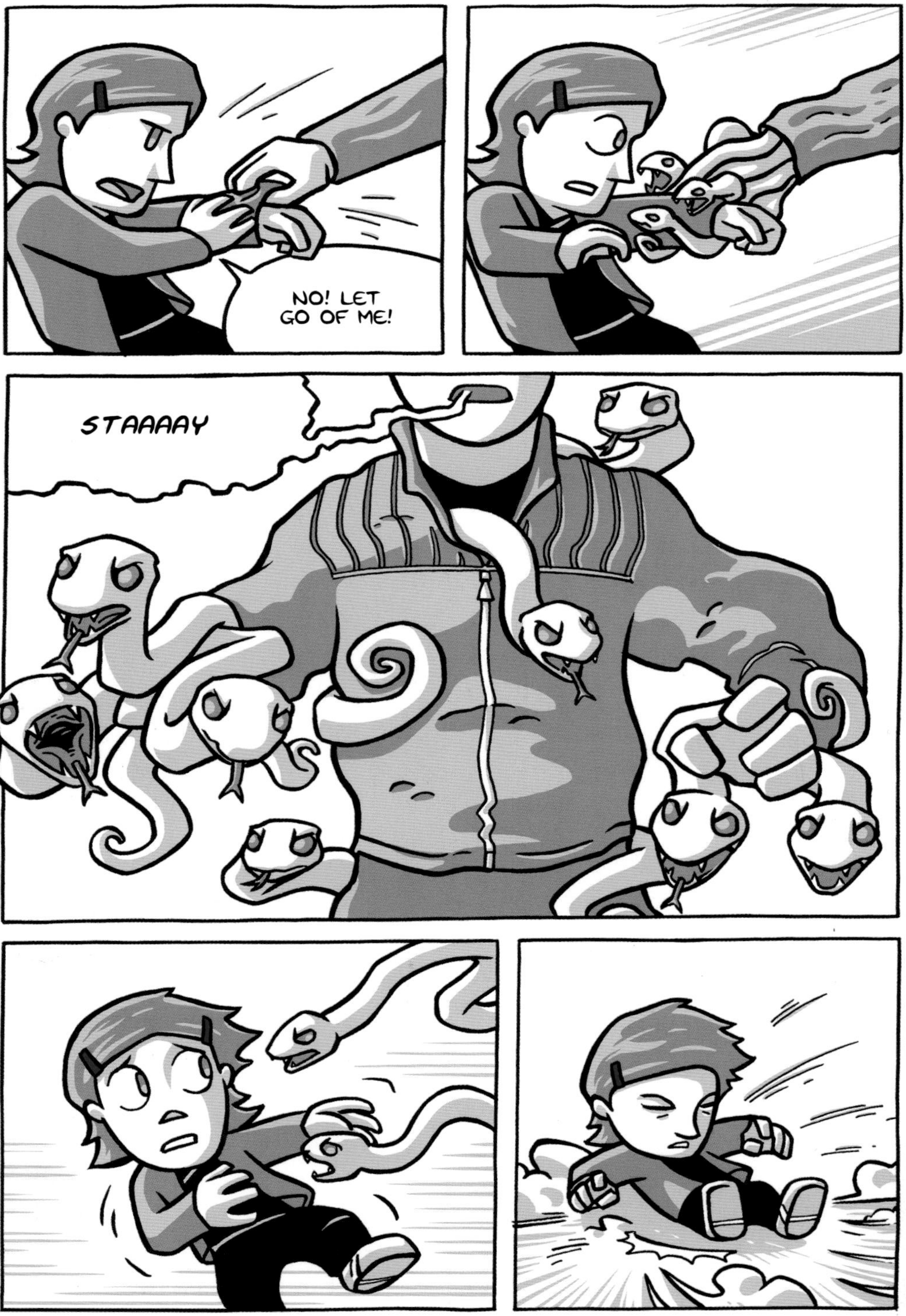
NO! LET GO OF ME!
STAAAAY

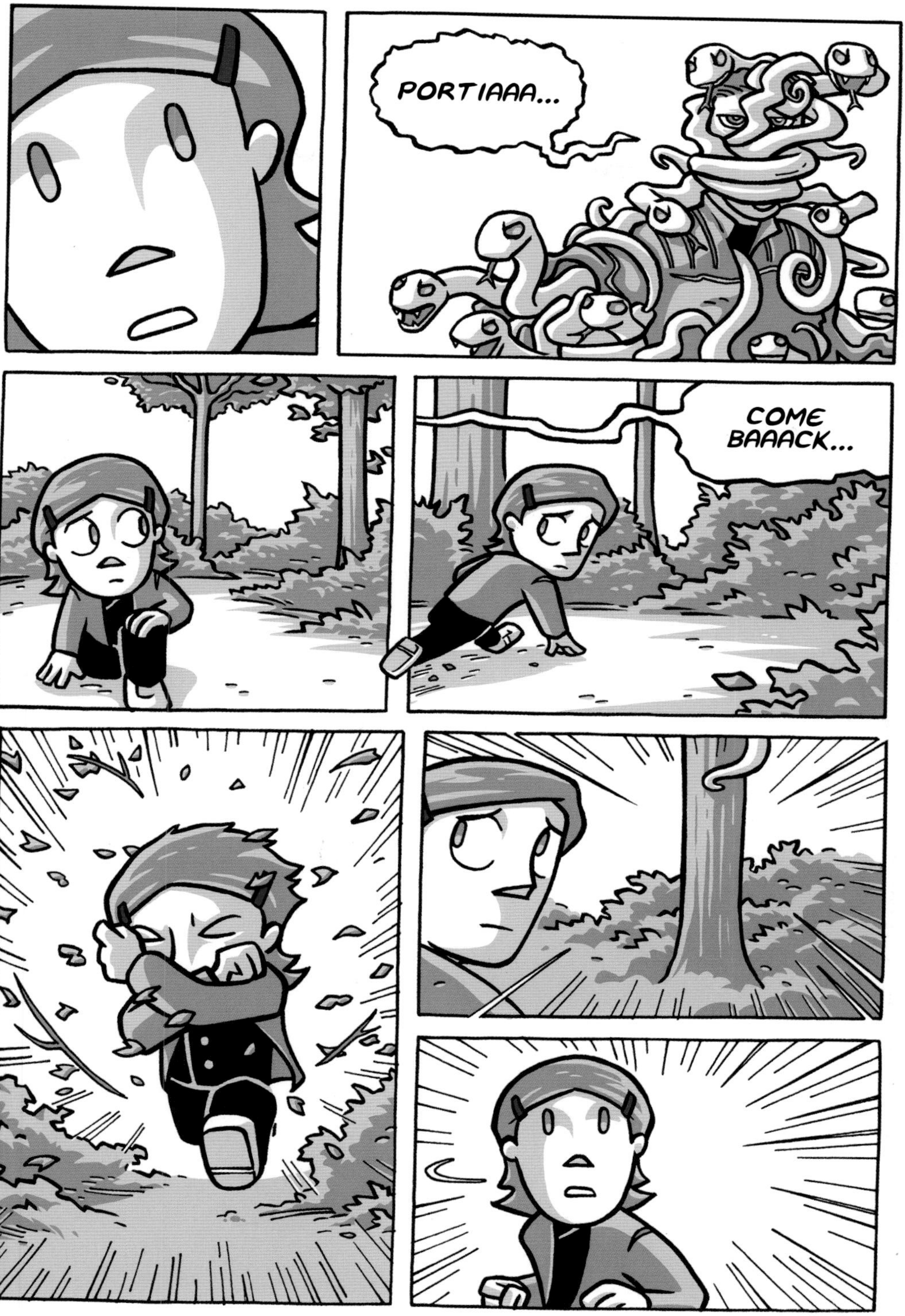
PORTIAAA...
COME BAAACK...

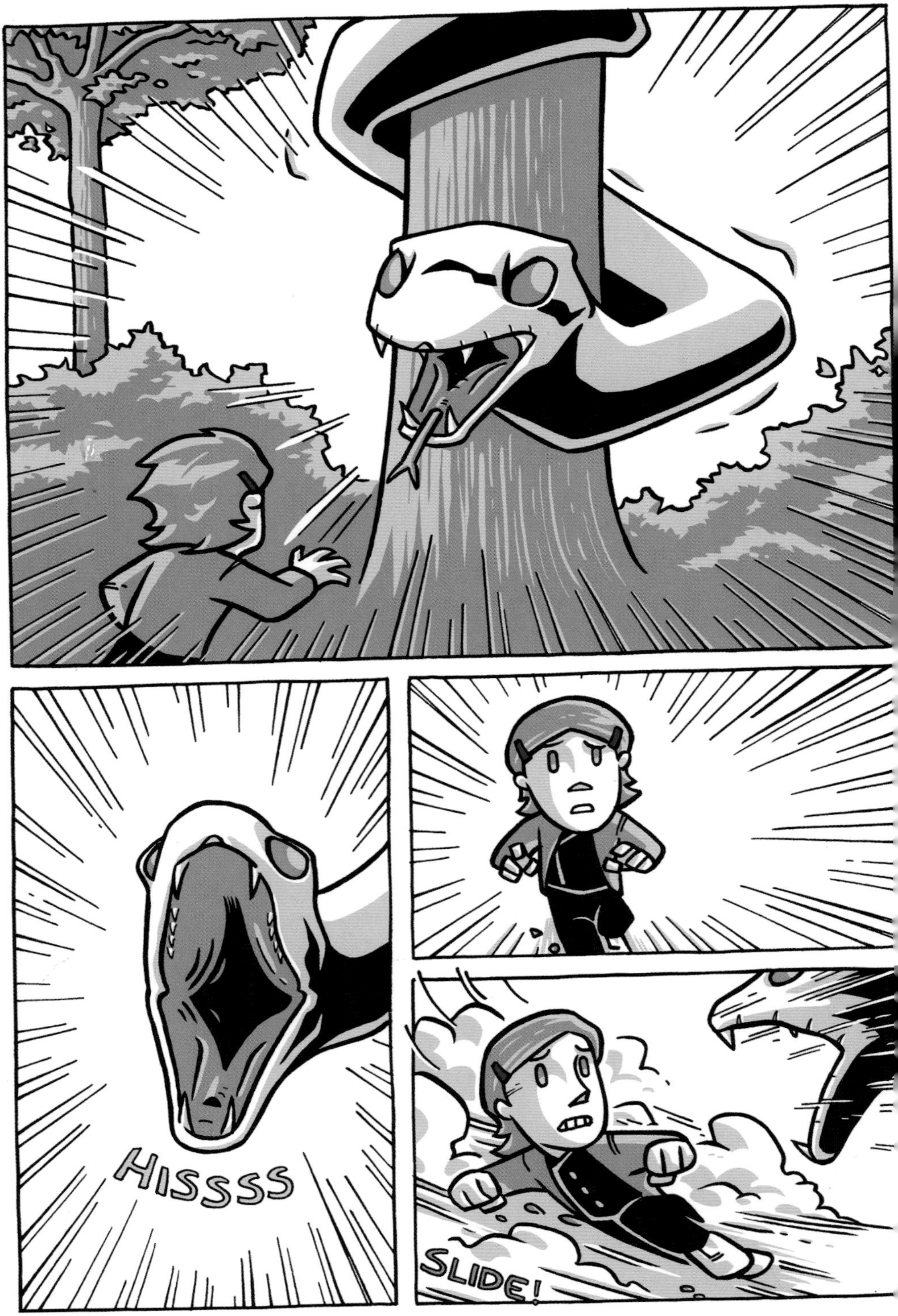
HISSSS
SLIDE!

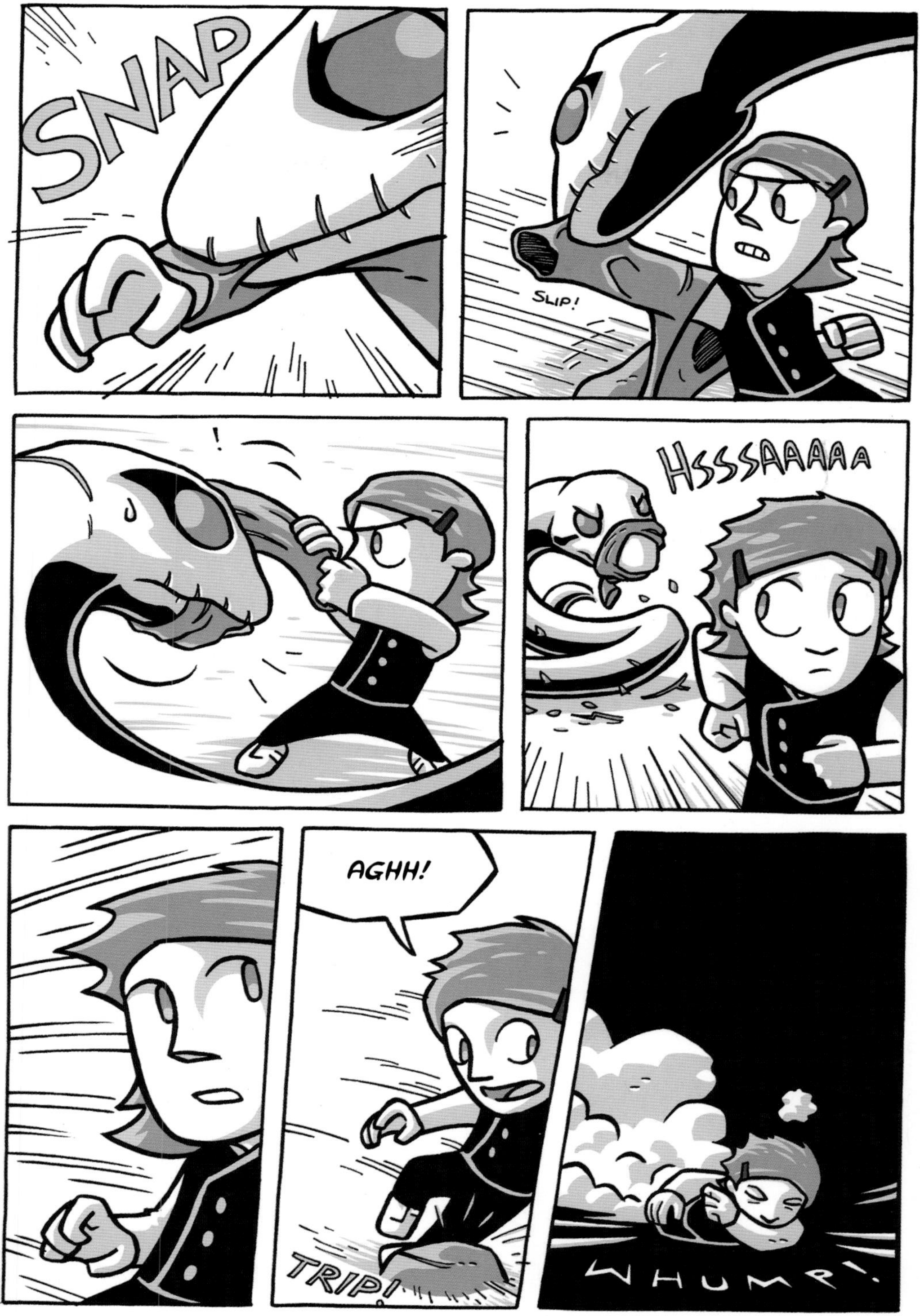
SNAP
SLIP!
!
HSSSAAAAA
AGHH!
TRIP!
WHUMP!

HISSSSSS

JELLABY.

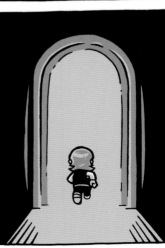

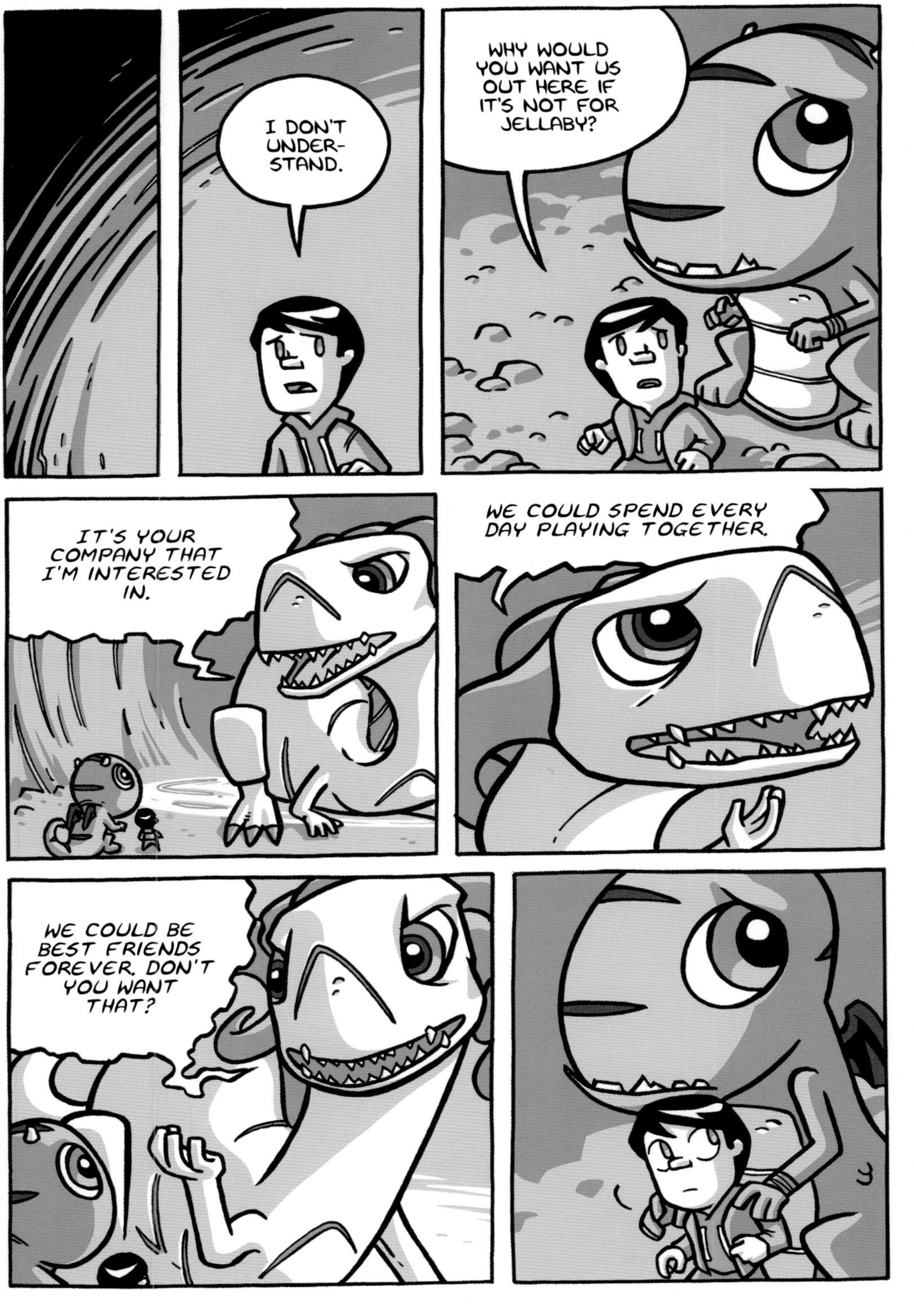
I DON'T UNDER-STAND.
WHY WOULD YOU WANT US OUT HERE IF IT'S NOT FOR JELLABY?
IT'S YOUR COMPANY THAT I'M INTERESTED IN.
WE COULD SPEND EVERY DAY PLAYING TOGETHER.
WE COULD BE BEST FRIENDS FOREVER. DON'T YOU WANT THAT?

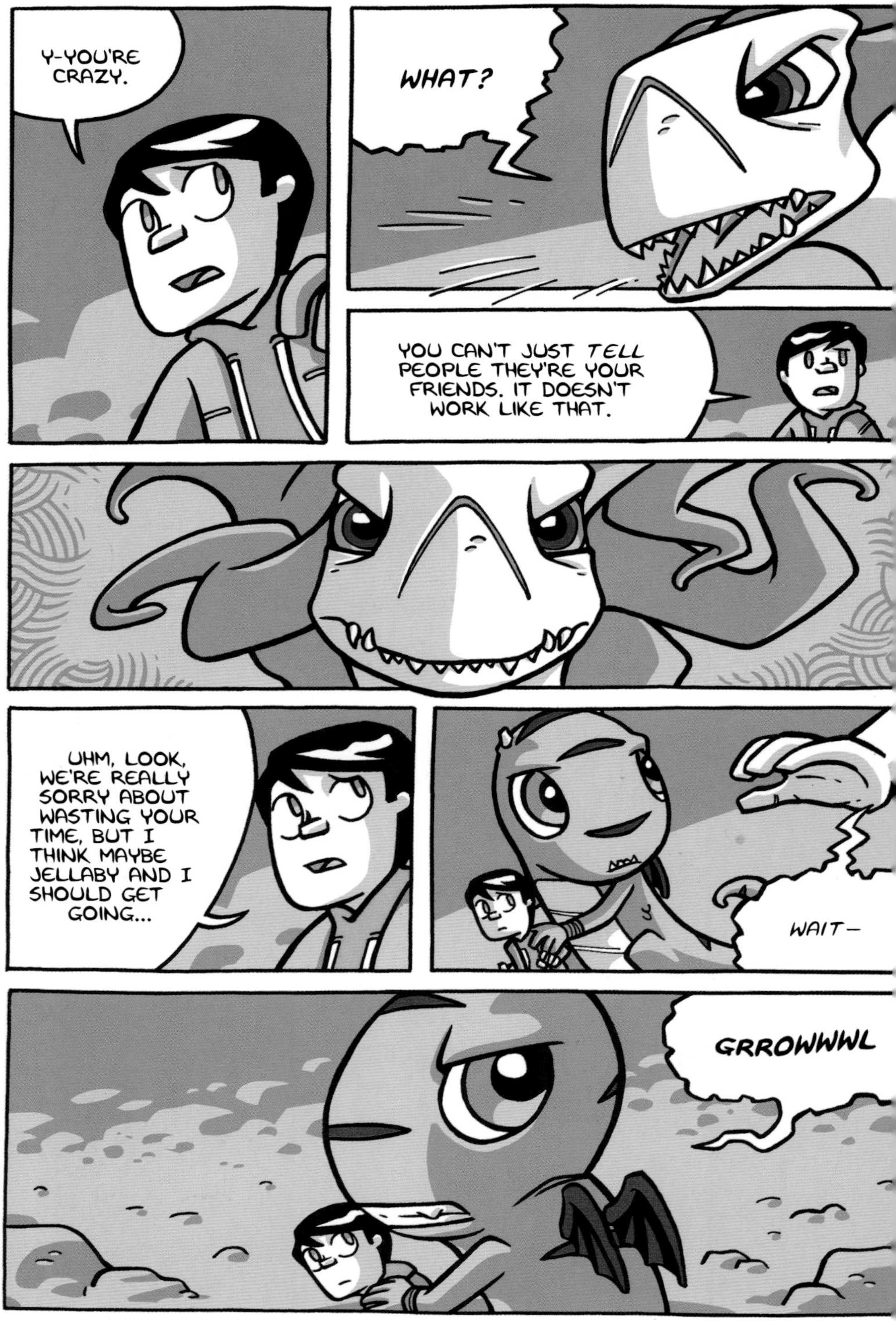
Y-YOU'RE CRAZY.
WHAT?
YOU CAN'T JUST TELL PEOPLE THEY'RE YOUR FRIENDS. IT DOESN'T WORK LIKE THAT.
UHM, LOOK, WE'RE REALLY SORRY ABOUT WASTING YOUR TIME, BUT I THINK MAYBE JELLABY AND I SHOULD GET GOING...
WAIT-
GRROWWWL

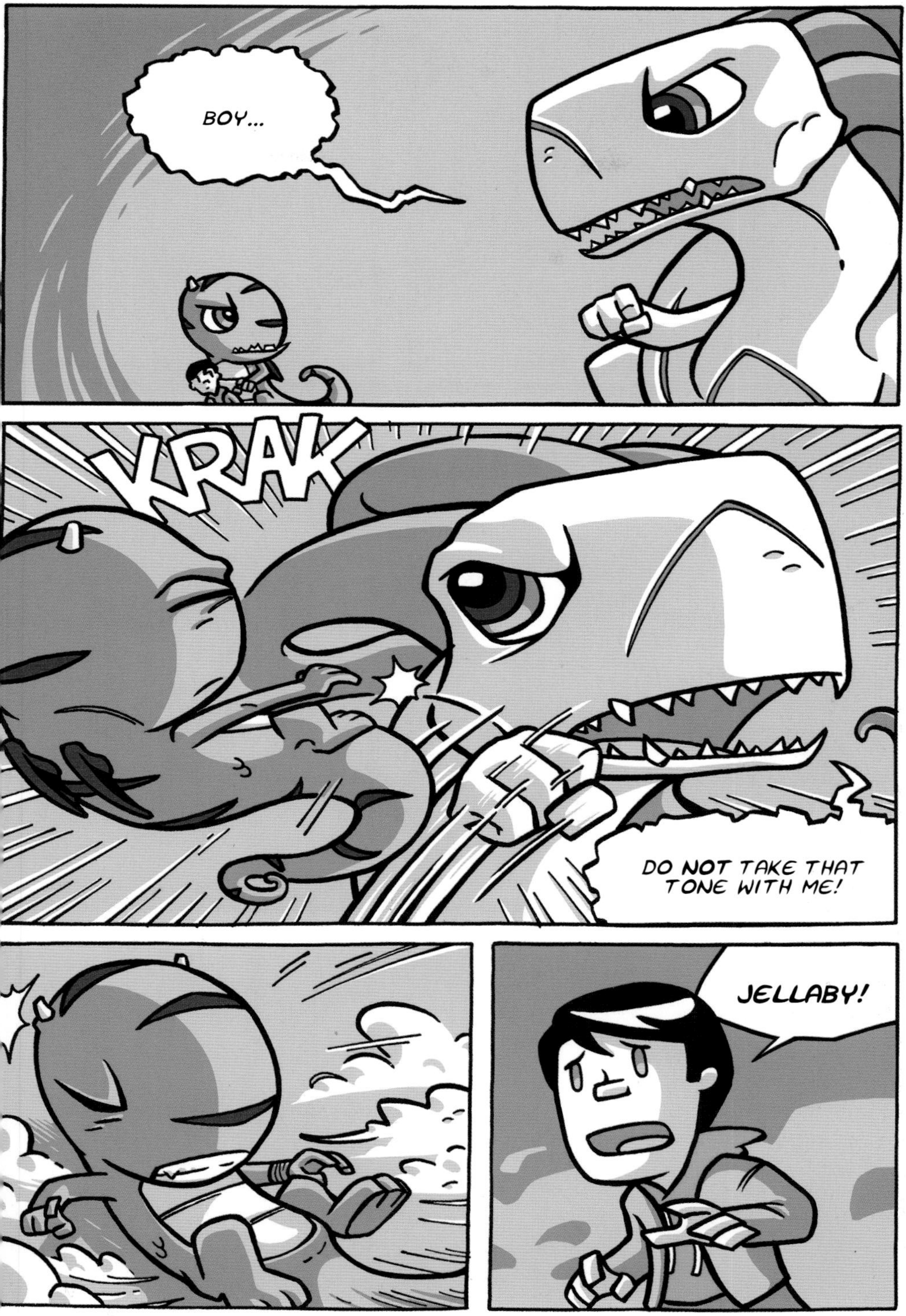
BOY...
KRAK
DO NOT TAKE THAT TONE WITH ME!
JELLABY!

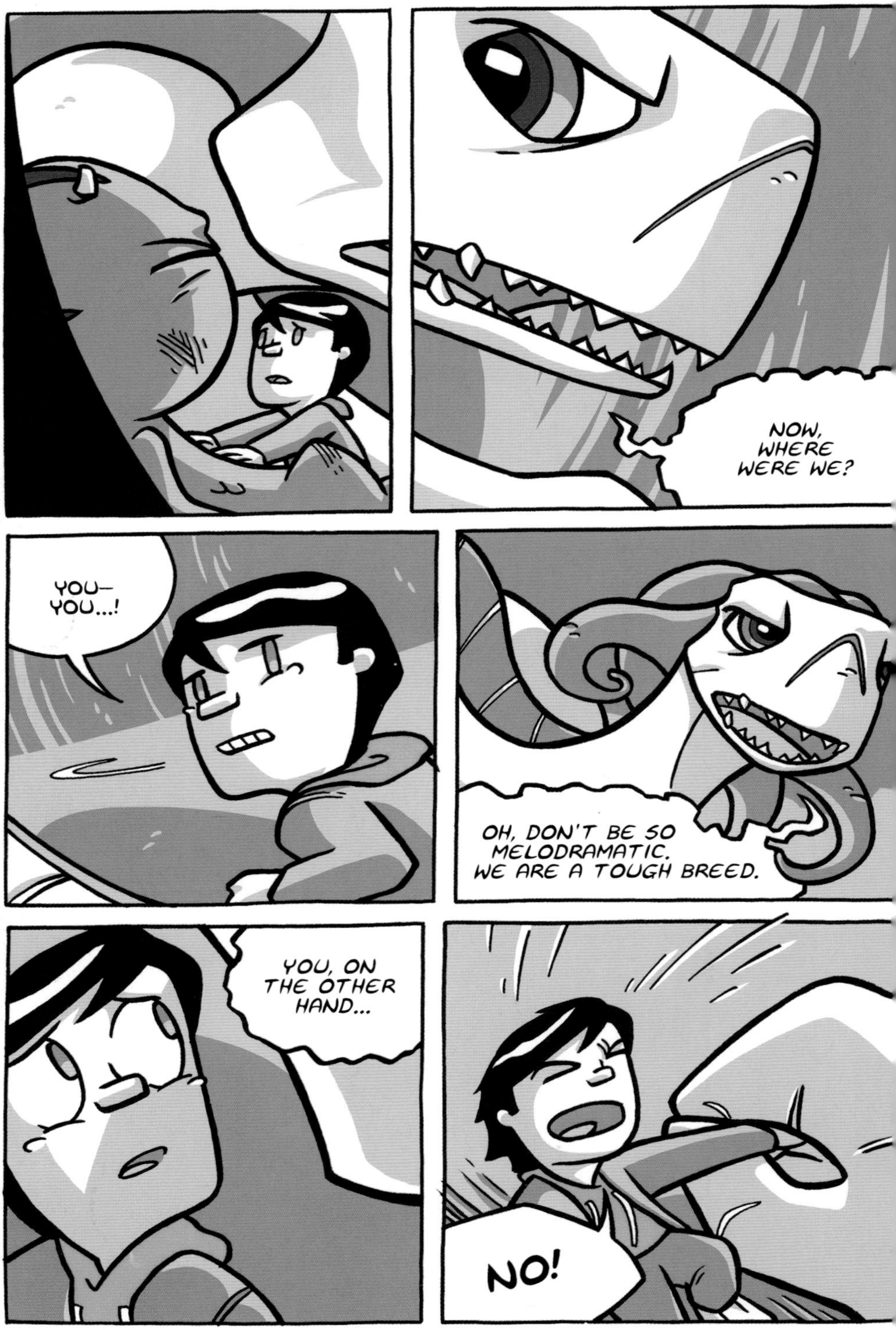
NOW, WHERE WERE WE?
YOU— YOU...!
OH, DON'T BE SO MELODRAMATIC. WE ARE A TOUGH BREED.
YOU, ON THE OTHER HAND...
NO!

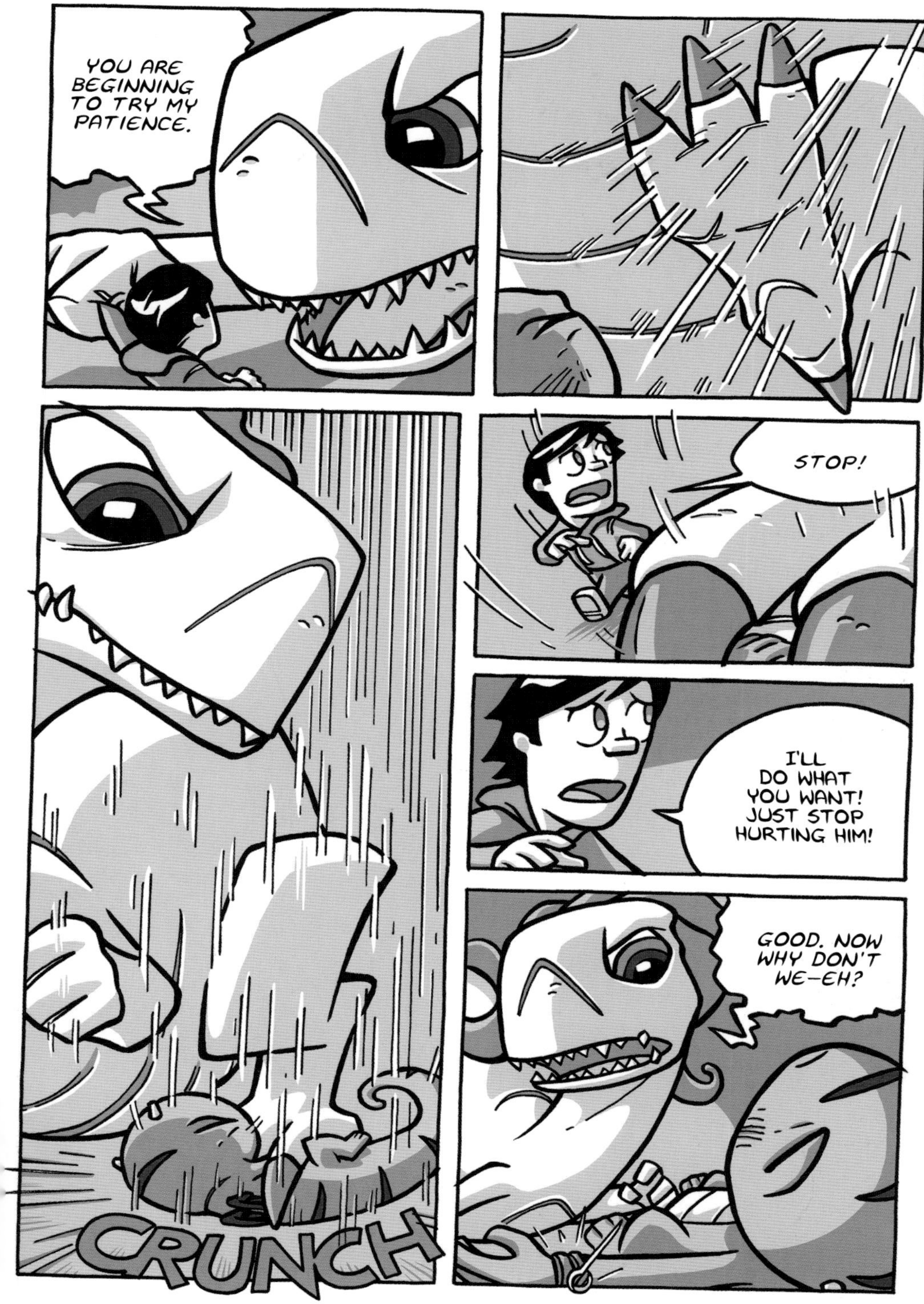
YOU ARE BEGINNING TO TRY MY PATIENCE.
CRUNCH
STOP!
I'LL DO WHAT YOU WANT! JUST STOP HURTING HIM!
GOOD. NOW WHY DON'T WE—EH?

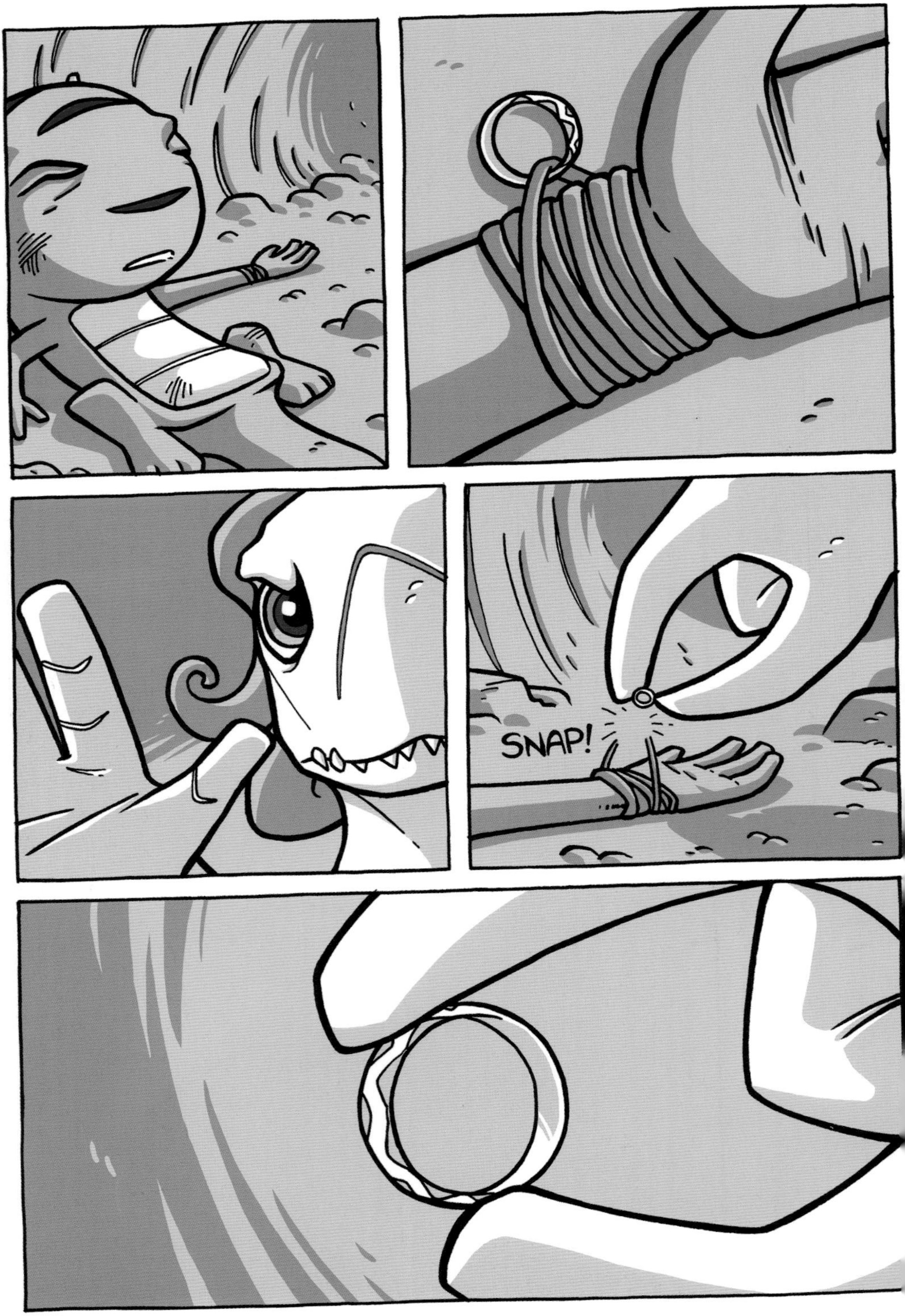
SNAP!

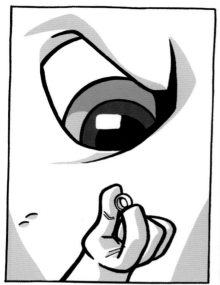

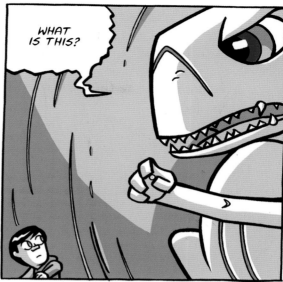
WHAT IS THIS?

I-IT'S A RING.

I KNOW IT'S A RING. WHAT IS ITS IMPORTANCE?

HOW SHOULD I KNOW?

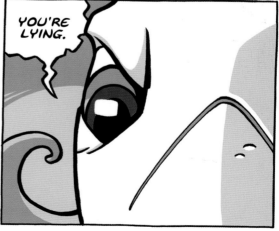
YOU'RE LYING.

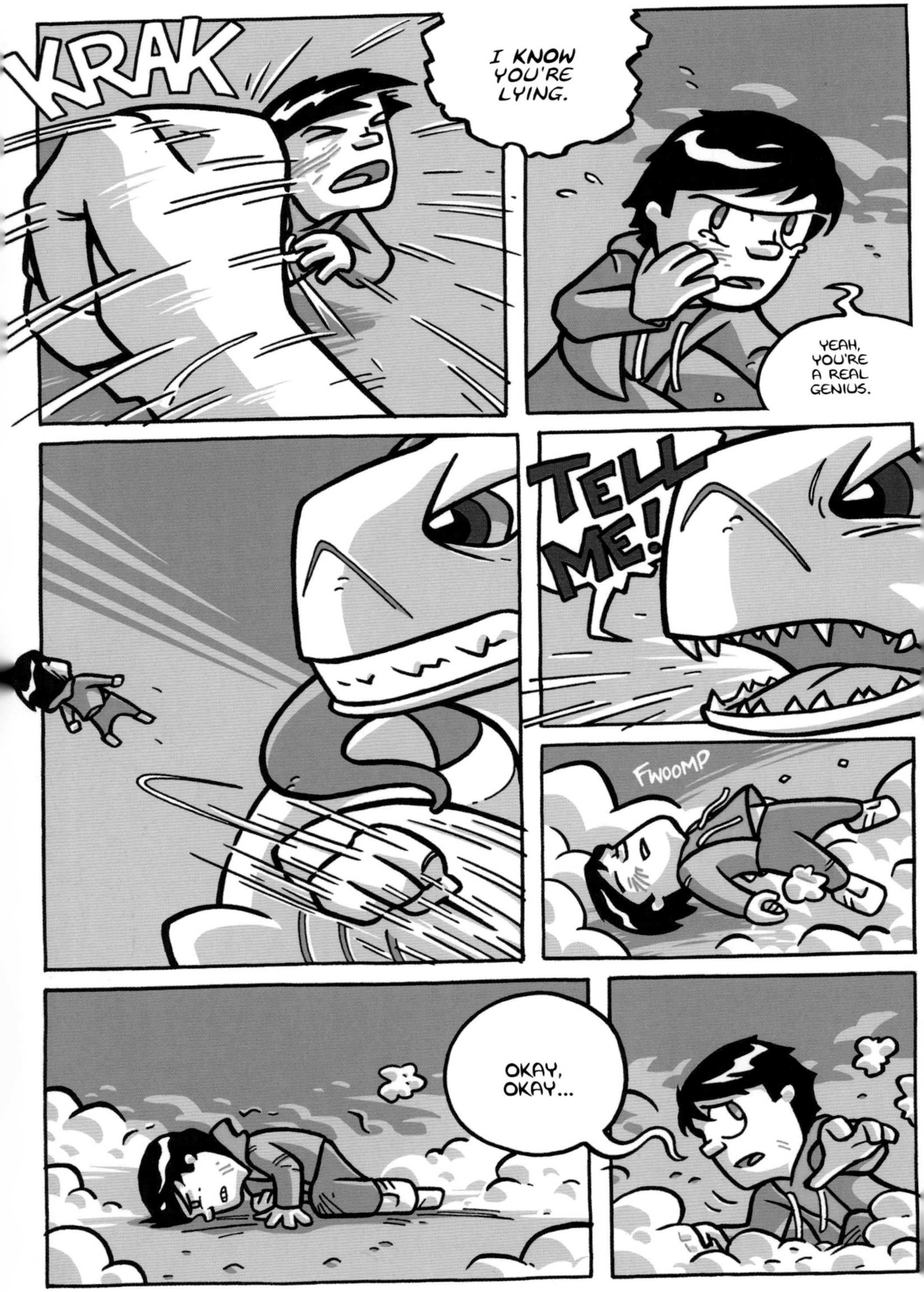
KRAK
I KNOW YOU'RE LYING.
YEAH, YOU'RE A REAL GENIUS.
TELL ME!
FWOOMP
OKAY, OKAY...

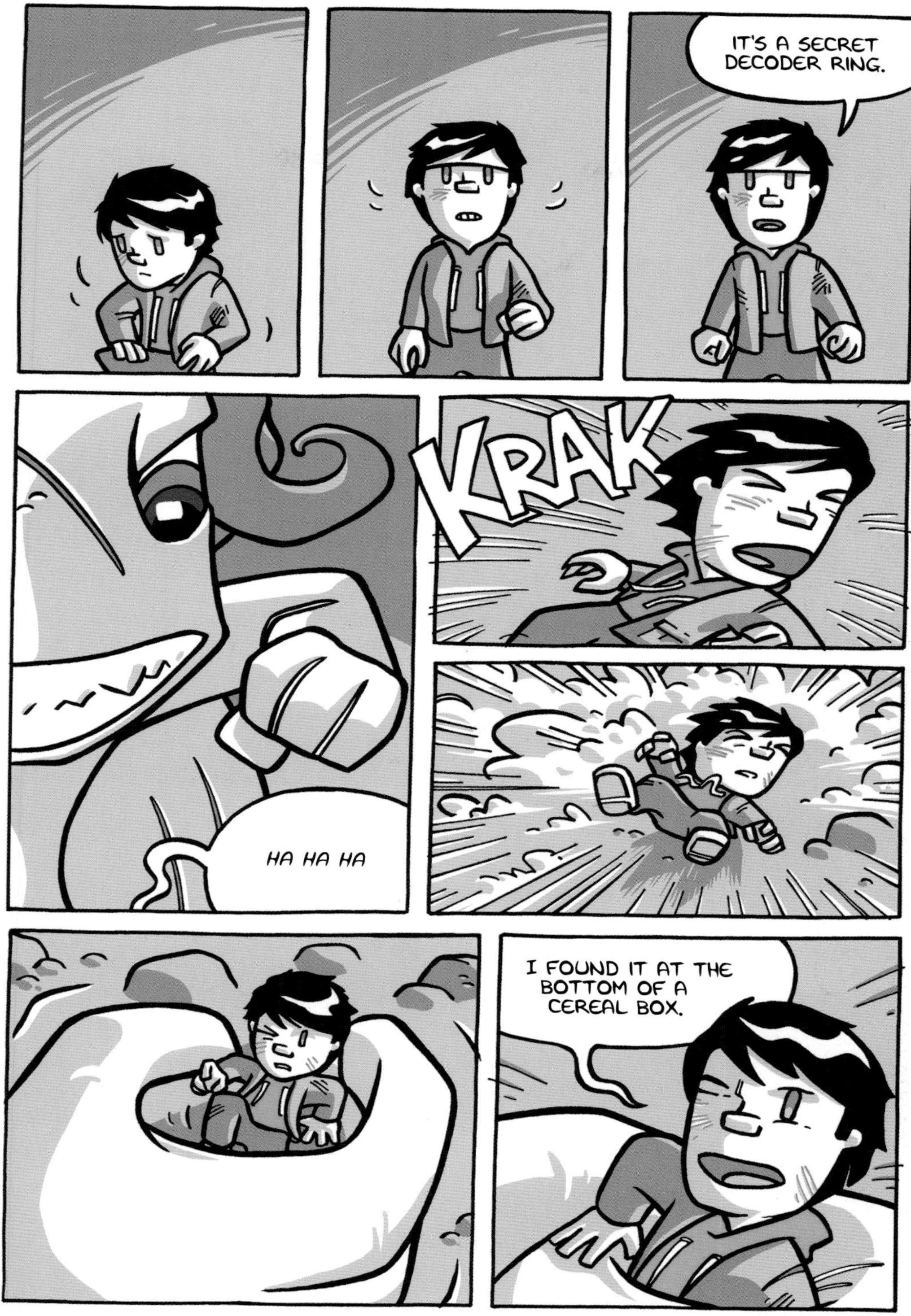
IT'S A SECRET DECODER RING.
KRAK
HA HA HA
I FOUND IT AT THE BOTTOM OF A CEREAL BOX.

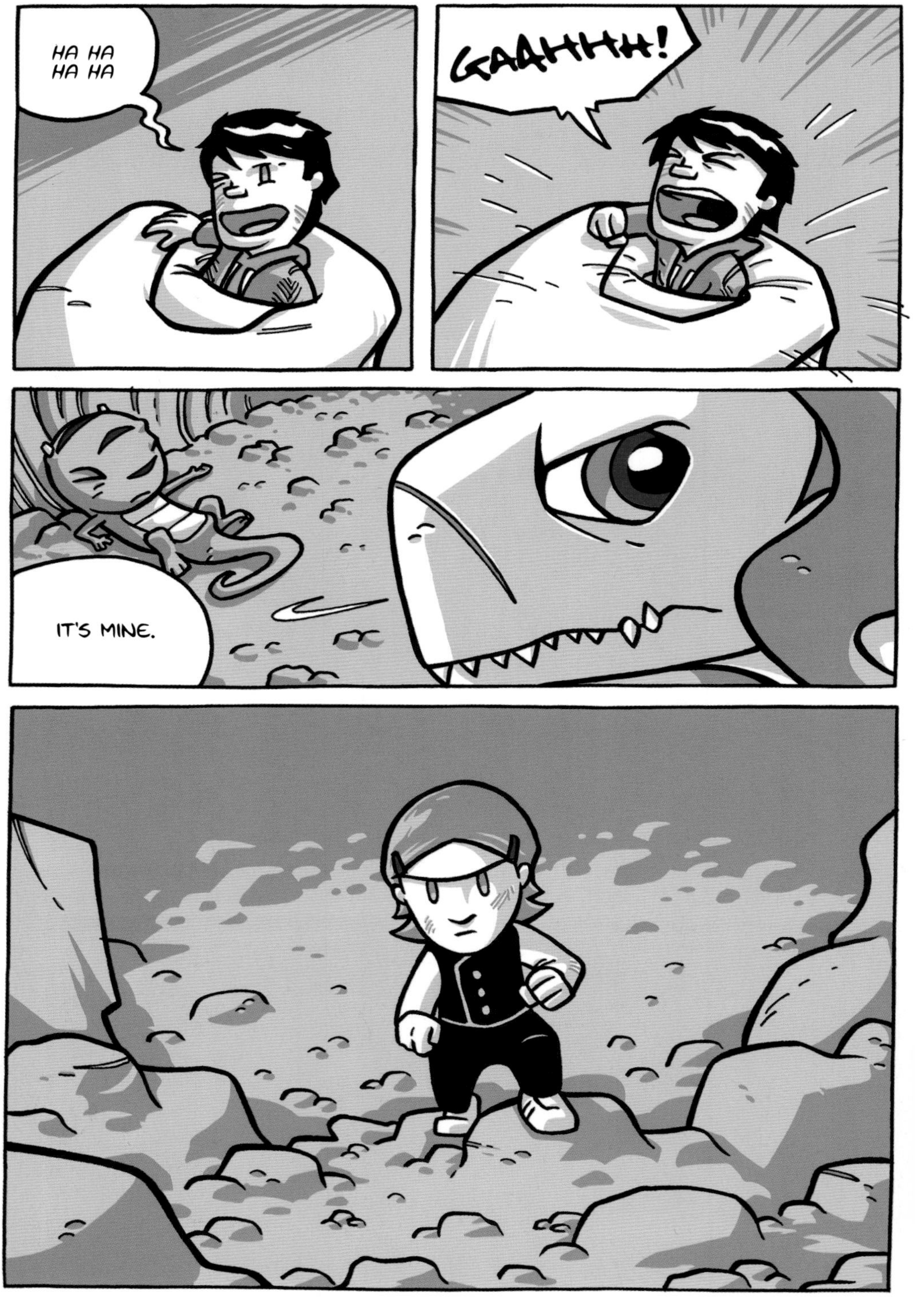
HA HA
HA HA
GAAHHH!
IT'S MINE.

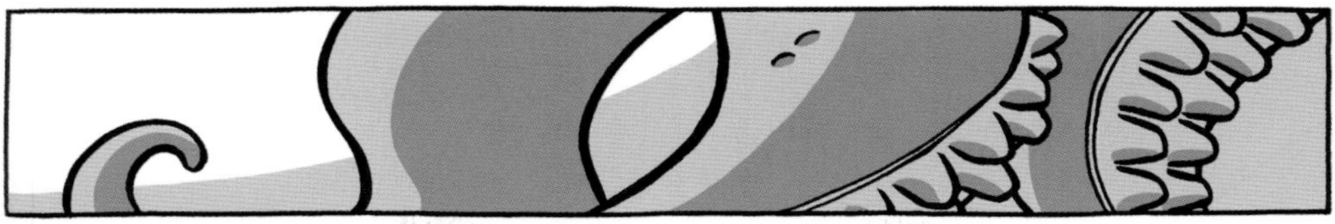

CHAPTER SIX

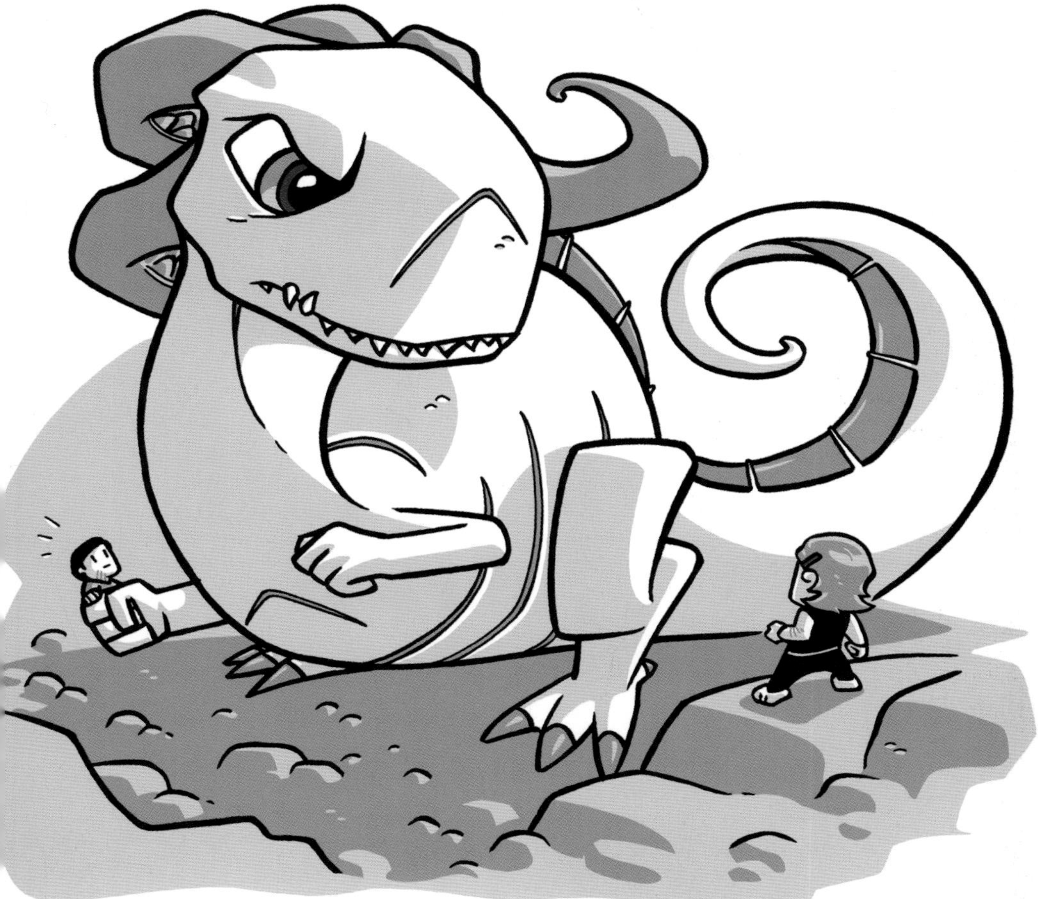

LET THEM GO.

HA! WHAT A DELIGHTFUL LITTLE FIRE-BRAND YOU ARE, MY DEAR.

YOU ARE HARDLY IN A POSITION TO MAKE DEMANDS.

WELL, YOU'RE NOT GOING TO MAKE MANY FRIENDS IF YOU CRUSH THEM ALL.

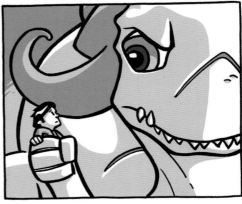

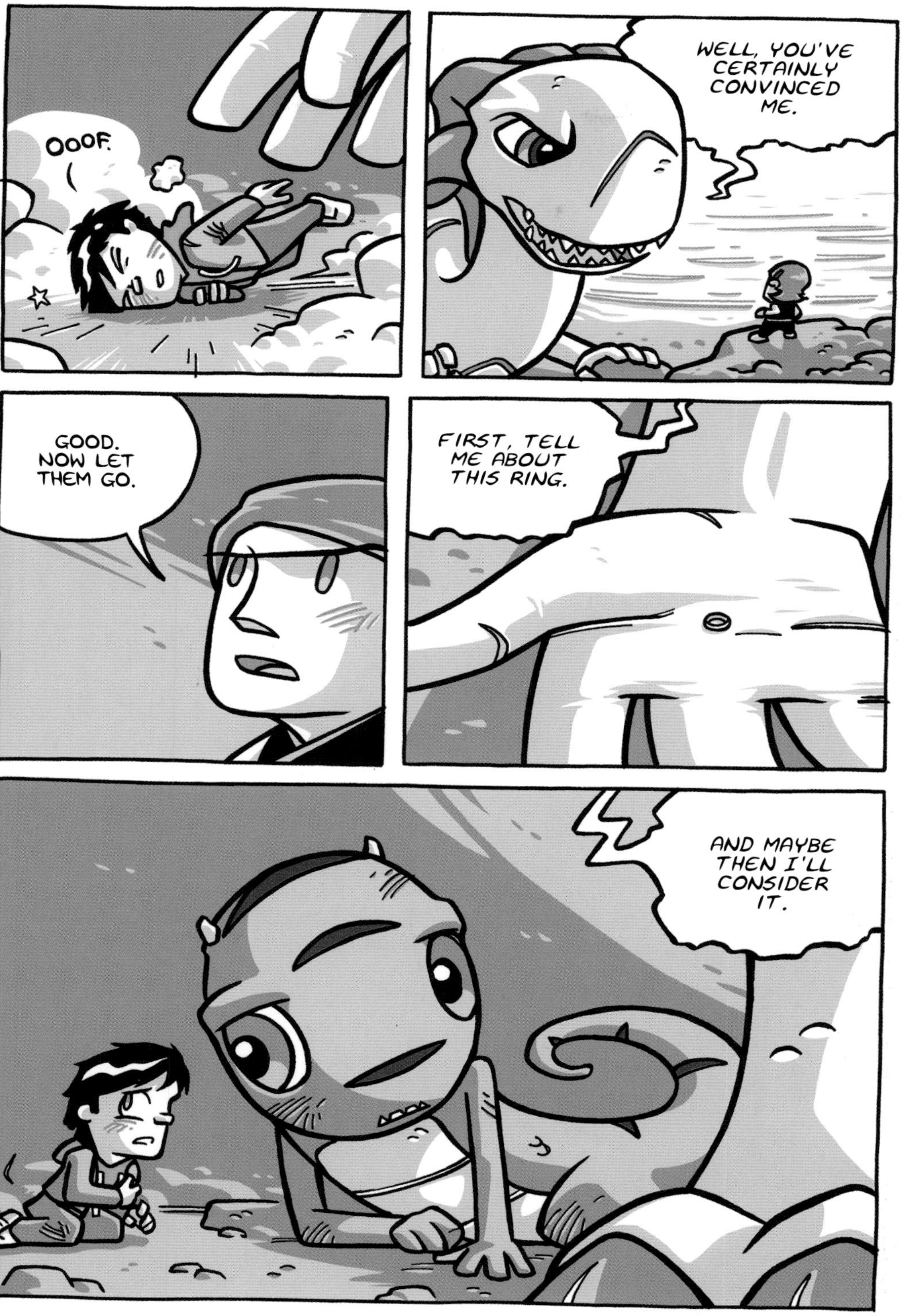
OOOF.
WELL, YOU'VE CERTAINLY CONVINCED ME.
GOOD. NOW LET THEM GO.
FIRST, TELL ME ABOUT THIS RING.
AND MAYBE THEN I'LL CONSIDER IT.

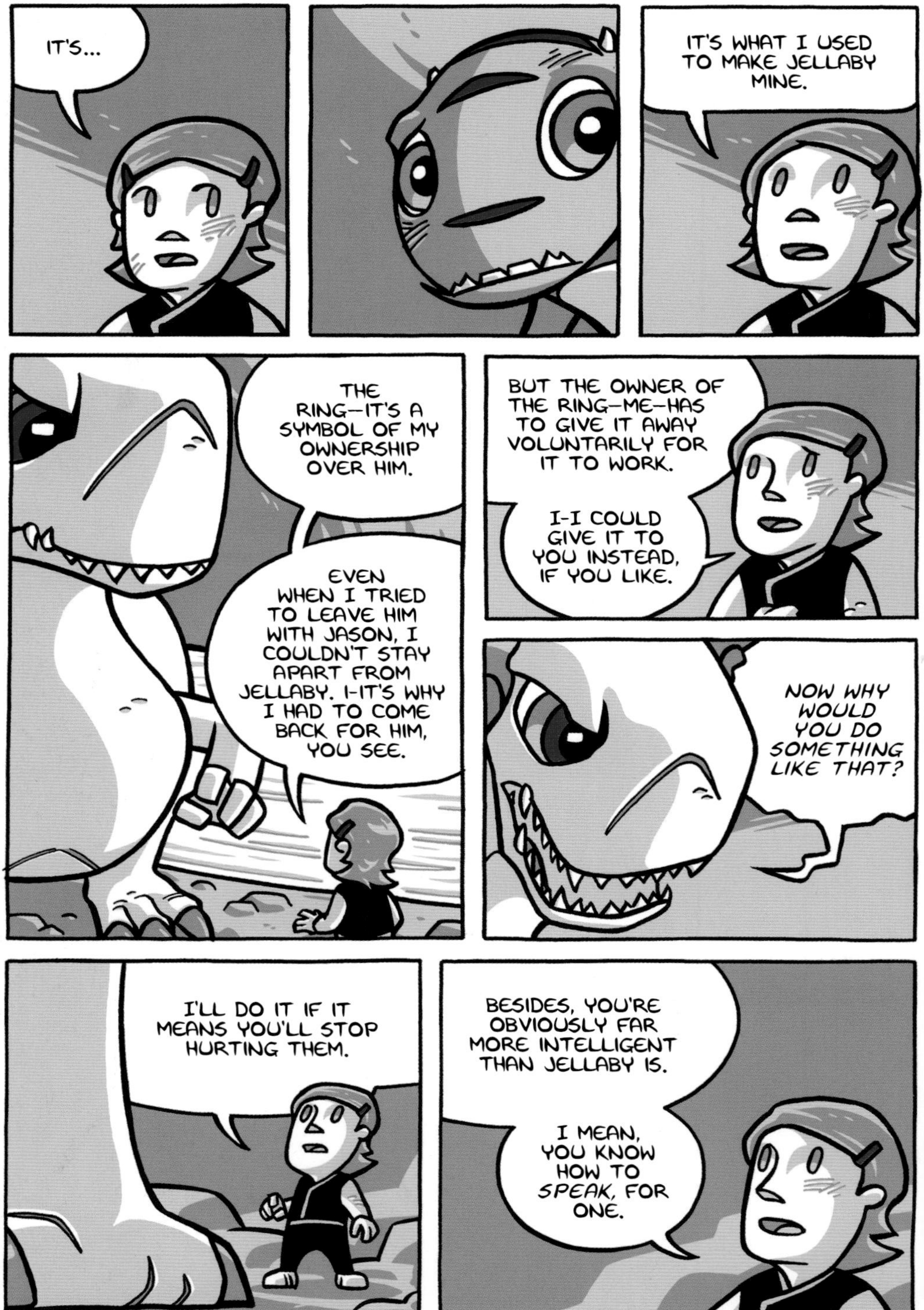
IT'S...
IT'S WHAT I USED TO MAKE JELLABY MINE.
THE RING—IT'S A SYMBOL OF MY OWNERSHIP OVER HIM.
EVEN WHEN I TRIED TO LEAVE HIM WITH JASON, I COULDN'T STAY APART FROM JELLABY. I-IT'S WHY I HAD TO COME BACK FOR HIM, YOU SEE.
BUT THE OWNER OF THE RING—ME—HAS TO GIVE IT AWAY VOLUNTARILY FOR IT TO WORK.
I-I COULD GIVE IT TO YOU INSTEAD, IF YOU LIKE.
NOW WHY WOULD YOU DO SOMETHING LIKE THAT?
I'LL DO IT IF IT MEANS YOU'LL STOP HURTING THEM.
BESIDES, YOU'RE OBVIOUSLY FAR MORE INTELLIGENT THAN JELLABY IS.
I MEAN, YOU KNOW HOW TO SPEAK, FOR ONE.

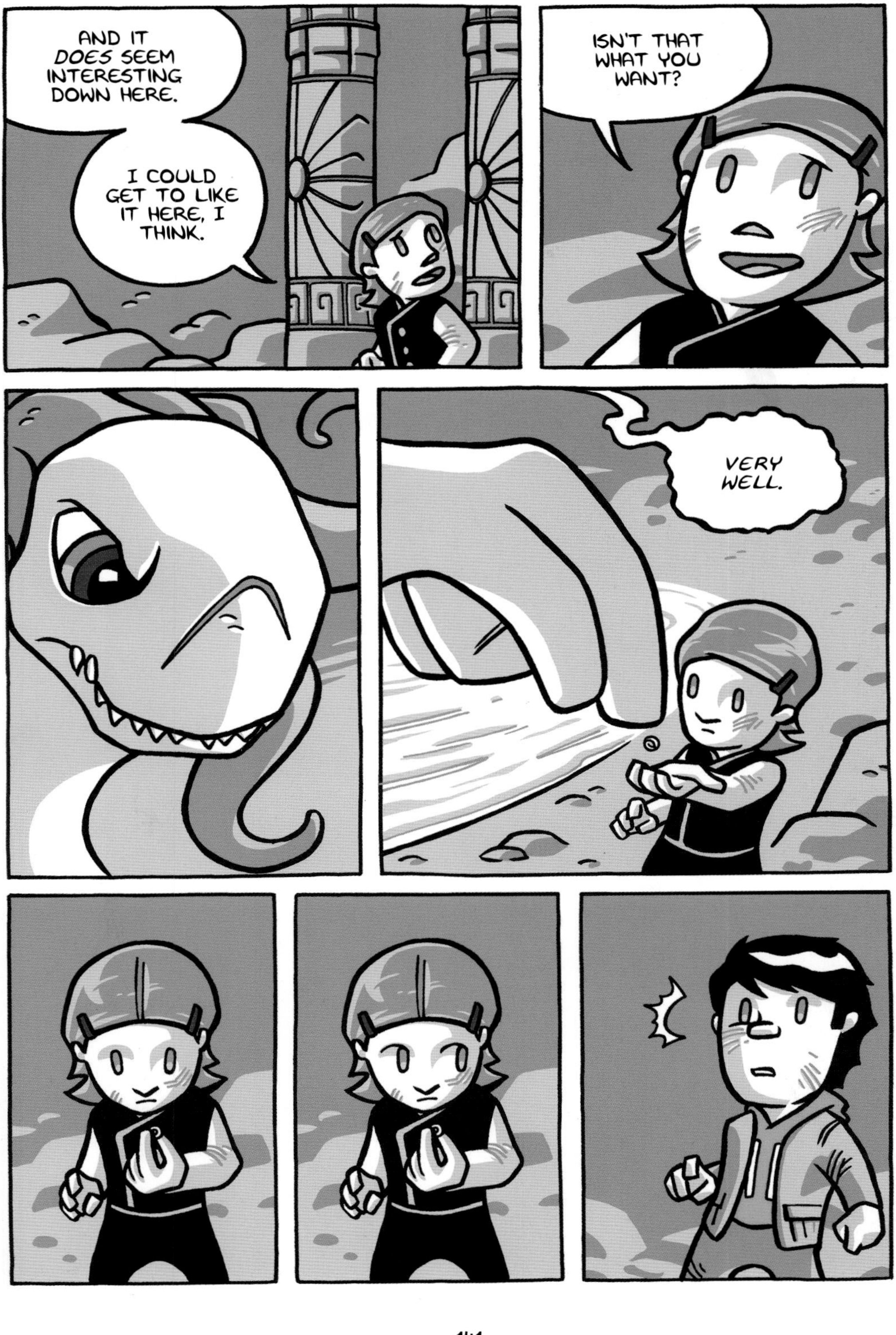
AND IT *DOES* SEEM INTERESTING DOWN HERE.
I COULD GET TO LIKE IT HERE, I THINK.
ISN'T THAT WHAT YOU WANT?
VERY WELL.

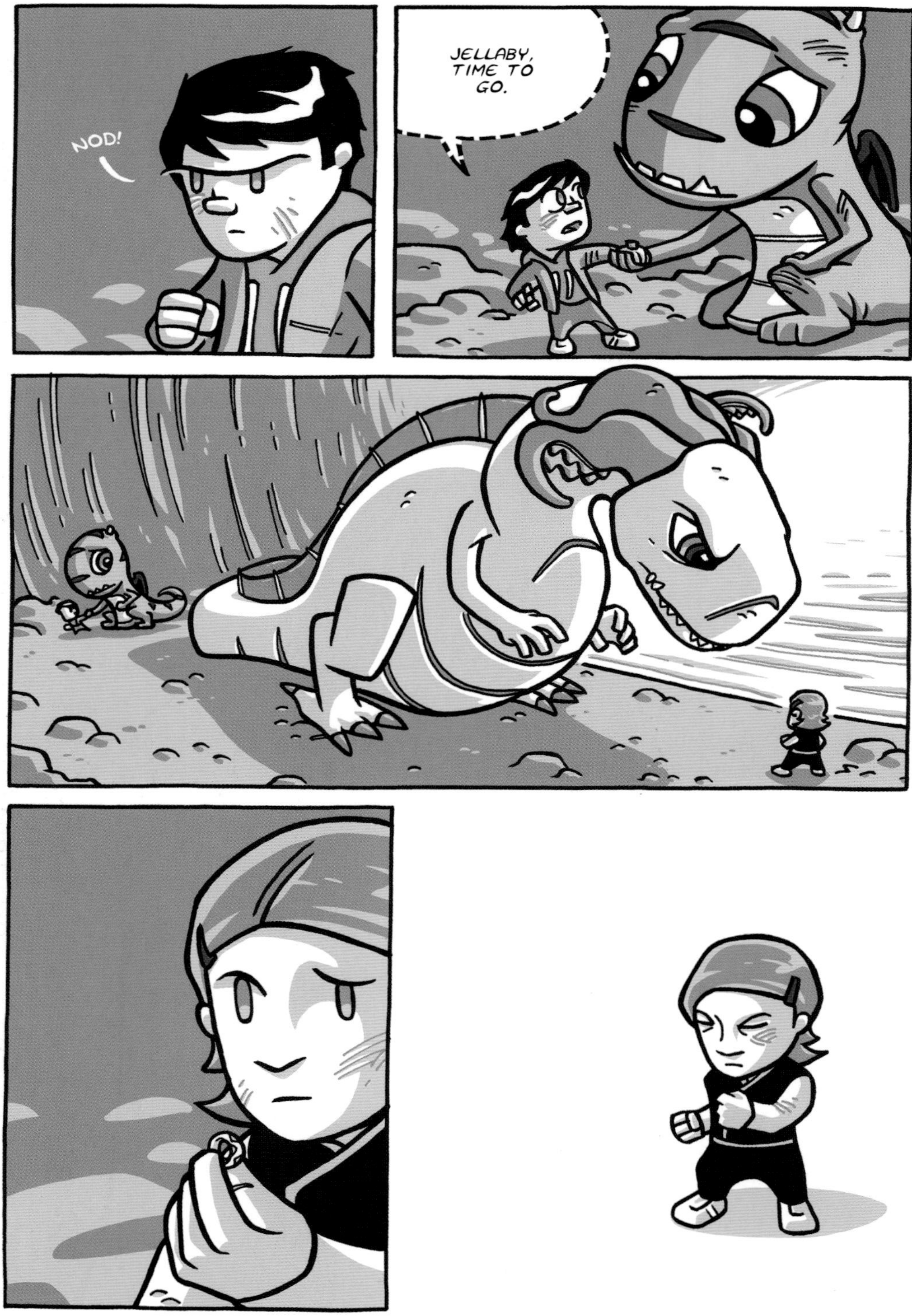
NOD!
JELLABY, TIME TO GO.

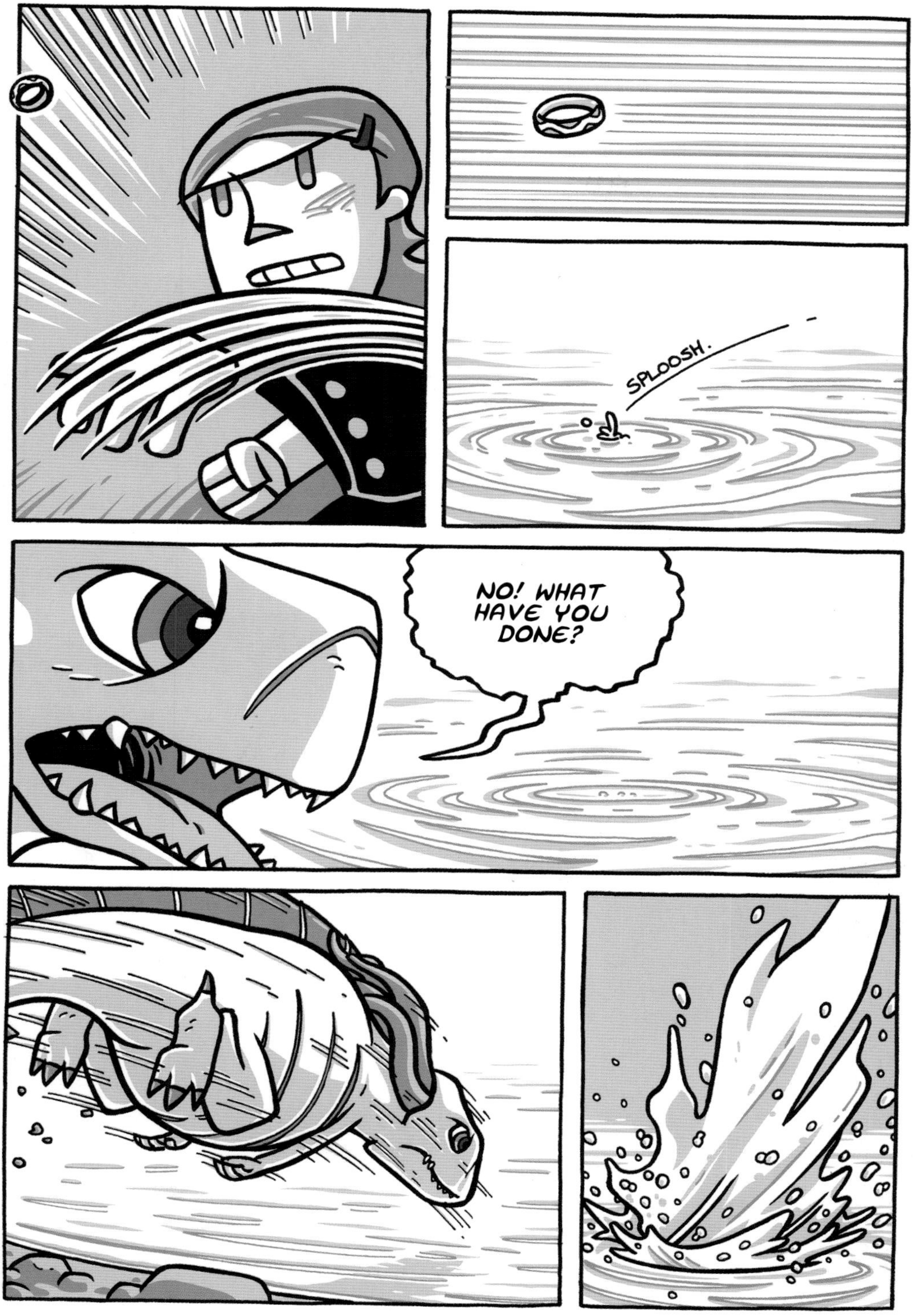
SPLOOSH.
NO! WHAT HAVE YOU DONE?

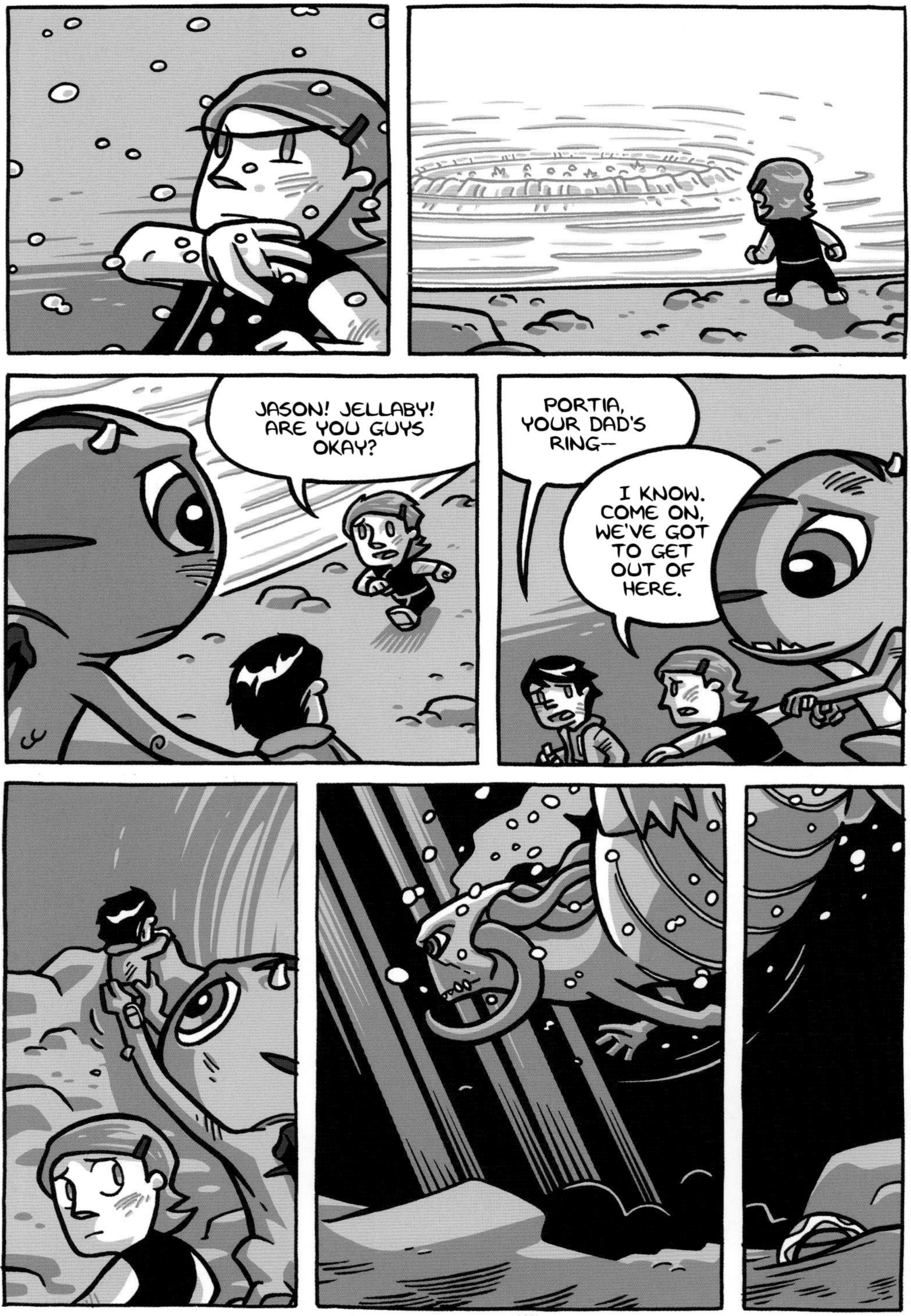
JASON! JELLABY! ARE YOU GUYS OKAY?
PORTIA, YOUR DAD'S RING—
I KNOW. COME ON, WE'VE GOT TO GET OUT OF HERE.

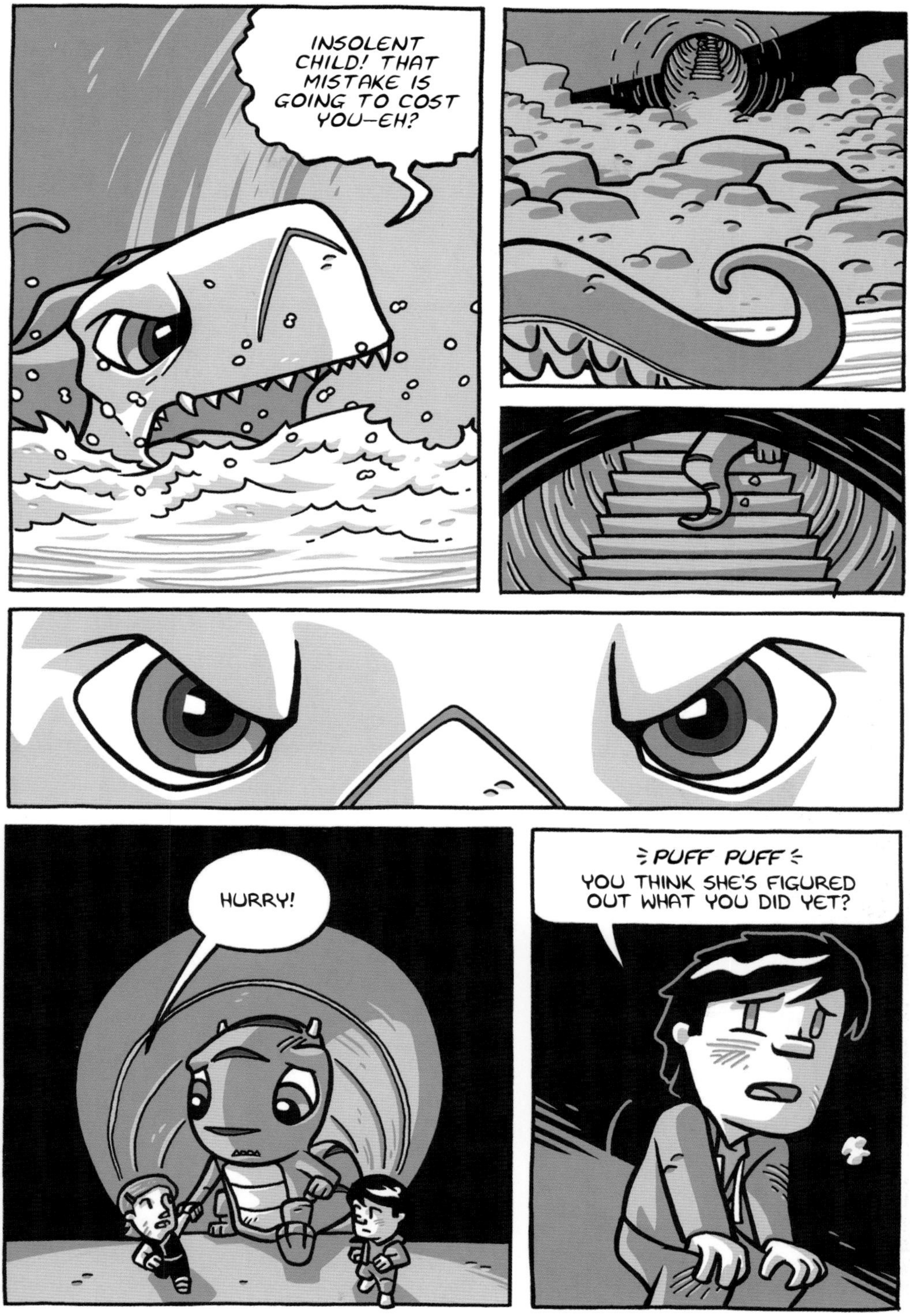
INSOLENT CHILD! THAT MISTAKE IS GOING TO COST YOU—EH?
HURRY!
PUFF PUFF
YOU THINK SHE'S FIGURED OUT WHAT YOU DID YET?

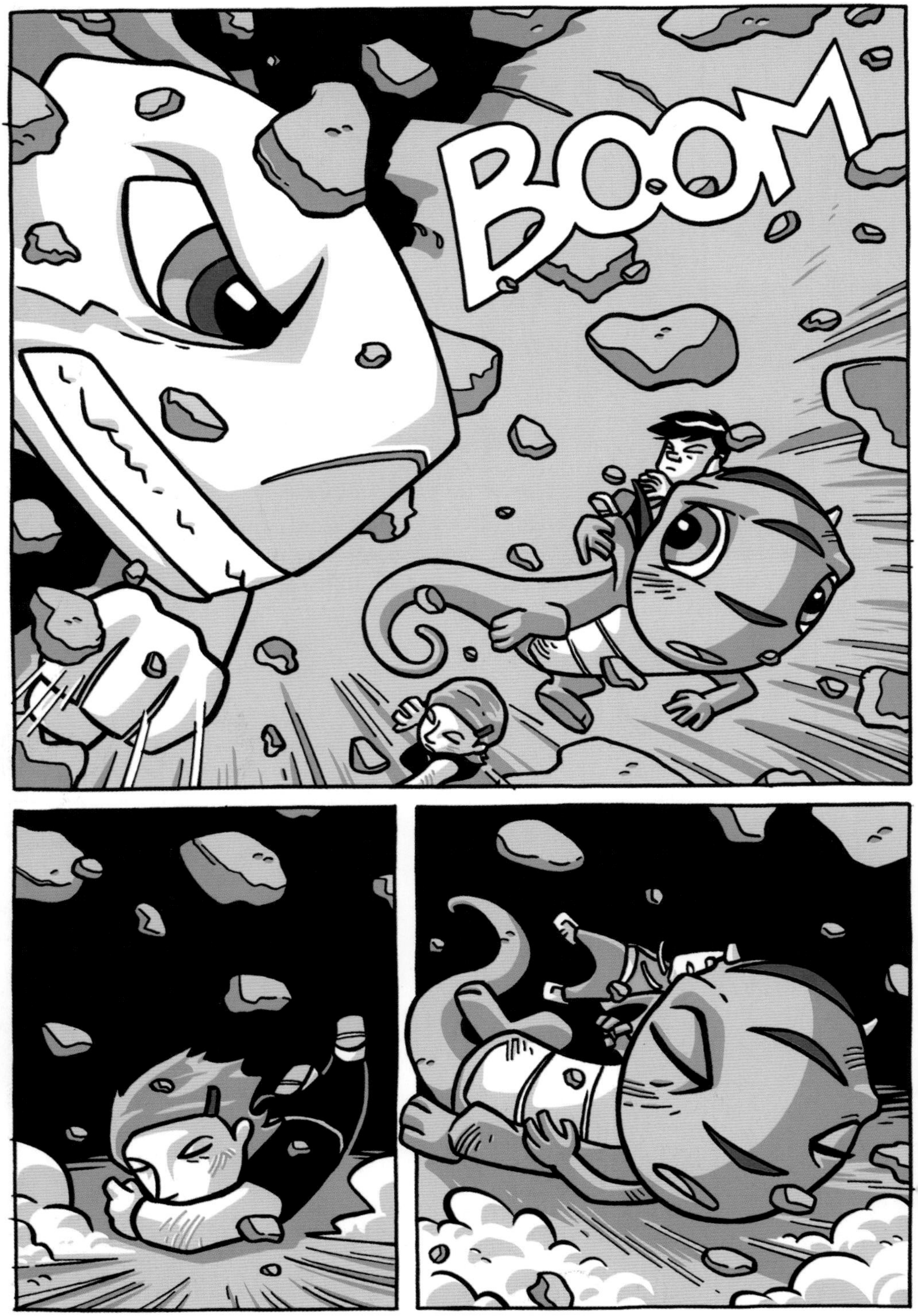
BOOM

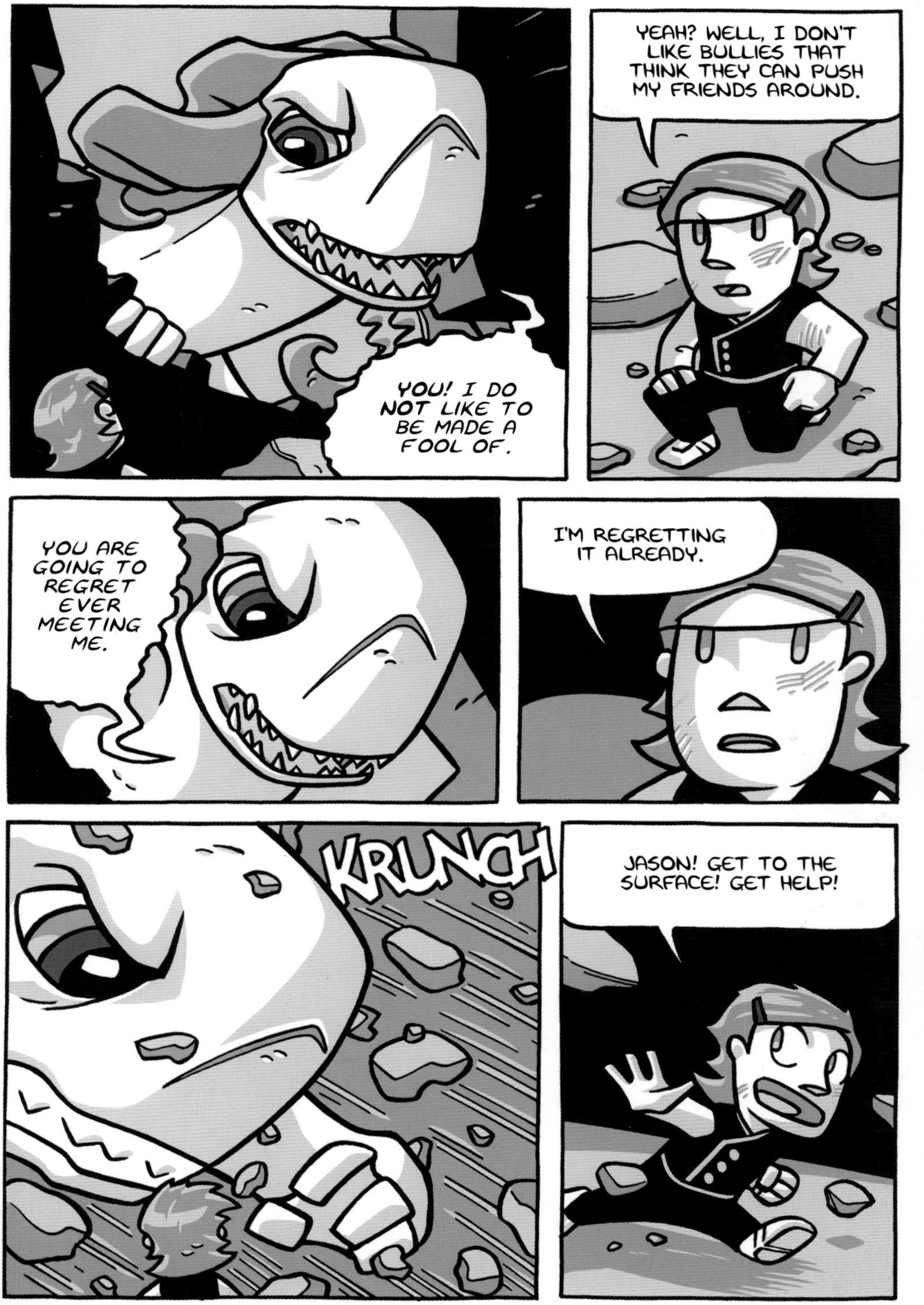
YOU! I DO NOT LIKE TO BE MADE A FOOL OF.
YEAH? WELL, I DON'T LIKE BULLIES THAT THINK THEY CAN PUSH MY FRIENDS AROUND.
YOU ARE GOING TO REGRET EVER MEETING ME.
I'M REGRETTING IT ALREADY.
KRUNCH
JASON! GET TO THE SURFACE! GET HELP!

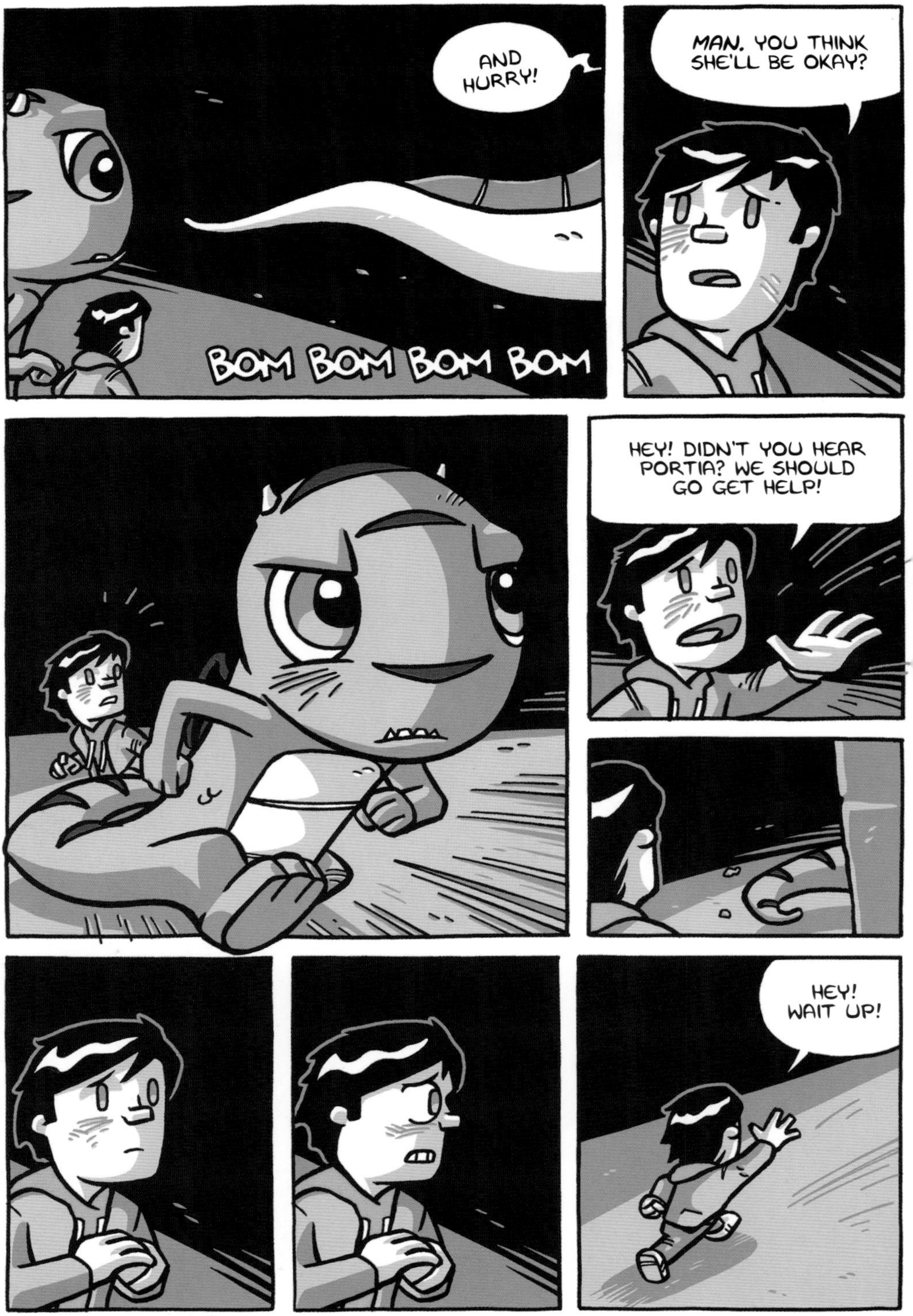
AND HURRY!
BOM BOM BOM BOM
MAN. YOU THINK SHE'LL BE OKAY?
HEY! DIDN'T YOU HEAR PORTIA? WE SHOULD GO GET HELP!
HEY! WAIT UP!

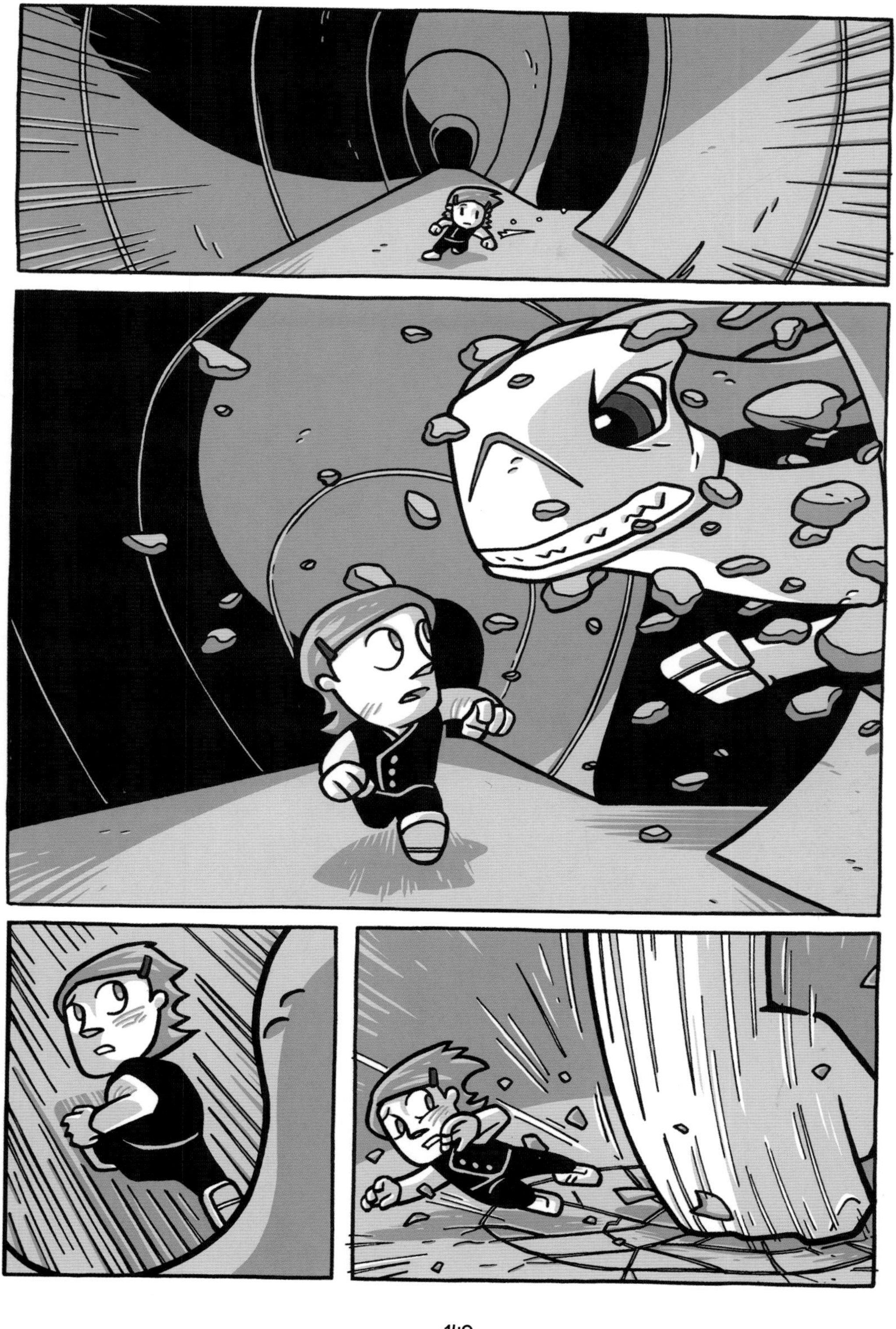

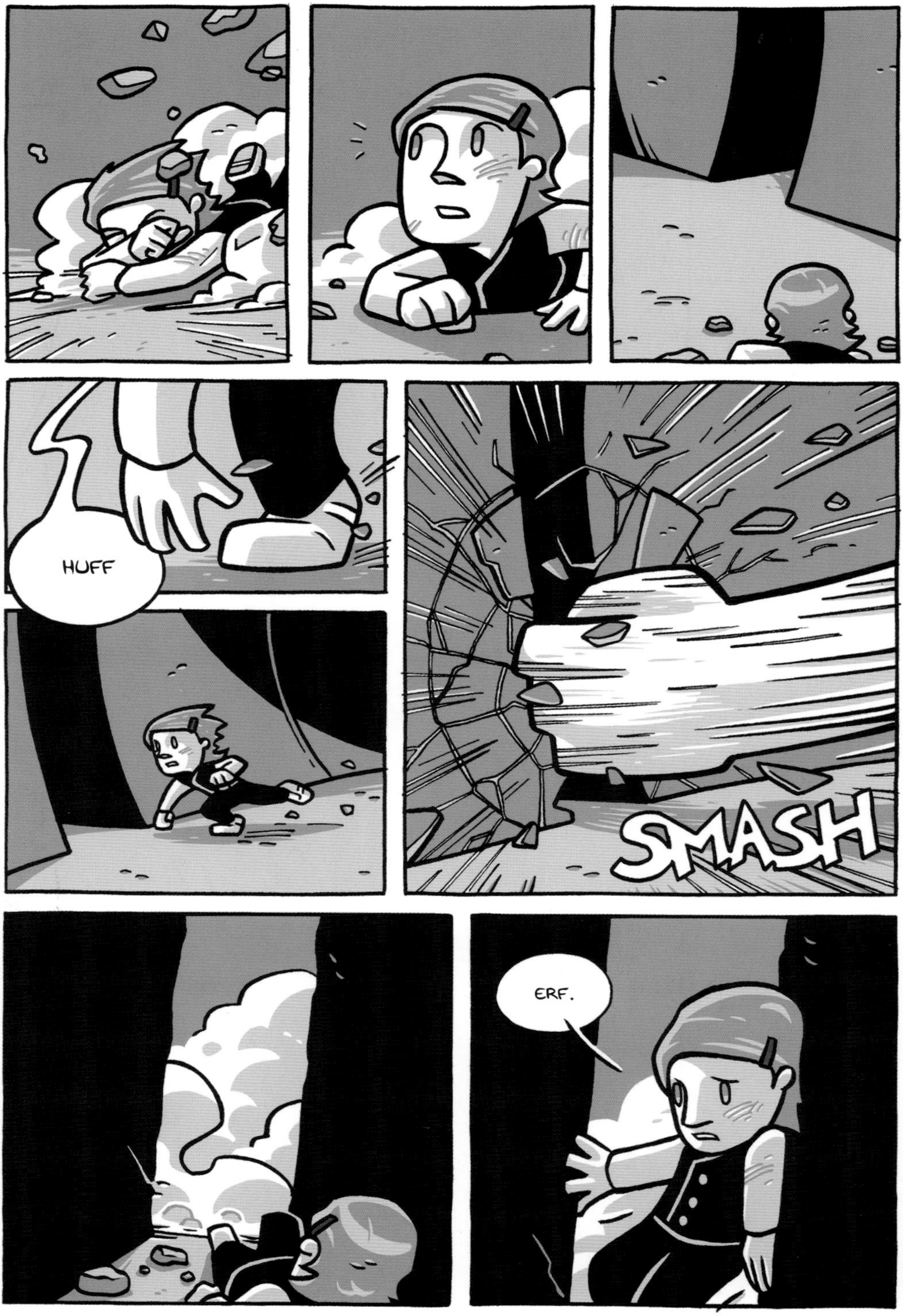
HUFF
SMASH
ERF.

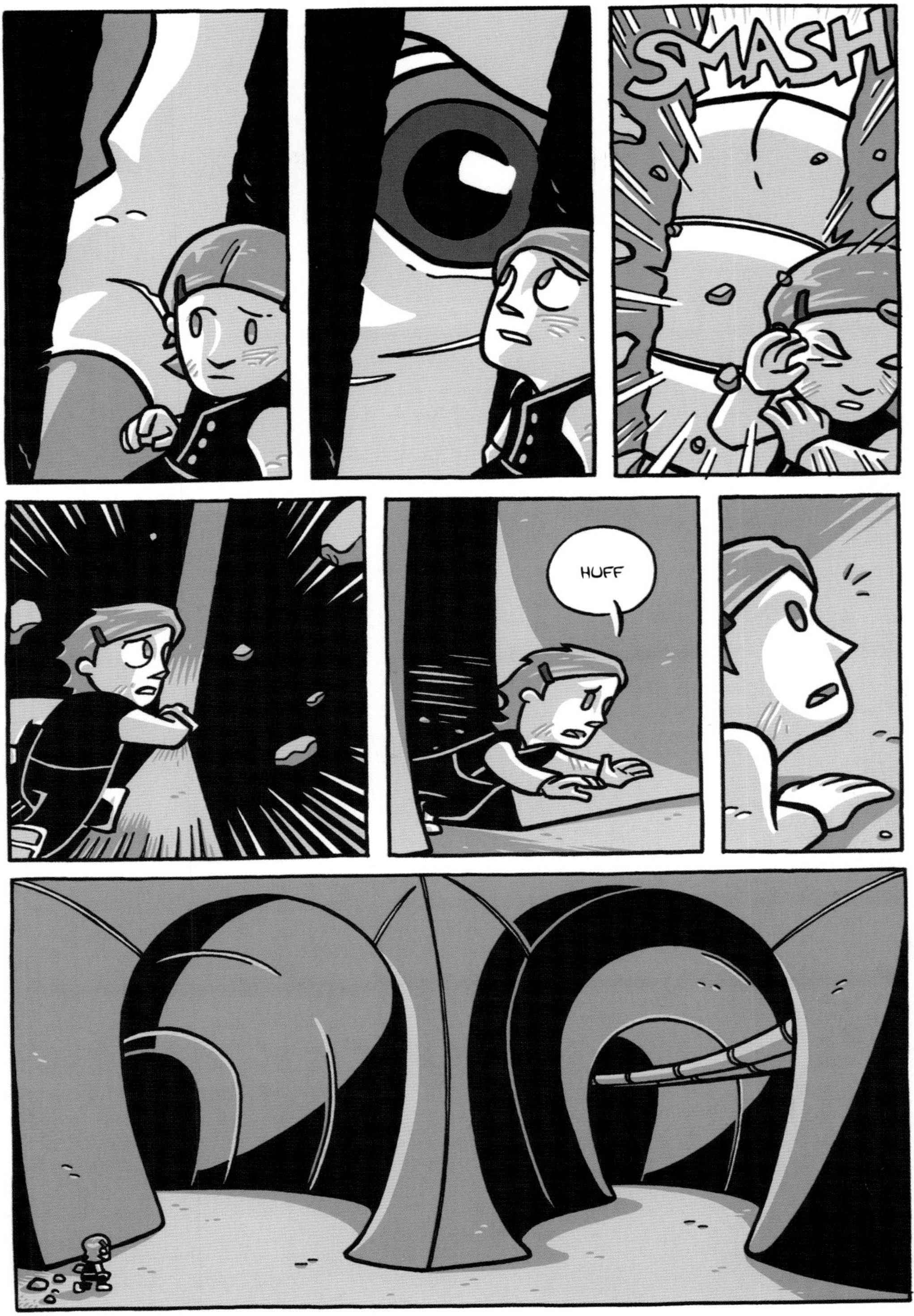
SMASH
HUFF

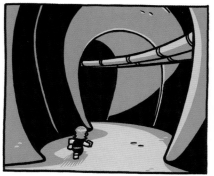

OH NO.

PORTIA!

WHAT ARE YOU DOING UP THERE?

WE CAME TO HELP!

...I THINK WE TOOK A WRONG TURN SOMEWHERE.

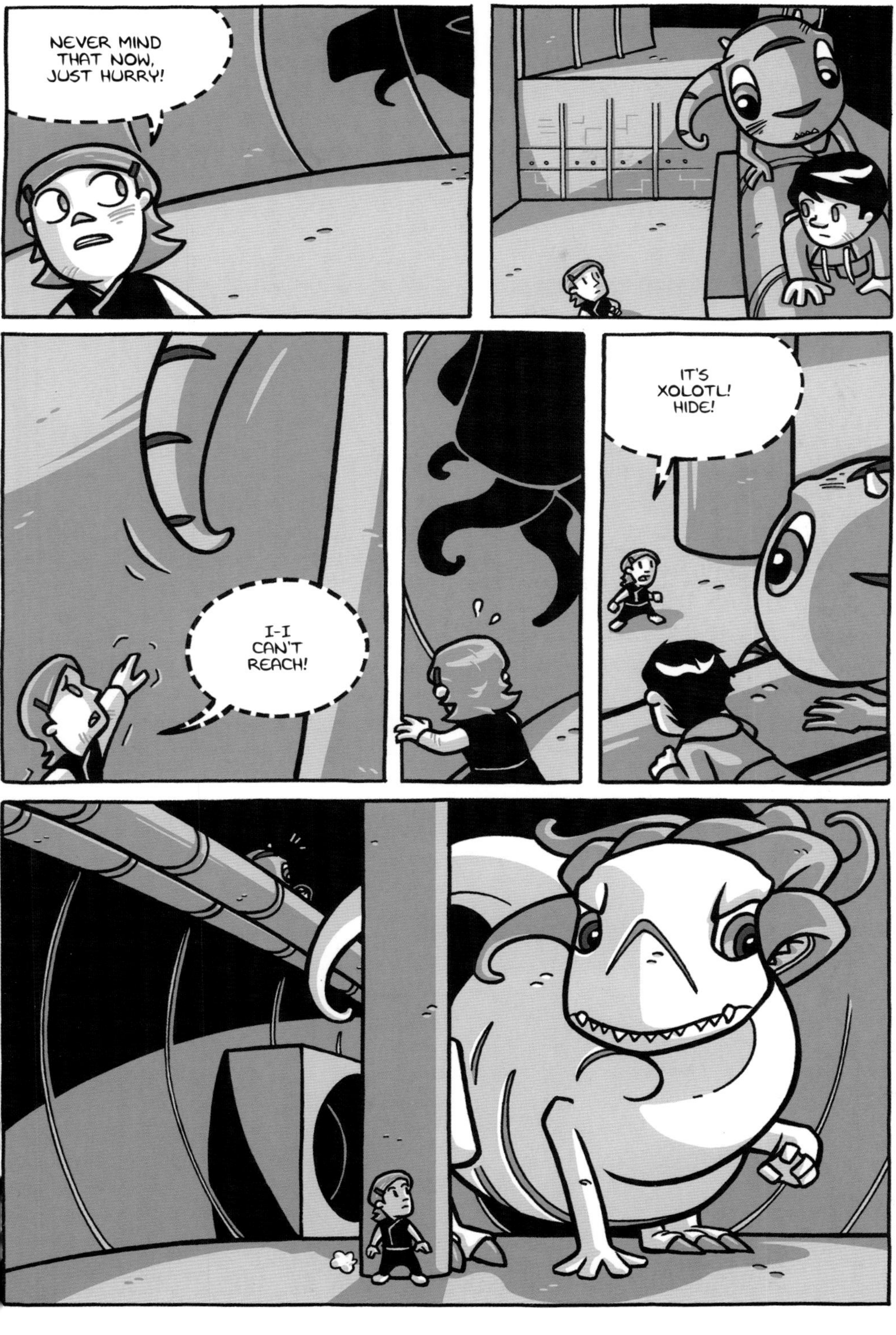
NEVER MIND THAT NOW, JUST HURRY!
I-I CAN'T REACH!
IT'S XOLOTL! HIDE!

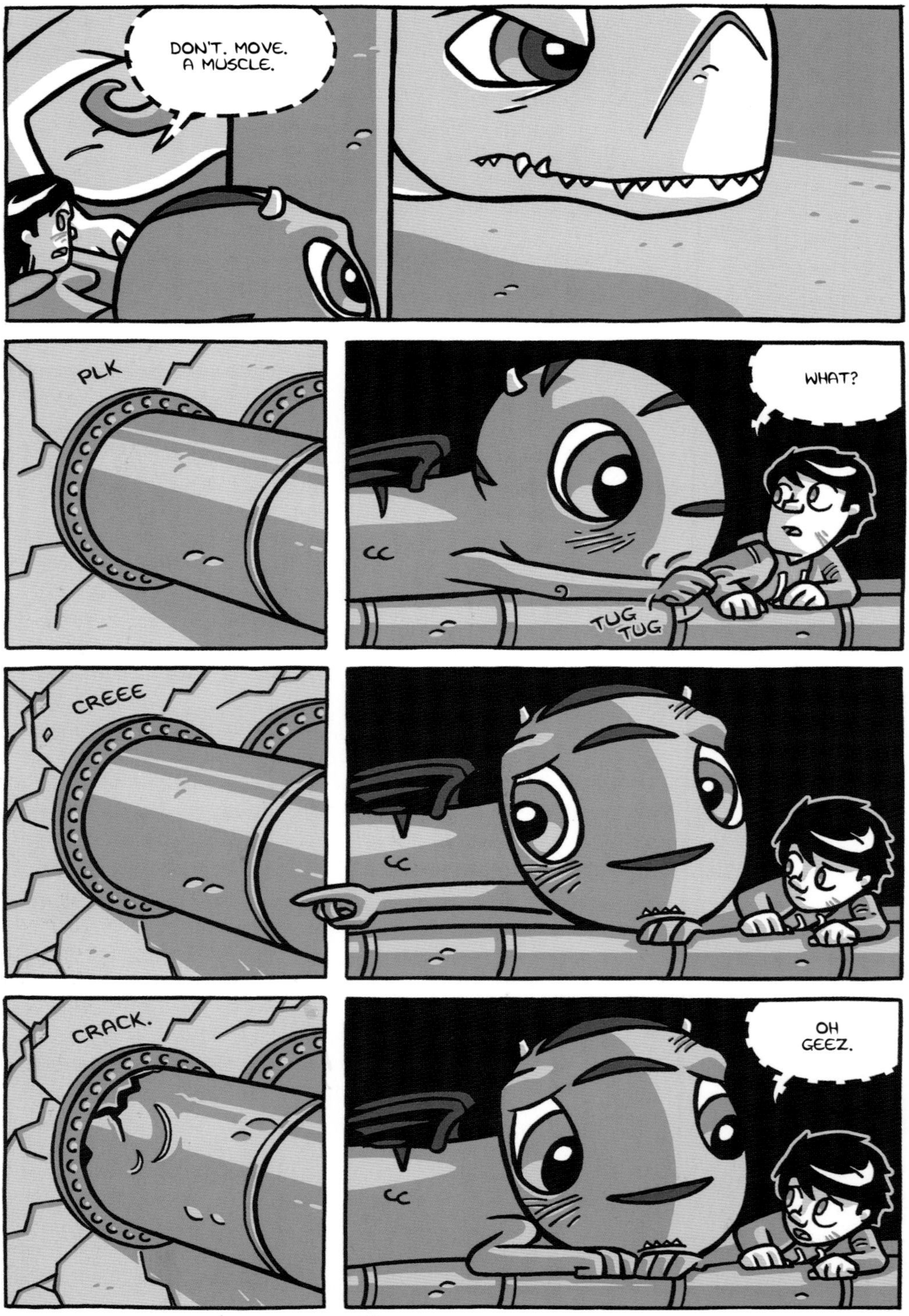
DON'T. MOVE. A MUSCLE.
PLK
WHAT?
TUG TUG
CREEE
CRACK.
OH GEEZ.

SQUEEE

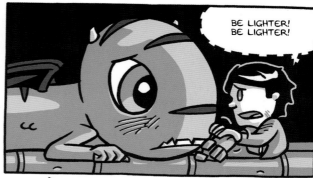

BE LIGHTER! BE LIGHTER!

CHUNG.

FLAP FLAP

FLAP FLAP

IT'S WORKING!

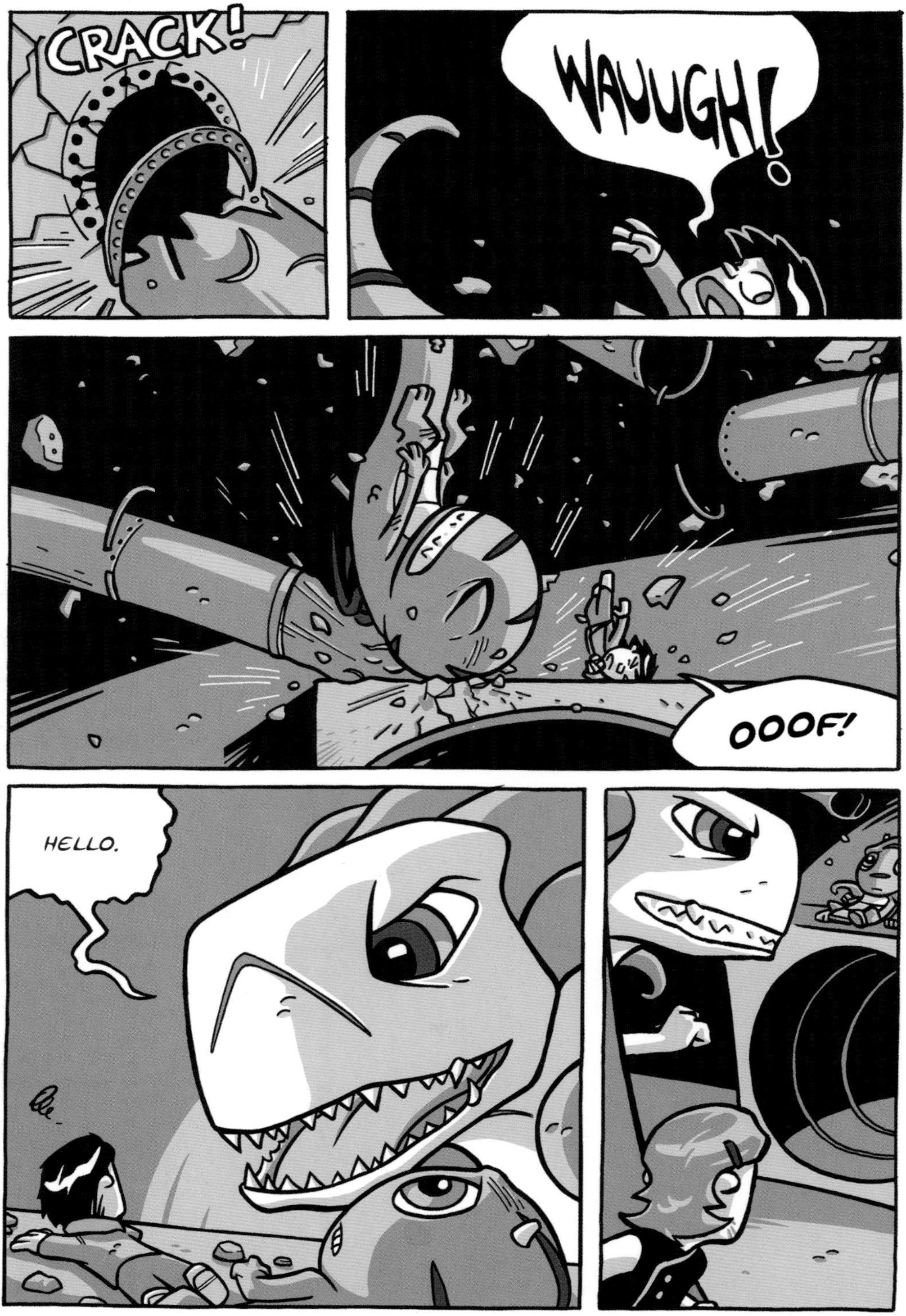
CRACK!
WAUUGH!
OOOF!
HELLO.

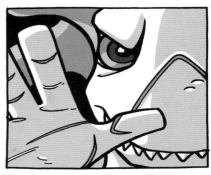

SHUCK

GRROOAR

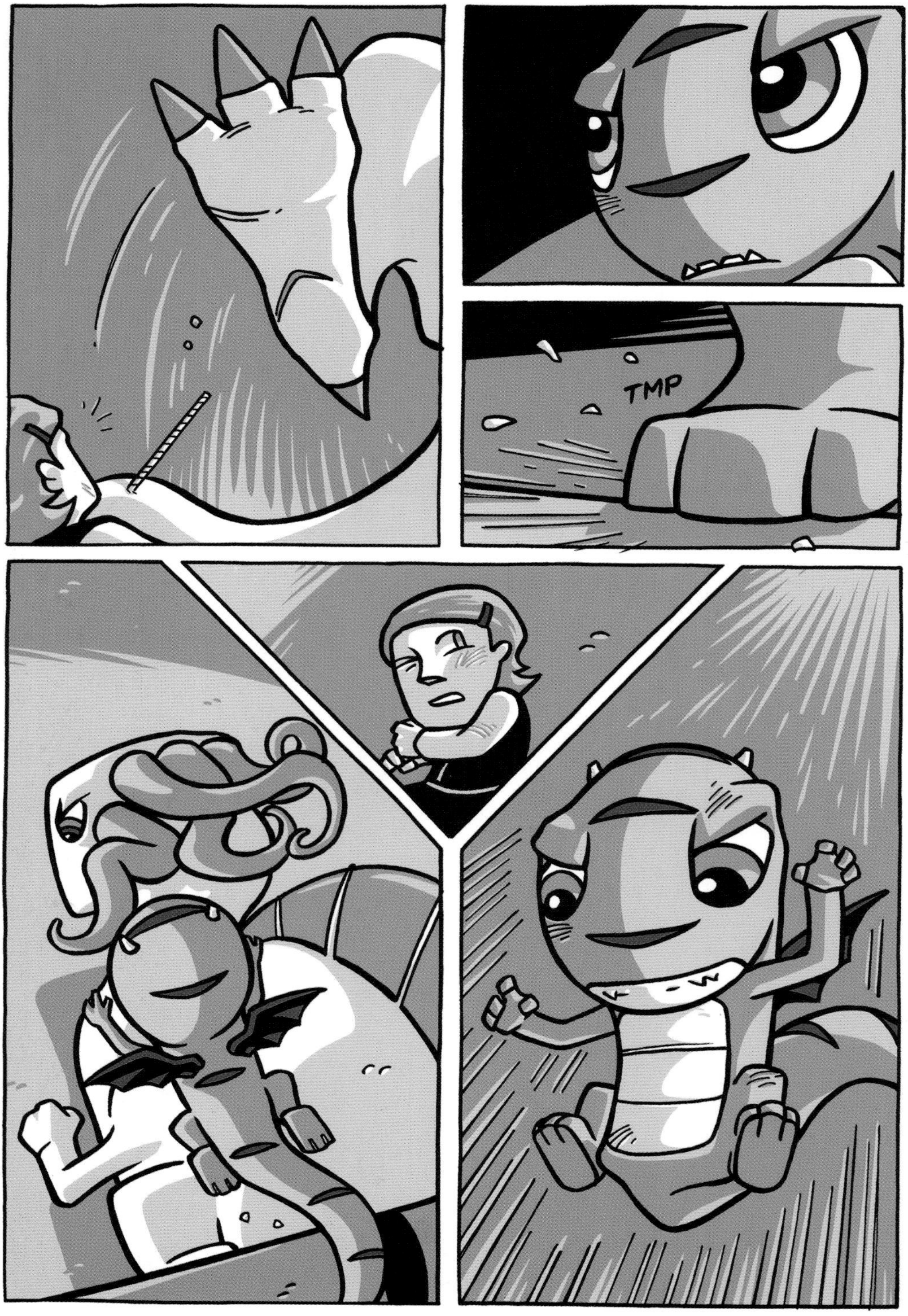
TMP

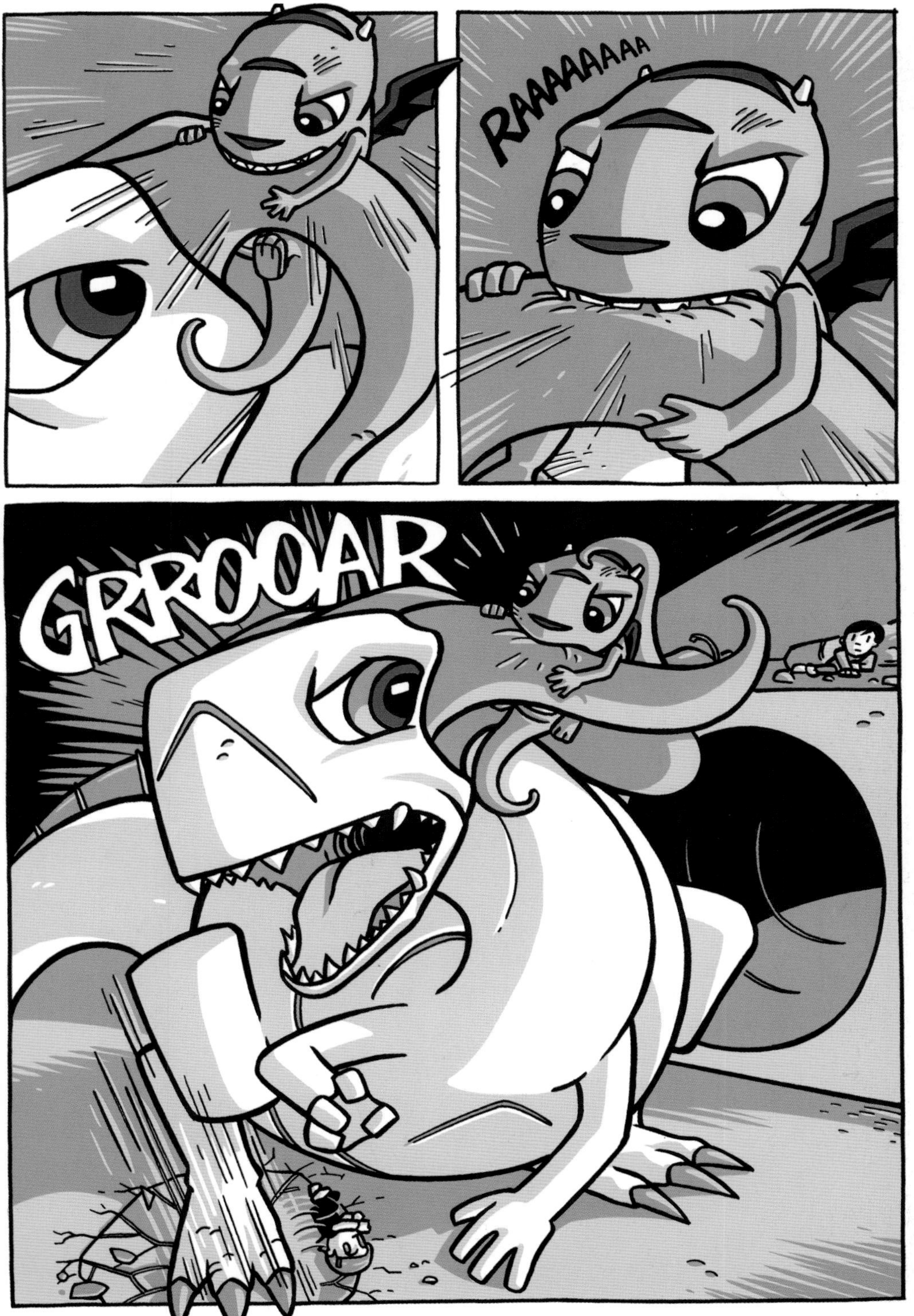
RAAAAAAAAA
GRROOAR

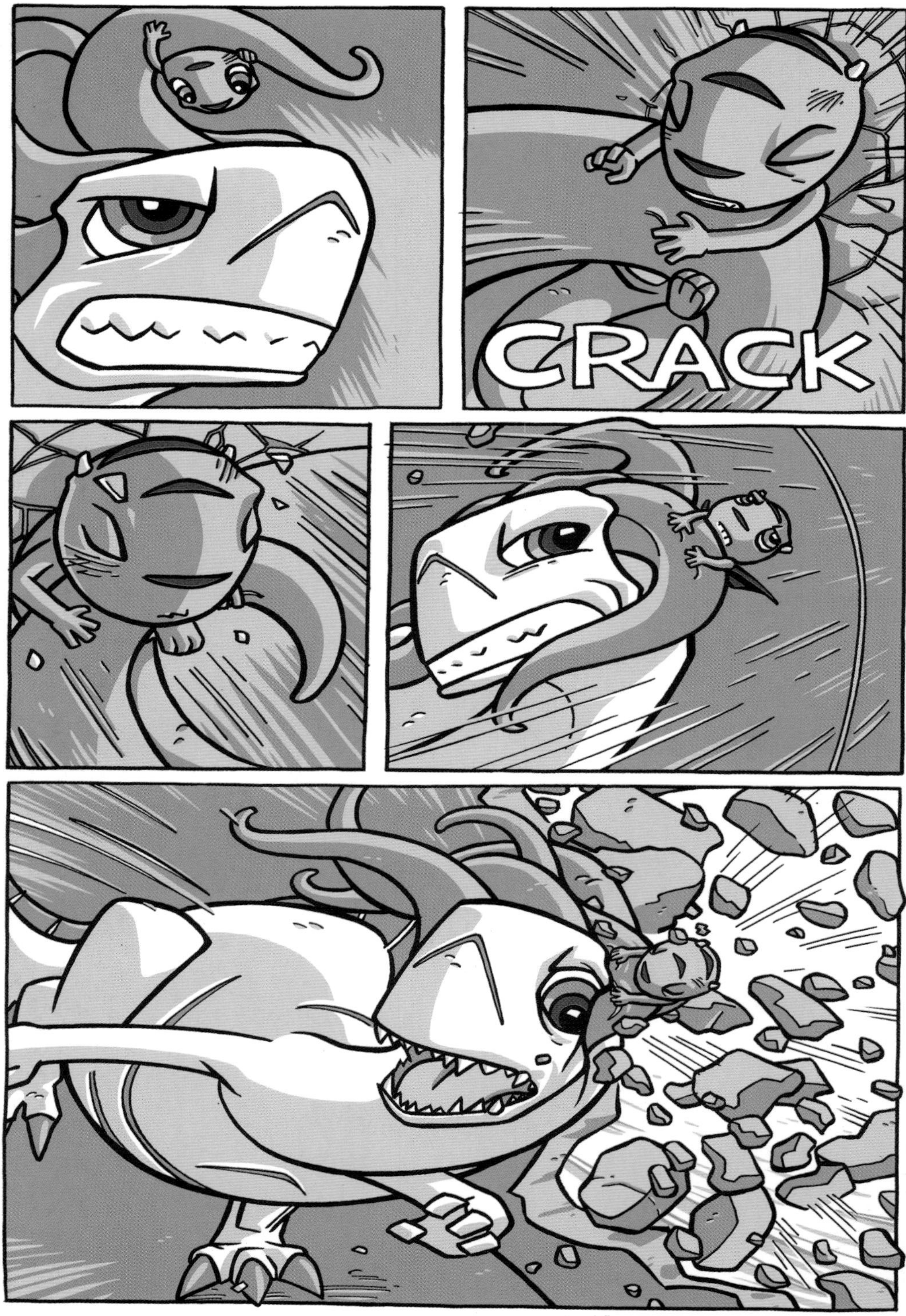
CRACK

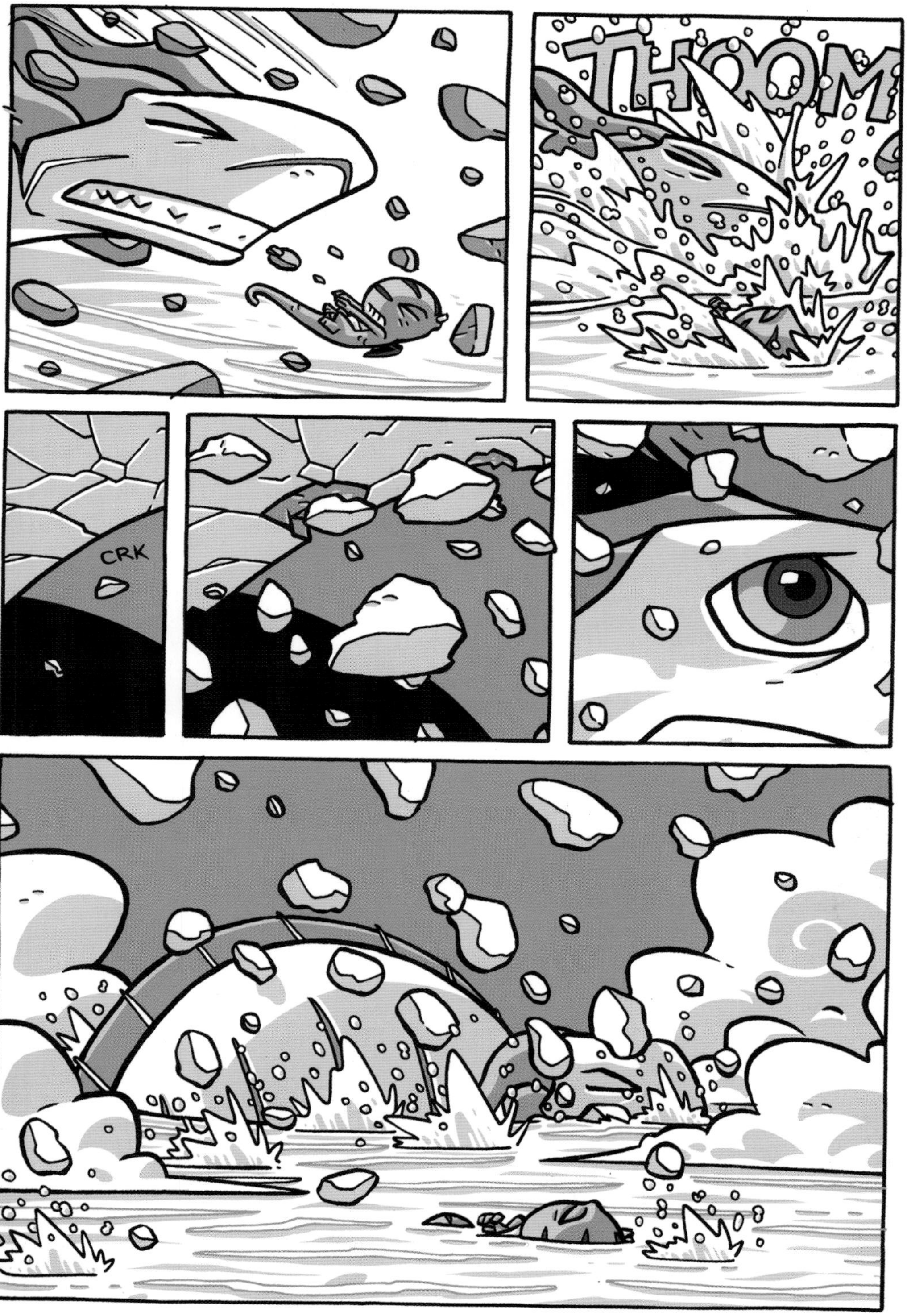
THOOM
CRK

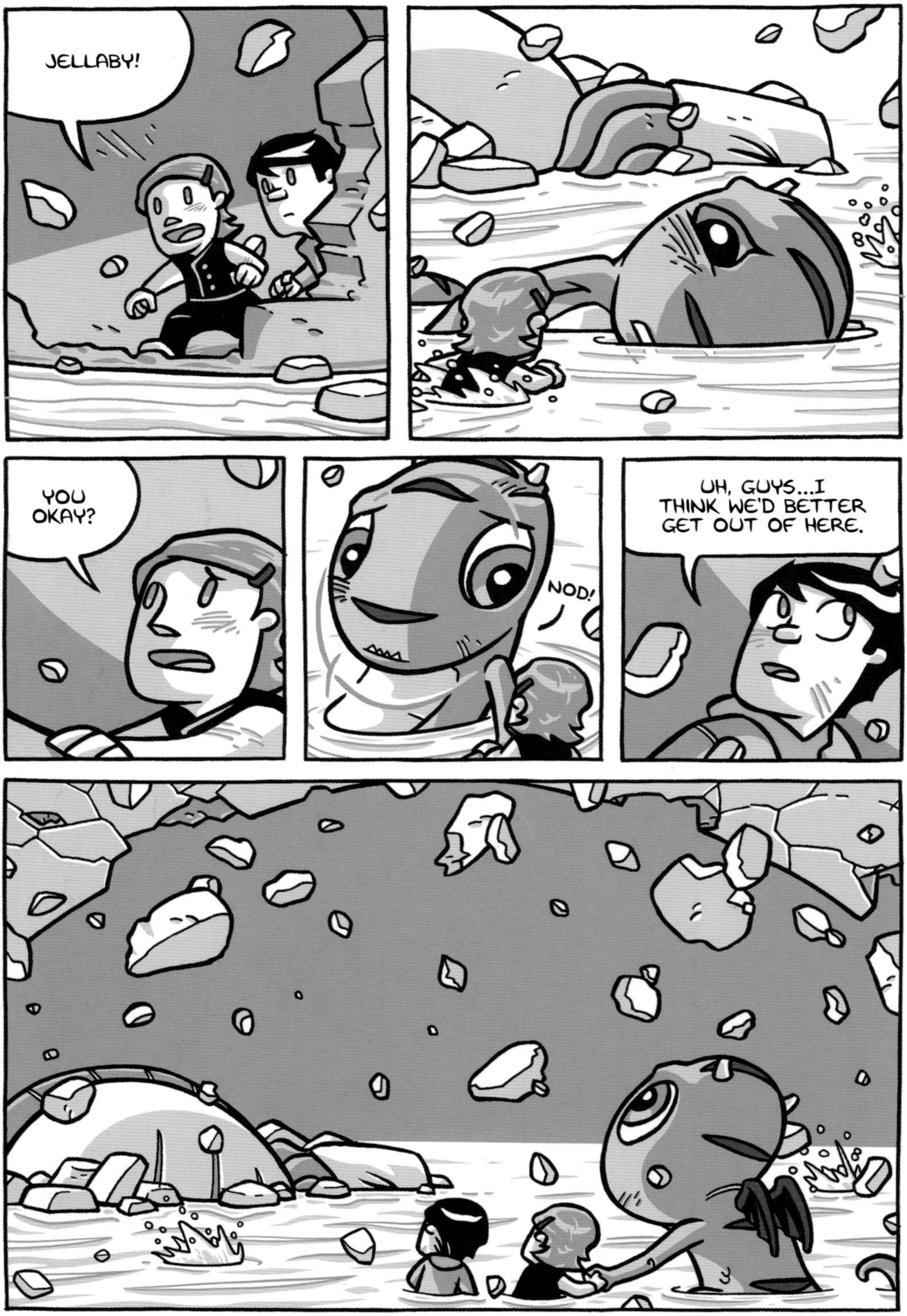
JELLABY!
YOU OKAY?
NOD!
UH, GUYS...I THINK WE'D BETTER GET OUT OF HERE.

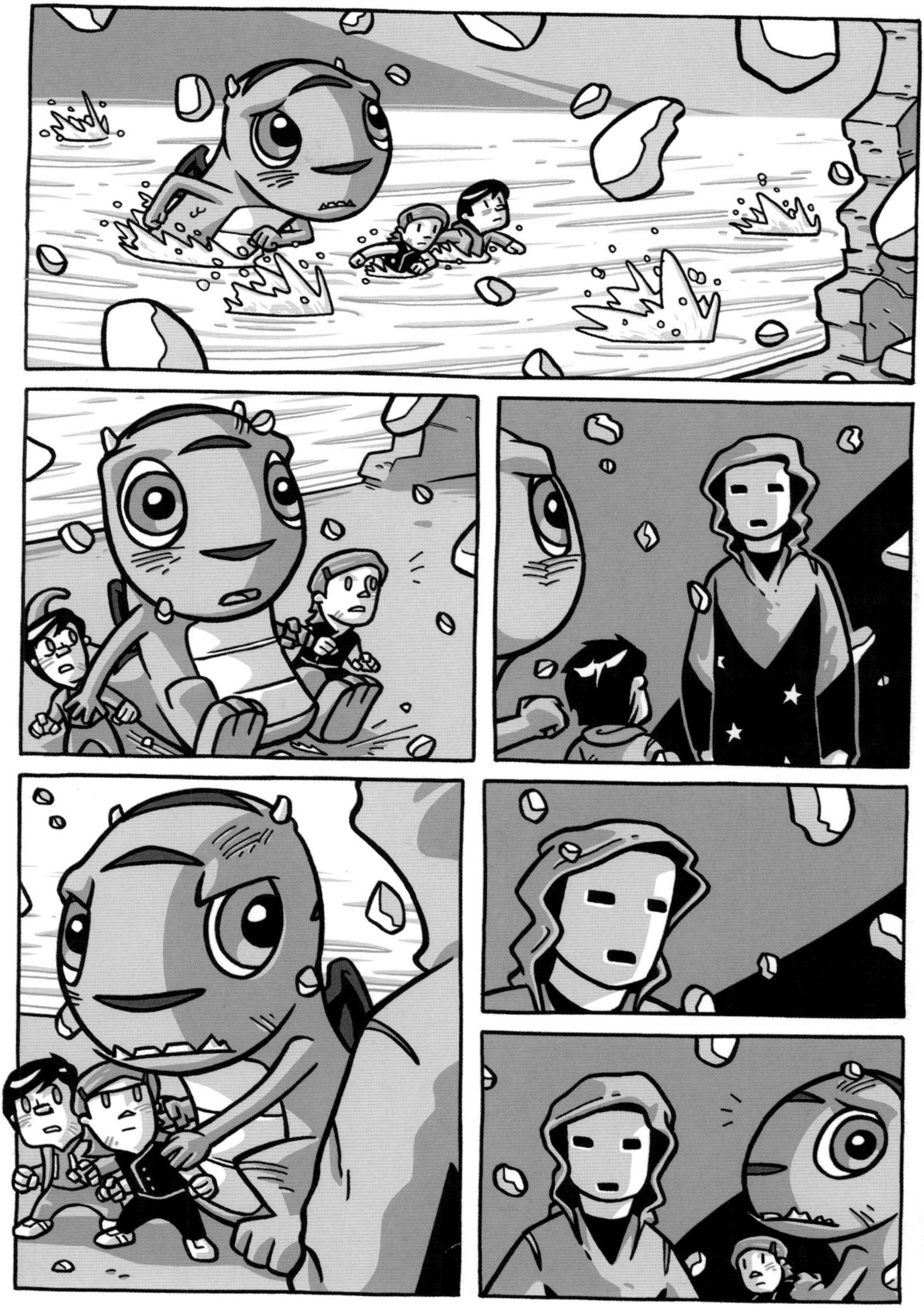

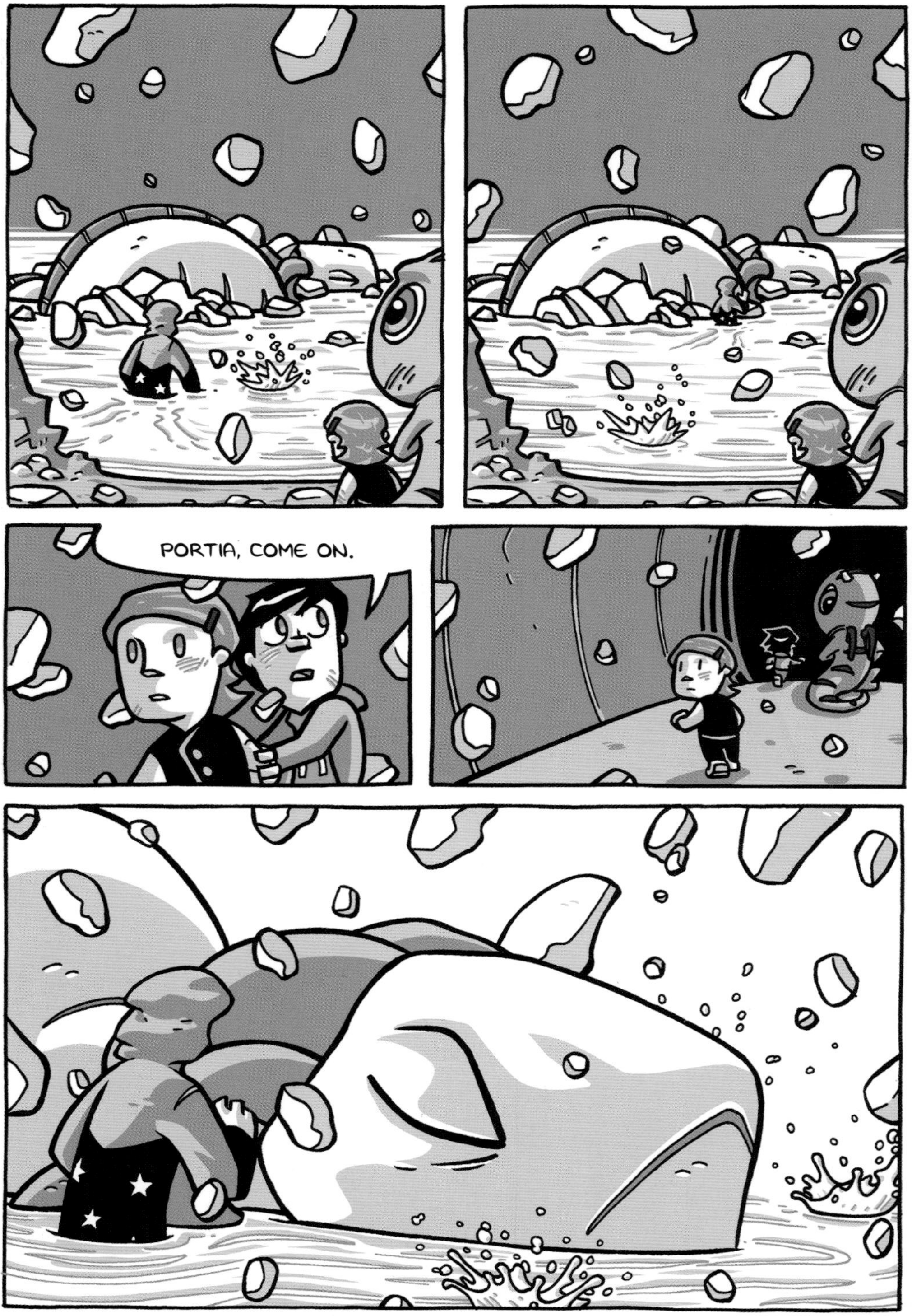
PORTIA, COME ON.

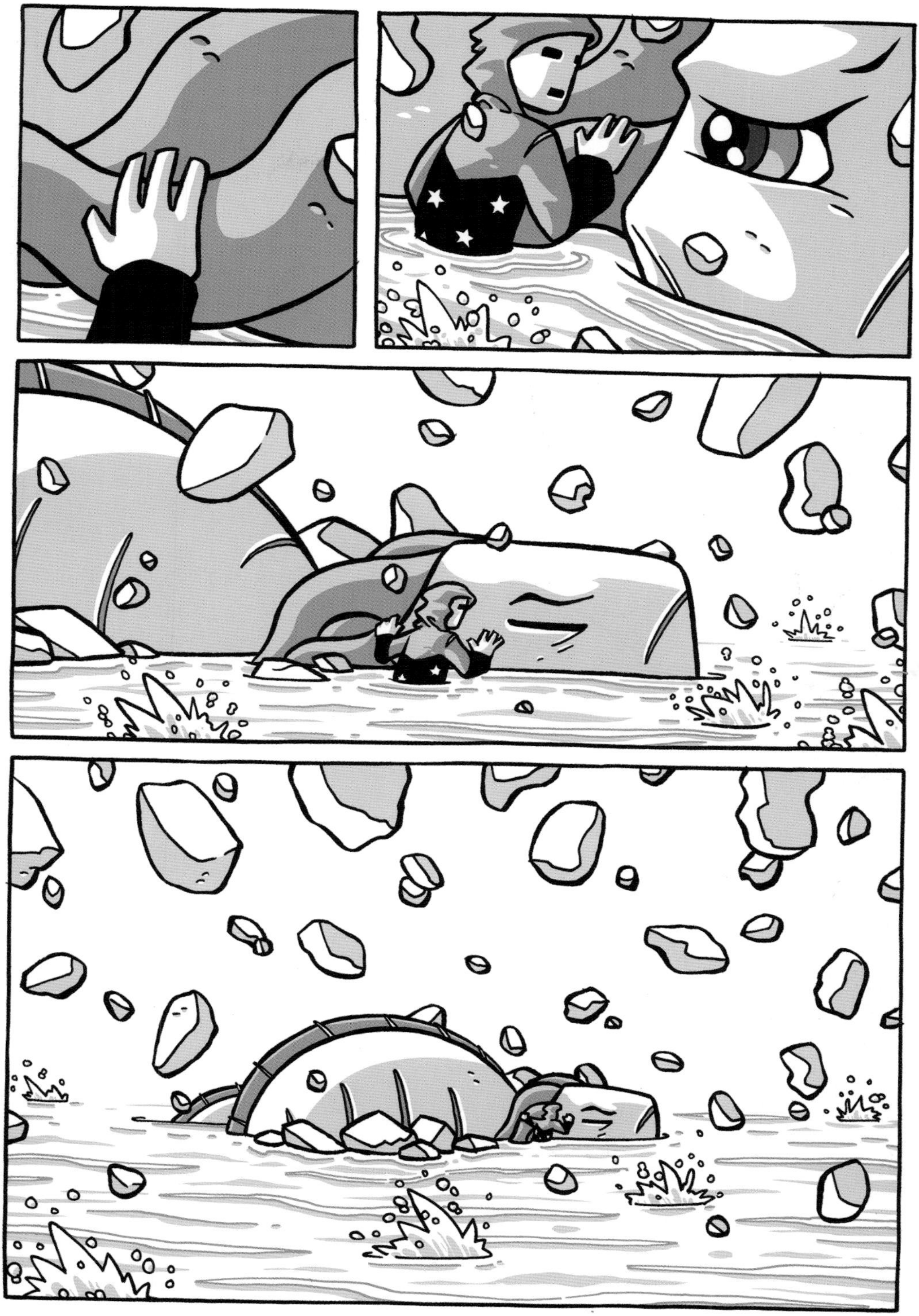

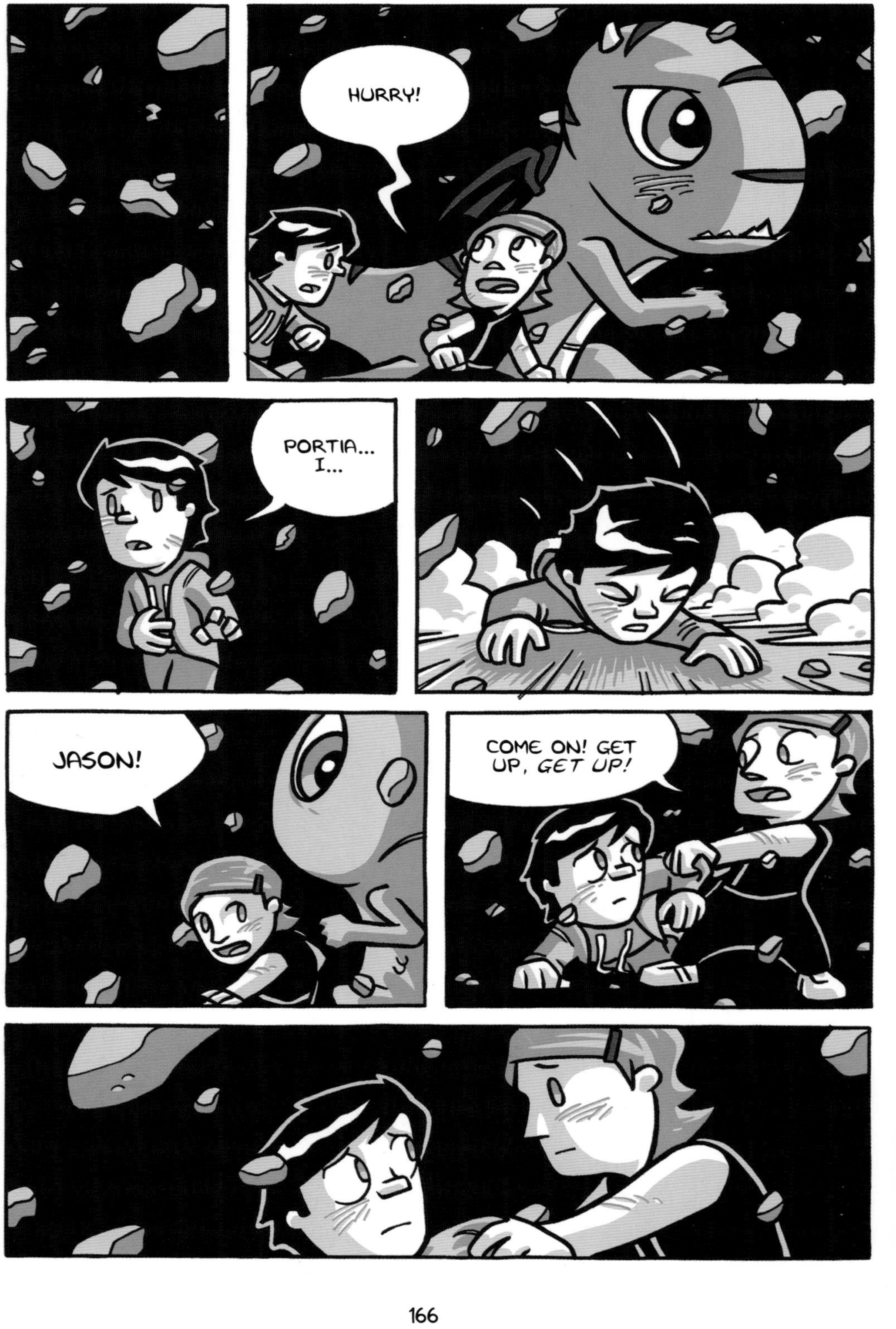
HURRY!
PORTIA... I...
JASON!
COME ON! GET UP, *GET UP!*

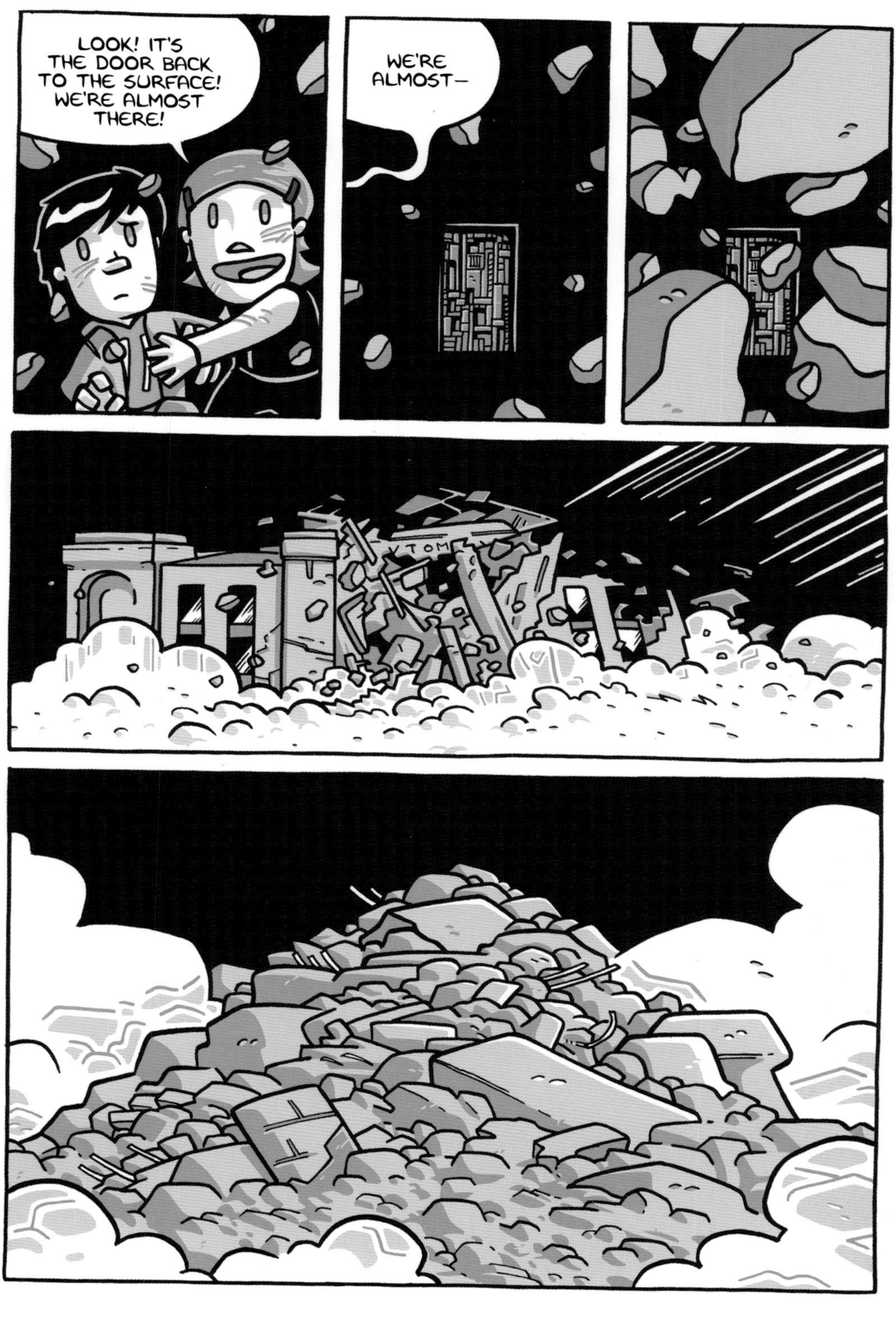
LOOK! IT'S THE DOOR BACK TO THE SURFACE! WE'RE ALMOST THERE!
WE'RE ALMOST—

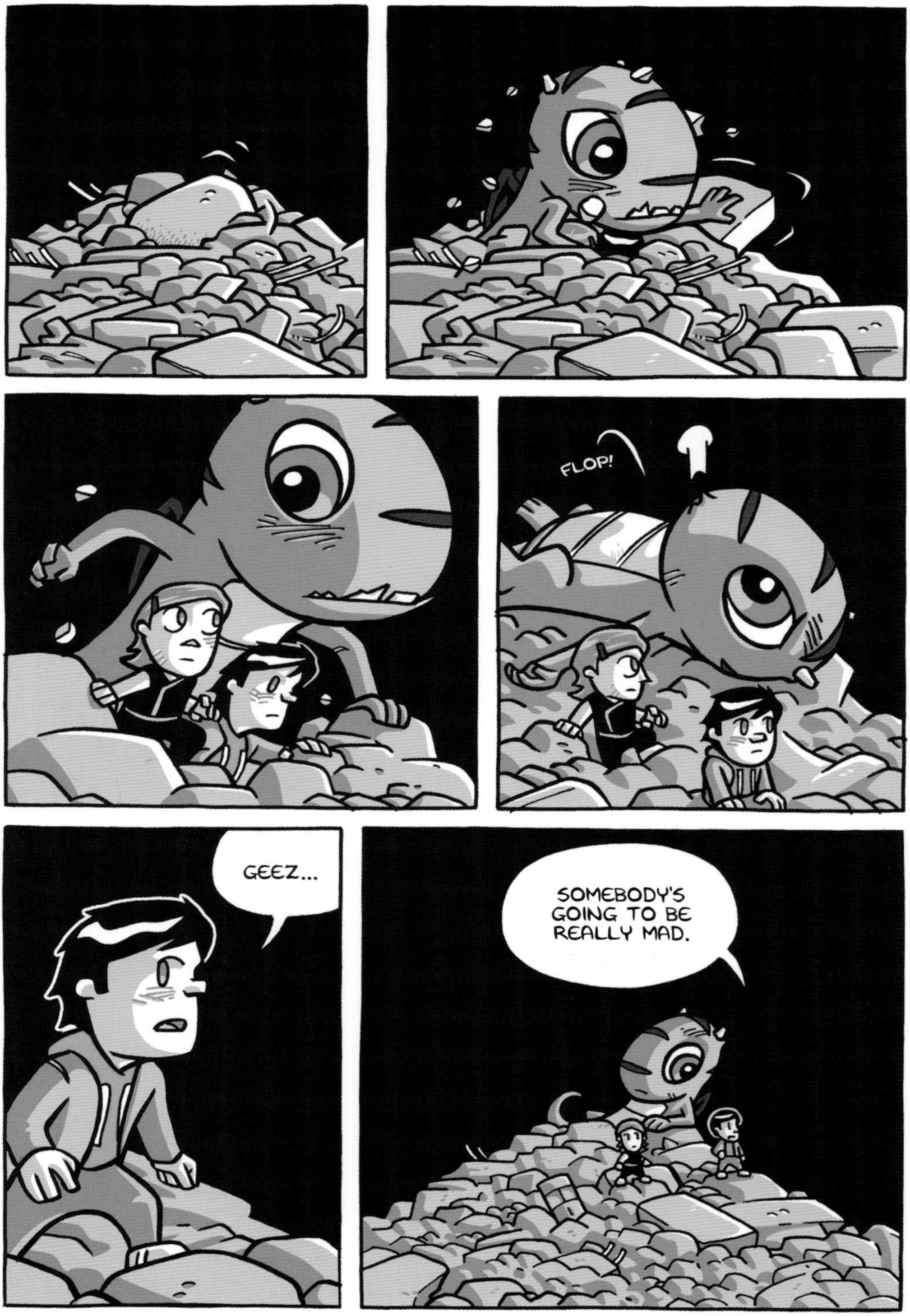
FLOP!
GEEZ...
SOMEBODY'S GOING TO BE REALLY MAD.

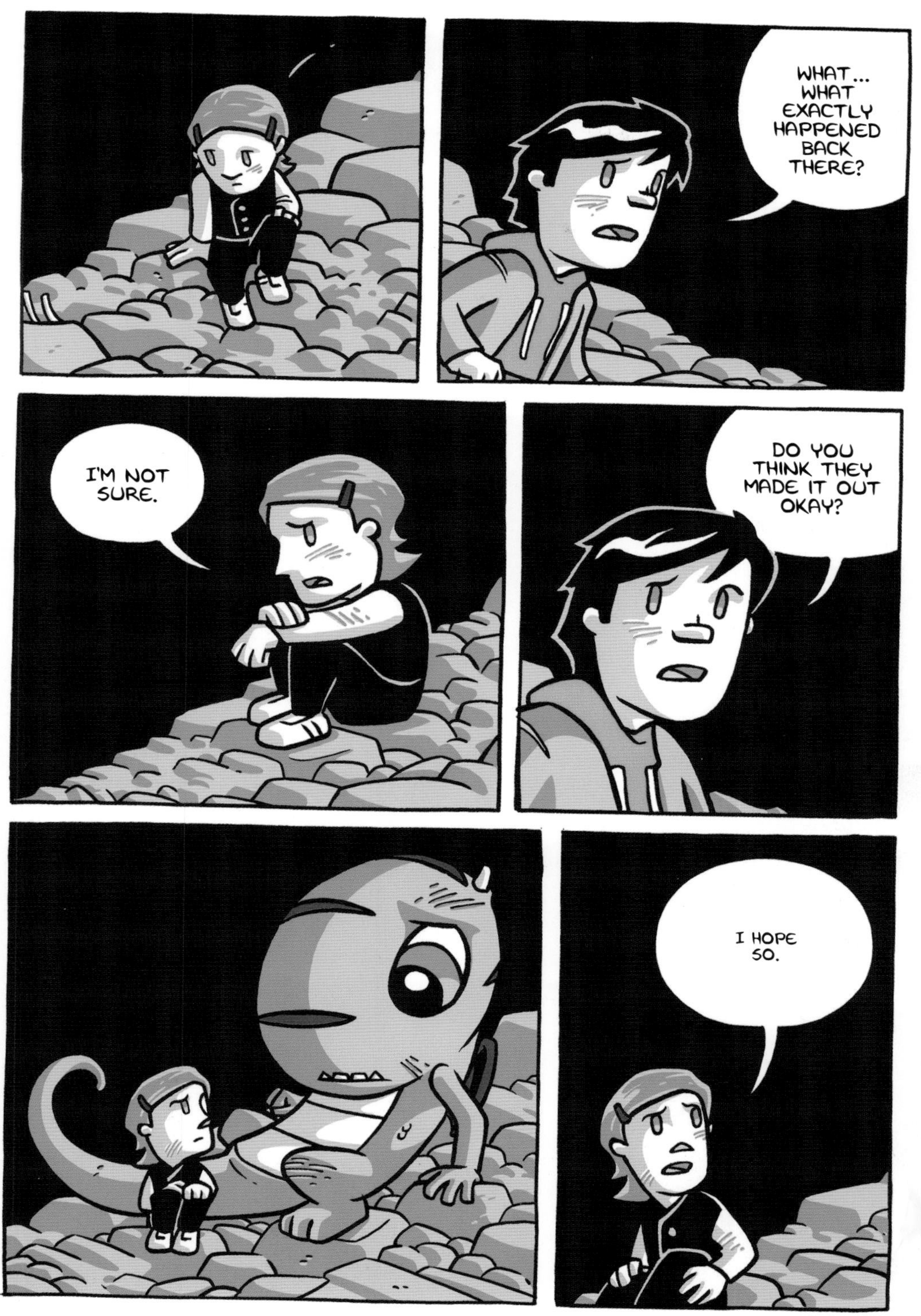
WHAT... WHAT EXACTLY HAPPENED BACK THERE?
I'M NOT SURE.
DO YOU THINK THEY MADE IT OUT OKAY?
I HOPE SO.

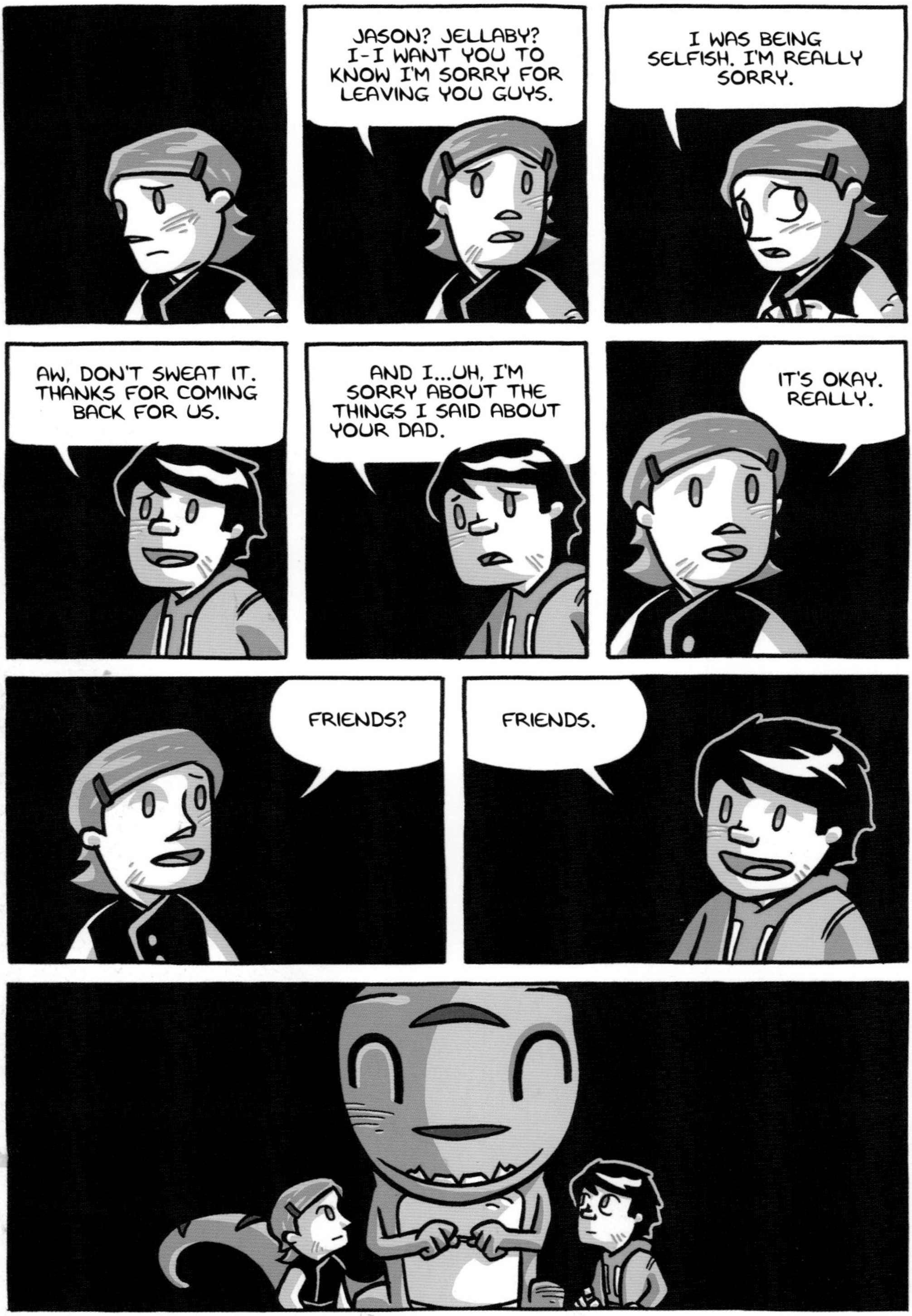
JASON? JELLABY? I-I WANT YOU TO KNOW I'M SORRY FOR LEAVING YOU GUYS.
I WAS BEING SELFISH. I'M REALLY SORRY.
AW, DON'T SWEAT IT. THANKS FOR COMING BACK FOR US.
AND I...UH, I'M SORRY ABOUT THE THINGS I SAID ABOUT YOUR DAD.
IT'S OKAY. REALLY.
FRIENDS?
FRIENDS.

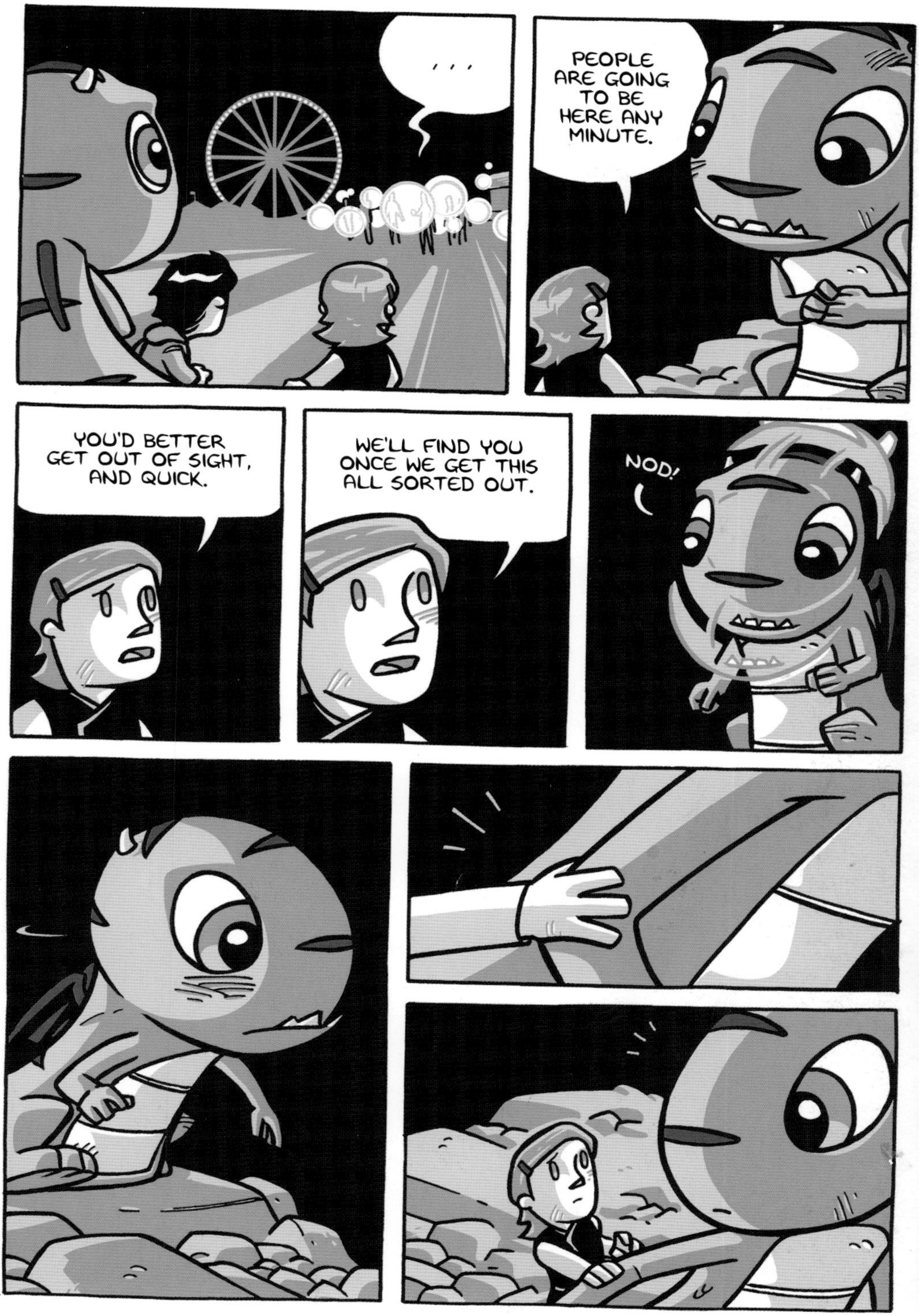
. . .
PEOPLE ARE GOING TO BE HERE ANY MINUTE.
YOU'D BETTER GET OUT OF SIGHT, AND QUICK.
WE'LL FIND YOU ONCE WE GET THIS ALL SORTED OUT.
NOD!

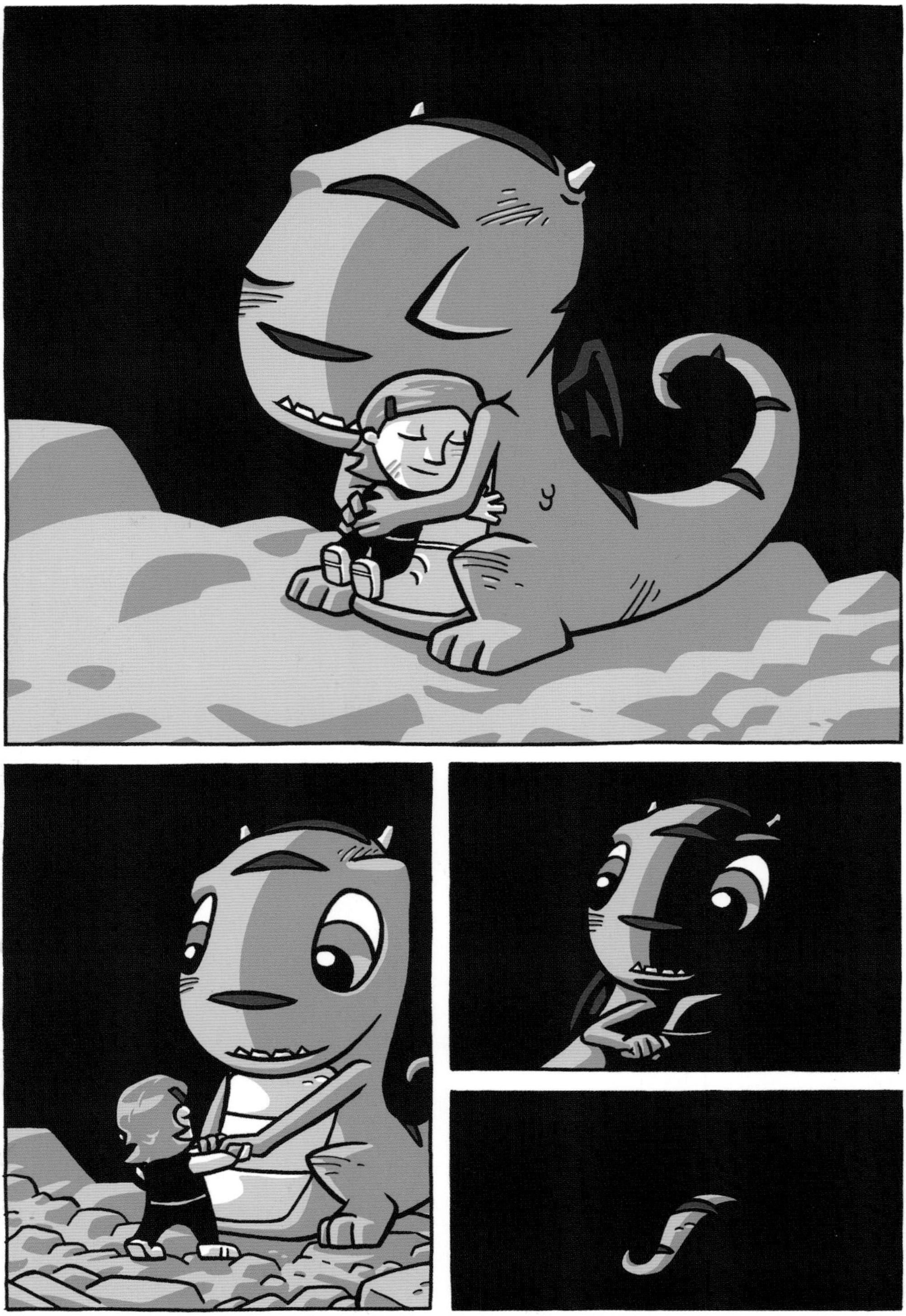

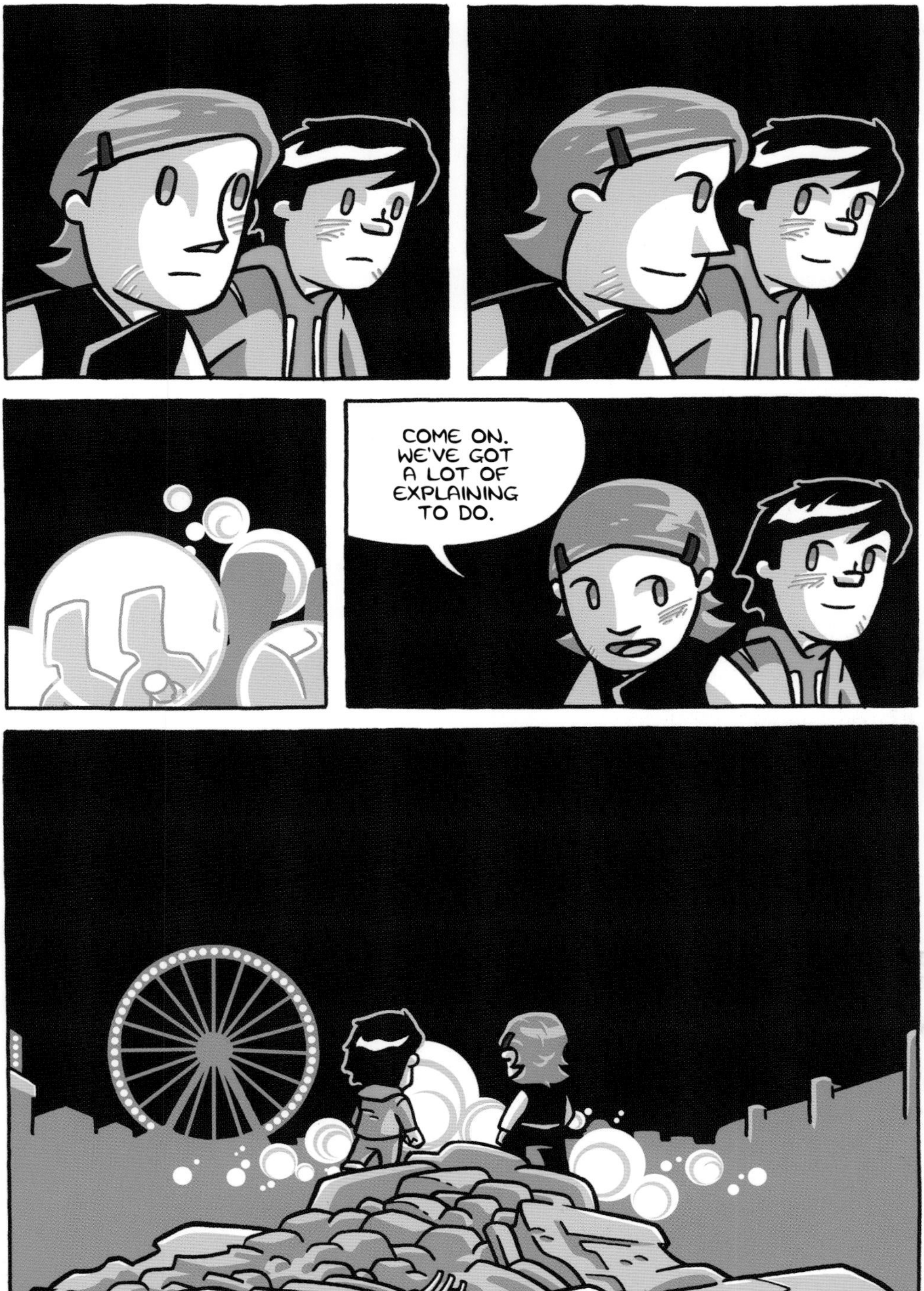
COME ON. WE'VE GOT A LOT OF EXPLAINING TO DO.

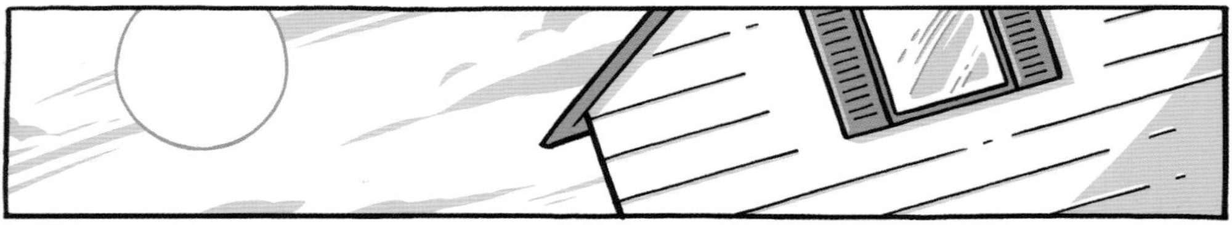

EPILOGUE

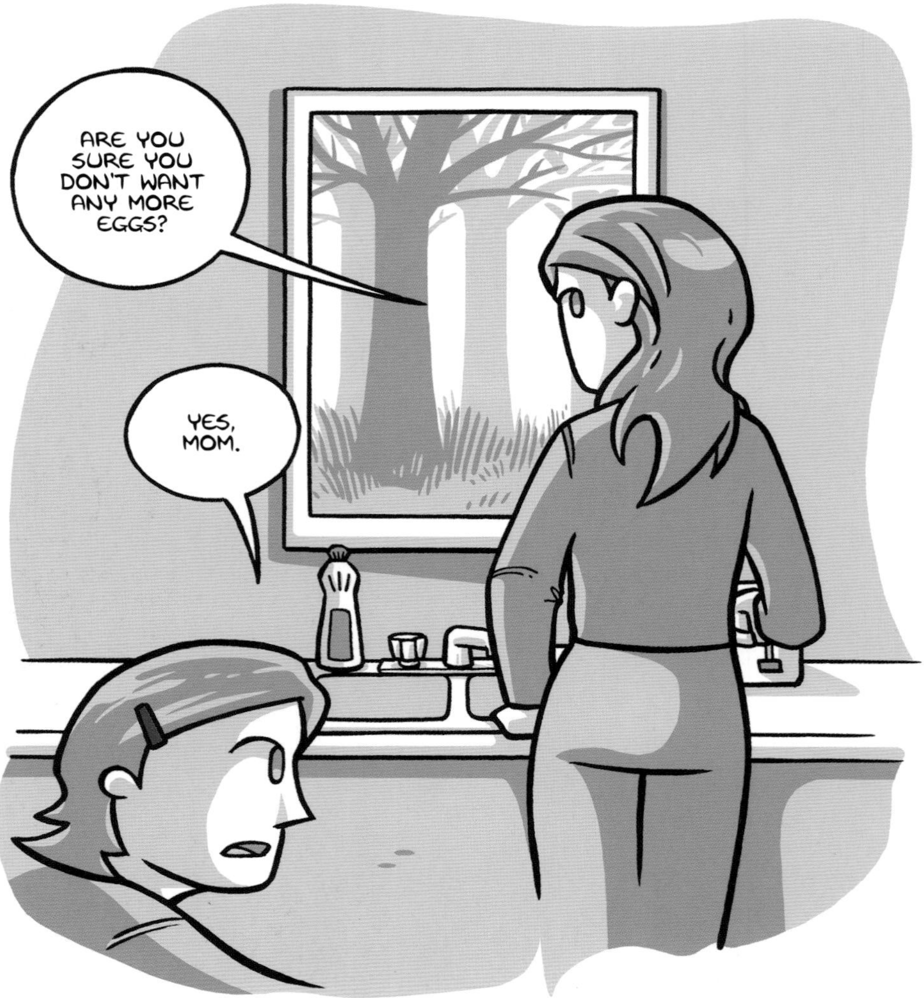
ARE YOU SURE YOU DON'T WANT ANY MORE EGGS?
YES, MOM.

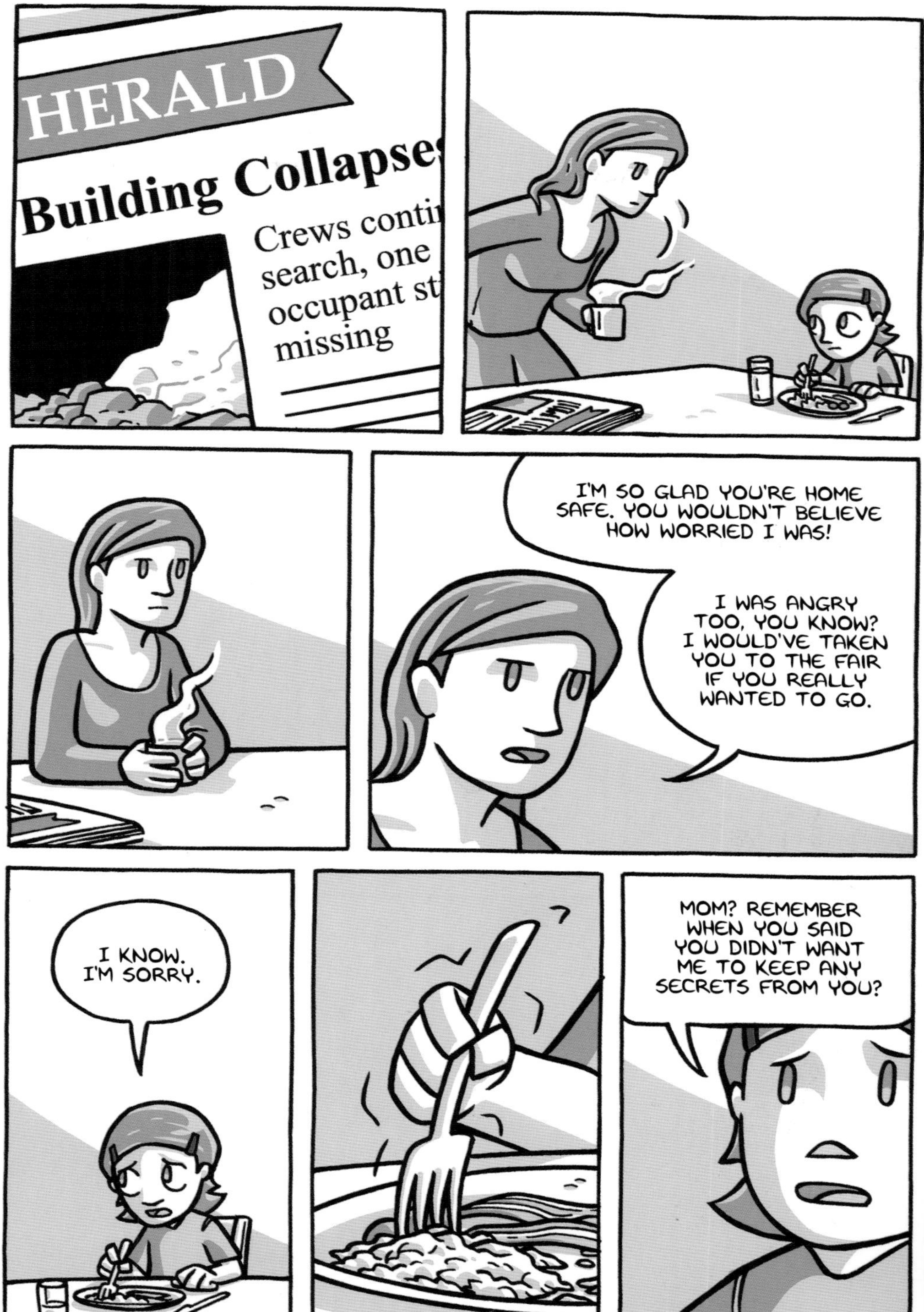
HERALD
Building Collapses
Crews conti
search, one
occupant st
missing
I'M SO GLAD YOU'RE HOME SAFE. YOU WOULDN'T BELIEVE HOW WORRIED I WAS!
I WAS ANGRY TOO, YOU KNOW? I WOULD'VE TAKEN YOU TO THE FAIR IF YOU REALLY WANTED TO GO.
I KNOW. I'M SORRY.
MOM? REMEMBER WHEN YOU SAID YOU DIDN'T WANT ME TO KEEP ANY SECRETS FROM YOU?

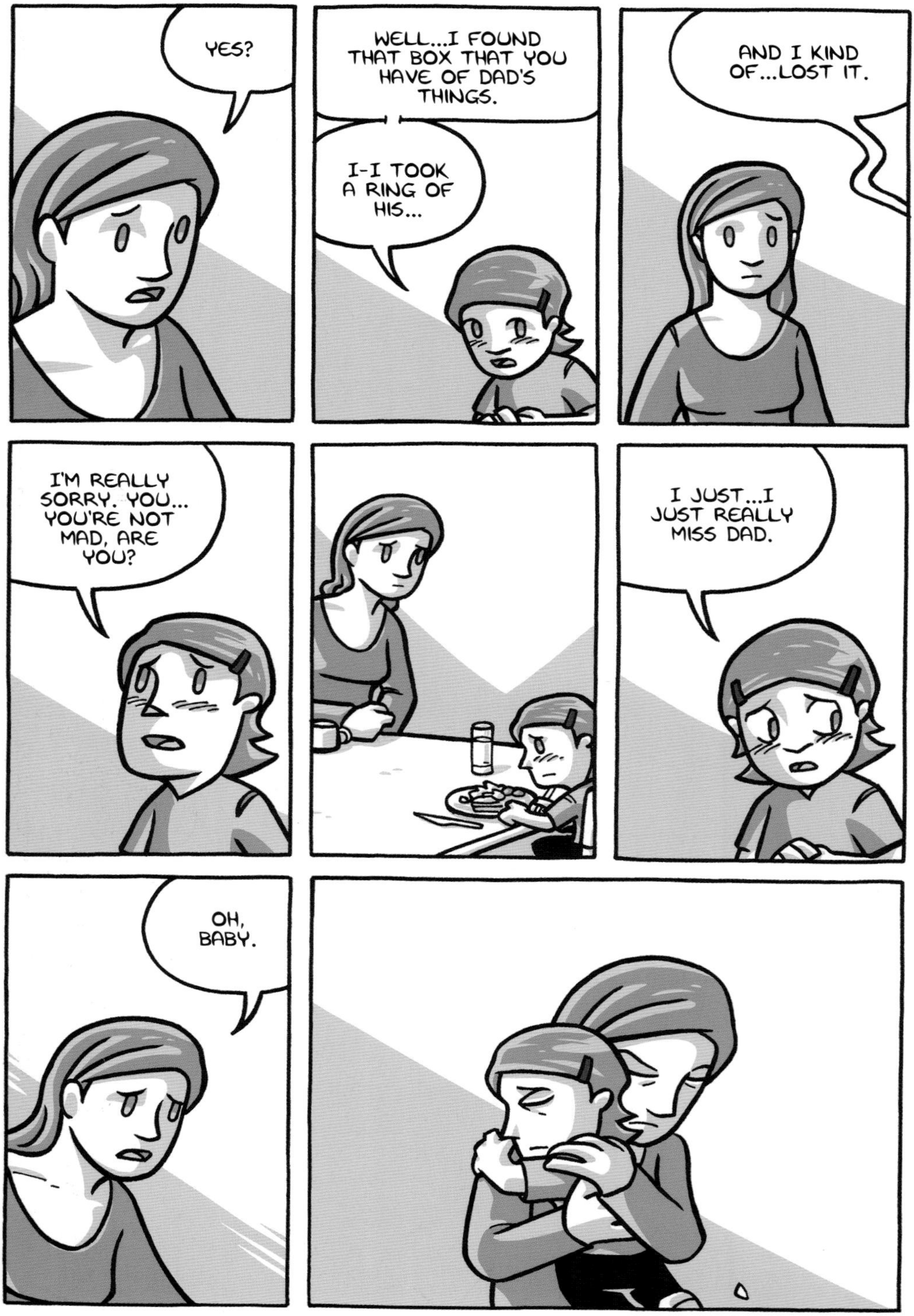
YES?
WELL...I FOUND THAT BOX THAT YOU HAVE OF DAD'S THINGS.
I-I TOOK A RING OF HIS...
AND I KIND OF...LOST IT.
I'M REALLY SORRY. YOU... YOU'RE NOT MAD, ARE YOU?
I JUST...I JUST REALLY MISS DAD.
OH, BABY.

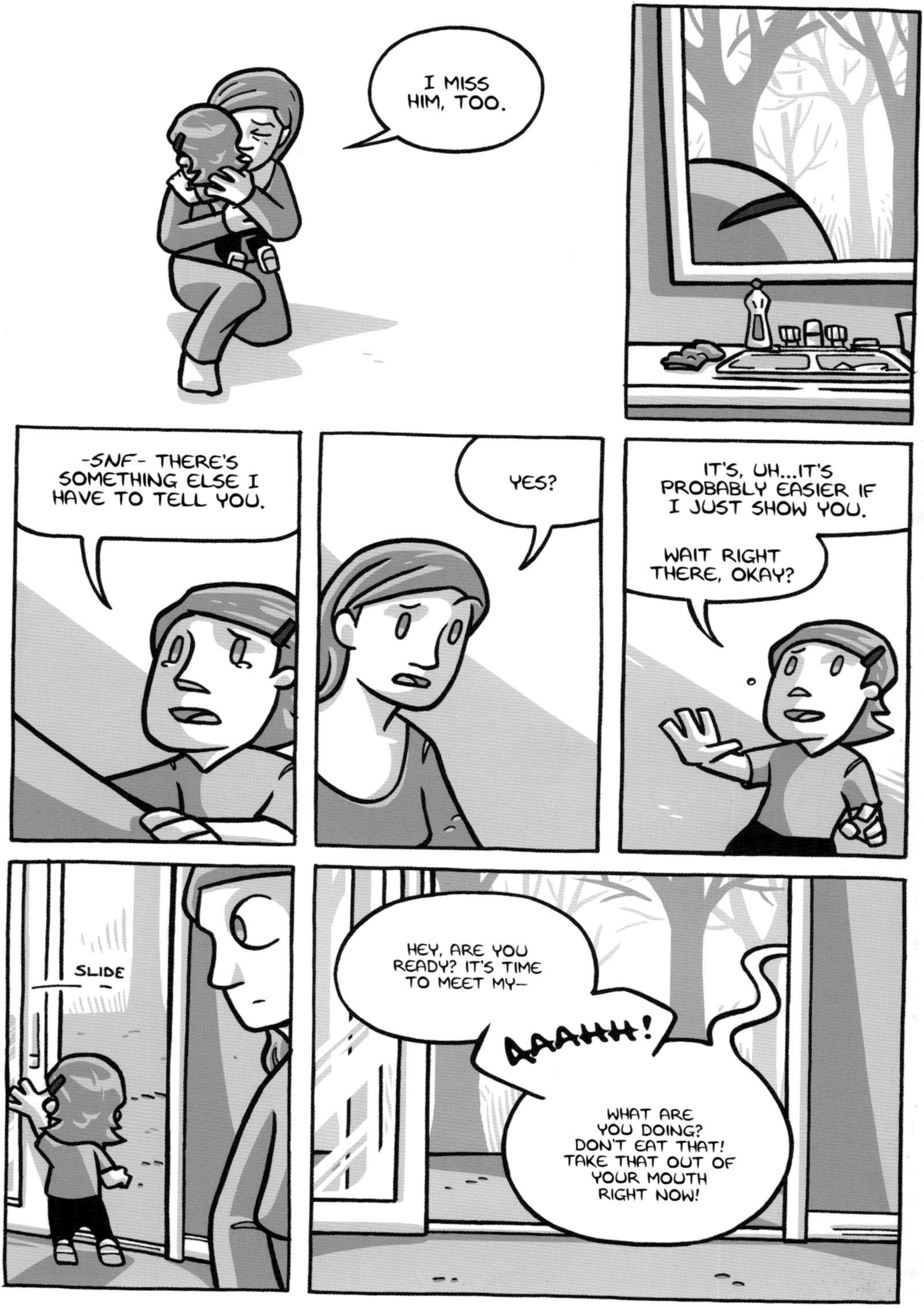
I MISS HIM, TOO.
-SNF- THERE'S SOMETHING ELSE I HAVE TO TELL YOU.
YES?
IT'S, UH...IT'S PROBABLY EASIER IF I JUST SHOW YOU.
WAIT RIGHT THERE, OKAY?
SLIDE
HEY, ARE YOU READY? IT'S TIME TO MEET MY—
AAAHH!
WHAT ARE YOU DOING? DON'T EAT THAT! TAKE THAT OUT OF YOUR MOUTH RIGHT NOW!

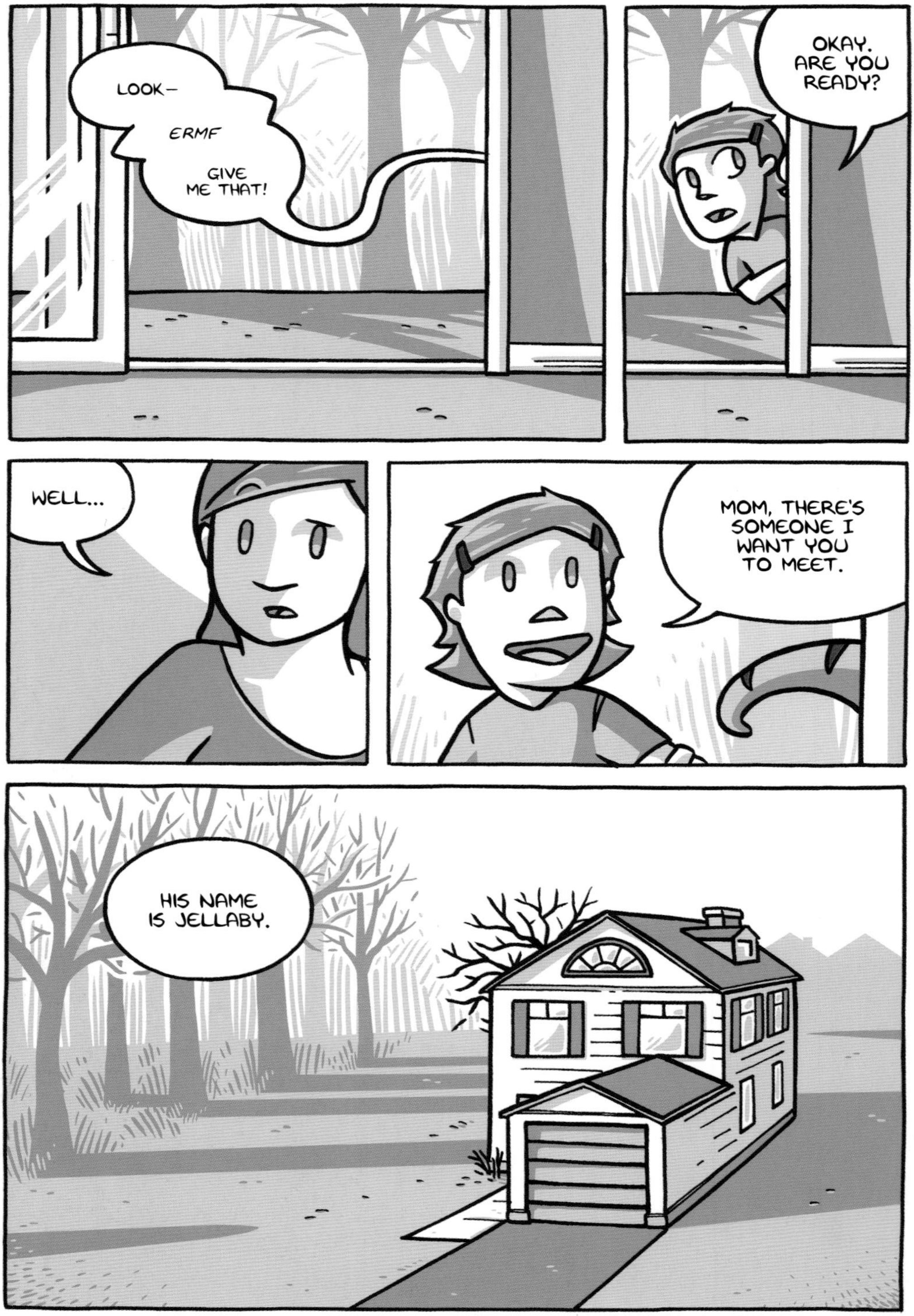
LOOK—
ERMF
GIVE ME THAT!
OKAY. ARE YOU READY?
WELL...
MOM, THERE'S SOMEONE I WANT YOU TO MEET.
HIS NAME IS JELLABY.

About the Author

Born in England and raised in Hong Kong, Kean Soo settled in Canada, where he planned to embark on a career in electrical engineering. However, he discovered that he'd rather draw comics instead. Kean began posting his comics on the Internet in 2002, and later became an assistant editor and regular contributor to the all-ages *Flight* anthologies. Kean was nominated for an Eisner Award and received a Joe Shuster Award for Best Comics for Kids for his work on *Jellaby*.

Kean still loves going to the CNE (the Canadian National Exhibition) for the tiny donuts and the rides. He enjoys riding on the Wave Swinger, but his absolute favorite is The Zipper, which is probably the only ride that makes him genuinely fear for his life.

Portrait of the author by Hope Larson

Sketches

XOLOTL   JELLABY

Top: Some early sketches of Jellaby and Xolotl. I based Xolotl's design on the Mexican axolotl, a type of neotenic salamander, which has since become a critically endangered species.

Left: An early study of the underground setting for Monster in the City.

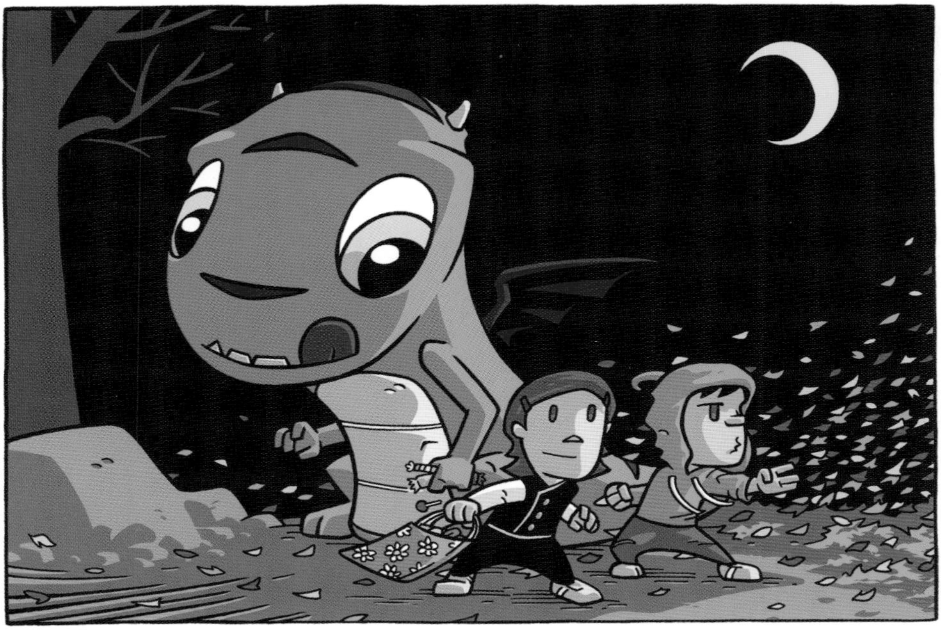

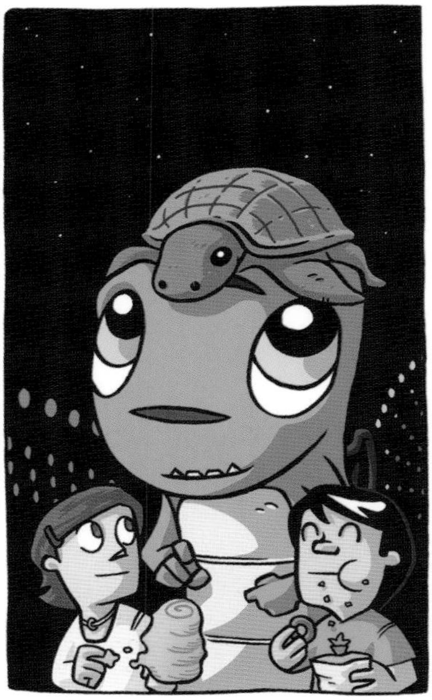

Above: Various pieces drawn for friends during the production of Monster in the City.

Right: The original Monster in the City cover, published in 2009.

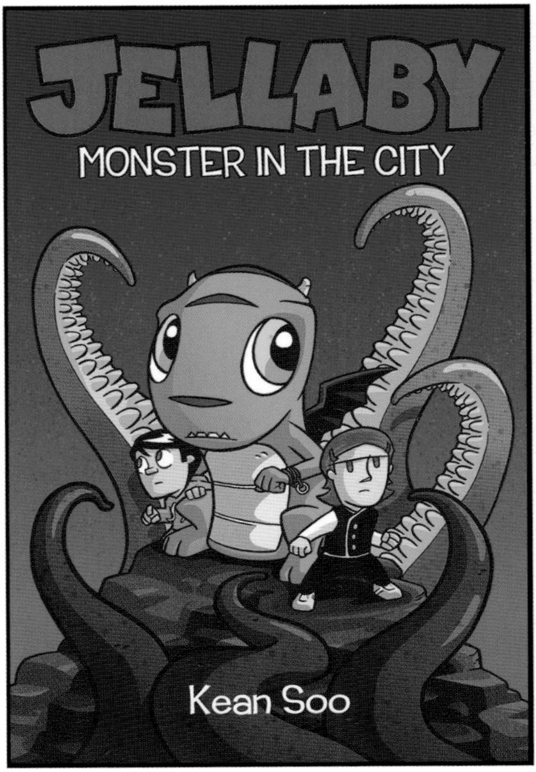
JELLABY
MONSTER IN THE CITY
Kean Soo